THE

PERFECT HOMECOMING

ALSO BY JULIA LONDON

HISTORICALS

The Devil's Love

Wicked Angel

The Rogues of Regent Street

The Dangerous Gentleman

The Ruthless Charmer

The Beautiful Stranger

The Secret Lover

Highland Lockhart Family

Highlander Unbound

Highlander in Disguise

Highlander in Love

The Desperate Debutantes

The Hazards of Hunting a Duke

The Perils of Pursuing a Prince

The Dangers of Deceiving a Viscount

The School for Heiresses (Anthology): "The Merchant's Gift"

The Scandalous Series

The Book of Scandal

Highland Scandal

A Courtesan's Scandal

Snowy Night with a Stranger (Anthology): "Snowy Night with a Highlander"

The Secrets of Hadley Green

The Year of Living Scandalously
The Christmas Secret (novella)
The Revenge of Lord Eberlin
The Seduction of Lady X
The Last Debutante

CONTEMPORARY ROMANCE AND WOMEN'S FICTION

Pine River

Homecoming Ranch
Return to Homecoming Ranch

The Fancy Lives of the Lear Sisters

Material Girl
Beauty Queen
Miss Fortune

Over the Edge (previously available as Thrillseekers Anonymous series)

All I Need Is You (previously available as *Wedding Survivor*)
One More Night (previously available as *Extreme Bachelor*)
Fall Into Me (previously available as *American Diva*)

Cedar Springs

Summer of Two Wishes
One Season of Sunshine
A Light at Winter's End

SPECIAL PROJECTS

Guiding Light: Jonathan's Story, tie-in to *The Guiding Light*

NOVELLAS

"The Vicar's Widow"
"Lucky Charm"

THE
PERFECT
HOMECOMING

JULIA LONDON

Montlake
Romance

Text copyright © 2015 Dinah Dinwiddie
All rights reserved.

Published by Montlake Romance, Seattle

www.apub.com

Amazon, the Amazon logo, and Montlake Romance are trademarks of Amazon.com, Inc., or its affiliates.

ISBN-13: 9781477821619
ISBN-10: 1477821619

Cover design by Laura Klynstra

Library of Congress Control Number: 2014915842

Printed in the United States of America

For the loyal readers who have stuck with me on the trails
through the lives of many characters

PROLOGUE

Beverly Hills, One Year Ago

Emma Tyler was at work, in the break room of Cypress Event Management, when she first heard about the devil child. Apparently, Cayley Applebaum was a skinny, curly-haired, twelve-year-old brat with a sense of entitlement so vast it rolled off of her in big tsunami waves. She had no limits on her cell phone and was perhaps the most spoiled of the children who roamed in packs up and down Santa Monica Boulevard. She lived in a Beverly Hills mansion in a magic bubble of infinite privilege and, like most of her friends, was accustomed to regular routines that included massages and facials, New York shopping sprees, and birthday parties that cost as much as art-house film productions.

Cayley was the only child of Reggie Applebaum, a film-industry mogul and power broker. He possessed buckets of money, and on the occasion of Cayley's bat mitzvah, he'd hired Cypress Event Management—CEM, as it was known around town—to produce a party. He'd said, *money is no object.* He'd actually said those words, as if they weren't a completely laughable cliché. Money was *no object* for a party for a twelve-year-old? Could anyone even say that with a straight face?

Reggie could, and he did.

Emma was fascinated by the tales of this kid. The planners working the event held court in the break room, reenacting Cayley's demands and tantrums with many expletives. Emma wondered who produced children like this? By what failure of parenting did darling little toddlers become demons in a few short years?

Emma was a vice president at CEM, but she didn't actually do much event planning herself. Her boss, Melissa, a well-preserved woman with an impressive collection of Chanel suits and handbags, said Emma lacked "people skills" and "empathy" for their most important clients.

Emma didn't disagree with that assessment. She'd never been an event planner to begin with—she'd landed her job at CEM some years ago by sleeping with one of the members of the board of directors. She'd taken the job because she'd liked the *idea* of event planning. But it turned out that she wasn't very good at execution. She couldn't click with brides and anniversary couples. She was one to speak the truth and had a hard time distinguishing which truths people were willing to hear and which ones they weren't.

But dammit, Emma had tried.

A few months into it, while working a divorce party—an inanity of the first order—Emma had agreed with the honoree that she did indeed look fat in her cocktail dress. After that, it looked as if Emma would be fired. Before Melissa could fire her, however, an important wedding had hit a snag. On the day of that wedding, the flower delivery van was hit from behind on the way to the venue and many of the arrangements were lost. The florist wanted to go with half the original order, arguing that he couldn't possibly replace what was lost and get it across Los Angeles in time for the ceremony. Emma had been the only one available to deal with the disaster, and she'd handled it beautifully. She'd told the florist the truth: The couple had paid thousands for flowers, which was a drop in the bucket of what they'd put into a smear campaign if the flowers didn't arrive as ordered, on time.

"Is that a threat?" the florist had asked.

"It's just the truth," Emma had said. "Oh, and by the way, I know someone with a helicopter."

"What's that got to do with anything?" the flustered florist had demanded.

"If I were you, I'd pay to have that shit airlifted over Los Angeles rather than face the fallout of not delivering flowers to a Hollywood star's wedding. But that's just me."

The last of the flowers arrived just as the violinists began to tune their instruments.

Once Melissa discovered that Emma was good at cutting through chaos and handling bad situations that popped up, she saw her employee in a new light. Eventually, Melissa came to appreciate that Emma didn't mealymouth her way around vendors and promoted Emma to vice president. She instructed her staff to call Emma if things broke.

If a vendor wasn't delivering, staff called Emma. If a venue canceled on them, staff called Emma. If a twelve-year-old girl was calling the shots and screwing everything up, they definitely called Emma.

Paul and Francine, two very competent, bullshit-tolerant planners, told Emma they couldn't deal with the kid. "Cayley changes her mind every day and we can't *book* anything. Now she wants to cancel the audiovisual vendor and it's *two days* before the bat mitzvah."

Emma was almost eager to go with Paul and Francine to meet this child, if for no other reason than to lay eyes on her.

The first thing Emma noticed about Cayley was that she had an insufferable habit of sneering at her mother, Tallulah.

Correction.

Tallulah was the vessel who had brought the little shit into the world, but she was no mother. She deferred every decision to the pubescent monster and quaked in the marquee glow of her daughter's displeasure. Emma wanted to slap both of them.

It became quickly apparent to Emma that in spite of the kid, the bat mitzvah would be stunning, even by Hollywood standards. CEM had booked the Beverly Hilton and would erect three distinct lounges. The first lounge was for younger children who were forced to accompany their siblings and parents to this event. Those children would be treated to little bowling lanes with Nerf pins and plastic bowling balls, a bouncy castle, a big foam pit for jumping into, and a face-painting station. Teens who were not as privileged as Cayley, who had to work summer jobs for spending money, had been hired to babysit.

The main lounge was built for Cayley and her friends. Cayley had decreed it would be pink. The teens would feast on cheeseburger sliders, Chinese food, and french fries served in cones. Cayley had planned entertainment stations to include temporary tattoos, a smartphone bling station, and of course, a *Guitar Hero* stage complete with microphones and a running video. But what Cayley was clearly most enamored with was the three photo booths that would grace the teen lounge.

As if all that wasn't enough, CEM had hired a handful of "party motivators." These were out-of-work actors hired to walk around and make sure the brat and her friends were having a good time.

The motivators had been Tallulah's grand contribution. "I just worry that the kids will be a little self-conscious and won't want to take advantage of all the great party treats," she'd apologetically explained to Emma in a high-pitched, wispy girl's voice.

"Heaven forbid that the kids actually pick themselves up off the pink velvet beanbags and walk around the pink lounge," Emma had said, and ignored the dark look Francine shot in her direction.

"Yes, well, that's a vulnerable age," Tallulah explained.

Well then, thank God for party motivators!

"God, Mom, you're so *stupid*," Cayley had said as her fingers flew across her phone, and Emma couldn't help but agree. "Anyway, those party people are all, like, *old*. I don't want them there."

"We've already hired them, honey," Tallulah said.

Paul and Francine exchanged a wary look, and the adults held their breath, waiting to see if Cayley would look up from her phone and insist they fire the four party motivators, or forget her displeasure.

When her fingers continued to fly across her phone, Francine carefully turned the attention back to the event.

The third lounge was intended for the adults. Cayley had become nearly hysterical when at first it appeared the adults would actually mingle with their children, and in the end, she'd gotten what she wanted—a separate lounge. It would not be pink. She'd agreed it could have a bar, and even a buffet. Apparently, Tallulah had suggested movies for the adults to watch, to which Cayley had agreed, but had recently changed her mind in favor of what she thought was a better idea: karaoke. She'd also agreed to have seating with power outlets and televisions hung overhead. That way, parents could watch sports while staying plugged into the world they'd abandoned just beyond the Hilton's doors.

But as they reviewed the plans for the adult cave, Cayley changed her mind again. "No," she said. "They don't get that."

"Oh honey—" Tallulah started.

"*No*, Mom," Cayley said sharply. "It's *my* party. I don't get TVs! Why should the parents get TVs?" She shouted this while texting.

"We've already planned it. It won't hurt—"

"I said *no*," Cayley said in a voice that reminded Emma of *The Exorcist*.

Paul and Francine looked helplessly at Emma. She knew what they were thinking—to cancel the AV equipment and setup two days before the event was an expensive change, not to mention a coordination nightmare.

This was where Emma excelled. She stood up and looked to the big glass back doors and the stunning view of the Pacific Ocean. "Cayley, can we step outside? I want to ask you something."

"What?" Cayley looked up from her phone. "*No*," she said, sneering at Emma. "Ask me here."

Emma bent over so that she was at eye level with Satan's Spawn. "It's about the photo booths," she said low.

Cayley hesitated, sizing Emma up. She finally stood and walked to the back door.

Once they were outside, Cayley impatiently demanded, "What?" And returned a text.

"God, you're despicable," Emma said.

That brought Cayley's head up, her brown eyes as big as teacups. "*What* did you just say?"

"You heard me."

Cayley gasped. "You can't talk to me like that!"

"I just did," Emma said, and folded her arms. "So here's how this goes, Cayley. Your overdone bat mitzvah is two days away. You're going to go with everything we've planned, with no more changes, or CEM walks. You don't want CEM to walk, because you know what that means, right?"

Cayley hesitantly shook her head.

"It means no party." Emma leaned closer. "It means *no photo booths*. All the crap you've been telling your friends about this party? Who's going to be there, who will get photos with who? Not happening. The adults get TV, and you get photo booths.

Another *no* out of you, and your friends will be talking about you next week, but not in the way you planned."

Emma didn't give the brat an opportunity for rebuttal. In her mind, the obvious had been stated, and that was that. She turned around and left a gaping little girl behind.

"Well?" Tallulah asked when Emma stepped inside.

"Ask her," Emma said, looking at Cayley as she shuffled in behind her.

"Okay, you can have your stupid TVs," Cayley muttered.

The next day, Melissa asked Emma to attend that damn bat mitzvah in case there was trouble. Emma sighed heavily. "You realize I may very well kill that little twerp."

"Try not to," Melissa said as she fit a gold-and-diamond-encrusted bangle around her teeny wrist. "Paul and Francine have their hands full as it is."

"I suck in situations like this," Emma reminded her.

Melissa smiled. She was a size zero, and in a bright orange sheath, she looked a little like a plastic straw. She patted her tiny hand against Emma's cheek. "Just don't talk," she suggested.

Emma arrived at the Beverly Hilton a few minutes late because of traffic, and found the party already in full swing. The teen lounge looked like the inside of a Pepto-Bismol bottle, with disco balls scattering the pink light around the room while the DJ played an endless loop of One Direction. Emma had to agree with Cayley—the party motivators roaming around did look kind of old.

In the adult lounge, the adult party motivators, otherwise known as cocktail waitresses, wore identical tight black skirts and white blouses and sleek ponytails.

The party was packed. No one was going to miss Reggie Applebaum's event; the guest list was a who's who of Hollywood film-industry royalty. Emma knew some of them personally, knew others by name. Some knew her, too, but kept their distance. Emma was used to that. It wasn't as if she was part of their circle. And she had a reputation around town for being cool and distant and a bit of a slut.

All true.

Emma didn't mix well with others, a truth that had plagued her all her life. Neither did she trust easily. And she preferred quick sex to relationships. None of these traits lent themselves to having lots of friends.

Emma also had a reputation for being beautiful, at least by Hollywood standards. Which meant that she was thin and blond. She had no qualms about admitting she was pretty—she had never understood women who demurred if anyone mentioned their good looks, or women who said things like, *No, I'm not pretty, my nose is too big,* or *my mouth is too wide,* or the worst, *you're much prettier than me.*

Emma knew what exactly she was, inside and out, ugly and beautiful. And had she been reluctant to recognize the surface good looks, there had been plenty of studio reps who had tried to convince her to take up acting, knowing that her face would trump any concerns about acting skills at the box office. But she had no desire to act or to be part of the film industry. She knew too many of the players and what they were like. She didn't really care about the star wattage at this party, either—she'd never been overly impressed by stardom . . . except for the time she'd met Steven Spielberg.

Anyway, tonight her job was to make sure everything was running smoothly. Reggie Applebaum was an important client for CEM. He'd hired them for a couple of studio events, and CEM wanted bigger gigs. The only way to get bigger gigs was to make sure that Princess Brat's party went off without a hitch. Whatever it took.

A long afternoon moved into evening, and the stilettos Emma wore were beginning to make her feet ache. Francine, holding a plate laden with food, found Emma watching the little kids bowl. "Have you eaten?" Francine asked as she chomped on a carrot.

Emma looked at the carrot and briefly pondered the improbability that root would become a desired food source. "No."

"Go eat," Francine urged her. "Things are calm. Paul and I have this."

Emma took Francine up on the offer and walked into the parents' lounge to the buffet. She picked up a plate and studied the selection of food, but nothing appealed to her. As she debated the selections created by one of the hottest chefs in Hollywood, someone stepped up to the buffet beside her. Emma glanced up and felt her heart do a little skip.

"Hi," the man said. When Emma didn't speak or turn away, but stared at him, he smiled curiously at her. "Sorry . . . have we met?"

Alas, only briefly. But it had been a moment Emma had never forgotten. Cooper Jessup looked just as tall, sexy, and robust as he'd been when she'd met him in Costa Rica a couple of years ago. His hair was dark and wavy, his eyes the shade of the fog that rolled in off the ocean. He met all the criteria of her secret desires—he made her blood rush. That made him kryptonite, dangerous to be around.

"Yes, we've met," Emma said, remembering herself, and extended her hand. She was almost afraid for him to touch her. "Costa Rica. The Marty Weiss birthday party," she reminded him. "I'm Emma Tyler, with CEM."

"Oh, that's *right*," he said, and took her hand firmly, shaking it. "I thought you looked familiar. That birthday party was bananas, wasn't it?"

"Totally," Emma said, and smiled a little. Cooper was a founding member of Thrillseekers Anonymous—a boutique company owned by four longtime friends, all men who loved physical activity. They'd come to Hollywood as stuntmen, had developed a stunt-training and stunt-choreography business, but had wanted more. Their love of extreme sports had morphed into the idea to stage extreme, heart-stopping sport outings for the rich and famous.

Everyone around town knew about TA because their clients were the A-listers that they all aspired to be. TA had developed a clientele by guaranteeing complete privacy for their outings—they had the means and know-how to evade the most ardent of the press corps. Rumor had it that TA took sheiks to surf monster waves, and dropped movie stars from helicopters to ski down rocky, snow-covered slopes. They zipped across ancient gorges with industry power hitters and climbed remote rock faces or drifted down the Amazon River on a raft with film crews. There was no sport, no daredevil activity that the four of them would not try.

So Emma had heard.

She also knew that on occasion, they were asked to do something out of the ordinary, something that was not really about extreme sports, but about the wives and children of their most lucrative clientele. Such as Marty Weiss's birthday bash on a private island off Costa Rica a couple of years ago. He was a rich businessman from Chicago, whose wife had given him the pop star Audrey LaRue and a jungle birthday theme for his sixtieth. TA had hired CEM to help plan it all. Emma had been called down when the local staff agency couldn't fill all the service slots they'd needed.

"Cooper Jessup, you are holding up the line!" A woman's head with stylish red hair appeared just around Cooper's arm. She eyed Emma suspiciously.

Emma knew her, too. She was Jill Jefferson, an actress on the popular sitcom *The Crowleys*.

"Hi, Jill," Cooper said, and smiled at her. "Do you know . . ." He winced apologetically and gestured to Emma.

"Emma."

"Emma," he repeated. "We worked together in Costa Rica."

"Costa Rica?" Jill asked, smiling as if that amused her, and looked at Emma again with an expression that seemed accusatory, as if she suspected Emma had engineered a trip to Costa Rica to be with Cooper.

"Thrillseekers Anonymous hired us to help with a birthday party there," Emma said.

"Ah!" she said, and smiled. "I'm Jill." She extended her hand with a desperate-to-be-recognized air.

"Yes, of course, I know you," Emma said, giving her what she wanted. "We've met."

"We have?" Jill asked, knowing very well, Emma suspected, that they'd met at Haley Rangold's wedding shower. Haley was Jill's costar on the sitcom and the true breakout star. And Jill? Emma bet Jill would be one of those perennial actresses, always finding work, never finding true fame.

"Haley Rangold's wedding shower," Emma reminded her.

Jill laughed. "Oh my God! It was my horrible karaoke, wasn't it?" she asked, and put her hand on Cooper's arm to gain his attention, to turn his gaze away from Emma. "Haley made me do it," she said with a roll of her eyes. "She kept insisting. It must have been really awful, because it became a clip on *EW Online*. Tell him how bad it was," she urged Emma.

"I didn't hear the karaoke," Emma said truthfully.

"You must have!" Jill said, laughing, her gaze fixed on Cooper. "I'm sure everyone in the neighborhood heard it."

"I heard your toast."

"My toast! Did I toast Haley?" Jill asked with a playful roll of her eyes. "I'm always toasting her on the show. She insists."

"Not that toast." Emma hadn't heard any toast to Haley at all.

Jill looked at Emma. "What toast, then?"

"You toasted yourself, remember?" Emma said. "You toasted yourself and unmarried women, and then talked about how you wanted to get married." Emma did not add that the toast had turned into a long and tipsy rant about how awful men were in general and how badly Jill wanted one that she could actually marry. *That* clip was probably looping on *Radar Online*.

Jill's smile froze at the reminder, and Cooper's brows floated upward with surprise. "Is that right?" he drawled, looking at Jill.

Jill flashed a brief, forced smile. "Oh, I probably did," she said dismissively. "Of course I'd like to be married someday. Wouldn't everyone?" She stepped around Emma and Cooper. "Nice to see you again, *Emma*. Is there any fruit?"

"Yes," Emma said. "Down at the end."

Jill wandered off, her dress skintight, her legs long and lean in her heels.

Cooper shifted to stand beside Emma, leaned down, and said low, "I don't think you were supposed to remember that."

"Probably not," Emma agreed with a slight shrug. "But it's impossible to forget. The speech was long and kind of whiny." She glanced up at Cooper.

He hesitated, as if he expected her to make a joke of it. When she didn't, he chuckled. "You're a firecracker, aren't you? That's no way to win friends and influence people, Emma Tyler."

"I've heard that."

He laughed again and, with a shake of his head, moved on.

This was the way it usually went for Emma. Socially awkward and tactless, as her parents had always said. Hard and flinty. That was a phrase from the novel *Jane Eyre*, which Emma had read in high school. She remembered how struck she'd been by those words when Jane used them to describe herself. It was as if Jane were describing Emma, and the phrase had stuck with her all these years.

Emma may have been hard and flinty all her life, but she'd never intended to hurt anyone. In her head, the things she said never sounded as people perceived them. Jill had surely known which toast Emma meant, and if she didn't, how else was Emma to say it? When she tried to shade the truth, she sounded ridiculous—she had no feel for telling stories. Something was wrong with her in that regard.

Emma watched Cooper move down the buffet, admiring him. She could still recall the sight of Cooper in swim trunks, helping fat old men zip down to the beach. He'd been all rippling muscle and sweaty sheen, glorious to behold. But Emma . . . Emma had made a date with one of those fat old men, and she'd missed Cooper's departure from the island.

Not that it mattered. She never went near him. Men like him—handsome, competent, sexy men—had the power to crush.

Cooper caught up to Jill, and they struck up a conversation over the shrimp before disappearing into the crowd.

Emma ate a piece of chicken, and the party wore on.

Some of the parents with young children began to leave. A few drunken young men took over the kiddie bowl and bouncy castle, a big no-no, and it took some doing by Paul to get them to leave. Emma decided to close down the kiddie lounge before more drunken teens or young adults attempted to commandeer the rented equipment. By the time they'd finished deflating, the karaoke was going strong in the adult lounge and the kids were swarming the photo booths, unable to get enough of themselves.

Emma sent Paul out of the kiddie lounge to check on Princess Brat. "I've got this," she said, gesturing to what was left of the cleanup. There wasn't much to do but pick up the pins and balls—someone would come tomorrow and take care of the rest. And the best part was that karaoke wasn't so loud in this lounge. Emma could actually hear herself think.

She had gathered up an armful of Nerf bowling pins and was carrying them across the room when she heard the door open. "Kids' lounge is closed," she called out.

"Need some help?"

Emma glanced over her shoulder, startled to see Cooper. A smile spread her lips before she could even speak. "As a matter of fact, yes. Did you come to rescue me?"

"I did," he said, and walked into the lounge and bent down to pick up a stray bowling ball. "Karaoke is definitely not my thing, so . . . I thought I'd wander around. Where is everyone?" he asked, gesturing to the room.

"Dispatched." Emma nudged a box with her shoe, maneuvering it around until she had it in front of her, and knelt down to stack the pins inside.

Cooper grabbed some pins and squatted down beside her. "Is it just me, or do parties like this make you wonder why anyone thinks kids are a good idea?" he asked as he put the pins and bowling ball into the box.

Emma laughed. "The little ones are cute."

"True."

"But the teens? I'd like to tee them up and kick them right out of Beverly Hills."

He grinned. "You don't like kids?"

"I *love* kids," Emma said. Children didn't make judgments about her. They didn't care if she was tactless. "I love kids who aren't from Beverly Hills," she amended, and smiled at him. "Kids who don't get facials and massages."

"Or get to choose their own nannies," Cooper said.

Emma gasped with delight. "You read about that, too?" she asked, referring to an *Us Weekly* article about a certain supercelebrity who allowed his children to choose their nanny. They'd been through six in the last year alone.

"I may or may not have flipped through a magazine recently," he admitted with a charmingly self-conscious smile. "But it's unbelievable, isn't it? When I was a kid, I was hardly allowed to choose a shirt for school, much less a nanny. Not that there were any nannies floating around where I grew up." He stood, gathering up some of the foam squares that had been lost from the pit. "And believe me, if I'd spoken to my mother like I just heard the guest of honor speak to hers, I would have been skinned alive and left to hang in the Texas sun."

"Same here!" Emma agreed as she gained her feet. Her mother had never let Emma get away with anything. Her stepsister, Laura, could get away with everything. Not Emma.

"Have you ever done a bat mitzvah like this?" Cooper asked Emma as he tossed the foam blocks back into the pit.

"I've never done a bat mitzvah at all! I had no idea so much was *expected*. I mean, the girl is turning thirteen, not twenty-one."

"Right," he said with a chuckle. "It's a lot of work. Looks like it might have been a complicated event."

"Not really." Emma glanced up; Cooper was looking at her. Sort of studying her, his gaze discerning. She realized she was having a conversation with him, an actual conversation. She nervously tucked a strand of her hair behind her ear. "Complicated is like a wedding anniversary I was involved with a few months ago. A *polygamist* wedding anniversary."

Cooper blinked. A grin spread across his face. "Get out."

"I am so not kidding. Four cakes," Emma said, holding up four fingers and wiggling them at him. "And that was only the beginning. There were four wives who all had completely different ideas for the event."

Cooper laughed as he picked up a riding toy. "Tell me."

"Well, the first wife thought it ought to be a barbeque. Nothing too fancy, and trust me, she was none too fancy," Emma said with a laugh. "But the second wife wanted a big formal sit-down dinner at a hotel. She was the loud, opinionated one. She convinced one of the other wives to be on her side, and it looked as if she was going to get her way, but then the newest wife—who looked like she was eighteen to their thirty- or forty-something—said she wanted a dance."

"A dance," Cooper repeated, as if he was trying to imagine it.

"Like a high school dance," Emma said, thinking back. "Which I think was not cool with their religious beliefs, not to mention all the awkwardness around deciding who gets the first dance with the hubby. Oh, and they wanted the event to happen in two weeks."

Cooper laughed at the absurdity of that as he tossed more foam blocks into the pit. "So what happened?"

"Well," Emma said, warming to the tale, to actually talking without annoying him, "I was called in at the last minute to help get it resolved. So I drove out to their house in the Palisades—" She laughed. "That house had four master suites and umpteen bathrooms and my God, the *kids*! There were kids everywhere, like it'd been infested. And the wives, holy shit—they were all so mad, they talked over each other. I wasn't much help, either, because I couldn't really concentrate, you know? I kept thinking, how do you *do* this? How do you pass him around? And none of them seemed to like each other, so I *really* didn't get it." She laughed and shook her head. "I like to think I'm open to different lifestyles. But that one? It confuses me."

"I don't get it either," Cooper said, walking back to where she stood. "I can't seem to wrap my head around one wife, much less four."

"Exactly," Emma said. "Our planner, Gage, kept pleading with the wives to agree and finally got them to a compromise on a sit-down barbeque. He pitched it as being an under-the-stars event. You know, out in the open to accommodate all those people."

"Sounds reasonable."

"*I* thought so," Emma said. "But then the youngest wife? The cute eighteen-year-old with the curvy figure and no kids?" she said, sketching out a woman's figure. "She told the old lech what she wanted and that was that. He told the other wives to stuff it, they were having a dance. And they did. But with four separate cakes."

Cooper laughed roundly. "I'm sure *that* went over well."

"It was *the* most uncomfortable party we've ever thrown, and I've been to more than a few. You couldn't have bulldozed through the tension in that grand ballroom. Oh, and our great idea for putting it under the stars went the way of the dodo bird, too. I had to scramble to get a venue." She smiled and sat down on top of a table. "What about you?" she asked, kicking off one shoe, and then the other.

"We've never done anything like a bat mitzvah, and after today, I can promise we never will," he said. "TA does extreme sports, not this kind of thing . . ." He paused and smiled lopsidedly. "Unless Reggie Applebaum asks."

Emma tossed back her head with a bright laugh. "I guess we *all* do what Reggie Applebaum asks, right? So what is the most complicated event TA has ever staged?"

Cooper had to think about it. "The Costa Rica gig ranks right up there," he said with a nod. "Rigging a zip line just to push a bunch of out-of-shape guys down it is not my idea of a good time. But the most complicated?" He leaned up against the table where she sat, his arms folded across his chest, his hip against her thigh. "You know Marnie Banks McCain, right?"

"We've met." Marnie Banks was a wedding planner in town.

"She planned the wedding of Olivia Dagwood and Vincent Vittorio."

"So *she* got that gig!" Emma exclaimed. Olivia and Vincent had been the hottest stars on the planet a couple of years ago. Every wedding planner in town had wanted that event. "CEM threw all that we had and then some at that one. How long did that marriage last, anyway? A hot minute?"

"Not even," Cooper said with a snort. "Olivia and Vincent wanted to be married where they'd filmed a movie, in the Rockies, of all places. They wanted to hike up to the place of a scene where they'd determined they had 'fallen in love,'" he said, making invisible quotes with his fingers. "That location is not exactly accessible, which is where we came in. And that was how the wedding from hell came to be," he said with a shake of his head.

He told Emma how a freak thunderstorm had knocked out the only bridge across a very steep ravine and had separated a group including the bride, groom, Cooper's partner Eli McCain, and Marnie, from the rest of the wedding party.

It sounded like an unbelievable and ludicrous weekend, complete with a bickering bride and groom and the successful rigging of snow blowers to shoot sandwiches and apples across a ravine until the stranded party could be rescued. Emma laughed with delight as Cooper entertained her with a description of shooting peanut-butter-and-jelly sandwiches across the ravine. "You're lying!" she accused Cooper, playfully shoving his shoulder. "No way that happened."

"It happened," Cooper assured her. "It will go down as one of the most bizarre weekends of TA's corporate life."

"Honestly, it amazes me that no one has been hurt in all the things I've heard TA does," Emma said. "How do you keep from getting hurt?"

"Oh, I've been hurt," he said with a laugh. "I guess I've got a secret weapon."

"What's that?"

Cooper dug into his pants pocket, then held out his hand and opened his palm.

Emma leaned over to look at it.

"Go ahead, pick it up."

Emma took it from his palm and examined it. It was a charm of some sort, silver and small, about the size of a nickel. The charm was scarred, the engraved image worn. "St. Christopher?" she asked, squinting at it.

"Yep. My grandfather gave it to me when I was a kid. My brother had gotten into some trouble . . ." Cooper waved his hand. "My brother was *always* in trouble. We were little demons, always blowing things up, always rigging our rockets onto our bikes, that sort of thing. My grandfather was the superstitious type. He gave my brother and me each a St. Christopher medal and made us promise to carry it always so we'd be protected from harm."

"And you've carried it all this time?" she asked skeptically.

"I sure have. I know, surprising, isn't it? Can't believe I haven't lost it."

"So *that's* the secret to not dying on a TA outing," she said dubiously as she handed it back to him.

He laughed. "I don't really believe this medal protects me. But I like the sentiment behind it, and I'm not opposed to putting a little trust into the power of positive thinking." He returned the charm to his pocket and looked at her. "What's *your* secret?"

The question startled Emma, and for a moment, she feared that Cooper knew about her reputation, knew what she did.

"Your secret weapon for parties like this," he clarified.

But it was too late—Emma's confidence had been shaken. "Oh," she said, and laughed nervously as she slid off the table. "I always wear pointy-toed shoes in case I need to kick some ass."

Emma stuffed her feet back into her shoes. She turned around. Cooper was standing, too; she hadn't realized how close she was to him. But there she was, only inches from him, so close she had to tilt her head back a little to see his face. His smile drew her in like a siren call. She could see the dark gray circle around his irises.

She imagined she could feel his energy, all male, potent and strong. Good God, she wanted to touch him.

Don't touch him! "Isn't someone waiting for you?" she asked.

"No." His gaze slid to her mouth. "Is someone waiting for you?"

"No one that matters," she answered honestly to his mouth.

Cooper's smile softened. He made no move to touch her, but his gaze lazily wandered over her hair, her face, her body. "We should get out of this room. Why don't we go grab a drink and listen to the drunks sing a few tunes?"

"A drink," she repeated softly.

"Or two," he said, "depending on how bad the karaoke is."

The low spark in his eyes was distracting. It was sexy. It was trouble. "I'm not very good in big groups. I mean, as a participant."

"Sounds like my brother. No one would believe he's an introvert, either, but he is."

What did he mean by that? He thought she was an introvert? *No, Cooper, it's far more screwed up than that.*

"You can take a break, can't you?" Cooper asked. "Reggie has taken a very keen interest in the karaoke machine. This is your opportunity to butter him up, and we both know you should never pass up an opportunity to butter up Reggie," he said with a bit of a smile.

The rush of guilt and disgust Emma felt was because she'd already buttered up Reggie. She drew the corner of her bottom lip in between her teeth and looked at his very sensual mouth. She would like nothing better than to get a drink with Cooper, to continue this innocuous conversation, to be easy. But Cooper wasn't like the guys she usually had drinks with, and her belly was beginning to churn.

"Come on, it will be fun," he said.

Emma couldn't remember the last time she'd been so attracted, so *tempted.* But this attraction was impossible for her, for all the secret reasons that, for a brief moment, she had thought he knew. What did he really want, anyway? To be friends? Please, men never wanted to be friends. So what did he want? A grope in a back room? Probably. It was always that, always physical, wasn't it? Men always wanted to touch her body, to push it, squeeze it, knead it.

Emma suddenly moved closer, so that her body touched his, daring him to do it, to put his hands on her. *Come on, show me what you want!* she silently shouted at him. She tilted her head back and said, "Do you *want* me to come?"

Cooper looked confused. His brows dipped as he studied her, but still, he made no move to touch her. "I'd like you to come, yes," he said, sounding uncertain.

His response was so different than what Emma expected that she didn't know how to react. He'd just complicated things completely by proving he was *not* like other men. He'd passed up the opportunity to grope her, to kiss her, to fill his hands with her breasts, and Emma did the only thing she could think to do in that confusing moment—she turned away from him and started for the door. "Sorry," she said, "but I have to work."

She walked out of the kiddie lounge and left that gorgeous man standing there.

Emma didn't see Cooper again until the end of the evening, when almost all the guests had gone home. By then, she was in Reggie's limousine, his wife and daughter having been sent home in another limousine. Reggie smelled of bourbon and cigars and his hand was between Emma's thighs. He was leaning toward her when something outside caught his attention, and he rolled down the window to yell at an underling. Cooper happened to be standing on the sidewalk, waiting for his car. His gaze caught Emma's as Reggie rolled up the window.

"Fucking morons," Reggie said, and slid his hand up, between Emma's legs.

"Stop it," she said, and pushed his hand away. She looked out the window and imagined Cooper's eyes.

ONE

One Year Later
Los Angeles, California

The day Carl Freeman's call for help came into Thrillseekers Anonymous—something to do with his very public, level-five, megadeath divorce—Cooper and his partners decided who would manage the request with corporate sophistication: Rock-paper-scissors. Eli McCain's rock crushed Cooper Jessup's scissors, and as a result, Cooper had to get on the 405 on a Friday afternoon and drive to Carl's Wilshire Boulevard office.

It would be an understatement to say that Cooper was not a happy camper when he arrived at the low-slung, nondescript office building. First of all, he hated stuff like this. TA had done a lot of lucrative stunt work for Carl's studio and they wanted to keep doing that work for him. Which meant that occasionally, they had to do things they weren't exactly set up or eager to do. Cooper couldn't imagine what Carl wanted, but "divorce" and "thrillseekers" did not seem to him to go together.

Second, Cooper hated to see a grown man cry, especially over a messy marriage.

Third, he was beginning to wonder where his life was going. He was thirty-eight years old and he'd just driven through some of the nation's worst traffic to talk to this guy about that messy marriage. This was definitely not something Cooper had thought they were signing up to do when he and his best friends had established TA. But lately, this sort of thing seemed more the norm than the exception. And if this was the norm, Cooper wasn't sure where it left him or TA.

Carl was on the phone when his secretary showed Cooper into his office. It was done up in industrial-chic décor; even the tinsel wrapped around an iron menorah was made of chain link. Carl's desk was glass and chrome, his chair metal. He waved Cooper in and gestured for him to sit in a similar, but much smaller, chair. Cooper was a big guy, three inches over six feet, and that chair was too small for him. He remained standing.

"Okay, listen, I need to wrap this up. I've got someone in my office." Carl paused, then laughed. "No, not her. But if you have her number . . ." More laughter, and Carl clicked off, tossed the phone down on the glass desktop without a care, and threw his arms wide. "Cooper! Long time no see," he said, as if they were old friends instead of the mere acquaintances that they were.

"No kidding," Cooper said, extending his hand. "I think it was *Avenger*—"

"So listen," Carl said, his entire demeanor shifting abruptly. He began to pace around his expansive office, nervously running a hand over his balding head and either ignoring or missing Cooper's extended hand. Carl was not what one would call handsome. He was short, a little overweight, and his eyes were fairly close together. But Carl was the kind of guy who exuded power. It was in the way he carried himself, the expensive suits, the priceless watches and fast cars. Cooper knew a dozen men just like him.

Carl gave a strange little laugh. "I honestly don't even know where to begin," he said, his eyes darting nervously to Cooper and back to the floor. "There's a woman who has screwed me over. A blond, gorgeous woman."

That description fit roughly half the women in Los Angeles.

"She's a little strange," Carl added. "Works at Cypress Event Management. I think she's a VP there. You've worked with CEM, right?"

"Yes," Cooper said.

"Emma Tyler is her name. Know her?"

Cooper blinked. Yeah, he knew Emma Tyler. Carl was right— she was blond and gorgeous, an Elizabeth Taylor of the modern era, tall and thin with expressive green eyes that held one's gaze a fraction of a second longer than was necessary. She had lush lips, curves in the right places, and her smile was incendiary.

After that chance meeting at the bat mitzvah about a year ago, Cooper had noticed these things about Emma from a respectable distance. In spite of being incredibly attracted to her, he hadn't pursued her after that night, because he was fairly certain he'd gotten the brush-off. Although, frankly, he was still a little uncertain what had happened at the Beverly Hilton.

And he'd started to date Jill after that event.

Emma was very attractive, but Cooper had heard enough things about her since that night to know she wasn't his type. Her reputation around town was not good. This, Cooper knew because his partner Eli had married Marnie Banks, and Marnie had told Cooper that Emma was not a nice person. At first, Cooper wasn't sure what Marnie meant. He thought Emma was friendly enough, if a little too matter-of-fact. If anything, he'd thought she was a loner, an observation he'd made to Marnie.

Marnie had snorted and rolled her eyes. "If that's what you want to call it. But she has more than a few *friends.*"

Cooper looked at Carl now, trying to imagine what business he'd had with Emma. A party? A birthday or anniversary event for his wife that had gone south?

"Come on, come on, you know who she is," Carl said impatiently. "She's got legs up to here," he said, gesturing at his thick neck. "Small tits. Long blond hair. And she has that look, like she doesn't give a shit."

And green eyes with heavy lashes, Carl forgot that. But Carl was right, Emma had a way of looking right through you . . . but not until after she'd looked directly at you, luring you in with a perfect, sultry smile. "Yeah," he said, and ran his hand over his head, feeling doubly uncomfortable now. "I know who you're talking about."

"Well, she has screwed me over," Carl said irritably. "I've got to get it cleared up or I'm dead. You have no idea."

"Okay," Cooper said uncertainly. If this was nothing but a lover's spat, he didn't know if he could keep himself from strangling Carl for making him get on the 405.

"Can you just . . . just sit, please," Carl said. At Cooper's hesitation, Carl said, *"Please."*

Cooper suppressed a groan and relented, fitting himself on that chair as best he could. He felt ridiculous, especially when Carl suddenly pulled a chair around, and sat directly in front of Cooper, so close that their knees were almost touching.

"I'll be honest, Cooper," Carl said low, as if they were sharing some desperate secret. "I'm in a lot of trouble. A *lot*. I need some help."

"I think you might have the wrong idea about TA—"

"No, no, listen. I know you guys do some things that aren't exactly adventures," Carl said. "You did Olivia Dagwood's wedding, you did that big birthday bash down in Costa Rica. And what about that security thing you did for Audrey LaRue?"

This was exactly Cooper's worry—people had gotten the wrong impression of them. "Those were things we couldn't get out of," Cooper said quickly. "But TA doesn't—"

"Here's the thing," Carl said, clearly an expert at cutting people off before they could say no. "I'm going through a divorce. A *bad* one. You know my wife, Alicia, right? Well, she's coming after me with both guns blazing, going after everything I have. She even wants my *boat*," he said, and his eyes took on a sheen of panic. "She rented a big house in Malibu that I have to pay for and she bought a new car, and she sends me credit card bills each month, and she's just shopping, shopping, *shopping*." He paused and scrubbed his forehead a moment. "So I was trying to work things out, you know? And I *had* her, Cooper, I had her!"

Cooper didn't know how or where Carl had her, and he didn't care. He was very uncomfortable hearing the details of his divorce. He preferred to get his news on these touchy Hollywood subjects like everyone else—directly from *TMZ*.

"She's out for blood. I mean, you know how women get when they catch you with your pants down."

No, Cooper didn't know. He'd always been faithful in his relationships. His problem was an inability to stick around for the long haul, or, as Jill had said as she'd walked out on him, *You're a fucking commitmentphobe.* But dammit, he was faithful.

"My attorney says, give her what she wants, because if you don't, she's going to drag your ass into court, and the judge isn't going to view your behavior favorably," Carl continued, rubbing his temples now.

"I don't know what this has to do with TA—"

"And I did, I gave her everything. And we're at an agreement, right? But one night, a little after Halloween, she calls up and tells me she wants this medal that belonged to her grandfather. Medal of Honor, Korean War. She gave it to *me* when her mother passed, but okay, I get it, and I'll give it to her. I know exactly where it is and I say, 'Sure, why don't you come over. We can have dinner. Maybe we can patch things up, Alicia. You know, for the sake of the kids.'"

He leaned forward, his eyes on Cooper's. "And she said, *Yes, Carl, we can,*'" he said, tapping his fist against Cooper's knee. "She said, 'I'm going to Vegas with the girls, and when I get back Sunday, I'll come over to get it, and we can talk. I don't want to drag this out. But I need that medal.'"

"So give her the medal," Cooper said, confused by Carl's story.

"Well, that's the thing—I was going to. But then it was gone."

"You lost it?"

"I didn't *lose* it. I know exactly where it was. It was sitting on my dresser. It was there every day, every night until . . ." He sighed and fell back against his chair.

"Until?" Cooper asked, still not following.

"Until Emma Tyler. She was, you know, *over.* Just a weekend thing with her, no big deal. You know how she is—she gets around."

No way, Cooper thought. Carl Freeman? She was with *Carl*?

"Anyway, Emma takes off before I even wake up, and honestly? We didn't do anything but fool around a little. She had her period or something, I don't know, she wasn't into it and seriously, a waste of my time. But we were in my room, and it wasn't going anywhere, and I got bored and fell asleep. The next thing I know, Alicia is standing there and she's holding up a pair of panties. And she is *pissed,* man. She said, *Just give me the fucking medal, Carl.'* But it was gone."

"Damn, Carl," Cooper said. "How do you live with so much drama?"

"I know, right?" Carl said, almost tearfully. "So I'm looking, I'm looking, and I figure out what happened. I was straight with

Alicia," he said, throwing up his hands. "I tell her I've misplaced it, that I will ask my housekeeper, Tiffany, about it, but Tiffany was on vacation, would be gone through Thanksgiving, so I couldn't ask her right then. And Alicia gets this weird look on her face, almost like she's happy, and she says, 'You know what else was in that medal box, you dumb fuck? My mother's wedding ring. My mother's four-carat *wedding ring*!'"

Carl threw his hands out wide and stared at Cooper. "Get it? Alicia put that ring under the medal on purpose! She was banking on me not finding that medal and the ring she hid under it. Now she's going to take me to court. She's going to throw out the settlement and go for the jugular. She's *got* me, Cooper. Emma took that medal, and Alicia's going to clean me out."

"So . . . just call Emma and ask for it."

"You think I didn't do that right away? She denied it, and then she wouldn't take my calls. So I sent one of my guys over there, and he comes back and it's Thanksgiving, and she's not there, and I figure, okay, she'll be back after Thanksgiving. So I try again. She won't pick up the phone. I send my guy there again and he tells me she took off."

"Took off—"

"Like . . . *fled*."

"Fled!" Cooper did his best not to laugh. "That doesn't make any sense, Carl. Why would she—"

"She's somewhere in Colorado. She told me she inherited a ranch or something, that's all I know. I'm willing to pay, Cooper."

"For what?"

"For what!" Carl said loudly, perturbed. "To find her! To go and get it, what do you think?"

"No," Cooper said instantly. "We're not private eyes."

"You have no idea how important this is to me, Coop. It's worth—literally—millions of dollars."

Cooper didn't care if it was worth the gross national product to Carl, he wasn't getting in the middle of this. He tried to stand, but Carl put his hand on his shoulder. "I'm begging you."

"Just get online and find another medal like it," Cooper said impatiently. "Buy another ring."

"Won't work. The medal is engraved with his name. It's a star with this blue ribbon. And the kicker is I don't know what that ring looked like—I never saw it. Alicia would know instantly if it was a fake. Listen, Cooper, you guys know the mountains. I just need someone to go and confront Emma and bring back that damn medal and ring—the box, the whole box. Or I'm going to end up in court and lose my shirt. Alicia has been waiting for me to do something to give her the ammo she needs to take it all, you know?"

"No, I don't know, Carl," Cooper said, and stood up. "I can promise you that TA doesn't want any part of the divorce business. I'm sorry—"

"No, no wait!" Carl said, and jumped up. "I'm not asking you to get in my business, I'm just asking you to go and get it back. Pay Emma if you have to, I don't care. Just get it."

"No thanks," Cooper said, and started for the door. "Listen, Carl, I'm sorry—"

"*Wait!*" Carl shouted. He hurried to his desk and grabbed a pen, then began to look for paper.

Cooper watched him, feeling sorry for him in a weird guy way. No man liked the idea of a pissed-off wife; women could be lethal when they wanted to be. But that didn't mean he was going to let TA anywhere near this.

Carl whirled around, holding up a pink Post-it. "Just one weekend. That's it." He handed Cooper the Post-it with the figure he was willing to pay.

Cooper blinked with surprise. He glanced up at Carl. "That's a lot of zeroes."

"It's nothing compared to what I stand to lose if this goes to court, and Alicia says her attorney is going to get it on the court calendar *this month*."

Cooper looked at the figure again. No way around it—that was a *lot* of money. "I have to talk to the guys."

"Of course, sure you do. But maybe you could talk to them today?" Carl asked, looking as hopeful as a kid waiting to open presents on Christmas morning.

Cooper sighed. This was exactly the sort of thing he despised, the sort of "service" agency he feared TA was becoming. He looked at the figure again. "I'm not promising anything."

"No, no, of course not," Carl said anxiously.

"I'd have to do some digging around you know, to find out where she went."

"Sure, of course."

Cooper looked at Carl, debating. The man looked desperate. "I'll be in touch."

"Great, great," Carl said. "But do you think you could be in touch sooner rather than later?"

Dammit, how did Cooper manage to get himself into these things?

TWO

Pine River, Colorado

The first thing Emma saw each morning when she awoke at Homecoming Ranch was the snowcapped mountain peaks. Sometimes, the clouds were so heavy they stacked right on top of the mountains like cotton candy. Sometimes, the sun would begin to peek out from behind the mountains and cast a gold halo around them. Whatever the view, it was so different from what she'd known all her life, so refreshingly crisp. So *new*.

Emma had not expected to be so moved by it when she'd arrived on the doorstep of the ranch she'd inherited earlier in the year. Frankly, she'd never believed she'd spend any time here. Emma's father had left the ranch to her and her two half sisters, Libby and Madeline. But Emma's relationship with her biological father had not been good, and she'd convinced herself that she hadn't wanted anything to do with the ranch or the sisters she'd scarcely known about.

But sometimes, things happen. Sometimes, the last place you want to be is the place you end up.

Emma hadn't expected to stay more than a couple of weeks when she'd shown up a few weeks before Thanksgiving. She'd just needed a place to lay low, to think about things. She'd understood that she'd have to contend with Libby and Madeline, both of whom had been at the ranch since their father had died. Emma had guessed Madeline wouldn't like her unannounced appearance, but that Libby would be cautiously hopeful of some sisterly bond. So Emma had planned to tell them the first day that she wasn't staying, that she was just passing through.

But Emma never said that. Because when she was driving up that bumpy road to the ranch house, she'd felt a calm settle over her. The anxiety that had built up during the last weeks in LA began to ebb, and when Emma had stepped inside the house, into the warmth and the smell of something baking, she'd been as uncertain about what she was doing at Homecoming Ranch as she had been about quitting her job and leaving LA.

And then she'd discovered the mountains.

Of course she'd seen them, had driven through them a few times. But she hadn't actually *felt* them until she was up here, at roughly eight thousand feet above sea level. She'd felt them that first week, felt their energy reverberating in her, waking her up.

Emma had been at Homecoming Ranch for a few weeks now.

The winter was turning out to be fairly mild, and most mornings were bright and crystal clear. It made Emma feel alive and in tune with nature. It made her feel real. She could almost hear practical Madeline: *I don't understand. Of course you're real.*

Yeah, well, Madeline hadn't come here from LA. In LA, Emma woke to the unnatural swish of the fronds on her neighbor's plastic palm trees scattered around his pool. And then she went to work in an industry full of plastic people and manufactured lives. She was sick of staging lavish events for toddlers' birthdays, Mommy's divorce, and the inexplicably pointless but popular White Parties.

The sun was a little higher in the sky this morning, which meant Emma had overslept. She rolled to the edge of her bed and hung over the side, her blond hair spilling onto the floor as she reached underneath it. Against Libby's advice, Emma had taken this room at the far end of the upstairs hall when she'd arrived. Libby said this room was too cold, that the heater didn't work properly. She was right about that—the propane burner had only one speed: low.

Luke Kendrick—Madeline's fiancé, whose family had once owned this ranch—said this room had been a nursery when his brother Leo was born, but as a toddler, Leo had tried to crawl out one of the three side-by-side windows that faced the mountaintops, and his mother had been so freaked out by it that she'd turned it into a study-slash-sewing room. Apparently, no one had ever studied or sewn anything here—the shelves were empty and there were no furnishings but the cast-iron twin bed.

Emma groped around under the bed until her fingers brushed the handle of her worn bag. She pulled it out and dragged it up onto the bed with her. She'd bought the bag for her seventeenth birthday, shelling out more than five hundred dollars, which she'd earned babysitting and washing cars, for the plush leather and multiple interior pockets.

She arranged herself cross-legged; the bed creaked beneath her weight. It was a wonder she managed to sleep at all on this thing— it was at least as lumpy as the gravy Libby had made at Thanksgiving. Gravy was a food Emma didn't understand—it served no nutritional purpose and really didn't add much flavor to anything. She hadn't meant to start an argument with Libby about it, but Libby had asked her what she thought of the gravy, and Emma had stated her opinion about gravy in general and Libby's in particular, and Libby had taken exception.

That was another thing Emma didn't get—why did people ask questions when they didn't really want to hear the answers?

That awful gravy was another reason Emma liked this room— in here, she couldn't smell it, or any of the other nutritionally useless food Libby made. And the room was far from her half sisters, who had taken rooms across from each other at the top of the stairs. It was far from the living and dining area, where Libby and Madeline gathered with their men at night. It was far from Los Angeles, which Emma had left behind, maybe for good (she was still mulling that over, still meandering through the options for the next phase of her life), and it was far from the rest of her family, which consisted of her mother, her stepfather, and the fair-haired, most-favored daughter, Emma's stepsister, Laura.

The bottom line was that Homecoming Ranch was far from everything Emma didn't want in her life anymore and, bonus, it had a view of the mountains. Beautiful, majestic mountains, their peaks as old as the earth, their ability to withstand the force of the universe unconquerable. *She* wanted to be unconquerable.

She reached for one of the many blankets on her bed and wrapped it around her shoulders, then unzipped her bag and peered inside.

There wasn't much to see. Some underwear and hair things. A blue silk tie. A small picture of a dog, a black Lab with the obligatory red bandana around his neck. An engraved pen—*15 years of service*. A gold cuff link, a marathon medal, and two military medals still in their boxes. Did ex-military really wear those things, or did they stick them in drawers? Two tie clips; one onyx, one silver.

Emma took the items out one by one, laying them out in a row. These were her reminders of who she was, of the Emma she'd left behind in LA. These things were little pieces of her now, embedded in her aura, all traded for the bits of her soul she'd left in their place. All of them equally important to her now, and yet none of them adding up to the whole her. There were still so many pieces of her that were missing, either permanently lost or as yet unformed. So many holes in her, so many tiny parts that were ill-fitting and odd. Emma had no illusions about that—she knew what she was, how awkwardly she'd been constructed, how off-kilter she lived her life. She'd always known that beneath the pretty façade was something that wasn't quite right. Looks truly were deceiving.

She heard the sound of women laughing drifting up through the wooden floorboards and glanced at the clock on her bedside table. It was ten after eleven and she needed to get ready for work.

She had a part-time job helping with the care of Leo Kendrick, Luke's brother. Well . . . perhaps *job* was too generous of a word. She had a part-time commitment. Yes, that was it. A commitment. She'd needed *something* to do when she'd decided to stick around, and Leo had captured her heart.

Leo was chair-bound, his body twisted with Motor Neuron Disease. His regular caretaker, a nurse, was out on maternity leave. Emma wasn't a nurse by any stretch, and Leo's father, Bob, had been very concerned about that when Emma had casually suggested that she take care of Leo until Marisol could come back to work. "Leo needs specialized care," he'd said gruffly. "This ain't happy hour."

But Emma was fairly persuasive when she wanted to be and had talked her way into spending afternoons with Leo, sandwiched in between two temporary nurses with proper credentials who came to take care of the important things, like meds and feedings and cleanings. Emma was Leo's companion, the one who watched TV with him and rolled him out onto the deck for a taste of the sun.

Emma put her things back in the small tote bag and zipped it up. She leaned over the bed once more and shoved it underneath, pushing it to the wall. And then she made a mental note to stop in at Tag's Outfitters and get a lock for her bag.

She didn't want anyone to ever see these pieces of her. They were her secret, her ugly little secret.

She showered and dressed in tights and boots, and a long, boxy sweater. She pulled her hair into a messy ponytail that looked more like art, a trick she'd learned from a famous hairdresser she'd slept with. At least he'd said he was famous. It was one night; she hadn't bothered to check it out.

When she was ready, Emma picked up her handbag and made her way downstairs. The smell of coffee that had sat too long in a pot and fried butter assaulted her olfactory nerves as she descended, causing her to wrinkle her nose. She could hear her sisters' voices, familiar to her, but not familiar. They were the voices of women she'd never really known, of women who had appeared in her life when their father had died, forced, along with her, into an uncomfortable little family trio. Emma had known Libby briefly when they were children. Madeline? She'd never heard her name until she learned of her father's death.

This morning there was someone else, a third woman. When Emma walked into the kitchen, she saw Danielle Boxer. Dani owned the Grizzly Lodge and Café in Pine River and apparently had become a close friend of Madeline's, judging by how many times she showed up at the ranch each week.

"There she is!" Dani said brightly. She wore her long gray hair piled on top of her head, and a white Guayabera shirt. Emma never saw Dani wear anything but those shirts.

"Here I am," Emma said as she walked across the kitchen, then pushed back the yellowed curtains from the window above the sink and opened it to air out the room.

Madeline was sitting at the bar, Libby busy with something in a bowl. Dani was standing next to the bar, her weight all on one hip. Behind her, in the living room, the star that Libby had put on top of the Christmas tree was at a height that made it look as if Dani were wearing it jauntily on her head.

"What's going on?" Emma asked as she walked back to the fridge and opened it, removing a small container of nonfat Greek yogurt. She ate the same thing every day when she got up: one seventy-calorie container of nonfat Greek yogurt.

"Oh, I just came out to say hi," Dani said cheerfully. "I feel like I've got a new lease on life. I hired a kid—Jacob Saddler, you know him?"

Emma had met Jacob at the fundraising 5k run Libby had put together to help buy Leo a new van. Jacob was still young enough to stare at Emma as if she were a creature from another planet.

"He's going to work the front desk a few days a week so I can get out! Let me tell you, when Mr. Boxer was alive, I didn't put in these long hours. I had a *life*. I had a garden and my knitting club." Dani sighed and put her hands on her back and dipped backward. "It's taking a toll—my back is *killing* me."

"Oh no," Madeline said, looking up from a pile of papers she was reading. "Maybe you should see a doctor?"

"Goodness, I don't have time for doctors," Dani said, but she winced as she eased down onto a stool. "They're just going to want to cut into me. No sir, I'm not going for that. Give me a better idea."

"Lose some weight. That would definitely help," Emma opined. She opened a drawer and picked up a spoon. But as she closed the drawer, she realized that her remark had been met with complete silence. She looked at the other women.

All three were staring at her; Dani seemed a little stunned.

"Emma," Madeline said low.

"What?" Emma dipped her spoon into the yogurt. "She said to give her a better idea. A doctor would say the same thing."

"Then let the doctor say it," Madeline muttered darkly.

"Oh, it's all right," Dani said, smiling again. "Emma's right—I could stand to lose about twenty pounds."

"I'd say more like forty," Emma said, and licked her spoon. "I mean, if you want to help your back."

"Oh my *God*," Libby said to the open window.

"Dani, I am *so sorry*," Madeline said, her blue eyes beseeching her friend.

Dani laughed, but it sounded a little strained. "I guess no one can ever say Emma doesn't speak her mind," Dani said briskly.

"No," Libby said, and glared at Emma. "Definitely no one can say that."

"What?" Emma asked, her spoon halting midair. "She asked!"

Libby shook her head, pushed her dark, curly hair from her face. It was a nervous gesture of hers, a memory that had come back to Emma after a few days of being around Libby. As girls, there had been a period of roughly eighteen months when Emma's mother and father had reconciled and Emma and Libby had lived together. Funny, the things you remember about childhood. Emma couldn't remember a single thing she and Libby did together, but remembered how nervous Libby would get when their father was around, and she'd push her curls from her face.

"Come on, I want to show you the picture of my wedding gown. It's on the computer," Madeline said. She stood up and gestured for Dani to go ahead of her into the adjoining room. She followed behind, and as she passed Emma, she glared at her beneath her dark bangs.

Emma finished her yogurt and turned toward the sink. That's when she noticed Libby standing there, her arms folded, her head down. "May I ask you something?" Libby asked crisply. "Have you ever been tested for Asperger's?"

Emma laughed with surprise, but in all honesty, she'd been asked that question before. "No. Have you?" She stepped around Libby to the sink.

"*No.* But I have a filter."

"I have a filter," Emma said defensively. "Maybe it's not as good as yours, but I have one."

"You do not! I don't know why you *do* that," Libby said, gesturing at the empty bar.

"Do what?"

"Antagonize people! For God's sake, Emma, you don't tell a woman she needs to *lose weight*!"

"You do if she is complaining about the pain in her back," Emma countered. "Oh, come on, Libby. She's in obvious pain. She made it clear she won't have surgery, and the only other option is for her to lose some weight. She's as big as a house! Don't pretend you didn't think the same thing."

"But the difference between you and me is that I don't *say* it. I don't intentionally hurt people."

Emma glanced at the dining room door. "I didn't hurt her," she said, but could hear the uncertainty in her voice. "I would want someone to tell me, wouldn't you?"

Libby shook her head. "You're unbelievable sometimes." She mumbled something under her breath, the exact words lost under the sound of a car pulling into the drive. Emma supposed that would be some man, either one attached to Libby or Madeline, or one of the five veterans who stayed on at the ranch and engaged in the rehabilitation therapies set up for them. Whoever it was, almost certainly a man.

Emma picked up her bag and slung it over her shoulder. "Look, I'm sorry if anyone was offended," she said, but she wasn't really sorry at all. It was reflex, old habit, to say sorry when she wasn't. *You think you're so cute.* That used to be one of her mother's favorite lines to her when Emma said something she apparently wasn't supposed to say. *You're not that cute, girl. You better watch that mouth. You better lose that tone.* She wasn't sorry for something she couldn't seem to change about herself no matter how she tried. And for the record, Emma never said anything to be cute—she'd said what she had today to be helpful. Emma liked Dani. Was it the way she'd said it? That she didn't couch it in the vague, touchy-feely language of women?

Story of her life, assuming people wanted to hear the truth.

Emma walked down the hall to the entry. She took a coat off the rack and donned it, belting it tightly around her. She picked up a pair of earmuffs from the communal basket and donned them, too, and was sliding her hands into her gloves when the sound of the doorbell startled her. No one ever rang the doorbell. Until this moment, Emma didn't know they even *had* a doorbell. The people who came to the ranch generally just walked inside.

"Will you get that?" Libby shouted at her.

Emma pulled her earmuffs off and let them rest around her neck, then opened the door.

She would never know how much time actually passed before she managed to speak. Later, she would remember how her heart hitched with a little thrill of excitement at the sight of Cooper Jessup on the other side of that screen door, peering down at her, his dark hair hidden under a ball cap, the scruff of a beard on his chin. And then the panic, the sheer panic.

Her mind raced through all the improbable reasons he would be standing there in a canvas coat, jeans, and hiking boots, patiently taking her in, top to bottom. She hadn't seen him since almost a year ago in Beverly Hills. For a brief moment she wondered if it was coincidence, but that was impossible—how could he even know about this ranch?

She stared up at his dove-gray eyes, his almond-brown hair, and at last said the first word that came to mind, a truncated question of how or what had brought him here, what spirit had divined him, if he was in fact a ghost or a figment of her imagination. But all that she could manage to get out was a singular, impatient, "What?"

"Well, hello to you, too, Emma," he said, unaffected by her brisk greeting. "You remember me, right? I was hoping I'd catch you here. Have you got a minute?"

A tingling sensation began to crawl up Emma's spine. As thrilled as she was that he should come in search of *her*, there was no way that this could be good. No way could this be anything but very, very bad.

At her lack of response, he arched a dark brow. "Hello?"

Emma snapped out of it, retreating quickly into her turtle shell. "I don't have a minute. I'm on my way to work."

"Really?" He looked surprised. "Not even a minute? Because I've come all the way from LA just to talk to you."

"Hello?"

Libby had appeared from thin air to stand behind Emma. She peered at Cooper curiously, as if she were trying to recall him from some long-forgotten function.

"You don't know him," Emma said. "But take all the time you need to get acquainted. I have to go."

"One minute, Emma," Cooper said as she pushed open the screen door, forcing him to step back. "Like I said, I've come a long way."

"*Oh?*" Libby asked, her voice annoyingly full of delight. "You did? Are you a friend of Emma's?"

"Don't, Libby," Emma warned her. She stepped through the screen door, brushing past Cooper.

"Slow down," Cooper said. "Please."

Emma stopped on the top step and glanced back at him. "All right, what do you want?" she asked, and looked at the man's watch she wore loosely around her wrist.

"Emma!" Libby exclaimed, horrified as she always was by Emma's abruptness. "You don't need to be in such a hurry. It's not a *real* job—"

"Yes, it is a *real* job," Emma insisted with a withering look for Libby. Okay, so she'd had to talk her way into it and she wasn't being paid for it. But it was where she wanted to be, and it was honest work. It was *important* work. It wasn't a White Party for Chrissakes.

"I mean, it's not like you have to punch a clock," Libby clarified. To Cooper, she said, "I'm so sorry. I didn't—Emma, can't you at least introduce us?"

"Introduce who?"

Good God, here came Madeline to gape at Cooper, too. Emma was not going to do this. She *couldn't* do this. She wasn't going to watch hopeful Libby and disapproving Madeline study Cooper. She wasn't going to watch Cooper smile and chat them up. She wasn't going to pretend that Cooper was some old friend and introduce him around. She didn't owe Cooper Jessup money. She'd never slept with him. She hadn't asked him to come, and she wasn't going to stick around now just to be polite. What was the point of that? In the end, he would—well, who knew what he would do or why he was here, but Emma could hardly catch her breath, and she wasn't going to stay and find out. "There went your minute," she said to him, and started jogging down the steps.

"Where are you going?" Libby shouted.

Emma turned to answer and was startled to find Cooper practically on her heels. "What's the hurry?" he asked in a silky, cool voice. "You're running off like you just robbed a bank."

"The *hurry* is that I'm in a hurry," Emma said. She began to stride across the drive to her car. The four dogs that resided at Homecoming Ranch crawled out from beneath the porch with dusty fur and their tails wagging furiously to impede Emma's progress as they sniffed around her feet, delighted to have company.

Cooper leaned over and scratched the biggest one behind the ears. "You're in such a hurry I'm wondering if you're trying to avoid something," he said, and smiled.

It was a startling smile, and it reminded Emma just how devastatingly sexy he was. It knocked her off center a moment, but she quickly righted herself. She never allowed herself to sway off the precarious point that had become her center. The fall was too great.

"You're not trying to avoid anything, are you, Emma?" he asked, stepping closer. "You have nothing to hide, right? Nothing that maybe belongs to Carl Freeman?" He watched her closely.

Holy shit. Emma's heart began to pound painfully in her chest. *Carl* had sent Cooper up here? He'd finally stopped calling her, and she'd thought . . . she'd thought it was over, the whole ugly thing. "I don't know what you're talking about," she said, her calm tone amazing her.

"You know Carl, right?" Cooper asked, his gaze laser sharp and completely fixed on her.

"Yeah, so?"

"So he says you have something of his, and he asked me to come and get it back."

Now her heart was absolutely leaping about with panic. It was just a stupid old medal! It had been dusty and shoved off in one corner of his messy dresser, and it had looked as if it hadn't been touched in years! *Why* was he making such a big deal out of it? "I don't have anything of his. I hardly know him. How did you know where I was, anyway?"

"How?" Cooper glanced over his shoulder at Libby and Madeline, who were standing together at the top of the steps like two extras in a film, eagerly awaiting their cues. Cooper turned his gaze back to Emma and leaned in so close that she could see the stubble of his beard beginning to emerge. "Seems you mentioned Colorado during a little pillow talk. I did some checking around."

"Pillow . . ." Now Emma could hardly draw a breath. "Wow, and here I thought you Thrillseeker guys were more on the ball than that, Cooper. I hardly know Carl Freeman. He's obviously confused me with someone else, because I *definitely* don't have anything of his."

"You sure about that?" Cooper asked. "Because judging by how sure Carl is, and how all the color has gone from *your* pretty face . . . plus the fact that you appear to be shaking a little, I'd say that you *do* have something of his. So why don't you give it to me, and I'll disappear from this quaint little town and this scenic mountain dwelling, and you can go back to your not-real job or whatever it is you're doing up here."

Emma was going to faint. She squatted down and petted the four dogs who were absolutely nuts for attention from anyone, just so that she could find her breath. When she had it, she rose up again, fixed her gaze on Cooper as she'd fixed it on a thousand other men, and smiled. "Like I said, you're talking to the wrong person. Now, I really have to go to my job. My totally *real* job." She turned around and walked to her car. She had to fight the strong urge to sprint, and moved at her usual, languid pace. She climbed into her car, turned the ignition, and started down the caliche road, headed for Pine River.

She never once looked back.

Her hands were shaking so badly she had to grip the steering wheel with all her strength to keep from shivering her way off the road.

THREE

As he watched Emma's white Mercedes bounce down the road, Cooper was reminded of that over-the-top bat mitzvah last year, that deserted kiddie lounge, and the expression in Emma's eyes. He'd thought many times about the way she'd looked at him that night—like she wanted him and loathed him at once—wondering what it meant, what was going on in her golden head. With some hindsight, he'd decided it was a strange mix of want and trepidation.

He'd just seen that look again.

He felt a touch to his shoulder and turned around. Two pairs of blue eyes were staring up at him. The women bore a slight resemblance to each other in the color of their hair and eyes.

"I'm Madeline Pruett," said the one with straight, long, black hair and bangs. Her eyes were vivid blue. She extended her hand. "And this is Libby Tyler," she said of the other, whose eyes were a lighter shade of blue and her dark hair very curly. "We're Emma's sisters."

"Sisters?" he repeated, a little surprised by that. He'd uncovered a stepsister in LA. Laura Franklin was starring in a soap opera, and she'd laughed a little when he asked if she'd seen Emma. "No.

45

Would you think me a really horrible person if I told you I don't know or care where she is?"

Cooper had assured her that was none of his business, and had assumed the sisters had a rocky relationship.

"She's very difficult," Laura had said. "Something isn't quite right about her, you know? Buy me a drink, and I'll tell you about it."

Cooper had thought it an odd thing to offer—someone was looking for Laura's sister, and she was casting around for a date. "Let me take a rain check," he'd said. "So no idea where she might be?"

"No idea," she'd said, smiling prettily.

"Your mom?"

"She hasn't talked to her, either. They don't talk so much." Laura had stepped closer to him. "Like I said, buy me a drink." She'd smiled in a way that made Cooper think she was offering more. But he'd left it vaguely open, having no desire to have a drink with her.

He'd had no idea Emma had *more* sisters. No one had mentioned them.

"Half sisters," the one with curls clarified, as if reading his mind. "I'm so sorry that she, ah . . ." She winced a little, as if searching for the right words.

"Took off," Madeline finished for her.

"She was in a rush," Libby said apologetically.

Madeline looked at Libby sidelong, then at Cooper. "So! Are you two . . . ?" She made a swirling motion with her fingers. "Connected?"

"No," Cooper said.

"Then—"

"Oh, hey!"

None of them had heard Danielle Boxer walk out onto the porch. Cooper knew her because he'd taken a room at her lodge. The Beaver Room, to be exact, the creepiest room in the history of quaint inns. It had been fashioned to look like a beaver den, he supposed, with thick pine planks in the walls and a bizarre pine-stacking around the fireplace that looked like giant pickup sticks.

Ms. Boxer was the one who had told Cooper where Emma was staying, but he was still surprised to see the innkeeper here. This ranch seemed pretty far from the business of running her establishment, which, to this point, had appeared to be a one-woman endeavor. He wondered if Ms. Boxer had come up here to warn Emma he was asking about her.

"Mr. Jessup!" Ms. Boxer said cheerfully as she walked across the porch to join the sisters. "If I'd known you were going to come out so early, I would have offered you a ride."

"He's a friend of Emma's," Madeline said as if it were impossible to believe, while eyeing him curiously.

"I think "friend" is a little optimistic," Cooper corrected her. "I know Emma, but only casually."

"Oh!" said Libby brightly. "Are you a wedding planner, then?"

That question was so far beyond Cooper's ability to absorb that he could only stare at her.

"Of course not," Madeline answered for him. "I'm guessing law enforcement."

"Oh my goodness, she's not in trouble, is she?" Ms. Boxer asked. "We've had enough trouble with Libby here—"

"Dani!" Libby cried.

Now his curiosity was aroused, wondering what sort of trouble that curly-haired sister might have had. "I'm not law enforcement," he said.

"Whatever you do, why don't you come in for some coffee?" Madeline asked. "Maybe we can help."

"Thanks, but I don't have a lot of time. Would you mind telling me where she's working?"

Madeline and Libby looked at each other. "Is she in some sort of trouble?" Libby asked.

"No," Cooper said, shaking his head. She wasn't yet, anyway. "There's been a slight misunderstanding, that's all."

"What sort of misunderstanding?" Madeline asked.

"You'll have to ask her. I just hope to get it cleared up as quickly as possible so I can get on with some work I have in the area. If you could tell me where she's gone, I'd really appreciate it." Cooper smiled as charmingly as he could.

Madeline and Libby exchanged another wary look, but before either of them could decide how to answer, Ms. Boxer said, "She's gone into Pine River. She's keeping Leo Kendrick in the afternoons."

Madeline gasped. "Dani!"

"What?" Ms. Boxer asked. "That's where she is, ain't she? Leo lives on Elm Street, Mr. Jessup. I don't remember the house number, but you can't miss it. Little green house with a fence."

"Dani, please don't say any more," Madeline said, more forcefully.

"That's all I need. Thank you," Cooper said. "Nice to meet you all." He turned and strode for his rental car.

In his rearview mirror he could still see the women standing on the porch steps, the lights of the Christmas tree twinkling in a window behind them. They looked as if they were arguing.

He shook his head and turned his attention back to the road. He should have said no to Carl, he thought irritably, a straight-up, *no.* But after meeting with Carl that day, Cooper had gone back to the TA offices—offices that were littered with baby bouncers, stuffed dinosaurs, diapers, and baby wipes. Even the trash can that had once served as a makeshift basketball goal had been turned into a diaper pail. Cell phones were considered toys, and it didn't matter whose cell phone, either.

As Cooper tried to tell the guys about his meeting with Carl, he had to do it over the singing Elmo that was being persistently shoved in his ear by one of Michael Raney's twin toddler boys,

Braden or Brodie—Cooper couldn't tell them apart most of the time. The twins had come only a year after Michael's wife, Leah, had given birth to Daisy. It was a damn rabbit warren at their house.

Cooper had been more impatient than normal; he'd be the first to admit it. And he'd made a remark about the noise level in the office. He was pretty sure he'd said something along the lines of, "Elmo is distracting me," but it might have come out, "Braden and Brodie are worse than the monkeys in Costa Rica. Get Elmo out of my face before I drop-kick him out the window."

Of course Michael had gotten his back up. "Hey! No one calls those two monkeys except me," he said, pointing to the boys as they fought over a truck.

"You know what you are, Coop? Jealous." This, from Eli McCain, another of Cooper's partners, and the father of little Maya. "I know what you want," he'd casually continued in that West Texas drawl he'd never managed to lose after all these years in LA. "You want a wife and kids like the rest of us. Only you're too bullheaded to admit it."

That remark had rankled Cooper even more. These guys assumed just because *they'd* started producing offspring like some Future Farmers of America program, he must want the same thing. It so happened that Cooper had no idea what he wanted, but he did not want to babysit on the job. "I've got nothing against *your* slide into a soft belly and endless TV, Eli," Cooper said. "But we specialize in staging extreme sport outings for the rich and famous. *This*," he said, gesturing around him, "does not convey extreme sport *or* rich *or* famous. This looks like a romper room."

"Chill out, Coop," said Jack Price, the fourth and final Thrill-seekers partner. "We get most of our business online or by phone. No one comes to the office. No one is tripping over strollers except you. And Michael's boys only come once a week."

The twins came to the office on the day that Michael was "in charge" of them. Michael believed he was being a supportive father and husband, but in truth, he brought the tots to the office to be ruled by an inattentive committee of four grown men. It was remarkable to Cooper that Michael, who had always had such a sharp eye for detail, never seemed to notice the havoc those two wreaked. They were into every cabinet, every drawer. They liked strewing paper about and losing keys, and even that day, as Michael perused the contents of the fridge, Braden had lost interest in the truck and was laughing hysterically as he pummeled Cooper's ass with his little fists. At least, Cooper thought it was Braden.

"Since when is it un-PC to think maybe the workplace isn't the right place for babies?" Cooper had demanded of his partners, throwing his arms wide before swiping Braden up and holding him upside down, much to the delight of the boy.

"Since we all had them or have them on the way," Michael said, and shrugged at Cooper's incredulous look. Even Jack's wife was expecting their first child. "Times change, dude. You gotta roll with it."

"*Roll* with it? So, what, you're suggesting I go out and get a kid because you have?"

"I'm suggesting that maybe TA is changing. Maybe it's not the same outfit it used to be, and there's no real point to hanging on to the past," Jack had said calmly, as if he were speaking to a lunatic.

"Changing into what?" Cooper had demanded. "How about earning a living? How about getting the hell out of the city and doing something fun?"

"We still earn a living," Eli had said. "But maybe we work fewer weekends and maybe we don't hurricane surf."

Dammit, even now, Cooper was still pissed about that discussion. It had been only a couple of years ago that the four partners had been united in their life views—the more women and extreme sports, the better. They'd been well compensated for their adventures and were in high demand—

Well.

They *used* to be in high demand. Their ability to take some of the better jobs that took them out of the country into dangerous places had suffered when the herd of babies had started to grow and wives had gotten involved. It was like his three partners had walked off a movie set, leaving Cooper to hang lights or tidy up. He didn't like it. He didn't like feeling even slightly adrift.

But that afternoon, Cooper had felt more defeated than ever as he'd dislodged Braden from under his arm and handed him to Michael, who promptly set him down and handed him a wooden spoon. Braden beaned his brother almost instantly with it, setting off a round of screeching and tears.

"So what did Carl want?" Michael asked as he forcibly removed the wooden spoon from Braden's hand.

Cooper told them. About the medal, about Emma's flight to Colorado, to some place near Pine River.

"Emma Tyler!" Jack said, his eyes sparking when Cooper told them who the woman was. "Now *she* is one good-looking woman."

Cooper could not disagree. She was possibly the most attractive woman walking around Hollywood. Or Colorado, wherever she was. Too bad she was so strange. "Nevertheless," he'd said, "we are not in the business of chasing down people who steal trinkets from their lovers."

"I agree," said Michael. "Seems like a waste of our time. Why would he get mixed up with her, anyway? Everyone knows how she sleeps around."

"Oh yeah?" Jack asked, interested.

"Hell, I don't know," Michael said. "I've heard it."

"Who cares who she sleeps with?" Eli had said with a wave of his hand. "How much is Carl willing to pay?"

Cooper showed them the piece of paper on which Carl had written his offer.

For a moment, no sound but Elmo could be heard as the men stared at the zeroes scribbled on that paper.

"Well now," Eli said. "We *are* in the business of extreme sports. And we've got the canyoneering trip late next spring for Fox Studio execs. We haven't decided where, have we?"

"We have not," Michael said firmly. "And this seems like a perfect opportunity to go and explore some possibilities in Colorado, am I right? We've had good luck there, and it's a dry winter—Leah and I canceled our ski trip because there is no snow."

"Wait," Cooper had said. "Are you suggesting we go and look at mountain locations in the dead of winter?"

"Why not just consider this an opportunity to do some advance legwork on Carl Freeman's dime?" Eli had asked. He'd put his hand on Cooper's shoulder. "Just take a drive around, Coop. A look-see."

"*Great* idea," Jack said. "I'll draw up the contract with Carl."

"Come on guys—" Cooper was set to argue, but at that particular moment, he felt something wet on his leg. He glanced down. One of the twins had managed to get the lid off his sippy cup and had poured his milk on Cooper's leg and foot.

Cooper looked at that cherubic face, then at his three partners, all of whom were trying very hard not to laugh.

"Great. Just great," Cooper had said tightly, and had walked out of the offices before he'd said something he would really regret.

And he *did* love the mountains.

He'd even felt a little hopeful when he'd finally pulled into Pine River yesterday. It was high forties, a bright, sunny day, and he'd decided he wouldn't mind spending a little time here, maybe taking a trip over to one of the ski valleys one day. If Emma was going to run from Carl, this was a good place to go.

It hadn't taken too much digging to find out where, exactly, Emma had gone. She'd actually told her boss about Homecoming Ranch. "*I remember it had such an interesting name,*" the woman had said.

The drive out to the ranch had perked Cooper up. It was about eight miles out of Pine River, an old mining town that had sprung up on the valley floor high in the Colorado mountains. The mines were long gone, and the town had turned itself into a tourist destination for summer mountain sports. As the ski valleys were too far away to be considered convenient to Pine River, winter was the off-season for Pine River.

The ranch setting was a gorgeous location, a perfect postcard of welcome to the Colorado mountains. The house itself was set in a stand of alder trees, up against the mountain and Ponderosa pines. It was old and in obvious need of repair, but it still had its charm. The roof was a collection of steeply angled pitches over various rooms and floors. The ground floor of the house was built with stone, and the second story, which looked to have been added on at some point, was made of tongue-and-groove logs. Large plate-glass windows lined the front of the house and reflected the snow-capped mountains rising up across the valley.

In between the house and a red barn was a grassy area enclosed by cottonwoods. Faded Chinese lanterns had been strung through the trees, and three picnic tables were situated under the branches. From one tree, a tire swing spun lazily.

The only jarring element to the picturesque setting was the empty tent pads and partially constructed cabin.

Cooper had another look at them as he drove away from the ranch.

He drove out the gate marking the entrance to the property, and down the narrow, two-lane road that wended down to the valley. He passed beneath pines, spruce, and cottonwoods, past empty meadows. Eli was right—there could be some great opportunities for TA here. As the weather was abnormally warm and dry, Cooper was going to enjoy poking around once he was through with Emma.

Minutes later, Pine River came into view. Cooper entered the older part of town where houses sat beneath towering elms on streets laid out on a grid. It looked like Anywhere, America, with bungalow houses and neat yards. Cooper tried to imagine Emma Tyler living in this town, but he couldn't see it. She didn't fit. Cooper wasn't sure where Emma fit, actually, but it damn sure wasn't Middle America. It occurred to him that she might require her own planet.

She'd been shocked to see him, perhaps even a bit frightened, her eyes going wide. She had seemed to him even skinnier than the last time he'd seen her, and he wondered, why didn't the girl just eat? He didn't understand what was in her head. She was beautiful. He guessed that she pulled down a very good salary given her status at CEM, and was obviously good at what she did. She had everything going for her, but had a reputation for sleeping around, having a strange, distant demeanor, and merely tolerating everyone and everything around her.

All of those rumors were so wildly incongruent with the package of her that it intrigued Cooper in a don't-get-this sort of way. Maybe because he'd had a very different experience with her at the Applebaum bat mitzvah. She'd been sunny and engaging, and he'd really liked her . . . until that bizarre ending in the kiddie lounge.

And then, the kicker. There she'd been, in Reggie's limo. He would never forget her in the window of that limo, or her expression, framed in his mind's eye now. She'd looked resigned. Distant. Like the Emma of the kiddie lounge had checked out, and had been replaced by a sullen Barbie doll.

She'd obviously been unpleasantly surprised by him today. So why hadn't she just handed over the damn medal and sent him on his way? That's what he'd do if he were in her shoes—he'd just give the thing back and get on with life. Surely she knew he hadn't come all this way on a hunch. Surely she knew that he was certain she had it.

Cooper found Elm Street easily enough. The houses on this street looked a little older and more weather-beaten than some of the newer houses Cooper had seen on the edge of town. The houses were a midcentury style, with shutters and window awnings, their garages detached and suitable for only one car. He spotted a green house at the end of the block, a chain-link fence bounding the property. In the drive was a maroon-colored passenger van with elaborate flames painted up the sides. Cooper wondered idly what sort of business that was supposed to represent.

As he pulled to a halt in front of the house, he could see the recent addition to the structure. The paint wasn't quite a match; the owner apparently had declined to paint the whole house. Decking had also been added around the house, including a wheelchair ramp. That ramp, along with the flaming van, stumped Cooper. He couldn't begin to guess what sort of job Emma would have here.

He unfolded himself out of his rental, smoothed his hair back with his hands, and walked through the gate. But before he could make it up the walk, a man stepped out onto the porch. He wore a sweat-stained garden hat on his head and slowly came down the steps to meet Cooper, eyeing him warily. "Can I help you?" he asked gruffly, his blue eyes shining out from skin creased by mountain sun.

"I sure hope so," Cooper said amicably. "I'm looking for Emma Tyler. Is she here today?"

The man squinted at Cooper. "She's in trouble?"

"Everyone keeps asking me that," Cooper said with a chuckle. "Not that I am aware. I just have a message to deliver."

The man considered that for a moment, then offered his hand. "Bob Kendrick," he said. "Emma's inside with my son, Leo."

Judging by the man's age, his son was likely somewhere in his twenties or early thirties. Was Emma hanging out with some mountain guy? Was *that* what was going on here? That didn't seem her type, but then again, what did he know? Cooper supposed nothing about her would surprise him now.

"Come on, I'll show you in," Bob Kendrick said.

FOUR

I don't have a lot of time to fill you in on how Emma Tyler became vice president of Leo Kendrick Operations, because I'm, like, *super*busy.

Okay, I know what you're thinking, because Dad looks at me like that, too—like I'm a guy with Motor Neuron Disease who is sipping food from a straw, that's what I'm so busy doing. And that is totally true. But I'm also busy getting ready to go see the Broncos play the Patriots next week in Denver. That requires a *lot* of high-level thinking and planning for a guy without use of his limbs.

I'm Leo Kendrick, and it's true that I have MND, and it's also true that this football game is like the best thing that's ever happened to me. It wouldn't have happened at all had I not come at this like the certified genius that I am. That's no lie, just ask Stephen Hawking, the famous physicist who *also* has MND—anyone who has this disease is probably a genius. To wit: First, I had to convince the Methodist ladies to take me on as this year's charity case. Check. Then, I had to convince them to get me tickets to the game at Mile High Stadium, which they managed, believe it or not, because someone from Pine River knew someone. Check. Better still, they knew someone important and managed to get me into a *skybox*. I think that's because I said something like, what is the point of going all that way in a chair if you can't get into a skybox, and fortunately, everyone agreed about that. Check, check, and checkmate.

So I scored the tickets for me and my friend Dante, who gets his chemo at the same boring hospital where my doctors sit around playing tiddlywinks, but then I suddenly realized that the family van—a former *bread delivery truck*—was not going to carry my ass all the way to Denver, no sir. So I *suggested* to the Methodists that they might want to have an auction to raise money to get me a van, and they did, but they didn't raise enough, so Libby Tyler stepped in and put together this 5k race to benefit yours truly, and the next thing you know, I am the proud owner of a *sweet* van, man. It's like a military machine—they roll me into that thing like a nuclear warhead and lock me down.

But you know what I learned? There's no such thing as true glory without someone coming around to bitch about it. I'm serious as a heart attack right now. Believe it or not, some people actually complained that it wasn't "fair" that *I* got the van when I'm not exactly a certified charity, and my dad and brother agreed. My dad and my brother are just too proud sometimes, you know what I'm saying? I'm trying to think of something funny to say about it, but honestly, after all my hard work, it totally pissed me off. So I said to myself, okay, Leo, what does a genius do? A genius arranges everything with a *real* charity to make sure this van will be donated to people with MND and other assorted jelly-legged diseases when I'm gone.

Oh, I'm definitely going. I mean, it's not like I know when or anything, but trust me, the tires will still be new on the van when the MND people get it.

I also learned that being a Dudley Do-Right is *totally* exhausting, and the worst of it was that Marisol wasn't there to help me. You've heard about Marisol, right? The hotheaded sexy Latina who happens to be a nurse here in town? For the last two years she's been bossing me around and changing my diapers and making sure my bed is set at the perfect angle so I can watch my TV shows. And then she had to ruin it all by having a baby and taking maternity leave, and let me tell you, that little stinker Valentina could not have come at a worse time. But do you think Valentina cares how her entry into the world affects *me*? No way, man. She just cries and curls her hands into little fists and sleeps a lot. I told that little stinker *after* football season would have worked better for me, but you know how babies and saucy Latinas are—they wait for no one.

So here's where things get interesting. Get this—my dad didn't have anyone lined up to take Marisol's place, even though she'd been pregnant for like two hundred years, and he said something dumb like, *looks like it's you and me, pal,* and I said, *over my dead body,* which my brother, Luke, pointed out is not a good thing to say to Dad, because, you know, he's going to have to step over my carcass eventually. But I'm not so far gone that I'm going to let my dad change out my tubes and hose me down and other things I won't mention here because I might vomit. I guess Dad wasn't too keen, either, because he found this service, and they send these totally hot nurses out once a day to check things out and do all the stuff I am *never* letting my dad do. They're great, but they are expensive, and we couldn't afford for them to be lollygagging around all day long. In other words, I needed someone cheap to hang around in case I couldn't work the remote, and who should show up but Emma Tyler?

I know, *right*? Crazy!

But if you'd lived around Pine River for twenty-seven years like I have, you would know just how crazy life has been for all those Tyler women. It started with their dad, Grant Tyler. Here's the flat-out truth about Grant—he was a cheat and a player. He hooked up with any hoohaw that would admit him entrance, and there were a few. Emma and Libby have different moms, but at least each knew the other was out in the world. Madeline has an altogether *different* mom, and she was a complete surprise to them. They were to Madeline, too.

That's not all Grant did. He practically stole Homecoming Ranch from *my* dad, and then he upped and died and left it to those girls instead of giving it back like he said he would. And he left the ranch in worse shape than when he got it, so it's not worth as much as is owed on it. So when the sisters all met up in Pine River, they had all these expectations, like they'd really dig each other and could agree on what to do with the property. Anyone who knows women *at all* could have told them that wasn't going to happen, at least not the way *they* thought it would, and long story short, they're all living up there together trying to get along and figure out what to do with the ranch.

I'm happy to say the Kendricks are out of the running. I mean, sort of. Luke is going to marry Madeline, so he'll have one foot in and one foot out. But me and Dad? We like it in town.

So *aaaanyway*, Emma was the last one to come into the fold, and I swear I am not lying when I say it was obvious from day one that she had a thing for me. I mean, she kept coming around and hanging out even before Marisol had her baby. I mentioned this to Luke once. I said, "Emma is totally hot for me," and Luke said I was taking too many pain pills again, because no way would a woman as kick-ass gorgeous as Emma Tyler have a thing for me. He hypothesized that she was bored in Pine River and didn't have anything better to do, to which I replied with some ideas that are not G-rated, and I begged Dad to throw something at Luke's fat head, but as usual, Dad refused to participate in "you-boys-and-your-shenanigans" business.

Joke's on Luke, because it turned out I was totally *right*. I mean, who was first in line to hang out with me when Marisol had her baby?

Yep, Emma Tyler. Good—you're keeping up.

Dad said, "Look, Emma, we can't pay you anything," and she said, "I don't care," which totally proves my point, because why would she come to this dump if she wasn't getting paid? But she started coming around every day, showing up at noon, staying until at least four, sometimes a lot later. Contrary to what everyone thinks (well, Madeline thinks), she's really nice. But she is a little weird.

She tried to play *Deadly Dungeon Duels* with me, my newest video game, but she kept asking these existential questions, like, why dungeons, why not forests, and other dumb stuff. It was annoying, but it's okay. About that time, my right hand stopped working, and I can't do the controller with my left, so it didn't really matter. Emma and I started watching TV.

Check it—one day, I'm in bed watching *House of Cards* on Netflix, and I'm on episode eight, and it's totally intense, and who crawls onto the bed with me and lays there like we're a couple? And I said, "People are going to talk. I hope you're okay with that, because I sure as hell won't deny anything happened since I have a reputation to protect." She said, "I don't care—let them talk. I have a reputation to protect, too." Which is why I totally dig her.

But I said, "Well, look, Emma, this is okay as long as you don't talk or disrupt the streaming video, and for God's sake, don't ask me questions during *House of Cards*." She said she wouldn't, so we started streaming videos together.

Luke told me it didn't look good for me and Emma to be lolling on a bed in the afternoon streaming video from Netflix all afternoon. Personally, I think Luke is a little jealous because there was a time back in the day that chicks used to flock to *him*. Those days are over for sure, and even if they weren't, Luke is going to marry Madeline on New Year's Eve, and Madeline doesn't strike me as the type to put up with "shenanigans," as Dad would say.

During these afternoon video-viewing sessions, Emma's done a little talking. She's said things like, *you don't look at me like other guys.* Which I pointed out was probably because I can't turn my head. And then she would say this off-the-wall stuff that had nothing to do with the program, like, *sometimes I wonder what it would be like to be someone else—do you?* I can't snort anymore, but if I could, I would have to that question. It's not like I lie around wondering why me, why MND, but yeah, the idea of being someone else has definitely crossed my mind a time or two in the last couple of years.

She said some other stuff that I won't share because I promised Dani Boxer I'd tell her everything first, and I haven't had time to deliver the dirt. Anyway, I didn't need my superior intellect to guess where this was all going, so one day, I casually say, "You know, Emma, I'm not going to live forever." As in, not very long at all, but I didn't say that, as it tends to freak people out.

As expected, she got all flustered and said, "Why do you say things like that?"

I said, "Because you need to get a grip—I can't be your boo."

She said, "You can't be my *what?*"

And I had to sidetrack a little and explain to her the *Real Housewives of Atlanta*, but then I circled back around and said, "Look, I know you're totally into me, and that's okay. Lots of chicks are. And I don't mind you hanging around at all. But you need to know that it isn't really going to go anywhere, you and me."

Emma smiled in this funny way that made me think maybe I'd hurt her feelings. But then she said, "*Obviously* I know that. You're dying."

Hey, even I was a little shocked by that. But at the same time, I really dug it, because at least Emma Tyler can say it out loud. At least Emma doesn't pretend I'm going to somehow miraculously beat this thing and live. No one else around me can face it, much less *say* it. Only Emma and I can.

"Well, that's kind of beside the point," I said, because it was. "The point is that I'm just not that into you."

She sort of averted her gaze and said, "You're so funny, Leo."

Yes, I am. But I wasn't being funny then. And even though she pretended to think I was, I could tell she knew I wasn't being funny. She got kind of quiet and wouldn't say anything for a while, and then said she didn't want to watch another episode of *The Americans,* so you *know* she was pissed.

She got up and left my room, and I could hear her talking to Dad for a long time, and he was probably spelling it out for her: *Leo. Is. An. Ass.*

Hey, I wear the mantle proudly.

But the next day Emma was back and she was her same old self, and I thought things were cool and we both knew where we stood. But I didn't count on Hollywood showing up at my door. Isn't that the beauty of this life? Just when you think there's no hope, that things are going to be totally boring for the rest of your life, something pops up to make it interesting again.

FIVE

Emma knew Bob Kendrick didn't trust her. He followed her
around to double-check everything she did, from changing the
sheets to making Leo's protein smoothies. Once, he even leaned
over her shoulder to make sure she was recording the right show
for Leo.

That was okay, Emma understood. She wouldn't trust her,
either. She was accustomed to not being trusted—people seemed
suspicious of her right away. Mostly women. They always eyed her
as if they thought she was going to steal their husbands, which
Emma chalked up to her looks. She didn't consider herself con-
ceited in that regard, but realistic. Why pretend?

That's why she loved Leo so much. Emma had never met anyone like him. Not anyone with MND, but like *him*. She'd known
from almost the moment they'd been introduced that Leo was
similar to her because he called it as he saw it, too. He just had
more finesse with his opinions. He wasn't "socially awkward" as
Emma's stepfather always said of her. But like her, Leo was realistic; he knew he was going to die and didn't hide behind useless

hope or prayer or whatever it was that people did to keep from facing awful, irrevocable truths. And it was an awful truth, one that sometimes kept Emma awake at night. Yet she loved that Leo could look headlong at his reality. He was braver than anyone she had ever known.

Emma understood the rest of the world didn't think like she and Leo did, and it didn't bother her that men like Bob decided they distrusted her and then stuck there. So when Bob stepped into the kitchen and told her that some guy was looking for her, he looked almost gleeful about it, as if he'd finally been proven right—she was not to be trusted.

"I know," she said, and dropped the tops of Leo's drinking tubes into a pot of boiling water. What the hell was Cooper doing, following her here? Her pulse began to race again. She didn't like this, being the prey. She was always the one to do the stalking. Not as blatantly as this—she never had to put much effort into it, really—but still.

Bob squinted at her, his eyes disappearing into folds of skin. "So who is he?"

Emma glanced up, hoping her face didn't betray her. "Just a guy."

"*Just* a guy doesn't *just* show up in Pine River," Bob gruffly pointed out.

Emma shrugged and turned back to her task.

"Well? Are you coming?" Bob demanded.

Before Emma could answer, she heard Cooper's low voice in the living room, followed by Leo's. "Nope," Emma said, and reflexively hitched her shoulders, as if trying to shake off Cooper's voice from her skin. "Not coming. I've already talked to him and I don't have anything more to say. I have things to do."

"*No, no, no,*" Bob groaned, and rubbed his forehead with both hands. "Jesus, please don't do this here, Emma. Don't bring your drama into my house and around my son."

"*My* drama! You're the one being overly dramatic," she said as she removed the bottle tops from the boiling water and set them in a rack to dry.

"Oh, am I?" he said sarcastically. He leaned backward, glanced into the front room a moment. "You gotta come talk to him," he almost whispered, presumably so Cooper wouldn't hear him.

"No, I don't."

Bob glared at her with a *Law and Order* glint. He stepped closer—which took him across the tiny kitchen to the bar that separated him from Emma. "Just what are you hiding, girl?"

"*Nothing,*" she said, and ignored the tingling in the nape of her neck that said she was. "No law says I have to talk to every guy who comes to my door."

"Maybe, but he came to *my* door. Who is he? What does he want? How the hell do I know this guy ain't stalking you and looking for trouble?"

He had a point. Emma turned off the burner and faced Bob. "He's a guy from LA. That's all. He's no one to me, I swear." Jesus, *another* lie. For someone who always wore the truth as her shield of armor, that was two whoppers on the day. "As for why he's here? I don't really know. But he's not violent."

"You don't know that," Bob said.

The sound of Leo's laughter wafted into the kitchen. "Yep, she's got two eighty-five horsepower," they heard Leo boast. "She'll blow any car off the road."

Bob rolled his eyes, as he often did when Leo talked about that van.

"That's amazing," came Cooper's low, dulcet drawl.

"Is he an ex-lover or something?" Bob whispered loudly.

Emma snorted, as if that was as ridiculous as it was impossible. "*No.* You didn't have to let him in, you know," she said. "Most people see a stranger at their door and they don't let them in. Did you think of that?"

"Thought he was a friend of yours," Bob said, and stepped around the bar, squeezing past Emma to take a pan from the stove. "Listen, I don't give a rat's ass who he is." He paused to dip down and look her right in the eye. "But I won't have any drama around my boy. Got that?"

"Couldn't miss it," she said, leaning back from him. "Okay, okay, I'll get rid of him. But in the future, if you don't want drama, don't let strangers into your house! Hello!"

Bob frowned at her.

"I'm just saying," she muttered as she left the kitchen.

Leo was exactly where Emma had wheeled him a half hour ago—in his chair, his head propped up by two pads on either side of the headrest, his fingers unnaturally curled around a stick that Leo insisted kept them from closing up completely.

And there was Cooper Jessup, leaning up against the wall, his arms folded across his chest, long and lean and handsome. But it wasn't that which held Emma's interest. It had been Emma's observation that when people first met Leo, they often looked purposely blank so as not to let on to all the thoughts swirling in their heads, such as, *thank God, not me,* and *what is wrong with him,* and *what do I say.* They tried very hard not to stare at Leo and his useless appendages and the apparatus that was necessary to keep him upright.

But Cooper was looking directly at Leo like he was another buddy he'd run into. Maybe he'd been shocked when he'd first walked in, but now he looked completely relaxed, as if he chatted with guys like Leo all the time. He also looked like a sexy motorcycle bandit with his jacket and boots and the shadow of a beard on his chin. As if he had a history as long as the road and the moves to prove it, and Emma felt that funny tingle slip down her spine.

Don't do that, Emma. Don't look at him like that.

"I had a buddy from high school do the flames," Leo was explaining, always happy to talk about the van. "It's sick, right?"

"Yep," Cooper said. "I've never seen a van as cool as that."

"I got it to take me to a Broncos game," Leo said. If he could stand, he'd be hitching up his pants and puffing out his chest right now. "Going to see them play the Patriots. Got skybox seats lined up for me and my pal Dante."

Cooper's face lit up. "Dude, that's awesome," he said. "My money is on one of those two teams to win the Super Bowl."

"Broncos, right?" Leo said excitedly.

"Maybe. But the Patriots are looking as strong as ever."

"Do you know how hard it is to get tickets like this?"

"I can't imagine."

"It takes a *genius*. Here's how I did it—"

"Excuse me," Emma said before Leo could launch into his ever-expanding story of how he'd managed to obtain tickets and a van to a football game.

"Wha—what?" Leo stammered, unable to turn his head.

"He came to see me, Leo."

"Hey, are you trying to stop me from talking about the game again?" Leo protested. "It's such a great story! Okay, well, maybe it's time *you* told a story, Emma. What'd you do that brings Cooper Jessup here all the way from Los Angeles?"

"Why is there an automatic assumption that I did anything?" Emma complained as she moved between Leo and Cooper, frowning down at Leo.

"Correct me if I'm wrong, baby doll, but generally speaking, men don't come halfway across the country unless there's a love thing going on. Or to catch a fugitive. I mean do you *ever* watch *Dateline*? I know you don't have a love thing going on since you're totally into me, so the only other logical conclusion is that you're on the lam. Am I wrong?"

"You're so wrong you're embarrassing yourself," Emma said flatly.

"Then who is he?" Leo asked.

"Just a guy," Emma said, and whirled around, intending to keep Cooper from moving any deeper into the house or conversation.

But Cooper was one step ahead of her and had moved around her. "First of all, I'm not just a *guy*, I'm a man." He looked directly at Emma when he said it, and the emphatic way he said *man* radiated down her spine and made her knees begin to quiver. "Yes, I did come with the intention of speaking to you." He shifted his gaze back to Leo. "But not to apprehend her. I'm not a bounty hunter or a cop. But I do need to speak to her, if that's okay."

"Man, that would be *super*cool if you were a bounty hunter, bro," Leo said.

"But he's not, and he already spoke to me." To Cooper, Emma said, "This is where I work. So . . ." She gestured firmly to the door.

"Hey, what's *this*?" Leo exclaimed. "Is it possible that I could have been mistaken? I mean, the odds are *totally* against it, but this has all the markings of a lovers' quarrel."

"No," Cooper said in a manner that Emma found unsettlingly quick and firm.

"Hey, it's okay," Leo said. "Emma and I aren't together—"

"Leo, shut up!" Bob shouted from the kitchen where, apparently, he was managing to keep up with the conversation.

"Can't, Dad!" Leo said cheerfully. "My mouth is the only muscle that works, and if I don't use it, I lose it. Pardon, Mr. Jessup— you were about to tell me about this love affair?"

"I'm about to stuff a sock in that mouth!" Bob yelled.

"Ignore him," Leo said. "He has a tendency to feel left out."

JULIA LONDON

Cooper smiled. "I wish I had something interesting to tell you, Leo. I'm also in town to do some work." He gave Emma a self-satisfied smile that only made her feel wobblier.

"What do you mean, work? *What* work?" she demanded.

"I think what Emma means to ask is, what kind of work do you do?" Leo offered helpfully.

"She knows what work I do," he said. "I have a company with some buddies called Thrillseekers Anonymous." He explained TA to Leo, and added, "We've got a contract to stage a canyoneering event next summer for some studio execs, and I'm going to check out the area."

"That is *sick*," Leo said, his voice full of awe. "Dad, did you hear that?"

"I did," Bob said, appearing in the door that led to the kitchen, wiping his hands on a dish towel. "You ought to talk with my son Luke. He's been all over these mountains. He could show you around."

"Oh yeah?" Cooper asked, perking up.

"There's nothing around here that he'd be interested in," Emma said, throwing up her hands as if trying to keep the men apart. "You're wasting your time, Cooper. Go to Telluride and look around. That's better."

"Telluride," Cooper drawled. "Where is that, exactly, Emma?"

Bastard. She had no idea where it was, and he knew it.

"No, no, Dad's right for once," Leo said as Bob ducked back into the kitchen. "There are loads of places around here to rappel or ride white water, or even do some of the swinging Tarzan stuff I saw on the National Geographic Channel. Luke would totally show you around and he's probably done it all."

"I'd love to meet him," Cooper said.

"Then come over tonight. He'll be here. Hey! Why don't you come for dinner? Dad! He should come for dinner!"

"Leo, for heaven's sake," Bob said, appearing again with Leo's lunch in a repurposed half-gallon milk jug. It was two-thirds filled with the smoothie Emma had made before Cooper had shown up. "Before you go issuing invitations, you might ask the head bottle washer if there's anyone available to *make* a dinner," he said as he fit the jug into the apparatus he had welded onto the side of Leo's chair.

"Don't let this jug of delicious liquefied fish and vegetables fool you," Leo said to Cooper. "We still eat real food around here. Well . . . we might agree to disagree on the definition of *real,* but what I mean is that it's not all liquid—some of it, you can actually chew."

Bob said something under his breath. "It ain't fish and vegetables." He moved to stick the straw in Leo's mouth.

"No, Dad, wait!" Leo exclaimed. "I'm having a conversation here!"

But Bob stuck the straw into Leo's mouth, who was powerless to stop him. Leo began the laborious effort of drinking.

"You're more than welcome to dinner tonight if that's what Chatty Cathy here wants," Bob said, jerking a thumb at Leo. "I'll whip something up. Won't be gourmet, but it will be edible."

"You're kidding, right?" Emma said, startled by Bob's willingness to have Cooper over for dinner. "What happened to the complaints about stranger danger and not wanting any trouble? Now you're inviting him to dinner?"

"Leo wants him to come," Bob said with a shrug.

"You don't have to be nice to him! It's not like he's a friend of mine!" she exclaimed.

"Gee, thanks," Cooper said.

"See, now, this is the kind of thing I was trying to tell you the other day," Bob said, pointing a pair of fingers at her. "You got the wrong idea about how to do people. Inviting him to dinner is called hospitality. I don't know how you do it up there in LA, but in these parts, we ask people to come in and sit down."

"Jesus," Emma muttered heavenward. She was not in the mood for a Bob Kendrick lecture, any more than she was in the mood to deal with Cooper. She glared at the latter and pointed to the door. "Cooper, will you please come outside with me so Bob can give Leo his lunch?" She walked to the door and yanked it open.

Cooper glanced back at Leo and Bob. "You're sure it's no trouble?"

"Not at all," Bob said. "I'll call Luke now."

"Cooper, come *on,*" Emma said.

"See you, Cooper!" Leo said, having managed to get the straw out of his mouth, driven by a desire to have the last word. "Between Luke and Dad and me, we know everything there is to know about Pine River. And I mean *everything,* if you get my drift." He sort of waggled his brows as Bob fit the straw into his mouth once more.

"Looking forward to it," Cooper said, and followed Emma out onto the porch. Once outside he said a little curiously, "Actually, I don't get his drift at all."

Emma wrapped her arms tightly around her and gave him her best glare. "I can't believe you *followed* me here."

"Yeah, well, I can't believe you won't give me that stupid medal." He arched a dark brow at her.

"I told you, I don't have anything that belongs to Carl. Not one thing. He's desperate and he's acting like an idiot, and he happens to be very good at that."

"I won't disagree," Cooper said. "But that doesn't mean he's lying." He smiled a little, which made his eyes glimmer in the winter light. "But you know what? He seems pretty damn sure you *do* have it. He's so sure, in fact, that he was willing to pay me a lot of money to come up here and get it. So why not hand it over? Then you can go back to your life, and God knows I'll get back to mine."

Emma didn't like the way he sounded so eager to get back to his. And really, Carl had sent him out here for a forgotten old medal? *Why?* Emma curiously studied Cooper a moment. "What's a lot?" she asked skeptically.

"None of your business. But let's just say there were more than a few zeroes attached."

That made Carl a lot crazier than Emma had previously believed. God, she should never have gone to Malibu with him! Frankly, she should never have done a lot of stuff she'd done in the last ten years, but then again, she was her own worst enemy, never able to resist the temptation to hurt herself with bad-news men. Why she couldn't be normal, couldn't be comfortable with someone like Cooper, why she couldn't believe that was even *possible* . . .

Okay, so she was messed up. But she was not as messed up as Carl Freeman, apparently, and there was some consolation in that. "If you're taking money from him, that kind of makes you a mercenary, doesn't it?" she asked, hoping, she supposed, to shame Cooper off the porch.

Cooper looked surprised, and then he laughed. He was not easily shamed. "Money talks, baby. And if you took the medal from him, what does that make you?"

An enormous rush of shame swept through Emma. She knew what it made her. She knew how despicable she was. She folded her arms over her body, holding herself tightly. "That would make me a thief. Which I am not, which I keep trying to tell you. I didn't take his stupid medal."

"Hmm," he said dubiously, his gaze sliding down her body.

Great. She was a horrible liar. Emma was going to have to shift tactics. "What's really going on here? Are you doing this because I wouldn't let you kiss me in Beverly Hills?" It was a pure shot in the dark. She had no illusions about what had happened that night at Beverly Hills. But she also knew men did not like to be challenged on their game.

Lo and behold, her question had the desired effect. Cooper stared down at her in shock. "Are you kidding?"

"Not kidding. You wouldn't be the first guy who doesn't like rejection. Usually guys like you can't bear it."

"Guys like *me*?"

"Yeah," she said, nodding. "Guys who are used to girls wanting them. And then when one doesn't, they can't handle it."

He swayed back, his eyes narrowing. "In what universe did you reject me?" he demanded.

"You wanted me to have a drink with you. I said no." She shrugged, letting that stand as the Great Rejection of Beverly Hills. Say it enough, and they believe it.

But like that night in Beverly Hills, Cooper didn't bite. He suddenly chuckled, then shifted forward and touched her arm, his hand curling around her elbow and drawing her close. "Here's the funny thing about that, Emma," he said, his voice smooth and deep. He bent his head so that his mouth was very close to hers, and her pulse began to flutter like an army of hummingbirds. "If I'd wanted to have you that night . . . I would have *had* you."

She gaped at his audacity as a stronger, heart-melting shiver of delight raced through her. *Bravo!* she wanted to shout. She couldn't think of a time a man had *ever* said that to her, had ever been so bold with her. She glanced down at the hand on her elbow that was now beginning to trail lazily up her arm to her shoulder.

"Here's what's going to happen now," he said, his finger now sliding across her shoulder. "I'm going to be around town a few days, so you'll have plenty of time to think about the medal and what you want to do with it." He moved his finger on to her chin, drawing a tantalizing line from ear to ear. "I'll check in with you and see if you haven't decided to hand it over after all. Because we both know you have it." He touched her bottom lip, his finger lingering there, and he smiled in a sexy, self-confident way that reminded her of the male stars in the films Emma poured herself into to escape the truth of her life, and it sent another, much more aggressive wave of impossible desire down her spine.

Emma didn't like that. She didn't like that at all. She didn't like the way she was melting inside or had lost the upper hand. She didn't like the powerful tug of attraction, because that was where the bad news always started. She tried to bite his finger, but he was too quick; he yanked it away from her lip a hairbreadth before she snapped.

"I don't have to think about anything, Cooper. Hang around as long as you want. Get yourself invited to dinner at every house in Pine River for all I care. There is nothing to hand over."

His smile deepened. "You're a horrible liar," he said, and walked off the porch, pausing at the bottom to glance back at her. "I'll be seeing you around, Emma." He walked on.

"Ass clown," she muttered as he strolled casually down to the gate.

"I heard that," he called out as he went out the gate and got into his ass-clown car.

SIX

Emma Tyler had nerve, Cooper would give her that. Was she crazy? She thought she had *rejected* him? He hadn't known whether to laugh outright or put his fist through the wall with that one.

The thing about women that Cooper never seemed to get, had never come close to getting in his thirty-eight years, was how mad they would become for no apparent reason. *He* was the one who ought to be mad here, not Emma. He was the one who had come all this way, and yet, she acted as if *she* had somehow been wronged. And she was the one who had done all the wrong things!

Nope, he didn't get it, and if Eli were here, he'd say the reason Cooper didn't get it was Cooper's own fault, that he'd never spent enough time with a woman to learn how to understand them. *It's an art, Jessup. You don't suddenly just get it after a few weeks of dating. You have to study it.* He'd offered this up when Jill had ended it with Cooper for the second and final time. Yeah, well, Eli had never been Mr. Steady, either, but then he'd gone and fallen in love, and the moment he did, he was a goddamn expert.

The one thing Cooper did get after that ridiculous exchange on the Kendrick porch was that Emma had the damn war medal. He might not be an expert on women, but he was an expert on liars, thanks to his older brother, Derek, who had schooled him properly.

Derek was the biggest liar of all. He'd perfected the art of deception—about his addiction, about his whereabouts, about hiding from the law. There wasn't a single thing that Derek hadn't lied about in his life. There wasn't a moment of his life he hadn't tried to hide from someone. Well, he wasn't hiding at present, but he was probably still lying while he did his time for armed robbery.

Cooper grimaced to himself as he drove back to the Grizzly Lodge and Café. He'd had a voice mail from his mother, a cheerful message that Derek was being released. "Just in time for Christmas!" she'd happily crowed.

Yeah, great, just in time for Christmas.

Cooper still loved Derek in that way brothers have of loving each other, no matter what. But he didn't find his brother very good company. He resented the grief Derek had put his parents through, the constant disruption in his family life. Admittedly, Cooper had learned a few things from his brother. In the beginning, Derek had taught him a lot, like how to fish, how to scale cliff faces, and how to blow up old tractor tires and the like. And he'd unwittingly taught Cooper how to read a liar. Early on, even when Derek looked as innocent as a toddler on Christmas morning, Cooper could tell when he was lying.

Eventually, the police could tell, too, and the law had caught up to Derek.

Now, thanks to Derek's training, Cooper could see the look in Emma's eye and sense that she wasn't being exactly truthful, either. He knew it was simply a matter of outwaiting her, and eventually, she'd give in and tell him the truth about the medal. Just like Derek. Because Cooper definitely wasn't going anywhere now, not after she'd tried to turn it around and make him out to be the guy who was chasing after her.

Women.

Cooper would try not to say "I told you so" when she did finally confess the truth, even if that completely reduced his satisfaction at being right.

➤━┥◆➤━○━◆┥━◄

Cooper had been in some dives in his life, but nothing had given him the creeps quite like the Beaver Room at the Grizzly Lodge and Café. It was all he could do to sleep in a room that looked like it had been gnawed by giant rodents, much less hang out. When he'd checked in, Ms. Boxer had said it was the only available one. "The Kisslers booked a wedding party here," she'd said apologetically. "Otherwise, I'd put you in the Peacock Room. But the Beaver Room is one of our most popular."

Cooper stopped in to clean up after his visit to the Kendricks. He called his mother to pass the time and listened to her talk excitedly about Derek's release. "I don't have a firm date yet, but I'll call you as soon as I know," she'd said. "You're coming home, right, honey? You're going to be here when your brother gets out, aren't you?"

He promised his mother he would—how could he refuse her exuberant plea, her excitement of having "her two boys" home for the holidays? He hoped he got credit somewhere for being at least a decent son, because the last place he wanted to be was in Huntsville, Texas just before Christmas.

When he said goodbye to his mom, Cooper had to get out of that room. Besides, it was genetically impossible for him to be in a place like Pine River on a day like this and not be outside. The weather was good, really good—no clouds, no breeze, nothing but blue overhead. He'd read in the local paper that the area had experienced an unusually dry couple of months. It was harming the ski industry, the article went on to report, but for Cooper, it was perfect. It looked like an excellent day to drive up Sometimes Pass and check out Cheyenne Canyon. Eli had mentioned it, and Cooper had read about it in one of the Grizzly Lodge brochures. *Remote Colorado wilderness! Pristine trails through spectacular mountain scenery. Hikers will be treated to the melodic sound of a rushing stream and the thrill of redheaded finches. The granite face of massifs and valley vistas will greet you as you descend to the floor of the canyon, where the state's best white water awaits.*

The trail was probably closed for the winter, but he hoped to at least get a visual to know if it was worth coming back.

Cooper strolled down to the store he'd seen on the main drag: Tag's Outfitters. He ducked in through the door of the adobe building and instantly felt closed in by the low ceilings and the sheer amount of stuff crammed into that massive interior. The establishment carried everything from clothes to mountain gear to enormous clay pots. In the front of the store, corralled by yellow tape and stacked one on top of the other, were Christmas trees. A variety of mishmash hung from the ceiling—piñatas, pots and pans, bird feeders. Blow-up pumpkins and turkeys and Christmas trees dangled, too, all of them carrying a layer of dust so thick that he could only assume they'd been batted away by shoppers for more than a few years.

In the middle of all that crap was a single, L-shaped counter. One half of it was piled high with papers and magazines. An enormous and ancient cash register dominated the other half. A massive man sat behind the register on a spindly stool, balancing himself with one foot planted firmly on the ground. His neck was as thick as Cooper's thigh, and he wore a scraggly beard and a stained canvas hiking hat.

"Hello," Cooper said.

The man responded with a slight lift of his double chins.

"I'm hoping you can give me some information," Cooper said. No answer.

Cooper glanced around the store, half expecting someone to appear to tell him the mountain man was deaf and dumb, but no one else seemed to be about except a man near the front of the store looking at snowshoes.

"I wanted to drive up and take a look at Cheyenne Canyon—"

"Can't," the man said. "Pass is closed."

"Sometimes Pass?" Cooper asked.

The man gave that lift of his chins again. "That's why it's called Sometimes Pass. Only open sometimes."

"But it hasn't snowed in weeks," Cooper said. "Wouldn't it be open?"

"They close it every winter," another voice said.

Cooper turned around to the man who had spoken. He'd moved away from the snowshoes and was standing in the aisle now. He was wearing loafers and jeans that rode so low on his hips there wasn't much keeping them up. His clothing was expensive; he gave off a hipster vibe.

"The county doesn't have enough money to plow that far out and it's easier just to keep it closed. I know another way into the canyon if you're interested."

With his heather-green sweater and upturned shirt collar, this guy reminded Cooper of the guys who wandered around West Hollywood—not someone who knew a back way into Cheyenne Canyon. "Oh yeah?" he asked curiously.

"A couple of the logging roads are open. The Forest Service is taking advantage of the weather to clear out some fire fuel."

Cooper glanced at the man behind the counter for confirmation.

"Don't ask me," the mountain man said. "Jackson here's the one who knows."

"I'm sorry, I should have introduced myself. I'm Jackson Crane," the man said, extending his hand. "Sorry to butt in, but I couldn't help overhearing. Tag hasn't been up in the mountains in years."

"Got all the gear you need, but I ain't no guide," the man agreed.

Cooper's gaze shifted back to Jackson Crane. He was a head shorter than Cooper, and slender. "I'll take you up," he offered.

Cooper must have recoiled slightly because the man laughed. "That must sound strange, but I only mean to be helpful. Tag will vouch for me."

"He won't rob or murder you, if that's what you're thinking," Tag said.

As if that was the first thing to pop into Cooper's mind. "I wasn't thinking that—"

"If you want to go, we should go," Jackson said. "There's a front coming through later and we'll lose light." He started for the front door, as if it had all been agreed.

What the hell? Cooper looked again at Tag, but Tag merely gazed back, unsurprised. Cooper couldn't think of a time he'd ever gotten into a car with someone he didn't know, especially a guy who dressed like a male fashion model. Not that he thought he had anything to fear . . . and he *did* want to see that canyon. So Cooper followed Jackson Crane out.

Jackson was standing next to a four-wheel-drive Jeep that had been jacked up on a big-wheel suspension. Another surprise—that was not the vehicle Cooper would have guessed Jackson would drive. Tag, maybe. But Jackson looked more like a Prius.

Jackson was busy clearing off the passenger seat when Cooper joined him. He glanced at Cooper and smiled a little before strolling around to the driver's side and stepping up and into the vehicle.

Cooper hesitantly put himself in the passenger side. "Who are you again?" he asked as Jackson started the Jeep.

Jackson laughed. "I'm a lawyer here in town. Sort of. I mean, I *am* a lawyer, but there's not much practice up here, other than the occasional divorce and a few wills. Oh, and Buck Ritchie's ongoing defense for cattle rustling." He looked at Cooper sidelong. "The dude can *not* stay out of trouble."

"I know the type," Cooper said. "I'm Cooper Jessup."

"Welcome to Pine River, Cooper," Jackson said, and gunned the Jeep, burning a little rubber on the main road out of town. "I hear you're in town to see Emma Tyler."

Startled, Cooper jerked his gaze to Jackson.

Jackson waved off his concern. "I had breakfast at the lodge this morning and Dani told me."

"Can't imagine why she'd have a reason to mention it," Cooper said, taken aback.

"You're right," Jackson readily agreed. "Other than there's not a lot going on right now, and she knows that I know Emma." He glanced at Cooper as he shifted gears. "Chill. It's a small town with nothing to do and not much other than Buck Ritchie to talk about, especially in the dead of winter."

That didn't exactly ease Cooper. He didn't like the idea of the town talking about him and his reason for being here, and hoped the music he was suddenly hearing in his head wasn't the theme song from *Deliverance.* "So," he said, trying to muscle his thoughts back to familiar ground, "you know Emma?"

"I wouldn't say I *know* her," Jackson said. "But we are acquainted."

Cooper imagined that everyone who came into contact with Emma could say the same thing: met her, didn't know her. "She's from here?" he asked curiously.

"Here? No, she's from Southern California. Her dad lived here.

That's how I know her—I worked for Grant Tyler for a few months. Right after I came on board he got sick and wasn't given much time. Talk about a mess," he said with a shake of his head.

"Oh yeah?"

"His finances, his love life, his kids, all of it," Jackson said. "He wasn't much of a dad. He had these daughters scattered here and there, and they didn't know about each other, and he sure as hell didn't have much contact with any of them. Emma's sister Libby tried to be a daughter to him, she really tried, but Grant wasn't interested in being a dad. However . . . he did want to try and do right by them once he knew he didn't have long. I mean, as much as Grant was able to do right." Jackson chuckled at that. "Let's just say virtue wasn't Grant's strong suit."

"So he left them the ranch," Cooper said, filling in the rest of the story.

"It was all he had left," Jackson said. "Once his ex-wives and the government and his creditors got their cut, Homecoming Ranch was it. And he was upside down on the mortgage to boot."

"In other words, not much of a legacy."

"Not much of a legacy, in need of repair, and really complicated overall," Jackson said. "I was the lucky one who got to deliver the news to the girls. I flew out to Los Angeles to talk to Emma. That's where I met her."

Jackson looked away, out the driver's window. There was something about his demeanor that made Cooper think that meeting hadn't gone well. "Did she know he was sick?" he asked.

"No," Jackson said, and suddenly downshifted, pulling off the main road onto a bumpy dirt trail. "They hadn't had contact in years, and honestly? She didn't seem that affected by the news, you know? Like she didn't care. I don't know what happened between her and her father, but there was definitely some bad blood there."

Cooper held on to the dash as they began to bounce up an old pitted logging road. "So is that why she's here?" he asked. "She came to claim her share of the ranch?"

"No, no, they did that last spring," Jackson said loudly over the bump and grind of the Jeep. "After Grant died, they all came out to meet each other and have a look around. The ranch had been set up for some destination events—Grant's idea to make some money, right? Family reunions, weddings, that sort of thing. And the girls decided they were going to make it work. That is, Madeline and Libby decided. Emma didn't want anything to do with it. The next day, she took off back to LA with some guy she called her boyfriend. No one had heard anything from her until she showed up here again, out of the blue, sometime before Thanksgiving."

So Emma was fond of taking off, Cooper thought.

"Not sure what her deal is," Jackson said, "but she's kind of interesting. I've got a buddy who works over at the body shop across from the city park. He says when the weather is good, she goes there in the afternoons and sits there watching the Wilson kids. They live on the other side of the park. He said she doesn't do anything but sit there and watch them. Sometimes she laughs, but once those kids go in, she leaves." Jackson shook his head and gunned it to get over some rocks. "I don't know why anyone would watch the Wilson kids—little terrors, all three of them. Dani says they're troublemakers at school. The dad works just shy of the law, and the mom, I hear, drinks her breakfast every morning. I don't know what Emma's fascination is with them." He suddenly looked at Cooper. "Oh hey, man, I'm sorry, I'm just talking out my ass—are you and she involved?"

"What? No," Cooper said quickly, thinking of her earlier today, suggesting she had somehow *rejected* him. "Nothing like that. She's got something that belongs to a friend of mine. I told him I'd get it back while I was out this way."

"Ah," Jackson said, throttling down to take a treacherous turn in the old logging road. "So you and she aren't . . . ?"

Cooper looked at him. Jackson shrugged. "Sleeping together?" Cooper drawled.

Jackson smiled faintly.

"No," Cooper said, eyeing Jackson curiously. "Are you?"

Jackson laughed. "Nope. I think that shop is closed up tight. Every man in Pine River has tried and gotten the cold shoulder."

That was interesting. From what Cooper had heard, that shop was anything but closed.

"So you're out this way for recreation?" Jackson asked, thankfully changing the subject.

"You could say that," Cooper said, and explained to Jackson what he did for a living.

Like most men, Jackson was enthralled by the idea of TA; it was every man's daydream. "I know some people who would be totally into that," he said. "Myself included. We should talk. I could hook you up with some potential clients."

"In Pine River?" Cooper asked.

"*No,*" Jackson scoffed. "Back east. Guys with *real* money."

Cooper found it interesting that this loafer-wearing, Jeep-driving lawyer in Pine River would know "real money" back east, but he didn't have a chance to ask him about it, because they came to an abrupt halt. An iron gate closed off the road before them, a yellow triangle with a warning against trespassing hanging slightly crooked. Jackson hopped out, walked up to the gate, jiggled the lock, then swung it open and pushed it out of the way.

He climbed back into the Jeep and put it into gear.

"I thought you said the road was open," Cooper said, noticing the sign on the gate that clearly marked the road as prohibited by the Forest Service.

"One man's 'closed' is another man's 'maybe.'" He grinned at Cooper as he drove the Jeep through the gate and up the road until it became impassable. At that point, Jackson stopped, retrieved some hiking boots from behind his seat, and donned them. "Come on," he said.

Cooper followed him up the road until they ran into snowpack. But from there, they could glimpse Cheyenne Canyon below them.

The view was breathtaking. A rush of adrenaline swept through Cooper; he could think of any number of things he would do in that canyon. It was narrow, with some interesting rock formations and, according to Jackson, a fast-running stream that poured into Pine River. Cooper had always been a lover of the great outdoors, and when he saw a vista like that, he felt he was standing as close to God's perfection as possible. Yes, he would definitely look forward to late spring when he could come back here to check it out.

They poked around the logging roads a bit more, but finding their way blocked more than once, they eventually drove back down to town. Jackson dropped Cooper at Tag's. "Thanks, man," Cooper said. "I appreciate it."

"Any time. Before you leave town, come around to my office and let's talk business. In the meantime, if you need anything, let me know."

Cooper said goodbye, watched Jackson drive away, and was digging in his pocket for car keys when his phone rang.

"Jesus, I've been trying to get you all day," Carl Freeman said testily when Cooper answered. "Where the hell have you been?"

"Cell service is pretty spotty up here," Cooper said.

"Well? Did you find her?"

"I found her."

"So did you get the box?" Carl asked, his voice rising with his eagerness.

Cooper steeled himself for the barrage that was coming. "Not yet."

"Not *yet*?" Carl shouted into the phone.

"Calm down, Carl. She says she doesn't have it. But I will get it."

"Alicia is busting my balls—you have no idea!" Carl ranted. "Her lawyer says that me losing this *fucking* family heirloom and her mother's *fucking* wedding ring is indicative of how I had no respect for her in our marriage! It's her dead mother's wedding ring, Cooper! I can't go to court and say that some one-night stand took off with that shit, do you *get* that? Do you understand how important this is? Do the *thousands* of dollars I'm paying you not indicate how important this is? I have about two weeks to get it back or it's court, Cooper. Two weeks!"

"Take a breath, Carl," Cooper snapped. "She's *here*. Give me a couple of days and I'll get it. I can't very well walk into her house and go through her things."

"Maybe you could find a way in—"

"*No*, Carl. I'll call you in a couple of days."

"You better," Carl said. "Because if you don't, I will smear Thrillseekers up and down Wilshire Boulevard. You'll be lucky to get a kid's birthday party." He clicked off before Cooper could speak.

Cooper fumed. This was the very thing he hated about TA— having to kowtow to a jerk like Carl Freeman. What he wanted was the extreme sports. What he couldn't abide was the kiss-ass end of the business.

Where he was going with it at this stage of his life, Cooper couldn't say, but it was clearly something that he needed to think about. And he would, just as soon as he could shake a certain blonde from his head.

SEVEN

Leo was not going to let it lie. Emma figured if she were sitting in a chair every day waiting for something interesting to happen, she would be relentless, too. But the difference between her and Leo was that she could take no for answer. Leo could not.

"I mean, it's like this," Leo said, his voice rattling along with the chair as Emma pushed him down the street, hoping that the fresh air and bright afternoon sun would divert his attention. So far, no luck. "We've all had those relationships that were never going to work out, you know? It's okay, Emma. You can tell me. I won't think any less of you, and in fact, I'll think *more* of you."

Emma stopped. She leaned over, braced her hands against her knees; the long tail of her hair slid over her shoulder and swung below her.

"Hey, why are you stopping?" Leo asked. "I'm kind of helpless, you know. If you pass out, I'm like, *stuck.*"

Emma slowly lifted up. She shifted around the side of the chair, tucking in the blanket around Leo. Bob had insisted on the blanket. He didn't like her to take Leo out. *Too painful for him*, he'd say curtly. *Too cold.*

Dad, it's not that bad, Leo would argue.

Emma didn't know how bad the pain truly was for Leo, but today, she thought she could see it around his eyes. And yet, he'd begged her, more than once. *Take me with you.* Anything to get outside of that little house. Anything to soak up a few rays, to breathe real air.

It occurred to her that maybe his incessant talking was his way of trying not to think about the pain.

"Are you all right?" she asked.

Leo peered up at her. Most of his muscles didn't work anymore, but his eyes were laser sharp and full of expression. "I'm *great*. The question is, how are *you*, Em? You don't look so good. Is it the heavy pushing? Or is it the interrogation?"

"Both. I haven't eaten." She pressed a fist to her abdomen, only now realizing she hadn't eaten since this morning. That was something else that had cropped up in the last few weeks—she couldn't seem to remember to eat until her body was on the verge of revolt. It was as if her mind was too filled with other thoughts to worry about it.

"Let's go back then, because that makes me nervous," Leo said. "I know you're acting weird because Cooper showed up, and I would totally help you if you'd just tell me what the deal is between you two."

"God," she sighed. "You're relentless! I really hate to disappoint you, Leo. I know how much you thrive on juicy gossip. But I really, honestly, hardly know the guy." She tried very hard to look sincere. But Emma could only look sincere when she was telling the truth.

"Really?" Leo asked, his voice full of deserved skepticism.

"Because it's, like, *super* strange that a guy would come all this way if you hardly know him."

He's not a guy, he's a man. A shiver ran down Emma's spine. *If he'd wanted you, he would have had you.* Okay, keep moving. She wasn't going to let Cooper's words play with her head.

"You *do* know him," Leo said.

"Seriously, will you shut up?"

"That's no way to talk to the true man of your dreams, but, because you're ultrasensitive, I will bow to your wishes."

"I'm not ultrasensitive, Leo." Emma had a sudden flashback to her mother, ten years ago. *Don't be so sensitive, Emma. It's not about you.* She shivered again. "I'm not even *sensitive,* doofus. I *don't know* Cooper. That's all there is to it."

Leo gave her a half-crooked smile. "You look like you're lying and like you totally want to kiss me right now. Well, don't. I don't want that big bruiser trying to fight me for you."

"Oh my God," she muttered, and walked around behind the wheelchair. She tipped it back and wheeled it around and began to push. "Sometimes I think you are the greatest guy in the world, you know? And then you'll be totally obnoxious like you're being right now, and I think, no, you're really the biggest *jerk* in the world."

"Thank you!" Leo said happily. "I know you may say that now, but you'll miss my sage advice when I'm gone. But don't cry for me, Argentina, the truth is I'll never leave you. You'll still be thinking about me when you're gimping around on a cane."

Emma gasped and gave the chair a hard jerk. "Why do you do that?" she demanded. "Do you think it's funny? Do you think it's shocking?"

"Isn't that our thing?" Leo asked, sounding surprised. "Aren't we totally honest with each other? I say it because it's true, and I don't shy away from the truth. Neither do you, Emma! So don't get teary-eyed on me. Are you getting teary-eyed?" he demanded.

"No," she lied.

"That's what I like about you, Em! You don't get teary-eyed for anyone or anything."

"Nope. I'm hard and flinty," she said, but the tears were burning the backs of her eyes.

"Come on," Leo said. "If I hurt your feelings, I'm sorry. I only meant to point out an obvious fact."

"You didn't hurt my damn feelings." She slowed her pace a little so that she could wipe away a tear. "It's *impossible* to hurt my feelings. But you don't always have to state the obvious, Leo. It's obvious already—get it?"

"Okay, well, that's even *more* obvious," Leo said. "But I get it. I won't state things that are obvious because they are totally obvious already, even though sometimes it seems things are *not* so obvious to the genius-challenged among us."

"Jesus, do you ever stop talking?" she cried to the perfect blue sky with breathless irritability.

"I think I have answered this question many times before. No, I never stop talking. You are, like, irrationally irritable, which says to me, there is more to this Cooper thing than you're willing to tell me," Leo blithely continued as she moved down the street toward Elm, as if she hadn't denied it more than once, hadn't asked him to stop talking one hundred times. "I just want you to get your stuff worked out beforehand so I don't have to worry about you."

"What are you talking about *now?*"

"Your stuff, your stuff!" Leo said impatiently, and paused to catch his breath. "Such as why you showed up in Pine River out of the blue, and why you don't want to talk about Cooper. *That* stuff."

"You know what?" Emma said, slowing her pace as they moved over the Pine River Bridge. "You're really lucky I don't push you into the river. Because the thought has crossed my mind about ten times in the last ten minutes."

"Threatening the totally handicapped. *Nice.* I *knew* I liked you."

On the other end of the bridge, Emma maneuvered Leo over a rough patch of pavement. But there was no access ramp onto the sidewalk, and when Emma tried to tilt Leo's chair back, she couldn't get more than one wheel onto the curb.

"What's happening?" Leo shouted at her.

"It's okay—" His chair tilted to the right. Emma struggled to keep it from tipping completely over and somehow managed to level it before Leo went spilling out of his chair.

"Go back. Go back across the bridge!" Leo said frantically.

"I can do it," Emma insisted, and studied the high curb for a way on. She was only vaguely aware of a car slowing. But when she heard the door shut, she whirled around.

Cooper.

"Need some help?"

"Yes!" Leo shouted with his back to the street.

Cooper walked around the front of his car, looking concerned, eyeing her as if he'd caught her stealing Leo. "What's going on?"

"Who is it?" Leo asked. "Who's there?"

"It's me, Cooper Jessup," Cooper said, and put his hand on Leo's arm. "The guy from this morning?"

"Thank God," Leo said. "We're having some trouble here."

"No we're not," Emma said quickly. "It's just that the curb is higher than normal."

"You have to save me, Cooper," Leo said. "She just threatened to dump me in the river."

Emma gasped and gaped wide-eyed with mortification at Cooper. "I was kidding!" she cried, but Cooper looked dubious. "I was *kidding,*" she said again. "Leo knows that."

"Maybe I do and maybe I don't. I'll let you know what I believe when I am safely on the sidewalk."

"Here, let me," Cooper said. He stepped in between Emma and

the chair, grabbed the handles of Leo's chair, easily tipped him back and put his front wheels on the curb, and then the back wheels. "There you go," he said to Leo. "I think it's probably a straight shot from here. Want me to push you home?"

"I've got it," Emma said, and elbowed her way in front of Cooper, shoving against his hard chest. He budged only a little.

"You okay, Leo?" Cooper asked again, unwilling to move until he heard from the horse's ass.

"Yeah, I'm okay," Leo said. "I guess I freaked out a little when this delicate little flower couldn't get me up here. And she hasn't eaten, so I am expecting her to faint at any moment."

"Why haven't you eaten?" Cooper asked, frowning at her.

"I ah . . . haven't had time," she said crisply. "But I'm fine. I'm not even hungry." She hoped he couldn't hear the rumbling in her stomach.

"Maybe you could take her to dinner," Leo said. "We could postpone our—"

"Thanks, Leo, but I have plans!" Emma said.

Cooper smiled slowly and easily at her fluster. His gaze wandered down her body, causing her starved belly to tingle even more. "That's okay," he said. "I've got plenty of time. I'll catch up with you tomorrow."

"I don't think so," Emma snorted.

"We'll see," Cooper said, and leaned around her to put his hand on Leo's shoulder. "You okay?"

"Could *not* be better!" Leo said. "You have made my day, Cooper Jessup. I'm so stoked you came into town."

"Okay, all right," Emma said, pushing against Cooper and leaning into the chair to get it moving. "We need to go."

"I'll see you tonight, Leo," Cooper said, and then caught Emma's arm, forcing her to stop and look at him. "I'll see *you* later, too," he said, his voice annoyingly and knee-bendingly stern.

"That's *great*," Leo said. "We were just talking about how Em's going to try and get out more. You know, socialize with people. I can't be her sun *and* her moon, you know what I'm saying?"

Cooper chuckled.

"He's not funny," Emma said. "Don't laugh at him. And don't get some idea that we're going to be friends, because we're not, Cooper. Not now, not ever."

"Ouch," Cooper said with a funny little smile.

"Leo and I really need to go."

"No we don't," Leo said.

"We'll see about the friend thing, *Em*," Cooper said with a wink, and leaned around her, giving Leo's chair a push to get it started.

Emma gave the chair another heave and began to move Leo along as quickly as she could.

"Thanks, Cooper!" Leo called out.

"Welcome!" Cooper called back.

She wasn't going to look back. She was *not* going to look back. Damn it, she looked back.

Cooper was standing on the sidewalk with his hands in his pockets, watching her. Expressionless. Virile. *Kryptonite.*

"Total hottie," Leo said, wheezing a little.

"Oh my God," Emma said. "Are you serious right now?"

"Well, he is. Way to draw him in, Em! I mean, if you get any warmer and fuzzier, we might have to call a fire truck. You want my advice?"

"*No.*"

"My advice is to be nice to him. It's no skin off your nose. Who knows, he might even *feed* you."

"I can feed myself," Emma muttered.

But Leo was right. She could be abrupt, especially when she was flustered. She'd never been a sweet girl, that was for sure. *Nothing but brass tacks and nails coming out of that mouth,* her mother used to say. Even as a little girl, Emma had understood she wasn't considered to be a nice girl, like Laura or Libby. If she could have figured out how to change that about herself, to become personable, she would have done it in a heartbeat. It sure would have saved her a lot of agony through the years. Unfortunately, having a way with words always seemed to elude her, like it had just now, with Cooper.

But then again, what was the nice way to tell someone to get lost?

Emma knew Leo was hurting when she wheeled him into the little house on Elm Street. He wasn't hungry, either, which seemed to bother Bob more than usual. "What's happened to your appetite, Son?" he demanded, as if Leo had eaten a jar full of cookies.

"I don't know, Dad. It could be the delicious selection of pulverized food you offer me every night," he said, and laughed. But even his laugh sounded a little off. When his care attendant came at four, Leo asked him to put him in bed.

He looked so thin and uncomfortable in that hospital bed, and there was a crease between his eyes that hadn't been there earlier. "Should I get Bob?" Emma asked.

"No, I'm fine. Don't worry about me," he said at Emma's look of concern. "I've got a full night lined up—it's the *Real Housewives* reunion show, and then hockey! I don't even have time to explain to you how important this game is for the Bruins."

"Thank God," Emma said, and smiled at Leo. She touched his temple.

"Cut it out," Leo said, his eyes twinkling above his permanently lopsided grin. "Dad will have a heart attack if he knows how into me you are."

"He already knows. I'll see you tomorrow," she said, and leaned down to kiss the top of his head.

"*Stop,*" Leo groaned. "Get out of here. But you better come back here with some gossip! The Methodist ladies are coming over tomorrow afternoon, and if I don't have some meat for them, they will draw blood."

Emma laughed. The Methodist Women's Group had adopted Leo as their cause. When they came to see him, they gathered around like hens, picking at the gossipy morsels Leo tossed out to them. "Don't stay up too late," she warned him. "You're always such a grump if you stay up too late."

"Hush, I can still catch the end of *Dr. Phil*," Leo said.

Emma left him lying there, his gaze fixed on the TV.

She gathered her things, said goodbye to Bob and the nurse, and drove down Elm Street to the main drag. But instead of turning right to head out of town toward the ranch, she went left, into town, like she did every day the weather was good. She drove past the faux-Western storefronts, past Tag's Outfitters, past the Grizzly Lodge. She drove until she reached the city park and playground on the other end of town.

Emma parked and walked to the wooden bench under the oak trees, taking a seat on the peeling paint, careful to avoid the old bird droppings. The faint smell of stale smoke wafting out from someone's chimney filled the air. It was a bright day, but cool, and the sun was starting its slide down behind the mountaintops.

Emma pulled her sweater coat tightly around her and wished she'd thought to bring gloves. She trailed her forefinger over the name carved into the seat of the bench. *Tashi.* She wondered if Tashi was a boy or a girl. If Tashi was grown or one of the teenage girls who hung out at the park and, once, overtook her bench with their cell phones and magpie chatter. She wondered if Tashi was happy or if Tashi looked up at the sunlight glittering through the bare branches of the oak tree and wished to be far from Pine River, in a different family with different siblings and parents and friends.

With the exception of Tashi's name, Emma liked this bench. Actually, she felt like she owned it. It was far enough from the playground so that she didn't look like a stalker, and yet close enough that she could see the kids.

The kids, *her* kids, were outside today as she knew they would be—they were in the park every afternoon when the weather was good. They were three siblings, two girls and a boy, all within six to eight years old. They lived across the street from the park in one of the identical Craftsman houses that filled this neighborhood. Sometimes, Emma saw their mother on the porch, a cup of coffee in her hand, watching them. But most of the time the children were alone, probably watched by their mother through the big plate-glass windows of her house. Emma could picture her preparing an evening meal with one eye on her children through the windows. Spaghetti, Emma mused, to be heaped onto big plates, over which the kids would report the details of their day.

The three of them were a tribe, always on the move. Emma loved watching the paths their imaginations took them each afternoon, carrying them deep into a fantasy world where their characters took shape, rising up so real that Emma could almost see them: superheroes, moms and dads, teachers, spies, bad guys and good guys. Emma wanted to go with them, to disappear into the world they'd created.

Emma had named the kids, too. Finn was the boy. He was the ringleader, instructing the girls what to do, and deciding what makebelieve would be played that day. Or at least it seemed so from where Emma sat. She'd named the girls Quinn and Brynn. They were very close in age. She liked how the two of them sported a different accessory each day—princess dress or cowboy hat, scepter or sword.

Emma had also envisioned a mother and father for these children, a hearth and home. She imagined them gathered around the kitchen table, coloring. Or after dinner, the family engaged in some board game, their Ozzie-and-Harriet parents lovingly admiring their brood.

Emma imagined all these things a few afternoons a week.

She was acutely aware that it was a weird thing to do. She couldn't even say why she did it. She wasn't crazy—she didn't need a trip to the psych ward like Libby had last summer. But for reasons that Emma had long ago allowed to escape her, these kids, this fantasy, made her feel good. It made her feel normal. Lovable. As if she could be part of something like this.

It would be easier for Emma to understand her compulsion to see these kids if she'd had a difficult childhood, but her childhood had been okay. Even when her mother had tried to reconcile with her absentee father, it had been relatively normal.

Emma was nine or ten when Grant had shown up in California with Libby in tow. Of course Emma had been thrilled that her father had appeared at her house to live, instead of the occasional holiday or quick weekend trip to the beach with her and her mother as had been the norm for the first years of her life. Emma had never really understood where her father went in between those short visits. She'd asked her mother about him, had even imagined that he was an important person, like a soldier, or the president—someone whose job was so critical that he couldn't come around more often than he did.

But then, like magic, he'd appeared on their doorstep with Libby, a robust figure, his smile as infectious as his laugh. "I'm going to marry your mother," he'd confided in Emma, and Emma had worshipped him.

Unfortunately, the reconciliation was a fiasco. Her parents never married. They survived only eighteen months of each other, and then it was over. Her father disappeared from her life again, and so did Libby. A few months after that, Emma's mother met and eventually married Wes.

Wes was a single father. Emma would never forget the first time she met his daughter, Laura. She was only a few months older than Emma and had short auburn hair, sparkling blue eyes, and a wide grin. She was sunny and outgoing—all the things Emma was not. Laura also had a motorized scooter, a huge point in her favor.

They were quickly friends and soon after, sisters. Emma adored Laura. They wore matching socks, braided their hair the same way, and giggled about boys. They attended public school together, attended sleepovers, and were elected cheerleaders to the same squad. They'd even experienced their first kiss on the same beach on the same night.

Emma confided everything in Laura. She believed Laura was just like her, a cosmic twin, the closest thing to her in mind and spirit as could possibly exist. It was a perfect union, a perfectly melded family. Perhaps the only imperfect thing about it was that Emma's mother loved Laura, too. Loved her so much that, at about the age of thirteen or fourteen, Emma had begun to feel as if her mother loved Laura more than her. Laura could do no wrong. Laura was effervescent and happy and, as her stepfather had explained, "socially adept."

"Whereas you can come off as sullen and strange," her mother had matter-of-factly added.

Still, Emma couldn't complain about her childhood. It was pretty good as those things go, right up to the summer of her seventeenth year. What happened that summer had not tainted her childhood—it had tainted everything going forward and had sent her spinning off in a destructive direction. That summer, she learned what men saw in women, what they really wanted from life: sex.

That wasn't all Emma had learned that summer. She'd also discovered just how hard and deep a slash of betrayal could penetrate a person. Bone deep. *Marrow* deep. Emma had been thoroughly slashed by two people she'd believed had truly loved her, social awkwardness and all.

"Ugh," she groaned, and looked away from the happy tableau of frolicking children for a moment. *Why did she do this?* Why did she relive the insanity of what had happened ten long years ago? It was over and done. And what the hell was she doing in this park every day? Trying to re-create her childhood? Or did she come to shake the pervasive feeling of melancholy that seemed to envelope her lately? Did she come to pretend that in some universe, families like this really existed? That not every family was a dysfunctional mess as hers had turned out to be?

Trying to figure out how her mind worked and what she was after was overwhelming for Emma. These days, it seemed like thinking in general exhausted her. She wanted only to exist for a time. Not think. Just be, quietly. Without drama, for God's sake. Without tall, dark-haired men with incredible gray eyes showing up to harass her about more things she didn't want to think about.

It was her own damn fault, but she still blamed Carl for the fact that her refuge here had been breached.

Carl.

Emma *definitely* didn't want to think of the night with him because it made her sick. She squeezed her eyes shut, trying to block the image of his bloated body and that hideous diamond ring twinkling on his pinkie. She remembered his square hands, and how he'd groped her. Men always groped, grabbing and squeezing like a kid with a mound of Play-Doh.

Emma hated herself for that night at Carl's. She *always* hated herself after nights like that. And though she'd managed to escape the worst with the excuse that she wasn't feeling well, she felt as disgusting as if she'd allowed him to use her completely.

And then she'd taken that stupid medal. But that's what she did. She let men grope her or worse, and then she took things from them.

God, if only Emma could understand what was wrong with her. She didn't *want* any of the things she took—they were meaningless items with no value other than that they'd been in a place where she'd happened to have been, being groped and hating herself. She'd even Googled it once—*stealing from so-called lovers.* Kleptomania was what WebMD labeled it, but Emma wasn't buying that. She didn't have any of the other symptoms of that disorder. She didn't have other compulsions or obsessions, and she didn't feel the need to steal from anyone but men she allowed to pick her up. What she had was an undeniable desire to take something from men before they took something from her.

There was no WebMD diagnosis for that.

Every time it happened, Emma vowed she'd never do it again. She bargained with God, promised to be good and do right. But then . . . then something would click in her brain and it was impossible for her to prevent it. Physically, emotionally, it was impossible.

Once, she'd even made an appointment and gone to see a therapist in Dana Point about it. Emma was fairly rational. She'd realized that what she was doing—the sleeping around, the stealing—was beyond nutty, and nutty things required intervention. The psychologist, a young woman with rectangular glasses and frizzy hair, had given her a sad smile and had said, "We have some work to do, don't we?"

Emma never went back. She didn't want to *work*, she didn't want to examine every angle of her life to discover why she did it. She knew *why* she did it. She just wanted to stop *doing it.* Give her the magic pill, show her how it was done, and voila, she'd be over it!

She'd just kept on, keeping to herself, trying to resist the urge and failing. But then her boss, Melissa, had called one day. *What happened to the candlesticks, Emma? We borrowed those from Haute Interiors.*

That call was the thing that turned everything on its ear. It had happened only a couple of days after Emma had left Carl snoring like a beach bum in Malibu, the medal in her purse. Emma had never once taken anything from work, had never even had the desire to take something. Why that night? Because Keith, the other vice president at CEM, had run his hand over her ass and told her he could make her scream? Keith was always saying things like that, and Emma had never felt the unbearable need to take something of his.

Maybe it was simpler than that. Maybe it was because Carl was calling her, leaving nasty messages on her phone about that medal. Or maybe it was because she had run into her stepsister that night.

Emma's contact with Laura had been sporadic over the last few years—a few family events here and there, the occasional funeral or wedding. Emma didn't hate Laura for what happened the summer of her seventeenth year. Still, it wasn't easy to see her, and every time she did, Emma was reminded of the betrayal and the wound that wouldn't heal. It was a slow, dull throb in the back of her head, replaying itself at the most unexpected and inopportune moments.

Laura had barely turned eighteen, Emma's eighteenth only a few short months away, when Grant Tyler had showed up in Orange County a second time. He'd told Emma that after all those years, he'd realized what a bad father he'd been to her. He'd been apologetic and contrite, and well he should have been, because he had been the worst of fathers. Emma had never heard from him after the reconciliation with her mother had failed, and her mother complained endlessly about his failure to pay child support.

But there he was, wearing expensive clothes and driving a Jaguar, a self-proclaimed new man, desperate to make amends and be the father to her he'd never been. He told her earnestly that she deserved it.

Grant was living in Vegas at the time and said he wanted nothing more than to show Emma a good time and rekindle the relationship they'd never had. *Come stay with me. I'm your dad, baby, and I want to know you, to know the* real *you, because your mother hasn't kept me up to date. You can shop, you can see shows, you can meet my friends. It will be fun, Emma, you'll see. This summer will change your life.*

And she could bring Laura, too! It all sounded so fantastic to the girl Emma had been that year, dewy-eyed and hopeful, ready for a good time. She'd felt truly special, thrilled that after spending the last few years listening to her mother's endless list of flaws in her, Grant didn't seem to see any of them. Here was someone who'd come all this way *just for her.* To know *the real her,* which her mother seemed to despise.

Somehow, Grant had managed to convince Emma's parents to allow her and Laura to spend the summer with him in his Vegas penthouse. Of course Emma had gone. She'd told Laura—her best friend, her confidant—how she craved that relationship with her father. She'd even confided that she harbored a secret fear—that somehow, she was partially to blame for her parents' failed reconciliation because of her inability to be "nice." Maybe this time, she'd eagerly said to Laura, her father would stick around. She envisioned him going with her to buy her first car, taking her to dine at good restaurants. Walking her down the aisle, becoming the curmudgeonly yin to her mother's yang, a goofy grandpa to her children.

All her life, Emma had envied her friends and the dads who loved them, who drove them to movies and out to the beach, who told their boyfriends they better have them home by midnight, and who teared up with pride when their daughters dressed to go out. Emma had wanted that, too, and Emma had believed Grant had really, truly, come at last to be that person for her. He'd ridden into her life like a knight, sporting a miraculous change of heart about being a dad and truly loving her, his flesh and blood.

Laura was the one person who knew how much hope Emma held for him.

The first few weeks in Vegas had been great. Emma and Laura had the time of their lives living in Grant's lavish penthouse with a rooftop pool. There were lots of parties and shopping and late nights with Grant's "friends," who would give them alcohol and pass joints to them and whisper that they could show them the world while grabbing their asses. Emma was willing to put up with it all, because she was Grant's daughter, protected by her status as his blood. She was his pet, his princess, and woe betide the man who took it too far.

But as the summer wore on, Grant became less and less available to her. When he came in late, he said he was working. Emma knew that meant he was gambling. That's how he'd afforded those digs. It came with the territory.

And then Laura met a guy.

"Who is he?" Emma had asked when Laura told her, eyes bright with the excitement of a new love.

"I'm not ready to say," Laura had said coyly. "I want to make sure it's going to work out before I tell you."

"You can tell me!" Emma had insisted. "We tell each other everything!"

"No, I can't!" Laura had said, laughing. "When it's official, I promise, you'll be the first to know."

"Does he have another girlfriend? Is he married? What does official mean, anyway?"

"Nothing like that. It's sort of complicated. He said he'd know when the time was right. Until then, I can't tell you!" And Laura had giggled like a girl.

Emma hadn't liked it, but she'd made a game of it, studying the young men who showed up at the pool, looking for any sign of affection from Laura. Emma had finally decided it was the lifeguard, and was convinced of that until the early morning she'd gone looking for Grant and had stumbled on Laura in his bed.

Emma had knocked softly, and when there was no answer, she'd turned the knob and poked her head into her father's room, intending to wake him up. She could still remember how the day's heat had already begun to seep in through the windows and up through the floor, how it had felt as if her skin was burning as she stared at Laura, alone and naked under the sheets of her father's bed, her face ashen.

And still, Emma was so naïve that she'd felt wildly protective of her stepsister, thinking Laura had used Grant's bed for a tryst with the boyfriend. *"Laura!"* she'd whispered. "You have to get out of here before he finds you!"

As she spoke, the bathroom door opened and her father had walked out wearing nothing but a towel, and Emma's whole world had turned upside down, tumbling over itself, splintering and shattering into shards of rose-colored glass. That day, everything Emma thought she knew, everything she thought she understood, went flying out that twelfth-floor window. She'd been so stunned, so repulsed, so *hurt,* that she'd fled Las Vegas, throwing her things in the leather tote that was now under her bed up at the ranch, hitching a ride to the airport. She'd called her mother from there, begging for a ticket home.

Laura had followed her a week later. Her arrival home was marked by a lot of shouting and crying, and in the end, Laura was deemed the ruined one, the used one. She'd been the victim of big, bad Grant Tyler, a terrible, horrible man. The catastrophe in Emma's world became all about Laura, and the pain of Laura and Grant's betrayal was insignificant to anyone but her. Laura had been cruelly used! Emma had merely been hurt. Was there really any comparison? No one seemed to care what Laura and Grant *together* had done to Emma. What they'd done to her all summer long.

When Emma couldn't speak civilly to Laura or sit at the dinner table with her, when she couldn't swallow the betrayal and move on as commanded by her parents, her mother had lost patience with her.

"You think you're the only one hurt by this? Think about Laura! Think what that bastard must have said, how he must have lured her in. She's *humiliated*, and the fact that you won't forgive her just makes it that much worse!"

"*Forgive* her?" Emma had cried. "She was sleeping with my father!"

"Don't say that," her mother had said angrily. "Never let me hear you say that out loud!"

"But it's true, Mom!" Emma had insisted. "They were having sex in his bed while I was in my room reading a stupid book."

Her mother had sighed and pressed her fingers to the base of her jaw and made little circular motions. "Why do you always do this? Why do you always make things so goddamn hard? This situation is bad enough as it is, and you're just making it *so much harder*, Emma! You're selfish! Why does everything have to be about *you*? Are you *jealous* of Laura? Is that it? Look, I can completely understand it if you are, but you don't need to kick her when she's down, don't you get that?"

"You have to be kidding," Emma had said flatly.

"I'm not! I can't understand why you make such a big deal out of something that happened to Laura!"

Emma was stunned. How could her own mother not see what had happened to *her*? "She *betrayed* me, Mom! She ruined my chance to know my dad, and he betrayed me, too! He came for me, and she stole him!"

"Oh, Emma," her mother had said, and with a sigh, she'd tucked in a stray wisp of Emma's blond hair. "You'e so naïve. Do you really think Grant came here for you? He came here for *me*. I've told you, he's always been crazy about me. He came to see if

I would leave Wes for him now that he's got money, and save him the child-support hassle."

Emma had been so stunned she could scarcely speak. "That . . . that's not true," she'd stammered. "He said he came for me."

"Whatever," her mother had said, and had smiled sadly. "I'm sorry, baby," she said, patting Emma's leg. "But that's what he wanted, and when he couldn't have me, I guess he used Laura to hurt me. You know the only reason I agreed to let you go to Vegas with him was because I thought it would be good for you to see something other than Southern California. I should have known you wouldn't see anything but despicable behavior." Her mother had gone on to say some other things that all boiled down to how Emma needed to get over her hurt because Laura was naïve, too, and hadn't known what she was doing, had been lured in by the big bad wolf, bless her heart.

Emma wished she could will it all away and forget that summer had happened. She wished she could simply forget how painful it was, and how twisted it was that she ached over Laura's betrayal. She'd never told anyone, but it somehow felt as if her father had cheated on *her*, had picked Laura over her.

It was sick, *so sick*, to be jealous of what had happened with Laura. Not what she'd done with Emma's father—that was disgusting. But in some twisted way, her father had preferred Laura over her. Emma *was* jealous, and that pain had turned into her secret, her dark, awful secret.

Emma had been trying to get over it for ten years. She lured men in. Not just any man—*never* good-looking men like Cooper who, if they could see past her looks, would be turned off by her personality. No, Emma went after older men. Men who were old enough or desperate enough or horny enough that they didn't care what she said, if she was nice or not. Men who would choose her over a woman like Laura, who was all smiles and sweetness. Emma wanted to be Laura, if only for an evening. She wanted to be the preferred one. So she sought the easy men out, enjoyed the attention, enjoyed watching their eyes light up with the possibility of touching her. She enjoyed a weird sense of victory when those men chose *her*. Not Laura. Her.

Of course that behavior came with consequences. The thrill of it ended when she allowed the man to catch her. Anything that came after—sex, if she had to, less if she could get away with it— felt dirty and cheap and empty. The moment the men chose her, the thrill was gone, and Emma felt so disgusting that she willingly left a piece of herself behind, then took something of theirs to remind her of how she'd been the one. If only for a night, she'd been the one.

The behavior had become habit now. She didn't think it had much to do with Laura and Grant anymore, but something so deeply rooted that it would take an axe to cleave out of her.

Sick, sick, sick.

Who could ever love her? She couldn't even love herself.

With ten years of hindsight, Emma knew that the blame lay with her dead father. She knew if he hadn't come into her life when he had, if he hadn't played on her young emotions and her desperate hope that he would really be the father she dreamed of having, none of it ever would have happened.

But that didn't make it any easier to be around Laura, or her betrayal any easier to accept. It didn't make it okay for Laura now to pretend that Emma had always been unreasonable, had always tried to make trouble for her. It didn't make it okay that in the course of family holidays, Emma's mother and stepfather preferred to sweep it under the rug and let it go that Laura had been fucking a middle-aged guy who just happened to be Emma's father.

Eventually, Emma stopped going to the Fourth of July barbecues and the Christmas parties. She retreated slowly from her family, tiny fragments of her leaving each day until she'd retreated so deeply from them and from herself that she didn't know how to make her way back even if she'd wanted to.

The night Emma unexpectedly encountered Laura, she realized two years had passed since they'd met. Laura had been as gorgeous as always with her dark auburn hair, her sky-blue eyes. She was more fit than Emma remembered her, toned and sleek. Her date was a real estate broker, one of the high rollers who appeared on TV shows about flipping houses.

Laura had smiled warmly when she saw Emma. "Wow, I wasn't expecting to see *you* here."

Emma hadn't known what to say. And as she'd searched for something, Laura had touched her hand. "You look great," she'd said. "Really great. You must be doing well."

"Ah . . . okay, I guess," Emma had stammered. "You look good, too, Laura."

Laura had beamed at the compliment. "Thanks! My trainer is Godzilla. He really works me," she said. "Hey, I'm starring on *Days of Our Lives*. Have you seen it?"

"Ummm . . . I haven't seen it." Emma's mother gleefully kept her informed of Laura's glam life.

"The storyline is so hard to follow. Did I or did I not kill my husband?" Laura said with a flippant roll of her eyes. "Let me introduce you to Josh Hyland," she said, and without taking her gaze from Emma, she reached to her right, touching her date's hand.

Josh Hyland turned toward Emma, and with a flick of his gaze, he made a quick appraisal of her and smiled appreciatively. "Who do we have here?" he asked, his eyes sliding to her breasts and up again.

"Josh, this is my stepsister, Emma."

"Well, well," Josh said, his gaze now taking her in like she was some fatted calf at market. "I don't know what's in the water in Orange County, but it's impossible to believe there are *two* women like you out there. But of course, you're related."

That salacious look of his, that smile, had flipped a switch in Emma. The hatches closed, the shutters came up. "We're not related. We're stepsisters."

"I meant, you came from the same house. So you share the same space, basically. Two gorgeous women sharing the same air." He winked at Emma, as if she should be happy with that assessment.

"We really don't share anything, to be honest," Emma said. "Well . . . except my father. I guess you could say we shared him." The words fell from her mouth before she could stop them.

Laura's mouth dropped open; she glared at Emma. "I don't believe you," she said, so softly that Emma scarcely heard her. Or maybe Laura had shouted it—Emma couldn't hear over the rush of blood in her own head, the result of being appalled by what she'd just said.

"Sorry—"

"There's an old guy over there, Emma. Maybe you should just go and do him and get it over with," Laura had snapped. She turned away, striding as quickly as she could without appearing to run, her long auburn curls bouncing above her hips, and Josh, looking confused, running after her like a dog.

That night, the candlesticks had ended up in Emma's car. Two days later, Melissa believed Emma when she said she'd picked up the sticks with many other things and had forgotten them. Of course Melissa would believe that—Emma was a vice president, a trusted employee. But taking those candlesticks had frightened Emma so badly that she needed to get out of town, to go somewhere and get a grip.

It so happened that Libby had called her early in the fall, wanting her help to set up a race. It was as good a time as any to go, and with stupid Carl pissed and wanting back the thing she'd taken in exchange for the piece of her she'd left in Malibu, Emma had snapped. She'd quit her job, packed up, and taken off.

She never dreamed that stupid pig would send someone after her. What was his deal, anyway? That medal had been in a box under some folded laundry. It had obviously been there a long time, unnoticed, unimportant.

The sound of a woman calling out startled Emma out of her rumination. Across the street, the mother of the children had stepped out onto the porch and was calling to them to come home. The three of them answered like little birds, then gathered up their toys and scampered across the playground.

Emma glanced at her watch; it was five o'clock. She'd agreed to have dinner with Madeline and Libby tonight. She was glad for it; she could use the company. And she actually kind of liked them—even Madeline sometimes. Maybe Leo was right; maybe she should try and be a little warmer and fuzzier. That notion struck Emma as so ludicrous that she actually laughed as she stood and walked to her car.

EIGHT

Dani had directed Cooper to the Stake Out when he asked where he might get a drink to kill time before heading over to the Kendrick house.

Dani had warned him that the restaurant was a bit of a meat market, but that appeared to be an understatement when Cooper walked through the swinging, saloon-type doors and into a loud din. It was only a little past five, but the bar was already packed with men in suits, or men in boots and flannel, and women in tight-fighting sweaters and jeans.

Cooper scanned the décor—elk heads, pine plank walls. Through the windows at the back of the restaurant, he could see a stunning view of Pine River, and a scattering of empty tables outside for use at a more agreeable time of year. The setting was pretty, but there was something about this place that made it feel cheap. Maybe it was the musty smell and plastic where wood should have been, or the linoleum where tile should have been.

Cooper walked up to the bar and ordered a bourbon neat. He paid for the drink, brought it to his lips—and noticed Emma sitting on a stool at the far end of the bar, sandwiched between a man who looked as if he'd just come down from the mountain and an elderly couple. Her expressionless gaze was fixed on him.

What was she doing here? He hated to think it, but he'd heard enough about her to believe she was here to pick up someone. He smiled a little sourly and lifted his drink.

Emma looked away.

Oh, no, Miss Tyler, you won't get off that easy, not this time.

Cooper started around the bar, silently daring her to avoid him. Emma visibly sighed, averted her eyes, and flipped her hair over her shoulder. Silky hair, the color of new corn, hair that shimmered in the low light. When Cooper reached her, he wedged himself in between her and the elderly woman beside her.

Emma stared straight ahead and said, "You're worse than a mosquito. I keep swatting you away, and you keep coming back to bite me."

"You didn't really believe you'd get rid of me with a few swats, did you?"

"No. But I definitely wished it."

Cooper propped his elbow on the bar, bending his head a little to see her profile. "What are you doing in here?" he asked. "You don't need to do this, you know."

She blinked, then slowly turned her face to him. "Don't need to do *what*?"

"You know . . . find company," he said.

She smiled as if that amused her and turned her body fully toward him. "Do you *honestly* think someone like me," she said, gesturing to her body, "would need to come to a bar like this to find company?"

When she put it like that, the answer was a resounding no. Emma was the sort of woman who could have who she wanted, where she wanted, when she wanted.

"It's none of your business, but I'm meeting someone. What do you want, Cooper?"

He was feeling a little stung for having stupidly assumed the reason why she was sitting here alone. "I came for a drink. But when I saw you here, I thought, no time like the present. We have some unfinished business."

She arched a brow. "No, it's definitely finished," she said casually, but she wrapped her hand tightly around her glass, giving her tension away.

"Let me buy you a drink and we'll talk about it." Cooper lifted his hand to get the bartender's attention.

"Hey—" She put her hand on his arm, pulling it down. "No thanks."

"Don't read too much into it. I'm just being friendly. We find ourselves in the same bar in Colorado. We're two acquaintances having a drink and talking a little."

Emma leveled a cool, green-eyed gaze on him. "How interesting that at first you thought I was here to meet up with some random guy, and when you find out I'm not, you decide you should buy me a drink, just like some random guy. Double standard, Cooper Jessup."

"Not at all the same thing," he said, although he felt another slight sting—Emma was right, he'd reverted to random guy without thought. "I know you, so this seems reasonable."

"I know you, too. But I don't want to talk to you and shouldn't have to. *That* seems reasonable, too."

"All the more reason to buy you a drink," he said. "I'm really not that bad. We've had a slight misunderstanding here, that's all. As I recall, we had a pretty good time the last time we saw each other. Remember?"

"I remember. But that was before you falsely accused me of taking something from someone."

"Not falsely," Cooper said, and smiled, nudging her with his shoulder. "Come on, Emma. A drink doesn't mean anything other than I'm trying to be nice."

"I'm not interested in nice. Haven't you figured that out about me? *Nice* is not in my vocabulary."

"Well, now you're just hurting my feelings," Cooper teased her.

That earned him a slight curve upward of the corner of her very lush mouth. How was it this woman wasn't on the silver screen? On the arm of every major player in Hollywood instead of doughboys like Carl? Even with that tiny hint of a smile, her eyes lit. She was unbelievably beautiful.

"Better I hurt your feelings now than later, don't you think? Because you and me?" she said, moving her finger between them, indicating them both. "We're never going to be drinking buddies."

"Wow, you are so *adamant* about that," he said with mock concern. "That's the second time today you've cut right to the bone. Okay, fair enough," he said, and lifted his hands in surrender. "No drink. We'll do this your way. Which, I will point out, is the hard way, but if that's what you want—"

"Great! Now that we've established we won't be having a *friendly* drink," she said, "there is no need for you to smash in between me and the lady behind you." She smiled and pointed away from the bar. "You can move on now."

But the pager on the bar in front of the elderly woman began to vibrate and blink. Her table was ready, and the woman slid off her stool and gathered her purse.

Cooper smiled victoriously as he plopped down on the barstool next to Emma. "Mind if I sit?"

"Cooper!" Emma gave him a little laugh, softening a little. "Seriously, go and bother someone else. I don't want to be *friends*." But she was smiling as she shoved his shoulder with her hand as if trying to push him off his stool. "Go away. Go back to LA and stunt work and Jill."

"You know about me and Jill, huh?"

"Who doesn't?"

"*You*, apparently," he said, and caught her wrist when she tried to push him again. "I haven't seen Jill in weeks. I think I'll stay right here. I've decided I like bothering you."

Emma groaned. She pulled her hand free of his. "I think you honestly believe that if you make a pest of yourself, I will confess something to you." She snorted. "Won't happen. I've seen a *lot* pushier than you."

"I'm not pushy, I'm determined. There's a difference. I've been hired to do a job and I'm going to do it."

"Determined. Pushy. Annoying. All the same thing," Emma said, and clinked her glass to his.

"You know what else? I think you like me bothering you," he said. "You know what they say, the bigger the bark, the bigger the attraction."

Emma laughed at his joke, the sound of it light and fluffy. It had a peculiar effect on Cooper—it felt almost as if he'd had a little too much to drink for a moment. A woozy, soft feeling swept through him on a whisper and evaporated into thin air.

"No one says that! You totally made it up!"

"Maybe," he said with a grin. "So look, you won't have a drink, you won't be nice, and so I'll leave you alone on one condition."

"No."

"Don't you want to know what that condition is?"

She shook her head no, but then said impatiently, "Okay, what?"

He looked around them and leaned in closer to her. Emma twisted around to face him, so that her knees brushed against his thigh. Cooper found himself staring into a pair of green eyes with gold flecks in them. "No one's around right now, Emma. It's only you and me. Hand to God," he said, pressing his palm against his chest, "whatever you tell me stays with me."

A smile slowly spread across her lips, illuminating her eyes again. Damn, but she was pretty when she smiled. Why the hell didn't Emma just *smile*? She could clear a path in this bar with that smile, could put the world at her feet.

"*That's* not a condition. That's begging."

"Here's the condition: you can kiss me like you wanted to do so badly that night in Beverly Hills if you tell me about Carl's box."

Emma blinked. And then she laughed. "You're funny, Cooper Jessup! And *weird*. Funny in a very weird way."

"Don't try and charm me, it won't work."

She laughed again and looked at his mouth, as if she was considering the condition. His blood was beginning to race a little.

"You have it all wrong. *You* wanted to kiss me. I never wanted to kiss you," she said.

"Not true," he said, his gaze on her mouth now.

"Totally true. You're not my type." She locked her eyes on his. "Not at *all*."

Her eyes were glittering with delight. Cooper could see how Carl had been drawn in—he probably fell the moment Emma smiled, probably promised her the moon and stars, because that's the kind of guy he was. Cooper was teetering, but he wouldn't fall. He knew when he was being played.

He leaned closer, rested his hand on her knee. "What's your type, Emma Tyler?"

"Older, fat guys."

He chuckled.

Emma didn't.

"Okay, so here's a new condition. I'll go back to LA like you want, leave you to mine Pine River for older, fat guys, if you give me that box with the medal in it. I know you have it, and for reasons that don't make any sense to anyone but you, you're lying about it. Listen, it's no skin off my nose, and it's no big deal to give it back. It will be forgotten by tomorrow, so why drag it out?"

Emma smiled coquettishly at his hand on her knee. She curled her fingers around his palm, and for a moment, Cooper believed she was going to tell him the truth. But when she lifted her gaze, there was a distance there. "Try and listen, cowboy," she said softly. "I don't have whatever it is Carl thinks he lost. Now *here's* an idea. I'll walk over to Tag's with you right now and buy you a trinket for Carl and you can take it back to him. How's that?"

"Unacceptable."

She laughed, amused. She picked up her drink, lazily licked a drop of condensation from the side of the glass as she considered him. Cooper languidly imagined those green eyes staring up at him from a bed somewhere. His gaze slipped to her mouth once more, and down, to the vee of her sweater, and the small, pear-shaped diamond that hung there.

He decided to try another tack before he did something stupid. Like touch her. *Kiss* her. Put his mouth on the hollow of her neck where that necklace hung, where he could feel her pulse. Or the spot where her neck curved into her shoulder. *Jesus, what are you doing?* "Okay, I give up," he blurted.

Emma blinked with surprise. "What's the twist?"

"No twist. I concede that you obviously don't have it, because no one would work this hard to hide something so meaningless."

Her lashes fluttered, with guilt or relief, he supposed, or a mix of both. "At *last*," she said. "Now may we please return to you being mildly acquainted with me in LA, and me here in Pine River not caring about you?"

"Sure," Cooper said, ignoring her digs. Maybe that worked on other men, but not on him. He drummed his fingers on the table. "Carl probably moved it and forgot what he did with it anyway," he said. "He doesn't strike me as the most observant kind of guy."

With one long, manicured finger, Emma traced a line around the rim of her glass. "Maybe his wife came and picked it up."

So she knew that it had belonged to his wife.

Emma swept her hair around and over her shoulder, exposing the nape of her neck to him.

Cooper looked away, took a strong slug of his drink. *Stop it.* Yeah, okay, she was beautiful, but Cooper was around beautiful women all the time. Beautiful *sane* women. Maybe Michael was right. Maybe he'd gone too long without a relationship, without regular sex. Too much testosterone was building up and all of that. "Anyway, I'm sick of talking about Carl Freeman," he said, and signaled the bartender.

"Well, *that* definitely makes two of us."

"So let's talk about something else," Cooper said. "Like why you took off from LA."

Emma arched a golden brow. "What makes you think I took off?"

"Because CEM told me you'd quit and left town. Your boss—Melissa, right? She told me that you were probably here in Pine River."

For the first time, Emma looked uncertain. "Wow. For someone who claims not to be following me, you sure sound like you've been following me."

"I've been looking for you."

"That sounds like a total violation of my privacy."

"I think having me look around for you is better than having a private detective look for you. That would have been Carl's next move. So anyway, why did you leave?"

"Well, it had nothing to do with Carl, that bald bag of wind," she snapped. "It's really not complicated, Cooper. I needed a change of view. Haven't you ever needed a change of view?"

"Sure. But I don't quit my job for one. I don't take off overnight."

She looked as if she intended to argue, but hesitated. She casually touched a lock of hair on his forehead, pushing it aside. He could feel the touch of her finger sink into his skin. "You're way off base," she said, and leaned across him and picked up his drink. She deliberately sipped from it, looking at him over the rim of the glass, and put the glass down.

Cooper couldn't help a small laugh. That move looked so practiced it seemed almost mechanical. He could just imagine it. *Innocently touch him, check. Drink from his glass, check. Smile and twist hair around finger, check.* "Does that really work? That drink-from-my-glass thing?" he asked, gesturing to his glass. "Do older, fat guys like that?"

Emma's eyes narrowed. She looked away, but Cooper caught her hand and held it. "I know when I'm being played, Emma. And you're playing me. You must have some secrets to hide."

She tried to pull her hand free. "You're annoying the shit out of me now."

"And you're starting to fascinate me." Even though he found her behavior objectionable and reprehensible—stealing was something he couldn't tolerate in anyone—he still found her oddly intriguing. What made a woman like her do the things she did? Say the things she did? "If I'm wrong, then explain to me why you're working for Leo Kendrick."

She smiled with amusement, and he noticed she no longer tried to free her hand of his. "*That's* your burning question?"

"It's not even remotely close to event planning."

"No, it's not," she agreed.

"So?"

"So, his nurse is on maternity leave. He needed someone to hang out with him during the day so his dad can take care of other things. And I needed—" She abruptly stopped midsentence and seemed to think better of what she was about to say. "I was happy to do it," she said, averting her gaze. "I *wanted* to do it."

That seemed oddly out of character from what Cooper knew.

Happy to do it. *Wanting* to do it. That was not the Emma who was currently residing in his head, whose hand was currently held in his. "Why?" he asked curiously.

"Why?" she echoed. "Because I love Leo."

Cooper didn't know exactly what she meant by that. He'd been surprised to find the man behind the flaming van was living in a chair, his body twisted and useless. "What's wrong with him?"

There was a slight, but noticeable change in Emma's careful expression. A sliver of concern slipping through, and then a sharper glance of pain. "He . . . he has Motor Neuron Disease. Like Lou Gehrig's disease. It destroys the muscles and they atrophy until he can't talk. Or eat." She looked down at her glass. "Or breathe."

Cooper felt a flush of guilt and sympathy under his skin, that rush of relief that by the grace of God, he wasn't afflicted with something so horrible. Emma's expression had gone placid again. Any sign of emotion had disappeared, replaced by a look of impatience.

"Well! On that cheerful note," she said, sliding off her stool and pulling her hand free of his, "I'm done." She hooked her purse over her shoulder and smiled, leaned in, her gaze on his mouth, stirring his blood, making him think of things that had nothing to do with Carl's medal. "This has been oodles of fun, but just so we're clear? Don't bother me again, Cooper." She brushed against his thigh as she squeezed out from between the barstools and walked away.

He didn't try and stop her. He watched her walk to the front of the bar until she disappeared into the main dining area.

He turned back to his drink. The bartender was standing there, his thick hands braced against the bar. "Another drink, buddy?"

"Yeah," Cooper said. "A double." He drained his bourbon and slid the empty glass across to the bartender.

NINE

"Scoot over, bitches," Emma said when she reached the booth her sisters had just taken.

"Emma!" Libby cried with surprise.

"What, you didn't think I'd come?" Emma asked, and waved a hand at her, indicating she should move over.

"Well, your text wasn't exactly encouraging. I mean, when someone texts *maybe* it doesn't actually mean yes," Libby said, seeming genuinely happy to see Emma. She scooted across the bench.

"Wow, you *did* come," Madeline said, nodding approvingly as Emma slipped in beside Libby. "I guess I owe you five bucks, Libs."

Emma smiled wryly. Madeline did not approve of her, but that didn't bother Emma; she figured Madeline was right to be wary of her. "I had to come, sweetie," Emma said with false lightness. "I couldn't risk missing out on the minutiae of your wedding plans, could I? We'll be reviewing them in detail again tonight, I assume."

"Every last one," Madeline said, and actually laughed. She seemed to be in an unusually jovial mood tonight, because she winked at Emma. "Even *you* can't bring me down."

Emma smiled. "I wouldn't dream of it. I hope the wedding is everything you ever wanted and more."

Madeline paused, waiting for a punch line.

There was no punch line—Emma did wish that for her. "Just because I don't want to hear about it every waking moment doesn't mean I don't wish you the best."

"Yeah, well, it doesn't necessarily mean you do, either," Madeline cheerfully pointed out. "Okay, *so?*" she chirped, leaning forward. "What's going on with the hunk who appeared from thin air?"

Emma looked between the two women. "You realize that you sound like a fourteen-year-old girl," she said, sinking back into the seat cushions.

"I can't help that I'm excited that someone interesting has come into town for *you.*"

"I think I'm vaguely insulted," Emma said, and twisted around. "Where the hell is the waiter? Why does it always take two mules and a cart to get a drink in this town?"

"Emma," Madeline said, tapping her hand. "Are you going to tell us?"

There would be no escaping it, apparently. Emma supposed she'd known that the moment she'd spotted them in the booth, engrossed in conversation, their dark heads leaning across the table toward each other as she sauntered over to them. She'd had a prickly feeling that they were talking about her.

But she wasn't ready to talk just yet, at least not before she had a drink, and even then she didn't know what she'd tell them. "What is it about everyone in this town?" she complained with a flick of her wrist. "Is it possible for a man and woman to exchange a few words without everyone trying to put a ring on it? It's ridiculous."

"Avoiding the question!" Madeline called out, pointing at her like a courtroom attorney. "No one is trying to put a ring on it. We just want to know who he is. I mean, it's not like total strangers show up at Homecoming Ranch every day."

"What are you talking about? Total strangers show up all the time. We do destination events, remember? We run a veterans' rehab center."

"Okay, they don't show up for you," Madeline amended.

"Fine," Emma said, giving in. "He thinks I have something that belongs to a guy we both know. He had to come to Colorado for something or other, I don't know, and he stopped by to ask about it." She lifted her palms up to indicate that was all there was.

"That's it? That's the reason he came all the way out to Homecoming Ranch? Why didn't he just call you? If he knew you were there, he must have had your number."

"I don't know," Emma said, squirming a bit. "What are you, a detective?"

"He's so *hot*," Libby enthusiastically continued, nudging Emma. "I mean, I'm totally in love with Sam, but I think that guy is freaking *hot*."

Inexplicably, that annoyed Emma even more. "Jesus, is sex all you guys think about?"

"It's not *all* we think about," Madeline said.

Emma groaned with exasperation. "I would really like to speak to a waiter." She looked back over her shoulder. "I could have downed two drinks by now."

"Wait, I'm confused," Libby said. "Who's the guy you and Cooper both know? And what does he think you have?"

"I don't know."

"What do you mean, you don't know? You mean that totally hot Cooper came all the way out to the ranch, without calling, to ask for something back from that guy and you don't know what he was asking for? Something doesn't smell right," Madeline pressed.

"Like, why *you*, why he came here, why didn't the other guy come himself, what he thinks you have—"

"A medal, okay?" Emma said, interrupting Madeline. She managed to catch the waiter's eye; he started for their table.

"A *medal*!" Libby exclaimed loudly, as if she'd never heard the word before. "What kind of medal?"

"I don't know, Libby, a medal. How should I know? A glass of cabernet," she said to the waiter, who appeared tableside.

Madeline and Libby ordered drinks, and Libby ordered an appetizer. "I don't know why, but I am so hungry all the time," she said sheepishly.

"Maybe you're pregnant," Emma suggested. "You should get a pregnancy test on the way home."

Libby's eyes rounded. *"No!"* she said, and laughed nervously. "No, I can't be."

"She's not pregnant," Madeline said.

"How do you know?" Libby demanded, but Madeline waved her off and fixed her gaze on Emma again.

Emma picked up the menu and began to peruse it.

"I think it would be nice if you invited Hot Guy for dinner."

Emma lowered her menu and pinned Madeline with a look of annoyance. "Do you, Madeline? And why would that be nice of me? Would it be nice to invite everyone in town who happens to be from California?"

"*No*," Madeline drawled. "But it would be nice of you to invite someone you know, who happens to be in town alone. It's called hospitality."

"It's called manipulation," Emma said. "And you're very good at it."

"Don't think of it as a date, because I know that's what you're thinking," Madeline doggedly continued, unruffled by Emma's remark. "We'll be there, won't we, Libs?"

"Of course!"

"Do either of you realize how aggressive you're being right now?" Emma blurted, searching for anything to get them to stop. "It may be *your* main goal in life to get a man, but it's not mine. It's none of your business if I know Cooper or not. And anyway, I don't like him, okay? Don't. Like. Him. It's not my problem if he's a stranger in town, and honestly, I couldn't care less. And finally, Madeline, you of all people should know I'm really not hospitable."

Madeline laughed. "Oh, I know," she agreed. "But I would love to see you untwist a little."

"Yeah, well, *that's* not going to happen," Emma said, and lifted her menu again.

"But . . ." Libby squirmed in her seat.

"Don't you start," Emma warned her.

"No, no, I'm not starting. You don't like him, fine. But don't you ever . . . don't you ever just want to . . . *you* know."

"Have sex," Madeline said flatly. "It's not a dirty word."

There was no way to explain to these women that she didn't want to have sex. Wait—that wasn't entirely accurate. Her body wanted sex—*real* sex, good sex—not the sex she generally had. And if she were going to have really good sex, it would be with someone like Cooper. Okay, it would be with Cooper. And that was definitely outside the realm of possibilities. It was all too complicated in her head. "I'm good."

"Okay," Libby said with a shrug. "It's your life. I'm just surprised, that's all, because you don't seem the type to be celibate *at all*. Madeline, maybe, but not you."

"Hey!" Madeline protested.

Emma smiled. "What makes you think I'm celibate?"

"You just said—"

"No, *you* just said. I'm not celibate. Anything but," she added, and felt a funny little flip of her gut.

"Really?" Madeline leaned forward. "Here's a question. How many guys have you been with?"

"Well, *that's* awfully personal," Libby said, clearly appalled.

"I know," Madeline said cheerfully. "But we're sisters, aren't we? Seems like something sisters would ask each other. Wouldn't they? If we'd known each other all our lives instead of a few months, would we not have asked this very question along the way?"

"Are you *drunk*?" Libby whispered loudly.

"No! Okay, I'll go first," Madeline offered. She looked around to see if anyone might overhear, then said low, "I've been with four."

"Congratulations," Emma said drily.

"You've been with *four*?" Libby exclaimed, as surprised as Emma was unimpressed.

"What? Is that too few or too many? Did you think Luke was my first?"

"Sort of," Libby admitted, which made Emma laugh with delight.

"Are you kidding? I'm thirty, Libby!" Madeline exclaimed as the waiter arrived with their drinks and deposited them on the table. When he'd gone, Madeline asked Libby, "How many have *you* been with?"

"Oh gosh." Libby squinted at the ceiling, her lips moving as she counted. "Five," she said. "Including Sam, of course. That sounds like a lot, doesn't it? I'm really not a slut. I mean, I always thought I'd marry my first."

That earned her a pair of looks from Emma and Madeline.

"Okay, all right, I'm old-fashioned that way," Libby said, waving her hand, clearly embarrassed now. "What about you, Emma? How many?"

"Too many to count," Emma said honestly.

"No, seriously," Libby said, nudging her. "How many?"

"I *am* serious. Too many to count." She didn't know if that was entirely accurate—she fooled around more than she had sex, really—but Emma was almost twenty-eight years old, and the last few years had not been good. She wasn't going to count, afraid of what she might discover.

"So you're a slut?" Madeline asked with a snort.

"Basically."

Madeline wasn't buying it, judging by the exaggerated roll of her eyes. "Okay, so don't play our little game. What about this—have you slept with anyone famous?"

Emma thought about that for a moment. "Fame is such a subjective thing—"

"Nope, no way. You're not going to turn a very simple question into philosophical bullshit and avoid answering. It's very simple, Emma. Anyone famous, yes or no?"

"Yes," Emma said. "Val Kilmer."

Madeline and Libby gasped at the same time. "The *actor*?" Libby asked in a bit of a squeal.

"No, the pizza delivery guy," Emma said. "Of course the actor."

"You *slept* with him?" Madeline whispered.

"Wasn't that the question?"

Madeline and Libby looked at each other and simultaneously burst into laughter. "Emma! You've been holding out on us!" Madeline cried.

"I have not! I didn't even know you until this spring, remember? I didn't realize I was supposed to arrive with my sexual dossier all typed up and ready to be handed out."

"That would have been awesome," Madeline said.

"You definitely should have told us if you slept with *Val Kilmer*!" Libby cried, and punched Emma in the shoulder. "That's big news! *So?* What was he like?"

Emma smiled. "Like all the rest of them," she said, and picked up her menu. Except that he wasn't fat. But he was older. "Nothing to write home about. What are you eating?"

Libby pressed for more details, but Emma stubbornly ignored her. She really didn't remember much about that night. She'd drunk too much at a party, and had ended up in his hotel room. Unfortunately, he'd had an early flight and was gone by the time she awoke the next day, taking a little piece of her with him in exchange for nothing but a raging headache.

When Libby and Madeline realized they'd get no more information from her, the talk turned to Madeline's wedding. It was to be held New Year's Eve in the barn at the ranch, the same place they'd hosted Thanksgiving. Emma didn't understand Libby's and Madeline's fascination with that barn, but she supposed it was at least something useful to come out of Homecoming Ranch.

To Emma's thinking, they had inherited Grant's problem—a run-down ranch that owed more than it took in. *Thanks again, Dad.* At first, Emma had been so angry about it. *That* was his dying apology to her? To give her another problem she didn't need? But Libby had seen that ranch as a new beginning and had desperately clung to it, even when Madeline and Emma wanted nothing to do with it.

So Emma did what she was apparently good at doing—she left. She left the problem with Libby, figuring if Libby wanted that ranch so badly, she could have it. She'd disappeared into her life in LA and had assumed Madeline would go back to hers in Orlando. She'd assumed everything would go back to the way it was before Grant had died. But then Madeline had begun to see something in that ranch, too, and had left Orlando behind for it.

Emma still had wanted nothing to do with the ranch, and God knew she wouldn't be here now had the candlestick thing not happened. But here she was, and she had to admit to herself, she was impressed with Libby's vision for it. Libby had smartly started a reintegration program for armed forces veterans who were struggling with PTSD and needed help learning how to reenter their lives after the wars of the last decade. She'd secured some grant funding, and they'd renovated the bunkhouse for them. Ernest Delgado, Homecoming Ranch's longtime ranch hand, was something of a den mother to the five men who were currently in the program. In addition to participating in some donated therapy programs, the men did odd jobs around the ranch.

Unfortunately, in the winter, there was not enough to keep five grown men occupied.

Moreover, the opportunities to grow Libby's vision were not great. The ranch was too remote, so far removed from services and medical facilities that no one wanted to come. Libby was working tirelessly to shore up the program, and Emma was truly in awe of her tenacity—she would have given up long ago.

Of all of them, Libby made life look so . . . *effortless*. After her bad meltdown last summer, the result of a relationship gone way south, she'd bounced right back. Now she took a little pill each morning and she was happy in love, full of big ideas and smiles.

Emma wished she could be more like that, but really, she was more like Madeline. It would probably kill Madeline if Emma ever said that aloud, but it was true. Like Madeline, Emma was straightforward, never afraid to say what was on her mind. That is where their similarities ended. Madeline had more tact and a surprisingly big heart. She could learn to love anything, like dogs and damaged veterans and widows. Emma couldn't seem to love anything.

Madeline wasn't ready to give up on Homecoming Ranch yet, either, it was apparent. She was going to marry here, maybe even start a family here. She was starting her life over here.

That was okay with Emma. They could keep this money-eating ranch for now. Personally, she'd put a lot of money aside and could even float the ranch for a few months if necessary, if for no other reason than to have a place to be. That was what Emma needed from the universe right now—a place to be, a place to figure out how to make her way back to the world.

But eventually, she'd leave. Emma knew herself too well. She'd go on with her life and forget her sisters. It was an ugly but certain truth about her.

It was Madeline who shook Emma out of her thoughts by mentioning Grant. "I ran into Grant's friend Sylvia Breslin," she said. "Know her?"

Emma shook her head.

"Yeah, of course," Libby said. "She's been selling real estate forever in this town. What about her?"

"So Michelle Catucci, the banker? She introduced us, and mentioned that I was one of Grant Tyler's daughters. You know, like that's my identity," Madeline said with a snort. "Anyway, Sylvia perked up. She said she'd heard about what had happened with Grant and his kids, and Libby's meltdown last summer—"

"Oh my God!" Libby exclaimed. "I swear, you have *one* small meltdown in Pine River and no one will forget it."

Libby failed to acknowledge that hers was a pretty spectacular meltdown, judging by what Jackson had told Emma—she'd taken a golf club to a man's truck.

"Don't worry about it," Madeline said to Libby. "Anyway, Sylvia said that just before Grant got sick, he'd been talking to her about buying some property in Vegas. And I was like, seriously? Because he couldn't pay his bills. But Sylvia said that's what she'd heard and thought he was planning to move before he got sick. She asked if he had ended up buying property there—you know, like I would have any idea."

The mention of Grant and Las Vegas was an unwelcome jolt of memory for Emma. She put down her fork, her appetite gone.

"Vegas," Libby said, her voice full of disgust. "That's just like Dad, to plan something without mentioning it to anyone. What would he do there?"

"Gamble, among other things," Emma said. "How do you think he made the money to buy the ranch in the first place? It's not like he ever held a real job."

"Who would know?" Madeline said.

"Seriously?" Libby asked. "I mean, do you know that for a fact? I didn't think you'd had much contact with him."

"I didn't," Emma said. "My mom kept in touch with him." She looked off, unwilling—unable—to think of how her mother had kept in touch with Grant after what had happened.

"So what was he like?" Madeline asked curiously.

"How the fuck would I know?" Emma said sharply, surprising even herself.

"Hey," Libby said. "She was just asking."

"You think I knew him any better than either of you? He was never around for more than a minute, and when he was, he made trouble for everyone. He was a prick."

"Hey!" Libby exclaimed again. "He was still our father."

"Yeah, right," Emma said. "And how'd that work out for you, Libby? He wouldn't give you the time of day even when he was on his deathbed."

Libby gasped.

Emma hadn't meant to wound her with that remark, she'd meant to make Libby see just how awful . . . forget what she meant. If Libby hadn't figured out what a prick Grant was by now, she never would.

"Well, I didn't know him at all," Madeline said, her back up now. "I don't know if he was a prick or a saint because I couldn't even pick him out of a lineup. You know what I remember about him? That he smelled like smoke. That's it, that's how much contact I had with my father. So pardon me if I am a little curious about the man who abandoned me. I just thought maybe you could give me some insight since you were closer to him than any of us."

"But I *wasn't* closer," Emma said. "I'm not close to anyone."

"No surprise there," Madeline said flatly.

"He was always nice to me," Libby said, sounding uncertain. "I mean, when he was around. Which he never was."

"He wasn't nice to me and he wasn't around. He lied about everything," Emma said. "That's what you need to know about him, Madeline. He was a lying bastard."

Madeline and Libby looked at each other. There it was again, that exchange of knowing looks between her sisters, the unspoken unity against Emma and her mouth. Emma didn't blame them one bit, and, in fact, she sided with them. Her sharp tongue had put a damper on an otherwise perfectly enjoyable evening with them, had perhaps even taken a bite out of their fragile camaraderie. Her only regret was that she hadn't meant to bite. Her reaction had been disturbingly visceral.

"I'm sorry," Emma said tightly.

"It's fine, it's all right," Madeline started, but Emma waved her hand.

"It's *not* all right. Look, I can't change—" She stopped. She wasn't going to apologize for who she was. She felt as if she'd been doing that for a very long time. "It's not my intent, *never* my intent, to hurt anyone."

"Then why do you keep doing it?" Libby muttered.

Emma glanced down at her hands. "Touché, Libby. I wish I had an answer for you."

"Well, that's news," Libby said pertly. "Can't remember the last time you didn't have an answer for everything."

Emma sighed. She signaled the waiter. "Check, please," she said.

"Madeline, is your mom coming to the wedding?" Libby asked, having turned away from Emma now, her attention on her other, better sister. She and Madeline began to discuss the wedding again, leaving Emma out.

Precisely where she belonged. Out.

TEN

At a quarter past eight, the three sisters emerged from the Stake Out. Emma was tired, ready to retreat to her room at Homecoming Ranch, but as she pointed her key fob at her car and clicked to unlock the doors, Madeline suddenly gasped. "My phone!"

"What about it?" Libby asked, glancing at her watch.

"It's not in my purse! I must have left it on the table."

"Okay, well, can you get a ride with Emma?" Libby asked, walking backward and away from them. "I'm supposed to pick Sam up at eight thirty and I'm going to be late."

"Sure," Emma said, and waved at Madeline, indicating she should go back and look for her phone.

"Thanks, Emma!" Libby hurried away from them.

A few minutes later, Madeline emerged from the restaurant. "It's not there. I think I left it with Luke. You can drive me to Elm Street, right?"

Elm Street! Emma suppressed a groan. She did not want to drive to Leo's, even if it was only a few blocks away and on the way home. She didn't want to see Cooper again. She glanced at her watch.

"What?" Madeline said to her hesitation. "I'm sorry if I am inconveniencing you, but it's like a block out of your way."

"If you were inconveniencing me, I'd say so. Just come on," Emma said, and stepped off the curb, headed for her car.

Madeline reluctantly followed.

Surely Cooper had left by now, Emma reasoned as Madeline searched her bag, muttering about all the places she might have left her phone. How long did a complete stranger stay at someone's house?

"Call Luke and ask," Emma suggested as she backed out of her parking space. "Use my phone."

"I would, but he keeps his phone in his pocket and never hears it. Do you know how maddening that is? What is the point of having a phone if you can't hear it and never answer it? Anyway, I'll just run in and get it."

When they turned onto Elm Street, Emma's exasperation swelled at the sight of Cooper's rental car in front of the Kendrick house. She unthinkingly sighed with displeasure.

Madeline made a sound of impatience and rolled her eyes. "Don't get your panties in a wad," she said. "I'll only be a second."

Emma pulled up at the fence. "I'll wait."

Madeline had hardly stepped out of the car when the front door of the house opened and light spilled out. Figures of two men emerged as Madeline went through the gate and half jogged up the walk.

On the porch, Madeline joined the two men, who Emma could now see were Cooper and Luke. Madeline threw her arms around Luke, then spoke to Cooper. Cooper turned to look at Emma's car.

Emma groaned and slid a little lower in her seat.

Whatever Madeline was saying went on forever. The three of them kept speaking, a regular conversation in spite of the cold.

Like they were old friends, catching up on many past years. Jesus, what could they possibly have to say to each other? *How was your dinner?* she imagined Madeline asking. *It was great, just great— haven't had Hamburger Helper in years.*

At last, at long last, Madeline and Luke went inside, and Cooper strolled down the steps and the walk, his hands shoved in his pockets and his formidable figure slipping in and out of the shadows beneath the mason-jar lights someone had hung up under the big elm tree.

Emma slid deeper into her seat. *Way* down, with a lot of wishful thinking that quickly evaporated when he tapped on her driver's window. *"Shit,"* she muttered. She slowly pushed herself up, rolled down the window, and killed the engine. He'd slid down on his haunches beside the car door, and she looked at his face framed in the window, at how the shadows made him look even sexier than he'd looked at the Stake Out.

"How was the Hamburger Helper?" Emma asked.

"What?" Cooper asked. "You mean the steak?"

Steak! Bob never made anything that didn't come from a box when she stuck around for dinner. She glared at the house.

Cooper smiled at her funnily. "It was good. How was *your* dinner? What'd you have, something light but heavy on the conscience?"

"Funny," Emma said. She really didn't like the way Cooper could see something in her no one else could see. She *did* feel guilty. And she didn't like the way he was looking at her now, like he knew what was going on in her head. Emma abruptly opened the door, intending to topple him over, but Cooper was pretty agile and managed to stand and move before she could. "Sorry," she said airily, and stepped out of the car.

It was cold; she leaned back against her car and folded her arms tightly over her sweater. She looked up at the night sky rather than into his piercing gray eyes.

The night was brilliant, a black swath of velvet between mountains, glittering with millions of stars that looked so close it seemed she could reach up and grab a handful. "It's a beautiful night, isn't it?"

"Hey!"

Emma turned toward the sound of Madeline's voice from somewhere near the house.

"Luke can't find it, but he says it's here. Just give me a couple of minutes more." She disappeared back inside.

"Unbelievable," Emma sighed.

Cooper leaned up against her car beside her and tilted his head back to look up. His shoulder grazed hers, and Emma found herself pulling in a little tighter. It was instinct, a natural reflex. Protect yourself at all times from the advances of men who looked like him, men who attracted her on a supersonic level.

"I never think about stars like this in LA, do you? It's like they don't even exist there. Everything is so phony there that it's really hard to imagine that there is this entire world out here," she said.

Cooper didn't respond. Emma glanced at him from the corner of her eye. He had shifted his gaze from the sky and was studying her. "What are you looking at?"

"Who, me?" His low voice trickled warmly through her like a good bourbon. "I'm enjoying the night sky as you suggested." He smiled. Heat began to sluice through Emma.

"Whatever," she said.

"I guess you think you won some little victory tonight," he said.

She didn't think that at all. But she said, "You're kidding, right? Because I haven't thought about it at all."

"No? Not even a little?"

"No." Emma abruptly turned around to face him, her shoulder against her car, her arms folded tightly across her. "Out of sight, out of mind," she said breezily. It was a lie, a huge lie. Cooper had been with her all through dinner, swirling around in the shadows.

"Funny . . . I thought about you," he said, and damn him if he didn't let his gaze slide down her body. "I thought, how am I going to get this girl to let go of that medal? Am I going to have to check her at every turn until we get this business resolved?"

Under any other circumstance, Emma might have invited him to check her now, check every inch and take his time. She wondered if he was thinking the same thing, because there was something veiled beneath his careful expression that made Emma feel a tiny bit short of breath.

"Would it be easier if I invited you to come up to the ranch and go through my things? Is that what you want?"

"Actually . . . that would be *great*," he said, and looked at her mouth.

She wanted to kiss him. It occurred to her in that charged moment that maybe she'd been going about this all wrong. Maybe the way to get rid of Cooper was to seduce him. She didn't exactly have the time or inclination to work out that reasoning, or how dangerous that thinking was for her, but brushing him off hadn't gotten rid of him, so maybe he would forget the medal in favor of wanting her.

"You look like you want to kiss me," Emma said flatly. "Are you going to try it, or are you going to deny that's what you want again?"

He chuckled and touched his knuckle to her temple. "I thought we'd been over this already and established that you are delusional. One of us wants a kiss, and it's not me. All I want is that medal."

"If that's what you need to tell yourself," she said, and shifted closer, her hand finding his waist and resting there lightly. He made no move to disengage from her hand. Emma wanted to remove it, to stop herself from doing something she would completely regret, but she was finding it impossible with the light of a million stars shining down on them on that cold winter night.

"I have a view of the mountain peaks from the window of my room at Homecoming Ranch. Every morning I wake up and think of the nearly twenty-eight years I've wasted looking at billboards." She tilted her head back and looked him directly in the eye. "It makes me wonder about what else I've missed." She eased forward so that her body was touching his.

Cooper smiled. He was allowing her to play this game with him, to see how far she would take it.

She would take it far enough that he would forget that stupid medal, she thought languidly. "I wonder what might have happened at the bat mitzvah if I'd let you kiss me."

Now Cooper grinned. He tucked a strand of hair behind her ear, and his fingers lingered on her neck. Sizzling spots of skin on a cold night. "Maybe if I'd let you kiss me, you wouldn't have slept with a married man," he said, and put his hand on her arm.

"I didn't sleep with Reggie. I just let him pretend he had a chance." That much was true. Emma had let him beg like the dog he was, had even allowed him to kiss her. And then she'd turned him down, had made him get a car to send her home . . . with his tie clip in her purse. Stupid bastard—as if she'd ever get mixed up with a married man whose daughter was an over-indulged twat.

"Women don't get in limos of rich and powerful men just to tease them." Cooper's hand went around her waist, drawing her closer.

"How would you know?" she asked. "Why would I sleep with someone like Reggie when I had someone like you practically begging for it?" She rose up on her toes, her mouth now directly below Cooper's. Her heart was suddenly galloping; she could smell his cologne, could almost feel his lips on hers.

"Who's begging now?" Cooper muttered.

He had her there. Emma touched her mouth to his.

She was instantly consumed by a conflagration of emotion and intense desire. She touched her tongue to the seam of his lips, pushing past them, into his mouth. He pulled her closer, opening his mouth to her assault. He cupped her face and nibbled at her lip, moving his free hand from her waist to her hip. He pushed her into his body, hard and solid, all the right angles and planes.

Cooper Jessup kissed Emma as thoroughly as she was kissing him, his tongue tangling with hers, his arm holding her steady, his body pressed against hers so that there was nothing left to her imagination. *She had never kissed like this, never!* She was always a disinterested partner, wishing for it to be over. But with Cooper, she felt molten, her body melting into his, ready to give in to whatever he would do to her. *Eager* for it.

Then Cooper suddenly put his hands on her arms and lifted his head. He firmly set her back a step or two.

For a few moments, Emma was confused by that. She should be fumbling to remove her clothes just now, and she ran her little finger over her bottom lip as she stared uncertainly at him.

Cooper's smile was confident. He casually swept hair from her cheek, like he knew her, like he had the right to touch her that way. "That may work on every man you've ever met . . . but it won't work on me."

What did he mean it wouldn't work? It *had* worked, judging by the bulge she'd felt in his pants and the way he'd kissed her. "You liked it," she pointed out.

"Of course I liked it. I'm a man. But I'm not Reggie. And I'm not Carl. I don't fall at the feet of a beautiful woman just because she kisses me. Like I told you earlier—I know when I'm being played. You think I will give up on the medal if you let me have a few liberties. But I don't take from women like that, Emma. With me, it's an equal proposition."

Emma recoiled from the truth about her intentions. "You're such an ass," she said, and tried to turn away, but Cooper pulled her back around to face him, locking her in place with both hands on her arms.

"Furthermore, the only thing you've done here tonight with that kiss is succeed in making yourself look guilty as hell."

She pulled free and pushed him back with both hands. She opened her car door, reached in, and honked the horn. And then she climbed into the driver's seat and slammed the door shut.

Cooper squatted down beside her before she could start the car and raise the window, his eyes eerily luminous in the light of the streetlamp. "I'll see you around, Emma." He was smiling as he spoke, but it wasn't a friendly smile. It was a hot, devilish smile. It was a determined, *I-will-win* smile.

"The hell you will," she said, and started her car.

Cooper stood up, gave her car two friendly taps, and then he sauntered off, like he owned this two-bit town.

Emma shouldn't have even noticed his exit. She should not have given him another look. It wasn't like she hadn't seen that very exit a million times in a million different films. But none of the film versions of that departure had ever made her feel so floaty.

Emma rolled up the window, then banged both fists several times against the steering wheel.

Jesus, what was she going to *do* with him?

ELEVEN

Are you keeping count? Only a few more sleeps until I head for an awesome skybox and the Broncos-Patriots game. Dad says I sound like a little kid, and maybe I do—but I've been dreaming about a game like this since I picked up my first pigskin when I was six and Mom enrolled me in Pop Warner football. I didn't even know about football, but Mom said I was like a moose in a china closet because I guess I was clumsy or something. I'll never forget it. She said, *If you need to crash into things so bad, go crash into other boys instead of my house.* She was kind of shouting it when she said it.

It was the best thing she ever did for me. Well, okay, maybe not the best, but I did love football. I played all the way through school and you probably wouldn't guess it by looking at me now, but I was so badass that I got a scholarship to play for the Colorado School of Mines. I know what you're thinking! That a bunch of engineers wouldn't be into football, but trust me, that team *rocked*.

I was headed for All-American when I started having trouble with my hand. Like, my hand would just stop holding a football, or stop holding a pen like there was no input from my genius brain. And then my foot started flopping around like a clown while I walked. It was weird, watching pens slip through my fingers and my foot flop around. Anyway, you know the rest of the story, MND, blah, blah, blah, and I had to stop playing. But I *still* love football, and now, after twenty-seven years, I get to see the *Broncos* obliterate the *Patriots.* That is every Colorado boy's dream, and I'm going to see it from a luxury seat!

I tried to convince Dad to get me some body paint so I could go *super* orange and blue, the Bronco colors, but Dad said no, he couldn't paint and it would be too cold anyway and he didn't think the world wanted to see my chest. Killjoy! I was pretty pissed about it, but Luke got me a great Broncos shirt and cap, and I'm ready.

I've still got plenty to worry about. You cannot imagine the effort it takes to coordinate and organize when you've only got a mouth to work with. Dad the Downer said we're going up Sunday morning and coming back that night, because we can't be away from all the breathing machines and crap that he pumps into me every day. So now I'm a little worried that it might snow, and if it does, Dad will drive my van like a grandpa, and we could be late. People, I can *not* be late. It will ruin everything for Dante and me if we're late.

Just in case, I've been studying up on alternative routes. I need to concentrate, and you'd think people would understand I have enough to do without worrying about everyone else in Pine River, but you know how it is, once you've established yourself as king of the hill, it's hard to get off, if only for a weekend. They still keep coming to me.

The Methodist ladies brought me a picnic basket full of stuff for my trip. Like baby wipes and big plastic bottles with crazy straws for all the stuff Dad has to give me, and it was really sweet, and I do love me some Methodist ladies—I mean, they are the reason I'm getting to go to the game after their big fundraisers, right? But I really don't have time for a hen circle right now. Then again, the Methodists can be counted on for the *best* gossip, and believe me, they already knew all about Cooper Jessup. It's like they're aliens with news antennas that come out of their heads the moment someone new comes to town.

This time, the ladies heard about the new guy from Dani. Well, color me mildly surprised, because it turns out, Dani apparently appreciates eye candy as much as the rest of them and has been telling everyone in town about the hunk from Hollywood.

As happy as I was to learn about Dani's hots for Cooper, all that talking and listening was exhausting. I'm not being sexist when I say that women have an unbelievable capacity to talk. I bet if you Googled it, you'd find it was an accepted scientific fact. If there weren't guys around, who would ever get them to stop talking? It's hard for me to admit defeat, but here goes—I was outmatched and I was unsuccessful in getting them to stop. They stayed a really long time. My plans for the afternoon—charting some alternative routes to Denver—were shot, and I had to ask Luke to call Marisol and beg her to come and help me look at maps.

Well, Marisol came immediately, because it turns out she likes to show off that stinky little hot mess of a baby. Valentina has a thatch of hair as black as night and socks that look like sheep. She won't even look at me because she'd rather sleep, which is really weird because usually little kids stare at me. Marisol stuck Valentina in one of those automatic rockers, and to sleep that kid went, like I wasn't even there. I'm giving her a grace period since she's brand-new, but sooner or later, she's going to have to learn who's boss around here.

So anyway, Marisol and I were poring over maps, and she was coding alternate routes in different colors when Emma showed up. Emma did this double-hop thing when she saw Marisol, like she wasn't expecting her at all, and she said, "Oh hey, hi, Marisol," and Marisol said, *"Um,"* and kept looking at the maps.

I explained to Emma that Marisol was helping me get ready for the game, because I didn't want her to think she was fired or anything, and Emma said oh, and then she wondered if I'd had my gruel, and Marisol said yes in that Latina way that essentially means, don't even think of stepping on *my* toes, *chica*, and Emma just walked into the kitchen. Sometimes she forgets to make a graceful exit. She forgets to say things like "Thanks!" Or, "Excuse me, hope you two have fun." She just walks off. I don't take it personally, because I figure she doesn't know what to say and just goes on. Anyway, she walked into the kitchen and I could hear her banging things around, being loud, and Marisol picked up the yellow highlighter and looked at me and said, "You're very stupid, Leo."

I said, "Stop flirting with me, Marisol. I'm busy right now."

And she said, "That skinny blonde is in love with you."

Well, tell me something I don't know already. People, what do you think I do all day with this ginormous brain? I think, I observe, and I am always one step ahead of you. I said, "Look, it's obvious she's totally into me, but she's not in *love* with me. She's in love with, like . . . sanctuary." I couldn't think of a better word because I'll be honest, my genius brain was one hundred percent focused on football. Marisol looked like she thought I was trying to speak Spanish or something and she said that didn't make any sense, but the thing is, it makes all the sense in the world. Emma is in love with the idea that there is a guy out there who doesn't want her for her body. I mean, I think she wants a guy to be completely into her kick-ass body, but she doesn't want that to be the first and only thing, you know? But then, she's kind of strange, and I think she's afraid if anyone ever looked past her perfect body, they wouldn't like what they saw.

Me, I'm *totally* into her body. That's what *I* want, but I can't do anything about it, so, *voila*, she's safe with me.

Emma knows that, too. That's why she's hiding out with me. I don't know exactly what she's hiding *from*, but hello, it's obvious to everyone she's hiding. People like Luke think she's hiding from something or someone. "Maybe she's on the lam," he said with a chuckle, but I could tell he'd actually wondered if that was true.

I'm a lot more astute than any other Kendrick in this house, and I *know* she's hiding from herself.

So, late one day Luke comes in with Cooper, his new best friend, and they're all excited because it's supposed to snow late in the week, and Luke's suggesting that they take a day or two and go skiing. This guy has been here a couple of days now, which I thought was all he'd planned, but now it looks like he's sticking around for a few more. Of *course* he's still here, because it's the holiday season and the ranch is running itself right now, and Luke has time on his hands and this guy likes to do the stuff that Luke likes to do, and Luke is *full* of ideas. Plus, Luke can be very convincing. Trust me, back in the day, he talked me into doing things that would have made my mom kill herself if she'd known.

I can tell Cooper digs it here, too. He doesn't want to admit it because that would be, like, super uncool to be from Hollywood and really dig Pine River. Anyway, we were sitting around and he and Luke were drinking beer, and Dad was shoving shit into a blender for me, and I asked Cooper how he knows Emma.

"Only casually. We worked a couple of events together." But when he said it, he looked like he'd just eaten something lumpy and couldn't swallow it.

I said, "Don't you like her?" Because even though Emma's a little odd, she's beautiful, she's funny in a nonobvious way, she tells it like it is, and she likes dogs. What's not to like?

Cooper looked like I'd caught him with his pants down, and believe me, he's not the kind of guy to get caught like that. He said, "I like her fine. I mean, I don't know her that well, but I haven't had any issues with her."

I thought that was a weird thing to say, no issues, and so did Luke, because he laughed. "Issues. Like what?"

Cooper shrugged and took a giant swig from his beer and said, "I'll be honest, guys—she's got a rep around Hollywood."

Well now, *that* remark totally made me feel the need to stick up for my woman, and I said, "Sure she does. She's different. But different isn't bad, you know? Like that kid playing basketball in New Jersey. You know who I'm talking about, right? The high school senior? He's like this huge basketball star, no one can block him, and he's got autism."

Cooper looked really startled, and so did Luke, who said, all confused, "What are you saying? Emma has autism?"

I am often amazed at how obtuse people around me can be. I was like, "*No*, dude, she doesn't have autism." Sometimes you really have to spell these things out. "I'm just saying she's different. She's not like the other girls, but she's still awesome. Like that kid in New Jersey."

Cooper said, "Right," but he said it in a tone that told me he didn't get it at all. So I said, "I bet you didn't know that she gave a big wad of cash to the Pine River afterschool program."

Luke was frowning like he thought I was making it up, and he was all, "How do *you* know, genius?" How can he still doubt my powers of observation? I said, "Because Debbie Trimble is on the board and she told me. She was as surprised as you, Luke, and I guess it's because you guys look at Emma and you don't think charitable works, right? They didn't even ask Emma for it. She heard Deb talking about it, and the next time Debbie was over, she handed her a check."

Cooper stared at me.

"She's like, super generous, and they're all excited about the improvements they're going to make in the spring." *Boo-yah.* Once again, I am king of information in Pine River.

Even Luke was impressed, because he said, "My God, what do you *not* know about Pine River?"

Well, nothing, but that is way beside the point here.

"So how come you never mentioned this before?" Luke demanded, all mad because once again, I knew something he didn't. I told him it was because it seemed kind of personal for Emma. Sort of like the Wilson kids, which, of course, Luke knows about because Jackson's told everyone. I mean, I know what it's like to want something so bad when you can only look at it. Like when you can't go out in the world and get what you want because your arms and legs don't work, or maybe because your heart is too broken. I explained all this to Luke, but it was Cooper I was watching. He was really quiet, just listening, watching me really closely like he wasn't quite sure I was all there.

I decided that night that I really like Cooper. I think he could get it, like, *really* get it. He just seems sharp, you know? Sometimes a person walks into your house and you get a sense about them, that they are really hearing what you're saying, and understanding it. Most people walk into this house and they are trying to think of something to say really fast so they don't have to address the elephant in the room—which would be me—or they are thinking about themselves. You can just tell.

But Cooper doesn't seem like that. He's cool.

And Luke *really* likes him. It's man love or whatever you call it when two dudes find someone just like them out in the world. Luke's been talking about Cooper and the stuff they've been doing, checking out all the places they could stage some sports in the summer like they're two little kids building a fort.

I remember when that used to be Luke talking about me and what we'd done together. We'd go way up in those mountains, and we'd build forts and hunt elk and ski and climb rocks—you name it. Mom used to get really mad at us and tell us she was going to sell us to a merchant ship if we didn't come home when we were supposed to, but Luke and I weren't really scared of her. We were *really* scared of bears.

Anyway, Luke and Cooper's excellent adventure makes me kind of sad. Not sad that I can't go—I got over that a while back. I'm sad that Luke has to replace me. Your brother is supposed to be there in the beginning and all the way to the end. Your brother is supposed to be exploring canyons with you in the winter. What really sucks is that I'm the lucky one in this deal, and Luke got robbed.

You know what I hate? I hate that I'm letting him down. I hate it worse than almost anything. Except maybe the Patriots. Anyway, I'm glad Luke has found Cooper who, let's be honest, is pretty good-looking and super smart. In other words, if you can't have me, he's a pretty good runner-up.

I just hope Luke doesn't forget how totally awesome I was.

Who am I kidding? That would be *impossible.*

TWELVE

Cooper had liked Luke Kendrick the moment he'd met him. He had an easy way about him, seemed very much at home running interference between his brother and his dad, and took ribbing in stride.

Their friendship had begun the night Cooper had dinner with the Kendricks. As Cooper had begun to describe the sort of sports they would like to stage here, Luke's eyes had lit with the possibilities. He'd been showing Cooper around for a couple of days, and it had been a blast.

Last night, the two of them had a beer at the Rocky Creek Tavern. "I know exactly where to take you," Cooper had said, pointing a beer bottle at Cooper. "I can't believe I haven't thought of it before. Trace Canyon. No one's ever back up in there except the Forest Service. There are some great gullies, some great rock faces. I'll take you up tomorrow if you have time."

Of course Cooper had time. He let the calls from Carl roll to voice mail; he didn't want his fun to be ruined with Carl's paranoia.

Like Jackson, Luke seemed to think the warnings about the canyon were more informational than instructional, and took Cooper all over Trace Canyon. They drove up logging roads and scoped out some great ravines for cliff jumping and temporary zip lines. The waterfall Luke had in mind was frozen, but in summer, he explained how it was the perfect place to rappel down to the pool below, then catch some white water another five hundred feet down.

Luke drove Cooper up the sunny side of Mount Cielo as far as he could, then pointed out where the rock face looked as if it had been sheared off by a giant knife. It was unthinkable to be this high up at this time of year without two skis strapped to one's feet, but the ongoing drought made it a perfect day for two men to play.

Luke apparently had the same thought. "Want to scale it?" he asked with a slightly maniacal grin—the sort of grin Cooper used to see on his partners. "I've got some gear in the back."

"Can we get up there?" Cooper asked, peering at the trail.

"It's worth a try," Luke said. "But we better do it while we can. Dad says a front's coming through tonight. This will be covered by snow tomorrow."

"Let's do it," Cooper said without hesitation.

It was a hard go, especially when they had to crawl over an ice pack, but they made it to the rock face. Cooper went up twenty feet just to test the theory that it would work for some soft studio execs. They both agreed it was doable.

Everything Cooper saw in Trace Canyon was perfect for what TA had in mind. Everything he saw was perfect for *him*. This setting— outdoors, mountains, small mountain villages—was where Cooper felt most at home. He was most comfortable with himself in the wild, when he had nothing but his own strength and stamina to rely on. It was a contest to him—how far, how high, how hard could he go? He had not yet found his limit.

The wind was turning and coming out of the north when they headed down from Trace Canyon. When they reached the point where cell service kicked in, Cooper noticed he had a missed call from his partner Eli.

Eli was a year older than him, a year or two older than Jack and Michael, and since they'd been boys, Eli had always acted like the elder statesman of their group, the voice of reason among the unruly. *Sure it's a good idea to blow up a beehive? Really think you ought to aim that gun at Jack?* To this day, Cooper valued his opinion. He called him.

"What's up?" he asked when Eli answered his phone.

"Carl Freeman called today and he was mad enough to kick his own dog," Eli drawled.

"That's mad," Cooper agreed.

"Says he can't get hold of you. What's going on?"

"I've been doing a little sightseeing," Cooper said vaguely. "Emma has it. She just doesn't want to admit it yet, which I explained to Carl. He needs to be patient. She's going to give in if for no other reason than to get me off her back."

"On her back, huh?" Eli said. "So the rumors about her are true."

"Funny," Cooper said, but Eli's joke settled wrong in him. He thought about the way she'd looked that night on Elm Street, her eyes shimmering, her smile a little pert. She was everything a guy could want—or at least everything *he* could want—and her reputation didn't feel right to him. There was a lot more to the story; he could feel it. But he didn't say that to Eli.

"Carl's a studio head," Eli said, and yawned. "Patience isn't his thing. What do you want me to tell him?"

"Tell him that I'll have it by the end of the week."

"I hope so," Eli said. "He's going to come at us with both barrels if you don't. I'll call him and talk him off his tiny little divorce ledge. So did you find any good spots for us?"

"Some *great* spots," Cooper said, and filled Eli in on Trace Canyon.

When he hung up, Luke was looking at him with an inquisitive expression. "I realize I've known you for only a couple of days," he said, "but I have to ask—what's going on with Emma? Anything we ought to be worried about?"

"No," Cooper said. "It's a misunderstanding." He explained to Luke that a mutual friend thought Emma had something that belonged to him and left it at that. He'd already said enough about Emma in front of Leo and had managed to get his back up. And besides, something Leo had said about Emma had intrigued Cooper, had made him think that maybe he didn't really know her like he'd thought. It was the mention of her donation to the afterschool program. That, on the heels of hearing about her interest in the kids at the park, and the job she'd taken with Leo was all so . . . unexpected. Unbelievable, really, given her reputation across LA. These new pieces of information about her didn't sound like a woman who didn't care about anyone but herself. They made Emma sound like she *did* care and maybe, that she longed for something.

"Madeline thinks she purposely tries to antagonize," Luke mentioned. "I'm not so sure about that. Sometimes, she pops off and says something off the wall, then looks surprised that she's offended anyone." He laughed, as if he found that amusing. "I may be wrong, but I just have a gut feeling about her. And God knows Leo can't say enough about her," Luke said, and grinned. "But then again, Leo thinks she's totally into him."

Cooper smiled. "Maybe she is."

"Whatever, I have to give the woman props when it comes to my brother," he added with a shake of his head. "We don't pay her a dime to come around and sit with Leo, you know? But she comes every day, and it's a great help to my dad. Not that he'll admit it," he said with a lopsided smile, "because Dad likes to think he's the only one who can take care of Leo. But she really has been a big help. She takes Leo outside and watches movies with him and reads to him. She makes sure everything is clean because Leo's immunity is not great. She does a lot for him."

Cooper silently considered that. It was all so curious, as if two different women were inhabiting that beautiful body.

"So when are you heading back to LA?" Luke asked.

"Soon," Cooper said. "But not for a few days yet." He still hadn't settled on how, exactly, to get the medal out of Emma. Maybe because he'd been enjoying the great outdoors too much to worry about Carl's problem for a bit.

"Great! If we get the kind of snow my dad says we're supposed to get, the best skiing will be up at Wolf Creek. We're close enough we could drive up early one morning and get a few runs in if you have time."

Cooper grinned. "I think that could definitely be arranged." It used to be this way with the guys of TA. Impromptu, spur-of-the-moment extreme weekends. It had been routine for so long. But now, Cooper couldn't remember the last time they'd decided at five o'clock on a Friday they were going to drive up the coast and do some windsurfing. He missed that more than he'd realized.

Yes, Cooper liked Luke a lot.

They chatted about some of the crazier sports they'd been involved in on the drive back to Pine River. Thick clouds were beginning to roll in, blanketing the valley in a dull gray light. As they neared the turnoff to Homecoming Ranch, Luke said, "Why don't you come up and join us for dinner? Libby and Sam will be there with Madeline and Emma. Maddie is making lasagna. She isn't much of a cook, but she makes a mean lasagna."

"I'm empty-handed," Cooper said, lifting his palms faceup. "And I'm dirty. I've been scaling rock faces."

"We've got showers," Luke said. "A surprising number of them, actually. I've got a clean shirt you can borrow. As for the empty hands, I picked up some beer today. It's in the back of the truck."

"I've imposed on you enough, Luke."

"This has been no imposition, are you kidding?" Luke scoffed. "I haven't been up in the mountains in a while. Come on, it will be a good time," Luke said. "And did I mention? Emma will be there, too. Maybe you can get back the thing she has." He grinned.

Cooper laughed. "I guess I'm in," he said, and frankly, he was grateful for the invitation. Anything was better than going back to the Beaver Room.

⤙⬦⬦⭘⬦⬦⤚

When Luke pulled into the drive in front of the house, Madeline bounded out onto the porch, but halted on the top step. Cooper opened the passenger door, and her face lit with delight. *"Hey!"* she said, hopping down the steps. "What a nice surprise!"

"Hello, Madeline," Cooper said.

"I invited him for dinner," Luke said, coming around the back of his truck. He planted a kiss on the top of her head. "Hope you don't mind."

"Of course I don't mind," she said, poking Luke in the ribs. "It's lasagna. That's all we ever eat around here. Come in, Cooper! Libby and Sam are in the kitchen."

Cooper cleaned off his boots as best he could, then walked in to meet Libby and her boyfriend, Sam Winters. Sam was a deputy sheriff, he said, and looked a little like Luke—big, muscular, and trim. He had the shadow of a beard and dark golden-brown hair that was longer than was stylish. He was quiet, and he didn't say much, but Cooper could see how much he adored Libby.

Libby practically leapt into Cooper's arms. "I can't believe it!" she said breathlessly, hugging him as if they were cousins instead of slight acquaintances. "Cooper, right? Is it okay if we call you Cooper?"

"Let him breathe, baby," Sam said low.

Libby laughed and pushed her dark corkscrew curls out of her eyes. "I hope you like lasagna. That's all Madeline ever makes."

"It's not the only thing!" Madeline protested from the kitchen.

"Cooper is going to shower in the guest bath," Luke said. "I'm going to grab a shirt for him to borrow."

Cooper and Sam chatted about all the places Luke had taken Cooper today as they waited for Luke to return with a clean shirt. Once Sam understood what Cooper was doing in town, he was very interested, too. "I don't know how you feel about fly-fishing, but I can show you some of the best waters in Colorado for it."

"Oh, please, say you'll go with him, Cooper," Libby begged. "Then I don't have to."

"You don't like to fish?"

"I have no idea if I like it or not. But I am very sure I don't like hooks in my face."

Cooper looked at Sam; Sam grinned fondly at Libby. "She's heard one too many tales from Tag down at Tag's Outfitters," he said.

Luke returned with a clean T-shirt and showed him to a shower. When Cooper had cleaned up, and had combed his fingers through his hair to tame it as best he could, he made his way back to the front of the house. He stepped outside and jogged down the steps to Luke's truck to toss his dirty shirt inside, and noticed that the temperature had taken quite a dip since they'd come up to the ranch.

Cooper returned to the house, pausing at the front door to clean the bottom of his boots again on the welcome mat. He heard someone on the stairs and looked up; a moment later, a pair of very shapely legs in skintight jeans came into view.

And then the rest of the body appeared, along with that cascade of blond hair and the sultry green eyes. The sight of him caused Emma to falter a bit; she paused on the bottom step, her gaze raking him up and down. "Well, well, look who's back for more."

He smiled. "You're awfully sure of yourself." She ought to be sure of herself, because she looked fantastic, her hair in one long tail, and her sweater hugging her almost as tight as her jeans. The memory of that completely calculated, but thoroughly pleasurable, kiss skated across Cooper's mind for what could possibly be the thousandth time. "You shouldn't be surprised to see me—I told you I'd see you around, remember?"

"Oh, I remember," she said, and leaned up against the banister, folding her arms across herself. "But most people call before they show up at someone's house. I'd love to humor your little detective work today, but unfortunately, I can't talk to you now because we're having dinner. It's *family* night. It's Libby's thing, and she gets very cranky when we don't all show up."

"Sounds like a great idea," Cooper said. He shifted his weight to one hip.

Emma frowned. *"Sooo . . ."* she said, drawing out the word, "you should make it quick. Go ahead, ask me if I have the thing Carl lost so I can say no, and then you can run back to town, and I will obey my summons to family night."

"I won't keep you," Cooper said, moving deeper into the hall. "In fact, we can discuss the medal you won't admit you have after dinner so you won't be late to family night."

She laughed. "And what, you'll just wait on the stoop? It's freezing outside, in case you haven't noticed."

His smile deepened. "I guess Luke didn't get the family-night memo. He invited me to have dinner."

Emma's brows sank into a frown. "Luke invited you to *family night?*" she repeated. "Did he clear it with Libby? Because she has some very specific rules about what is and is not allowed on family night."

"I guess," Cooper said with a shrug. "He didn't mention it when he invited me."

Emma's brows dipped. "That is so . . . *unfair*. I didn't know we could invite other people! Libby was very specific—*don't make any plans tonight, Emma, it's family night, Emma, don't let me down, Emma*," she said, mimicking her sister. "Whatever." She sighed, glanced at what looked like the entrance to the family room and pursed her lips.

That kiss slipped into Cooper's thoughts again and wended around, taking root. He didn't want to think about it. He damn sure didn't want to be another notch in her belt—which was exactly the way he'd felt when she'd kissed him under the stars. He liked to think he had some standards.

"Well," Emma said, and cast a look over him as she stepped off the stairs. Now she was standing in front of him, close enough that he could touch her. Cooper shoved his hands in his pockets to keep himself from it.

She looked up at him with a wry smile. "Don't think because you kissed me once that you can just waltz in here and make yourself at home."

He laughed, fighting the urge to touch her. "I think you really are delusional. Once again, I must point out that you have the facts wrong. You kissed *me*, Emma."

"Keep telling yourself that, big guy," she said, and walked to the door of the family room. She paused at the threshold and glanced over her shoulder at him. "Well? Come on, if you're coming. Trust me, you do *not* want to be late to family night." With that, she disappeared into the room.

Cooper didn't follow her immediately. He stood there, his head down for a moment, focusing on one slow breath at a time.

He didn't know what was in his head about Emma Tyler, exactly, other than the fact that it was very different than what had been in his head when he'd shown up in Pine River a few days ago. But he could tell from the way his body was reacting to hers, the way he was tolerating her indifference, that internally, he'd begun to play a little Russian roulette with the big ball of fire that was Emma. The woman who could disgust and mystify just by breathing, who could make a man feel his knees with a look.

And he was the guy who usually saw right through women like her, who avoided her kind of drama in his life. Yet here he was, struggling to keep his hands to himself. Wanting to dine with a family he scarcely knew because she would be there, too.

This could not be good.

This was slightly alarming.

THIRTEEN

Emma gave Madeline an accusatory look when she entered the living room. In return, Madeline beamed at her and said gleefully, "Don't look at me!" She moved past Emma to the dining room with a stack of plates. "Luke invited him, and I had nothing to do with it."

Emma didn't believe that for a moment. There was no point in talking to Luke, or any of them, for that matter. She'd never seen a group of people so eager to include a total stranger in their number. It was as if they'd been stuck up here on the mountain, waiting for someone to make it to the top and give them the news about the rest of the world.

Emma carried on to the kitchen, and went directly to the open bottle of wine, ignoring Luke, Libby, and Sam, who were all seated at the kitchen bar.

"Hello, Emma." It was Sam who'd spoken. For some reason, the things Emma said never ruffled him. And because they didn't, she had a special fondness for him. Sam was a recovering alcoholic, and oddly enough, sometimes Emma felt as if she and Sam were more alike than anyone else. They both sucked at letting go of things from their pasts, apparently. Emma smiled at Sam over her shoulder. "Hi, Sam."

Sam looked pointedly at her, then nodded at Libby.

"Okay, all right. Hello, Libby. Hello, Luke," she said with a bit of irritation, and turned back to her wine.

Someone grabbed her from behind, startling Emma so badly that she shrieked. It was Luke, who wrapped her in his ironclad band of arms and squeezed tight. "Hel*lo*, Emma," he said, and let her go, but not before tousling the top of her head.

"Hey!" Emma protested irritably, and tried to smooth the hair that had come loose from her ponytail.

"Oh hey, dude, there you are," Luke said.

That, Emma supposed, was Luke blaring the trumpets to announce that Cooper had come into the kitchen. But even if Luke hadn't said it, Emma would have known. She could *feel* him, his presence big and bold, pressing against her. She turned around, and of course, Cooper's eyes were on her. Firmly affixed to her, as a matter of fact. Boring holes right through her.

"Can I get you a beer?" Luke asked.

"Thanks," Cooper said.

Emma poured more wine into her glass. She took a fortifying sip, then turned around to face the group.

"Oh look, it's starting to snow," Libby said, peering at the kitchen window in front of which Emma happened to be standing. All heads came up and riveted on her.

As if Emma could possibly feel any more awkward. She put down her wine and walked out of the kitchen as Sam filled them in on the possibility of accumulation.

The dining room, with its wall of double-paned windows, had been added on to the original house and required two steps down to enter. Madeline was setting the table. She'd already fired up the potbellied stove for warmth, a requisite in the room at this time of year.

"I'll do that," Emma offered, taking the tray of silver from Madeline.

"Thanks," Madeline said. She watched Emma methodically lay out the silver for a moment, then pretended to straighten a left-over Thanksgiving centerpiece before leaning to one side to glance into the kitchen. She then scurried over to Emma like the rat she was. "So, he seems like a really nice guy," she said low. "Luke likes him a lot."

Emma paused what she was doing and glared at her sister. "What the hell, Madeline?"

"What?" Madeline asked innocently. "I'm just saying."

"You're just saying, my ass. Whatever happened to strong, independent women who don't need men? Whatever happened to letting things happen organically rather than trying to steer them?"

"Whatever happened to being less defensive?" Madeline countered. "Why can't you just be friendly and leave it at that? *You're* the one that keeps making a big deal out of him. Why is that, Emma? I mean, since you came to Homecoming Ranch, you've been . . ." She paused, pressed her lips together, as if she caught herself from saying something she didn't want to say.

Emma's head came up. "I've been what?"

"I don't know. Rudderless? Adrift? *Cranky?* And then this guy shows up, this big, seriously good-looking guy, and you act like he's poison. Of course we're wondering what's going on. If it's not a big deal, then why not be nice to him?"

"And while I'm busy being nice, I guess it doesn't bother anyone that he is badgering me for something I don't have?"

"Just tell him you don't have it," Madeline said. "You don't have to be such a . . ." Her voice trailed away and she averted her gaze.

"A bitch," Emma finished for her. She couldn't help but laugh a little at Madeline's guilty look. "Don't worry, it's not the first time I've been called that." She smiled wryly at the absurdity of everything—who would ever understand how difficult it was for her to be the sort of woman who always said the right thing? The kind of woman who instantly knew how to put everyone at ease? Emma had never grasped the softer side of her personality—if it even existed—even on those few occasions she'd really tried.

She was suddenly reminded of herself at fifteen, trying so hard to fit in when Laura had friends over for a sleepover. Laura had always included Emma, even when it was clear her friends didn't want Emma to be included. On one of those nights, they'd played a silly game, a loves-me, loves-me-not sort of game. When it was Brenda Kingsley's turn, she wanted reassurance from the others that she was cute enough, popular enough, for Jose Pachecho. To Emma, it had been a ridiculous question. In the rigid and cruel class system of high school society, of which they'd all been citizens, there was no moment when Brenda would be cute or cool enough for Jose Pachecho. Emma could see by the expressions on the other girls they were all thinking the same thing. *No*, she'd said to Brenda. *You will never be good enough for Jose.*

She hadn't said it flatly, or without some regard for Brenda's feelings. Honestly, Emma thought she'd said it as kindly as it could be said. Not so, Laura told her later. *You don't tell someone like Brenda that she's not good enough!* The girls hated her for being so mean, Laura said. Emma had tried to argue that they were all thinking the same thing, and maybe Brenda needed to hear the truth.

Laura had looked at her as if she were crazy. Of *course* they were thinking the same thing, Laura had said. But they would never *say* it.

"I don't know if I can pretend not to be a bitch," Emma said now, shaking off that ancient memory. "I'll try, but I think that horse has left the barn."

"I'm sorry," Madeline said, looking stung. "I shouldn't have said that."

"Don't worry about it. I don't care."

What Emma had meant to convey was that she wasn't easily wounded, but of course, Madeline didn't take it that way. "You *never* care. You're so damn hard to deal with sometimes, you know that?" she said, the injured party now, and walked out of the dining room.

"Yes," Emma muttered. "I know." A curl of shame wrapped around her heart, and she stared down at the box of silverware without really seeing it. How did anyone become something different than what they were at their core? It was hard as hell to live in this skin. *Nothing but brass tacks coming out of that mouth.*

The sound of laughter from the kitchen reminded Emma of her task; she finished setting the table.

When Madeline announced dinner was served, they all trooped into the dining room and took their seats. Somehow, whether by conspiracy or sheer dumb luck, Emma was seated directly across from Cooper. There would be no avoiding his intent gaze now. There would definitely be no forgetting that kiss now. Or the way he'd put her back on her heels. With him sitting across from her, his chin and cheeks shadowed by a beard, his hair finger-combed, there was no possible way Emma could avoid the lust and distrust and insecurity and interest that was beginning to leak into her belly in a confusingly sweet-and-sour mix.

As the salad was passed around, Luke regaled them with all the places he'd taken Cooper today. Which, to Emma, sounded like a big canyon where they'd climbed some rocks. That was the last thing she would do on a day like this.

"You should try it," Cooper said, and Emma realized he was talking to her.

She glanced around them to be doubly sure. "Try what? Trespassing into closed national forests?"

"Luke!" Libby said, glancing nervously at Sam. "You didn't take him up there to do that, did you? Those roads are closed."

"Yeah," Luke said with a wave of his hand, his eyes twinkling with amusement. "Maybe we crossed a boundary or two. You have to break a rule every now and then."

"Please don't suggest that to her," Sam said, pointing to Libby, and settled back, draping his arm across the back of Libby's chair. "We finally convinced her *not* to break rules, remember?"

"Point taken," Luke said to Sam, and smiled fondly at Libby.

Sam was referring to Libby's infamous meltdown last summer. Libby had lost it over a bad breakup and then would not obey a restraining order to stay away from her ex-douchebag's children, to whom she'd become very close. Which, in that way these things had of working themselves out, was how she'd come to be with Sam. As a deputy sheriff, Sam had enforced the restraining order.

"I meant canyoneering," Cooper said to Emma. "Climbing rocks. Sliding down waterfalls. It's fun."

"I'll pass," Emma said.

"You don't like the outdoors?"

"I like the outdoors just fine. But I don't like climbing rocks."

"Me either!" Madeline said. "Luke is forever trying to get me to do that with him. I'd rather eat nails."

"That's my girl," Luke said with a laugh.

"So what'd you think of the canyon, Cooper?" Sam asked.

"I thought it was fantastic. It's perfect for the kind of work we do. We want to stage one of our extreme outings here late next spring if we can get the approvals we need."

No, no, no . . . he was coming back? Emma couldn't get rid of him *now*, in the dead of winter! How long would he stay as spring turned into summer, when this place was beautiful and there were so many things to do? She knew the kind of guy Cooper was—he'd bounce from one sport to the next and never leave.

Wait . . . was *she* going to be here next year?

"You'll love it here in the spring and summer," Sam said, further ruining Emma's hope for peace. "There's a lot to do."

"That's what I'm hoping," Cooper said, and took a plate of lasagna Madeline handed him. "Thank you."

"There's really not much beyond climbing rocks, though," Emma pointed out, suddenly desperate that he not come back, desperate that she have this place to herself if she needed it. "And Pine River is far from any real city. The closest one is Montrose. There's only one decent restaurant in town, and it's not really even decent by LA standards. And there's one tiny grocery and Wal-Mart. No Trader Joe's here. No women to speak of. You'd be happier closer to Denver."

"Don't extend the welcome mat too far, Emma," Luke said wryly. "Sure wouldn't want Cooper to trip on it."

Cooper laughed. "I do appreciate your concern for me, Emma. But you don't need restaurants or groceries or even women to zip over forest." Luke and Sam laughed at that.

Emma shrugged. "I'm just saying," she said, and picked up her fork, stabbing at the lasagna.

"I think it's a great idea," Madeline said, sounding like a matriarch. "Are you originally from LA, Cooper?"

"No. Texas," Cooper said. "My partners and I grew up there."

"Texas," Libby said dreamily. "I always wanted to go there. It sounds so mythical. Cowboys and horses and big orange sunsets."

"Maybe it used to be mythical. Now it's like any state, just bigger and hotter."

"Your family is there?" Madeline asked.

"What's left of them," Cooper said, and looked down at his plate. "My dad died a few years ago. My mother is still there."

"No siblings?" Madeline asked.

Emma noticed the slight hesitation in Cooper's devouring of the lasagna. "I have a brother," he said.

"I feel your pain," Libby said. "I have two. Twins, even."

Cooper smiled.

"You never know what you're going to get when it comes to siblings. Isn't that right, girls?" Libby said, and laughed.

Madeline frowned. "Would you like to rephrase that?"

"Why should she? It's true," Emma said, and sipped her wine.

"That didn't come out right," Libby quickly clarified. "I mean that I consider myself to be very lucky." She smiled, clearly pleased with herself. But Libby couldn't possibly think she was lucky to have landed Emma as a sister. The idea struck Emma as so amusing, she couldn't help a laugh.

"Don't laugh at her," Madeline chided Emma, and smiled at the men. "I think what Emma finds amusing is that our father didn't clue us in as to each other's existence when he was alive. So to discover we *had* siblings was a very big surprise for us. I guess you never know what you're going to get in a father, either."

"I'm sorry," Libby said. "I made a very lame joke. The truth is that the three of us have a really complicated story." She smiled at Cooper. "But if you'd known my dad, you would never have guessed he wasn't Father of the Year. He was very personable."

That was Libby for you, always trying to make Grant into some sort of misguided saint, and it made Emma furious. "He was a *dick*, Libby," she blurted.

"Emma!" Libby cried.

"Well, he was. I don't think it's fair to me or Madeline to portray him as a good guy."

Libby colored slightly. "Look, I know he had his issues, but we all do. He wasn't malicious—"

"Are you kidding?" Emma said, suddenly sitting up, suddenly angrier than she'd been in a very long time, suddenly *raging* inside. "Do you really believe that? Let me tell you just how malicious he was, Libby. He *slept* with *Laura*!"

Had she really just shouted that? Judging by the number of mouths hanging open, she had. Emma sank back into her chair, curling her hands into tight fists as she sought her footing. She never let her emotions get the best of her. She kept it all at arm's length. She should never have said it, but Libby . . . *Libby!* Emma just couldn't listen to Libby defend him one more time.

"That's not funny, Emma," Libby said, her voice shaking.

"Wait, wait—who is Laura?" Madeline demanded, frowning at Emma as if she suspected her of intentionally causing trouble.

"My stepsister," Emma muttered.

"Oh, that's *right*," Madeline said, her voice full of surprise, her eyes widening with shock as she slowly sank back in her chair. "Seriously, Emma, is that your idea of a joke? Because she's, like, *your* age, isn't she?"

"Seven months older than me," Emma bit out.

"I don't believe you!" Libby said angrily, ignoring Sam's hand on her arm. "I know you didn't like Dad, but what you said is not true, Emma! Why the hell would you say something like that?"

"It *is* true, Libby," Emma said wearily.

"Oh really?" Libby demanded. "So when exactly did this happen? When he was dying of *cancer*?"

Emma rolled her eyes. "No. Obviously *that* wouldn't have happened. It was a long time ago, when I was seventeen. He'd invited Laura and me to Vegas. She'd just turned eighteen, old enough not to get him arrested, and . . ." She shrugged. It was impossible to even say it. It was still so goddamn difficult to wrap her mind around.

"And what?" Libby asked, her voice full of hurt now.

Why did Libby always carry so much hope that people would act right? Hadn't she seen enough in her life to know they rarely did? "They had an affair, Libby. It went on all summer long until I discovered it. Laura and Dad had a sexual affair for an entire summer."

"Good God," Sam muttered. Libby was staring at Emma in shock.

"I'm sorry," Emma said. "But I can't let you convince everyone at this table that Grant was a good guy in spite of the way he treated us. He wasn't a good guy—he was a total *dick.*"

"Oh my God," Madeline said. "He *was* a dick!"

Emma pointed at Madeline and said to Libby, "See?" realizing, for perhaps the first time, that if there was anyone who would share her outrage about Grant and Laura, it would be Madeline and Libby. Why hadn't she considered it before this moment?

"You know what I see? I see someone who is hell-bent on ruining everything about this family," Libby said angrily.

Emma hadn't intended to ruin the evening. She hadn't intended . . .

Oh hell, who knew what she intended anymore? That's what she always told herself, she didn't intend to do anything, and yet, she somehow managed to do it. Emma stood up and gathered some plates. "I'm not going to apologize for telling you the truth, Libby. But a word of advice—don't let it get to you. Don't let it screw you up. God knows I let it get to me, and look at me now. But the man is gone, and he's not going to come back and right his wrongs."

Libby shook her head and stared down at her plate.

Emma looked away from her wounded sister—and right into the eyes of Cooper.

He didn't seem shocked by her admission. He looked almost as if he'd expected it.

"Okay, well, enough of Grant," Libby said, waving her hands, erasing him from family night as Emma picked up more dishes and headed for the kitchen. "So! The big game is next week, huh, Luke?" she asked, desperately trying to turn the conversation to something else.

Emma walked into the kitchen and stacked the dishes in the sink. She heard someone come in behind her and assumed it was Madeline. She steeled herself for the lecture she was sure she'd get. But when she turned, it wasn't Madeline who'd followed her, it was Cooper, carrying a lasagna pan and the bowl of salad.

"I insisted on helping," he said. "Does that make it lucky you or lucky me?"

"*Shit*. You again," Emma groaned, and turned on the faucet.

Cooper walked up behind her and deliberately reached around her, his body against her back, to put the lasagna pan on the counter. Emma closed her eyes for a moment and let the feeling of him sink into her pores.

"I'm sorry," he said, his voice soft.

She opened her eyes, surprised by that. "No you're not. You deliberately put the pan there."

"I mean, I'm sorry about your father. That must have been very hard for you."

Bittersweet emotion began to close Emma's throat. He was sympathizing with her? She shot him a skeptical look. "Let me guess—next you'll ask if it's true, right?"

"No. I feel pretty confident that no one would make that up."

That much was definitely true.

"You must have been so disappointed in them both. I would have been. I understand how it must have made you feel."

Emma snorted. "How could you?"

"You know the brother I mentioned? He's in prison for armed robbery."

Emma stilled for a moment. She looked at him, waiting for a *but,* or a joke.

"Are you going to ask me if that's true?" he asked.

Emma blinked. "No . . . I feel pretty confident that no one would make that up," she murmured.

Cooper gave her a thin smile, as if they'd shared terrible secrets before.

"How . . . how long has he been there?"

"Fifteen years," Cooper said on a weary sigh. "He's due to be released in a matter of days. So yeah, I know all about how family can disappoint."

"I'm sorry," Emma whispered, and she meant it. She was truly, deeply sorry for him. She wouldn't want anyone to experience the hurt she'd felt in the last ten years.

Cooper carefully laid his hand over the one Emma had braced against the sink. "Thanks. That's nice to hear."

Emma felt something tender curl around them. She held his gaze, wondering if she should say more, worried that if she spoke, it would be the wrong thing. And he waited, as if he expected her to say something. But eventually, his hand fell away and he picked up a box of plastic wrap on the counter to cover what was left of the salad.

Emma watched him, imagining how a felonious brother could change a family. How it would unfairly tip the balance of a family, much like a stepsister sleeping with a father had tipped hers. At least in Emma's mind, everything in her family would always be measured against that single summer: their shared history that had occurred before Laura slept with Grant, and their fractured history after Laura slept with Grant. In Cooper's case, she could imagine that demarcation was everything before his brother used a gun to rob, and after.

Emma knew how isolating it could be, how alone it felt to be one of the innocents in the family upheaval. She knew how the trauma hovered like a shadow in one's peripheral vision. Always there, just beyond the present moment.

She and Cooper were more alike than she ever would have imagined, Emma realized as she turned back to the sink. His admission of a family tragedy made him seem more real to Emma.

Flesh and bone and sinew. Brains and thoughts and feelings. A man with hard planes and soft eyes and desire simmering beneath every breath, with the experiences in life to back up his hungers.

All very dangerous territory for Emma.

"Hey! We need another bottle of wine!" Madeline shouted, her declaration followed by laughter. Apparently, they'd been able to move on from Grant.

"I'll get it," Emma said, and brushed past Cooper—intentionally—and walked to the laundry room, where they kept a small wine cooler. She was moving in a bit of a fog now, unsure of what she was doing. After years of longing for someone to see her side of things, to understand how *she* felt, to have someone say they did, made her feel unbalanced. A little seasick. If Cooper understood that about her, how long before he'd understand other, darker things about her?

No, no, she could never let him see that side of her. She had to get this growing infatuation under control.

Emma flipped on the light in the laundry room. She dipped down and studied the wine in the cooler, selected a bottle, and stood. She turned back to the door, intending to leave.

But Cooper blocked the way. He was leaning up against the jamb, his arms crossed over his chest. His cool gray gaze was fixed on her, almost as if he'd already begun to see the darker things about her. Emma's blood began to swirl. He was not looking at her with casual interest, but with heat.

What was he doing? Did he want to kiss her?

Of course he wanted more. He'd seen through her, seen her hurt, and wanted to exploit it, right? Isn't that what men like him did? *Try it,* she thought. Moments like these were where she excelled. The sexual interest of men was her base of operations from which she'd launched her assaults for the last several years. She walked to the door and tilted her head back, staring up into eyes that were now all gray shadows. "What are you doing?"

"Not sure," he admitted.

Emma shifted the bottle of wine to the crook of her elbow and with her free hand, traced a line down his chest. "What would you *like* to do?"

He caught her hand and pressed it against his chest—hard. "I'd like to ask you to stop treating me like some poor dumb asshole. What are you so damn afraid of?" he murmured.

The question jolted her awake. She tried to take her hand back, but he held it firmly. "Maybe you should go, Cooper. You know, pack up and get out of town. Don't you have something to do tomorrow? Some canyon to jump over?"

"I don't think I'll be going anywhere tonight," he said calmly, as his gaze moved down her face, to her mouth. He touched the corner of her lips with his finger. "Snow's coming down pretty good. So try and lighten up a little, will you?"

Her blood stirred more. *Kryptonite.* It was happening; her body was betraying her, responding to this gorgeous, overly confident, and damn it, too masculine *man.* "What's a little snow? Maybe you should go now, before it gets too deep."

A smile slowly curved his lips. "You're a funny girl, you know that?" He ran his thumb over her bottom lip. "Sometimes I think you want a friend, and in the next moment, I think you don't. Sometimes I think you want me to make love to you. But then you talk and ruin the moment. I'm not sure what to make of you."

"I'm wishy-washy," she agreed. "But why do you care? Do you want to be my friend? Or do you just want to fuck me?"

Cooper arched a brow with surprise. He caressed her cheek with his thumb. "Honestly? I don't know." He touched her lip with his thumb again, resting it there.

How startling that Emma hoped it was some of both. She had just skated right out of her rink, and it panicked her. She lightly bit his thumb, hard enough to startle him. When he withdrew his hand, she dipped beneath his arm, putting some space between them, getting away from that heat. She left him standing there and walked back into the dining room with the wine, hoping like hell she wasn't glowing.

No one looked at her—they were involved in a lively discussion about some work at the ranch Madeline wanted done.

A moment later, Cooper followed, his gaze still firmly fixed on Emma as he took his seat across from her. That man had a way of looking at her that made her feel as if he could see every one of her thoughts. And the more he looked, the more lascivious thoughts she seemed to have. There were several strong desires floating around in her head now, thanks to him and those eyes. *Damn it,* why did he have to come to Pine River? Why *him* of all the candidates that stupid jackass Carl could have sent? Emma tried not to squirm, but she could feel the schoolgirl flush in her face.

Cooper saw it, too, judging by the hint of the smile on his lips.

Emma tried to concentrate on the talk of Madeline and Luke's wedding, and then about the current drought's effect on the ski industry as they finished another bottle of wine. She was grateful when Libby mentioned a movie she had seen.

"I know the director of that film," Emma said, grateful to have something to talk about. "He's married to a woman with three kids. But he's gay."

"No way," Libby said, wide-eyed.

"Actually," Cooper said, "he's separated. He's planning on coming out this fall before his next film is released."

Emma looked curiously at Cooper. "You know Trevor?" she asked incredulously.

"Know him well," Cooper said. "How about you?"

"Same here," she said. "I've worked a few of his events." What was that feathery, slightly nauseating swirl Emma was feeling now? That she and Cooper knew more people in common than just Carl and Jill? Emma didn't have many friends, but those whom she considered to be among her closest circle were people who didn't judge her. If Cooper knew them, too—knew at least one well, as he'd just said—didn't that mean in some strange way he must know a little of her, too?

"I just think it's so cool that we have *two people* here who know a famous director," Libby said excitedly. "Emma knows Val Kilmer, too!"

"Met him," Emma clarified, ignoring Libby's look of confusion. In Libby's world, copulation equaled near commitment.

The mention of Val Kilmer prompted a discussion of that actor's films. Safe ground, especially for Emma, who spent much time in movie theaters hiding from the truth of her life.

It was Libby who returned from the powder room with the news that the snow was falling heavily. They all stood up to have a look, and in doing so, realized the amount of time that had passed since they'd sat down for dinner. It was twenty past eleven.

There began a final clearing of the table, everyone pitching in to carry things into the kitchen, Libby overseeing the dishwashing. Emma volunteered to clean the dining room, and by the time she'd finished and returned to the kitchen, she found it deserted, save Cooper. He was sitting on a stool at the bar, a coin or something in his fingers, which he mindlessly turned over, again and again.

"Where is everyone?" Emma asked.

"They went to bed," he said. "Except Luke. He's rounding up a quilt for the couch. Looks like I'll be bunking there."

Emma's heart began to race. She glanced at the coin. "So what, I'm supposed to entertain you?" she asked crossly.

"I don't need to be entertained." He turned the coin over again, and she recognized the St. Christopher medal he'd shown her that night in Beverly Hills. "Don't feel as if you need to keep me company—I'm used to making my own way. You know . . . like you."

A shiver ran down her spine. "How could you possibly know what I am?" she asked, without rancor, but from a genuine desire to know.

"I'm good at reading people. And I think I'm especially good at reading you."

She mentally stumbled. She'd been labeled aloof and distant; no one had ever claimed to *read* her. The idea made Emma laugh unsteadily. "I'm going to bed, detective." She dropped the dish towel onto the bar and walked past him.

Cooper didn't try and stop her. Emma faltered at the door, not wanting to leave it like this, not knowing how else to leave it. Cooper Jessup had knocked her off her game completely, and Emma couldn't help but look back at him.

He was watching her go, just as she knew he would be. But his expression was not what she expected. It wasn't predatory. It wasn't the least bit wistful. It was . . . kind. *Kind.* Emma was used to disdain, to confusion, to lust. Not kindness! She hadn't asked for that, and in fact, she'd sort of asked him for anything *but* kindness. She nervously pushed a loose strand of hair behind her ear. "Good night," she said.

"Good night, Emma."

She fled up the stairs before she did or said something stupid. She felt completely out of her league now, confronted by a man she didn't know how to handle. What the hell was *wrong* with him? Why was he playing this game with her? It felt as if it had gone far beyond Carl's medal.

It also felt as if something soft was growing in her.

For some reason, Emma thought of Grif, the one true relationship she'd had in the last eight years. Grif . . . *God, Grif.* Three years ago she'd met him, and she'd known he was bad news before he ever said hello to her. He was a beautiful man, handsome and rough, and he could charm a woman right out of her bra with merely a look, a touch. Emma had known Grif would be attracted to her. She'd known he would want her. He was the sort of conquest she enjoyed, a man who was so sure of himself that she took perverse joy in walking away.

But Emma hadn't counted on wanting Grif. Once she'd realized it, it was too late; she hadn't known what to do with herself. So she'd strung him along, teasing him, and enjoying every moment of their dating life. It went on for weeks, the give and take, always holding herself just beyond his full reach. She liked Grif. She thought he was funny and thoughtful, and vaguely dangerous.

At last, Emma let him catch her fully. Grif wasn't like the men she generally pursued. He was young, he was hot, and he knew his way around a woman's body. He liked his sex a little rough, and Emma, well . . . she was up for anything. The sex had been explosive, perhaps the best set of orgasms she'd ever had. For a week, they'd existed like animals, unable to keep their clothes on for more than a quick trip to the store.

And then . . . Grif was done. He was completely done with her. Emma hadn't been surprised because she'd known Grif was just like her—it was all about the chase. After the prey had been caught, the rest of it was meaningless and empty.

Emma had *known* that would happen; she had known from the beginning she was nothing but another piece of ass to him. And yet, she'd allowed herself to be swept along by some ridiculous fantasy of love all the same because she'd been so physically attracted to him. She had presented herself to him as he wanted, had become exactly what women were to her father—a bird to be caught, and then mere flesh and bone, a port with a hole—and it had hurt no less than her father's betrayal.

Grif was different from the older men Emma chased, who "chose" her instead of some other blonde at that given time. Grif was different because Emma had really wanted him, and somewhere along the way, she had wanted him to want her, too.

It was a strange, crazy world in Emma's head when it came to sex.

Now she was confronted by a more complex problem. Cooper was like Grif in some respects. He was a beautiful man and Emma was strongly attracted to him. But she wasn't going to make the same mistake as she'd made with Grif. Because when Cooper had what he wanted from her—that damn medal—he'd be done with her, too. Any hint that he was interested in more than her body was just a ploy. And the more Emma dragged this out, the worse it would be for her.

In her room, Emma pulled out her tote bag and unzipped it. She turned it upside down and watched her prizes tumble onto her lumpy bed. She picked up the box with the medal and held it in her hand. She didn't bother to open it; she knew the medal was inside. She didn't *want* to see it, because that medal was all she really was to Cooper, and all she ever would be. That was all Carl had been to her. A thing. A trophy.

If Emma swallowed her pride and gave Cooper this medal, he would disappear. Being mean hadn't worked. Seduction hadn't worked. The only thing that would work to get rid of him before things got really complicated was to give him the medal. If Cooper had that, he would go back to LA and tell stories about her.

If she gave it to him, she would humiliate herself. But she would also spare herself the agony of wanting to climb a mountain she was incapable of scaling. Best to look at the mountain from afar, admire the peaks, but keep her distance.

So give it to him. Give it to him, give it to him, send him on his way. The longer he stays, the more he sees. The more he sees, the weaker you are.

It was the only thing to do, and yet it was so hard, almost unbearable to admit that she really was a liar and a thief and a slut with some very mixed-up ideas.

Emma rolled onto her back on the bed, put the box on her belly, and stared up at the peeling ceiling.

Shortly after she'd arrived in Pine River, she'd attended a yoga class with Libby. Yoga wasn't her thing, but Libby had convinced her. *Come on, you'll feel like a new person,* she'd said. Emma had needed to feel like a new person. So she'd gone.

At the end of class, with her hands in prayer pose, her thumbs pressed to her heart center and her head bowed, the instructor had said, "Today, be yourself. Your true, undefined self."

That particular comment had stuck with Emma and had pointed out a huge gaping hole in her: She didn't know who her undefined self was. She'd been defined by the summer of her seventeenth year for so long that she'd barricaded her spirit from the world. And in that yoga class, Emma had been struck with the unnerving realization that she didn't know how to set her spirit free.

"Maybe now," she said aloud. Maybe now was the time to be undefined, to step out of the borders of her boxed-in life.

FOURTEEN

Cooper was thirty-eight years old. His ability to close out the world when he was in an unfamiliar place—to sleep anywhere, like he had in his twenties—was considerably diminished.

The sleep he'd managed on that couch over the last two hours had been very shallow. He'd been aware of every creak and moan in this old house, and had even believed he could hear the snow falling. In fact, the snowfall became so loud that he worried it was a true blizzard and he'd be trapped at this ranch. He got up to peer out the big picture window, wearing only his boxers.

Not only had the snow quit falling, there were only three inches of it on the ground, if that—nothing that Luke couldn't manage in his Jeep.

Cooper was not trapped. He hadn't miraculously developed supersonic hearing.

He'd returned to the couch and slung an arm over his eyes. His nerves were electrified, his thoughts whirring. He kept thinking of Emma, of the way her eyes weren't exactly green, but neither were they blue. More like the color of a tropical sea. He thought about the way she'd interacted with everyone at the supper table, the invisible veil she put up between her and everyone else. As if she was present, but not entirely. Her gaze had found him occasionally, and the faint flicker of a smile across her lips would show before she quickly averted her eyes. She was afraid to look at him after he'd talked to her in the kitchen. Why?

Cooper also thought about the canyon he'd seen today. He must have drifted into sleep, dozing a little, because he was climbing the sheer face of a cliff, his hold so tenuous that a breeze would have dislodged him. He became aware of someone or something, and when he turned his head to look, he slipped from his hold.

Cooper's eyes flew open; a shadow passed in his peripheral vision. He blinked against the dark until he could focus in the dim light of a lamp that had been left on in the hall, and turned his head.

Emma was standing at the front window, gazing out. She was wearing an oversized shirt, and her legs, slender and shapely, were bare. Her hair fell down her back in one long silken drape, and Cooper was reminded of the feel of it between his fingers.

"It's stopped snowing," she said, her voice barely more than a whisper.

Cooper didn't speak; he lifted up to one elbow.

Emma turned around to face him. She looked ghostlike, framed in the window as she was. Cooper's curiosity was aroused, as was his body. "What are you doing?" he asked, his voice gravelly from fitful sleep.

Emma moved toward him, gliding across the braided rug like a wraith. Cooper tensed, wary of her intent. But when she reached him, she climbed on top of him, forcing him onto his back as she straddled his groin. He put his hands on her hips, his thumb sliding under the tiny strip of panty on her hip. Her hair spilled around her shoulders, her eyes shining in the low light. She was sexy as hell, and his body was responding, hardening against her.

Emma casually scraped her fingers down his pecs, across his nipples. She slid her palms to his shoulders, then leaned down to kiss him. God help him, but her mouth and tongue were so soft against his. Every vein in him began to swell with desire, and Cooper kissed her back, sinking his fingers into her hair, gripping thick ropes of blond silk in his fist. He knew she was using her body to toy with him, and yet, he couldn't keep from responding.

She shifted, her mouth sliding to his neck.

"This is beneath you, Emma," he said gruffly.

"*You're* beneath me," she murmured, and licked his ear.

"You don't even like me," he reminded her.

"Not true. But what does it matter? You like this," she said, sliding her hand in between their bodies and over his erection.

He hated the machination, the manipulation. He hated even more that he was aroused by it. He abruptly sat up and caught her wrist, forcing her to look at him. "My *dick* likes it. Don't confuse that with me. *I* don't like it."

"Come on, Cooper," she purred. "You want this." She surged forward, catching his head between her hands, kissing him.

Damn it, he *did* want it. He was male, he wanted sex, he *always* wanted sex, and part of him was berating himself for ruining a good thing. But he wasn't going to have sex like this. It was cheap and meaningless, it was overt manipulation, and this was not the way he wanted Emma Tyler. Cooper wasn't certain he wanted her at all, but if he ever did, it damn sure wouldn't be like this. He pulled her hands from his head and pushed her back. "That's enough."

"Liar," she said, and shimmied back, onto his thighs. She smiled as she began to trail kisses down his chest, her gaze on him, daring him to stop her as she moved to his groin.

Cooper grabbed her roughly by the arms and hauled her up. Emma gasped, wincing a little, but Cooper didn't loosen his grip. "I said *no*," he said firmly.

She laughed, the sound of it harsh. "You just lost your chance," she said, and shifted back, bracing her hands against his chest to climb off of him.

Cooper swung his legs off the side of the couch. "If we're going to have sex, the desire will be mutual. No power plays."

He saw the almost imperceptible hitch in her shoulders. "There will never be anything mutual between us, Cooper. I don't do things in the ordinary ways. I don't do ordinary love. Haven't you learned anything about me?"

She turned, as if she was going to leave the room, but Cooper caught her hand in his. "No one said anything about love, ordinary or otherwise," he said. "I swear to God I can't figure you out, Emma, but I'm not your adversary."

Emma hesitated; her fingers curled a little around his. It was nothing more than a brush, really, but in that darkened room, it felt a little to Cooper as if she were clinging to him. Her fingers scraping, however faintly, against a life ring.

And then her fingers slipped away from his altogether. "I never implied you were my adversary. I never said anything about you at all, other than you should go home. You *do* need to go, Cooper. So I came down here to tell you that I have it."

Cooper's head was still wrapped around the physical encounter between them and the notion that there could never be anything mutual between them. "Have what?" he asked impatiently.

She glanced over her shoulder at him. "What do you think?"

He realized what she meant. "Are you kidding?"

"You're surprised? You said you didn't believe me."

"Where is it?"

Emma reached for something on the end table. She took his hand and turned it palm up, then put the box into his palm.

Cooper opened the box, saw the medal nestled inside, and closed the box.

"Jesus," he said, and pushed a hand through his hair.

Emma floated down onto the couch beside him, looking deflated.

"Why?" he asked. *Why lie, why now, why take it in the first place?* God, there were so many things he didn't understand about this woman. So many little twists and turns that made no sense.

"Why?" she echoed.

"Why do you have it?" he asked her. "Why did you take it?"

She bit her lower lip and shook her head. "I don't know. It's just a weird thing," she said with a flick of her wrist.

"Then why didn't you just tell me? Why didn't you give it to me the day I showed up instead of dragging it out like this? Why even hide it?"

"Isn't it obvious?" she asked curtly. "I'm ashamed of myself. I would rather lie than admit I took that stupid box. But *you* . . you just wouldn't give *up*," she said, her voice filled with wonder.

Cooper fell back against the couch. He was relieved and he was oddly disappointed. Not that she had it—he'd known that all along. It was her explanation. He wished there had been something—she robbed Peter to pay Paul, anything other than *it's just a weird thing.*

"Thanks," he said.

"For what?" she asked with disgust. "For not lying?"

"More like for being honest."

She shifted, her back straightening, her hands going to her knee. "Funny, that's the thing about me that people find so annoying—I'm usually too honest." She stood up. "Okay, Cooper. You've got what you wanted. You can go home now. You're going to leave Pine River, right? No more pretending to look at cliffs or whatever it is you've been doing?"

The expression in her eyes was wistful, and that look did not match the words coming out of her mouth. "Is that what you want?" he asked uncertainly.

"*Yes.* I want you to go back to LA and not come back. Is that plain enough for you?"

Very plain, and Cooper was more than a little annoyed by her blunt honesty. And by his goddamn fickleness. A moment ago, he despised her for trying to use him. Now, he was stung she wanted him to go.

"What?" she demanded impatiently.

"I thought we were getting somewhere," he said simply.

"*Where?* Where were we getting?" she exclaimed. "You know what? We *were* getting somewhere," she said, sounding angry now. "But we got there too fast. And now it's over. So in the end, we got exactly nowhere, which is exactly where we were destined to go from the beginning."

He would have bought that explanation had she not spoken so angrily and looked so sad. Whatever was going on in her head was a spectacular mystery, and Cooper grudgingly admitted to himself that he was more interested than he wanted to be. "Okay," he said with a shrug. "I'll go."

"Good." She moved to leave the room.

"But I could also stay a little while," he said, uncertain where *those* words had come from. All he knew was that he wanted to unlock the mystery in Emma Tyler. It was like reading a thriller and being denied the last few chapters. He'd figure her out, and then he'd go. But in that moment, staying felt . . . important.

Apparently not to Emma. She whirled around to face him with a murderous gaze. "*Not* a good idea. Are you deaf, Cooper? Are you *dumb?* I want you to *go.* I want you to leave and never come back. In other words, get the hell out of my life!"

It made no sense to Cooper that he should stand up and grab Emma then, much less kiss her. But he did, kissing those words off her breath, nibbling them off her lips, his tongue sweeping into her mouth and swallowing them whole. Emma struggled weakly at first, but then responded to him, pressing against him. He was heating up again, his body swelling with desire. He kissed her neck, her shoulder. His hands swept up her body to her breasts, then down again, over her hips.

He didn't know how long he kissed her, but Emma shoved against him and backed away from him. She unsteadily touched her fingers to her swollen bottom lip. *"Bastard,"* she spat, and walked out of the living room.

Cooper could hear the stairs squeaking under her weight as she went up. He slowly sat down, an image of Emma shimmering in his thoughts. He was not an obtuse guy—she certainly spoke like she wanted him gone. And yet there seemed to be a major contradiction lurking in her. Maybe he was crazy, maybe he was trying to see something there because he wanted to make love to her—but he couldn't rid himself of the idea that she was not what she presented.

Emma Tyler was more intriguing than any woman he'd met in a very long while. He rubbed his scalp. He didn't have the time or the energy for this! He was too old for games. He was way past the point in his life that he would be strung along in ways and for reasons he didn't understand.

Yeah, he'd get out of the mountains before it snowed again, and head back to LA.

Cooper lay down, pulled the quilt over his chest. But his sleep was even more fitful than before.

>─┼─◆─○─◆─┼─<

He was dressed and ready to go when Luke came downstairs. Cooper was anxious to get off this mountain. He wanted the sunshine of LA, the predictability of women there. He wanted to see

Braden and Brodie and give them the kiddie sombreros he'd picked up at Tag's Outfitters.

Cooper told Luke on the slow drive down the mountain that he was heading out after their ski date. Luke had looked at him strangely, apparently waiting for Cooper to say something more, perhaps about the thing he'd come to get from Emma. But Cooper didn't mention it, and Luke apparently knew not to ask.

Luke dropped him off at the Grizzly. Cooper grabbed a bear claw pastry and coffee from the Grizzly Café, then went up to the Beaver Room and called his mother. "Hi, Mom," he said through a yawn.

"Coop, honey, I'm so glad you called," she said. "Derek called this morning. He said he's due to be released on the twenty-third to a halfway house, and then three months after that, he can come home! After all this time, I'm going to get him back!"

Cooper resisted the urge to rain on her parade. God knew his mom had long been the stalwart, making the twelve-hour round-trip between the oil fields of West Texas to the penitentiary near Houston to see Derek four times a year. She'd watched the prison tattoos bloom on Derek's arms, had watched the lines in his face deepen, the features harden, and still, she had that mother's eagerness to have her boy home.

Cooper's mother was not the least bit prepared for the kind of man who was coming back to her, and coming back only because he had no other place to go.

"Aren't you excited?" she asked.

"It's great, Mom."

"We can spend Christmas with him," she said, her voice bubbling with an enthusiasm he'd not heard for Christmas in years. "You're coming home for that, aren't you? You have to, Coop. This will be our first time together in *years*."

"Of course," he said. "I wouldn't miss it."

But he was filled with dread. Derek wasn't the fun-loving older brother Cooper's dusty memory could conjure up on occasion. When Cooper thought back to their life, he could honestly believe that Derek had tried to be something other than a thug and a thief. But there was something in Derek, a compulsion he could not overcome to get high and push the limits of the law.

Cooper promised his mom again he'd be home in time, then hung up. His next call was to Carl Freeman.

"It's Cooper," he said when Carl answered.

"I was about to send a posse after you," Carl said. "What news do you have for me?"

"I have it," Cooper said, and balanced the phone between his ear and shoulder as he opened the box.

"No shit!" Carl said happily, and then laughed loud and long. *"Boo-yah!"* he shouted. "She's got that gleam in her eye, Coop. She thinks she's getting the whole thing. Just wait till I show up with that fucking box."

"I'm looking at it right now," Cooper said. "Red-and-silver ribbon with an eagle in the middle." He pulled at the little tab of the velvet shelf the medal sat on and lifted it up, expecting to see a diamond ring beneath it.

There was no ring. *No ring.* Cooper put the medal aside and felt inside the box for a false bottom, and when he found none, his heart sank. *She hadn't. She couldn't have. Emma, no.*

" . . . stupid shit."

"What?" Cooper hadn't heard anything that Carl had just said.

"I *said,* it's not red and silver with a big eagle! It's a *star,* a fucking star! And it has *blue* ribbons! What the hell, Coop? What medal are you looking at? What'd she do, go and buy one at the drug store? I can *not* believe this! Do you even get what I'm trying to do here? What's at stake for me? You tell that bitch if she doesn't hand over what's mine today, I'm filing charges!"

As Carl continued to rant, Cooper stared down at the medal. Nothing made sense. Emma had given him the medal. She'd made a big show of it, handing it over, asking him to leave. Why in hell would she give him a *fake* one? She had to know that he'd figure it out very quickly, that he'd be back. And where had she gotten another one, anyway?

He looked closer at the medal. It didn't look fake. Cooper was no expert, but this one looked like a very real military medal. Could she have taken it from the ranch? There were vets out there, so it was possible. No, no, he couldn't believe it. He couldn't believe Emma Tyler would walk down to the bunkhouse and steal from a *vet*. But what other explanation could there be? Who else could this medal belong to? And moreover, why did Emma have more than one medal? Was it possible she was really just batshit crazy and went around stealing medals?

He sank down on the edge of the bed, his thoughts swirling and skipping around each other as Carl continued to rant about incompetence in general.

Emma had more than one medal. What else did she have? Did she only steal medals, or did she take other things, too?

What the hell was the matter with her?

"Yeah, all right, I've been played," Cooper said crossly into the phone when Carl screamed what a loser he was. "But she's got that goddamn medal. Give me one more day, Carl. I will get it if it's the last thing I do," he said, and clicked off the phone before Carl could shout at him again.

And then Cooper hurled his phone across the bed, hitting the pelt-covered headboard.

He was livid. He was absolutely, illogically, and undeniably *furious.*

FIFTEEN

It would have been a very bleak morning were it not for the pristine layer of snow that dusted the mountain peaks and weighed the boughs of the pines outside of Emma's window. All that new snow helped her believe the grit left from the night before would rub off.

Alas, that was a pipe dream, because she couldn't get rid of the grit.

She'd showered and dressed, and still felt grubby and tarnished after what had happened last night. She prepared herself as best she could to meet Cooper downstairs, to see the rejection in his eyes and feel the sting of humiliation under her skin. It took some effort, but Emma adopted an expression of indifference and went downstairs.

Cooper wasn't there.

"He went to town with Luke and Sam," Libby said.

"Left?" Emma said, thinking that Libby must somehow be mistaken.

"Yeah, he left," Libby said, smiling. "Why? Did you maybe want him to stay?" She poked Emma in the side.

"No," Emma said, ignoring the poke, and helped herself to yogurt. "I was worried you'd invite him to move in."

"I haven't yet," Libby said pertly. "But I wouldn't mind if he did. He's very nice and he's easy on the eyes."

Emma eyed Libby suspiciously.

Libby shrugged. "I can look, can't I?"

Emma sat at the kitchen bar with her yogurt. She pretended to flip through the pages of a magazine, but she didn't see the pictures or words before her. What she saw was Cooper's face. She shouldn't be surprised that he left without a word to her after what had happened. He probably was so eager to get out of here and away from her that he'd been prepared to hike out.

But *he* was the one who'd said all that *I can stay a little while* business. Why had he even bothered to say it if he didn't mean it? If there was one thing Emma couldn't abide, it was people who said one thing and meant another, which, obviously, he had. But still, she'd hoped maybe there had been something more in that last kiss . . .

Grow up, Emma. You made your bed, now you lie in it.

Unfortunately, Emma couldn't lie in the bed she'd made— she was too out of sorts. Miserable! Completely at odds with the person she had worked to become. Where did that leave her? Who *was* she now?

She picked up her purse and started for the door.

"Are you leaving?" Libby called after her.

"Yes!" Emma shouted back. Maybe for good. Maybe she'd get in her car and just drive until she ran into the ocean.

Emma didn't drive away from Pine River, she drove to work. She'd been there a half hour when Leo said, "Wow, *someone's* in a mood."

"Who, your dad?" Emma was folding towels with her back to

Leo. She knew he was talking about her, but wasn't willing or ready to discuss her mood.

"No, *you,* sweetheart," Leo pressed. "Someone piss in your Wheaties? Let the air out of your tires?" He paused to catch his breath. Leo wouldn't tolerate a mention of it, but it was obvious to Emma that his breathing was beginning to degrade. "Who ripped your rompers?" he asked.

She turned around. Leo was strapped in his chair, his head buttressed by two thick pieces of foam on either side, a strap around his chest. It was amazing to Emma that Leo was always smiling. Always! As if he hadn't a care in the world. She couldn't force a smile today, and her troubles were so insignificant compared to his. "Just because I don't run on at the mouth like you doesn't mean I'm in a bad mood," she said, trying to lighten her mood. Leo liked it when she talked that way to him. He liked to measure her response on his imaginary sass-o-meter.

"I am basing my expert opinion not on your silence, but how mean you look."

"Mean!"

"As mean as hornets at a picnic, as my mother would say. Mom definitely had a way with words. So what's up, Em? You can tell me."

"Leo—"

"Don't say 'nothing.' I hate when you say nothing when it's so obvious it's something. Make it quick, will you? The Methodists are coming over and if we're lucky, there is pie involved."

"Look, genius, you're leaving for Denver in a few days. I would think you'd want to conserve your strength for that, so maybe you should shut up for a while."

"Touchy," Leo observed as she walked around behind his chair to put the towels on a table behind him. "That's a sure sign of a bruised heart. I mean, all anyone can talk about is how rude you

are to Cooper, which says to me that you totally have a thing for him. Which, by the way"—he paused to draw a deep breath—"is an opinion I've shared around town. It totally makes sense, seeing as how you can't have me."

Emma's mouth gaped open. She raised her eyes to the water stain on the ceiling directly overhead and prayed that she would not bean this poor, defenseless man. "That's ridiculous, Leo. My heart is not *bruised*, for God's sake. I probably am rude to Cooper, but then again, I'm *rude*. And it doesn't matter, anyway, because he's gone back to LA."

"No way!" Leo said. "Dani didn't mention it when she was here at lunch, and she *definitely* would have mentioned it if he'd checked out. He doesn't like the Beaver Room, you know. That's my favorite room."

Emma walked back around to the front of Leo's chair and picked up the second basket of laundry.

"Hello, you're blocking *Days of Our Lives*," he pointed out.

Emma shifted to her left.

"It's okay to like someone, you know," Leo said casually, his gaze on the television. "You don't *have* to be an ice princess."

"I'm not an ice princess!" she snapped. "I'm direct, and I can't help it if people can't deal with *direct*. I choose my friends carefully, Leo. I'm not nicey-nice just for the sake of being nice and that does *not* make me an *ice princess*."

"Okay, just don't stab me with an icicle," Leo said. "How about 'cool cucumber'? Can I say that? Because I know you like being a cool cucumber. You work hard enough at it."

"You're really annoying me," she said. "That's just *me*, don't you get that by now? It's not an act; it's who I am."

"Please," Leo scoffed. "That's like me saying, yeah, I have MND, but that's just me."

"*Stop* it," she demanded.

"Come on, Em, what's really twisting you around?"

Everything. *Everything!* So much that she couldn't pick out one single thing that was the culprit behind her admittedly foul mood. Her whole life was twisted around and upside down all because of that damn medal! "Gee, where to start?" she asked snidely. "I don't like that you're going to Denver, for one," she said, and whipped a wrinkled towel out, snapping it dangerously close to the television. "There, I said it. I know you don't like to hear it, I know you don't like anyone disagreeing with your wants. And I know you really want to go, and how important the game is to you. But frankly, I'm worried about it." She looked at him. "You know what? I agree with Bob. It's a bad idea."

"*Oh!*" Leo said, wincing. "That's a dagger to my poor weak heart! Beat me, curse me, but don't agree with Dad!"

"And the worst of it is that I can't go with you," she said. "What if you need something? What if you aren't feeling well?"

"That's why I have a big burly nurse going with me. Plus Dad and Dante. I'll be fine."

"Dante has stage-four cancer, Leo."

"So he's a little weak," Leo said. "But I still have Dad and the nurse. And the two Methodist dudes who are driving us. That's plenty of people to worry about me while I worry about the Broncos."

"In other words, you don't need me," she said curtly.

"Not this time," Leo said easily, and drew another deep breath.

Emma suddenly felt defeated, utterly defeated. Even Leo didn't need her, the one person in her life who truly needed someone by his side 24/7. But wasn't that what she wanted? Hadn't she lived the last few years making damn sure that no one could ever get close enough to her to know her, much less *need* her? Hadn't she equated familiarity with the ability to hurt her and wound her? Theoretically, Leo should not be able to hurt her feelings, and yet, he just had.

"Great," she muttered, and moved across the room to stack the towels on an empty chair.

"Would you quit moving around? I can't turn my head. Come on, talk to me, Em. Tell me what's going on."

Oddly enough, Emma was frustrated enough that for once, she wanted to unburden herself. She wanted to say aloud the things that were rattling through her brain. And as Leo was the only person she could possibly bring herself to speak to about such personal things, she hesitantly moved toward the stool in front of him and sat down. "Am I allowed to speak during *Days of Our Lives*?"

"Silly girl. I DVR my shows in case someone like you has a life crisis. But it *is Days,* so this better be good." He flashed his lopsided smile.

"I gave him the medal," Emma said flatly.

That caught Leo off guard. "Wow. If I could raise my eyebrows, I totally would right now. You had the thing he wanted? And you gave it to him? And you lied about it?"

"Yep. All of that."

"That is like, *super* curious," Leo said. "What, you didn't like the guy or something?"

"I hardly knew him," she said. "I have a lot of things like it. Things I've taken from guys I hardly knew. But did know, you know . . . intimately."

For once, Leo didn't have an instant comeback. "That's *awesome,*" he said, his voice full of wonder. "That makes you like . . . a love bandit. And yet it begs the question of why?"

"I don't know," Emma said angrily. She spread her fingers wide over her knees. "It's weird, I know, God, how I *know,*" she said, feeling the agony of it. "Even saying it makes me kind of sick. And it's so wrong, obviously. Maybe even criminal. Not to mention unhealthy," she said, gesturing at her head. "But honestly, Leo, I don't want to really do anything about it. Or at least I didn't until now."

"An unrepentant bandit. That's the best kind, you know. That makes you a sexy jewel thief."

"Leo, I'm serious," Emma said with some exasperation. "It makes me despicable."

"Are you kidding? You could never be despicable, Emma! Okay, so you have a screw loose. Who doesn't?" He paused to take a deep breath.

He was frustrating her, unwilling to take her seriously. "I should never have said anything," she said, and stood up.

"Wait, wait," Leo said. "Please sit down. For the sake of argument, let's just agree that you have a major screw loose. I mean, by *any* definition this is prime nutter territory."

She cast a withering look at him. "You're not helping."

"Still, it doesn't make you bad, Emma. It doesn't make you despicable. It doesn't make you unlovable."

That word, *unlovable*, kicked Emma in the gut. She sucked in a sharp breath as if she'd actually been hit and pressed her palm against her abdomen. The painful twist she felt surprised her, and she slowly sank onto the stool again.

"What? What'd I say?" Leo asked. "Unlovable? Was that it? I said you *weren't* unlovable."

"Don't, Leo," Emma said, and swallowed. "You're not a shrink and it's not like I'm going to change."

"But you're *not* unlovable, Emma. Wait—is that a double negative? Look, what I'm trying to say is that you're lovable. Totally, completely lovable, even with this crazy thing you do. I mean, look at me, I adore you!"

Emma looked at him, expecting to see the twinkle of laughter in his eyes, but Leo looked as earnest as she'd ever seen him.

"I don't adore you in *that* way, I already told you. But I love you because you're you. You're like, drop-dead gorgeous, and you say what's on your mind, and you think about things in a funny way, and you'll watch a marathon of *Duck Dynasty* with me when I know you're bored and you don't make fun of me even once. You're *awesome,* Emma. And just because you took a medal from some guy—okay, *guys*—doesn't make you any less so."

Damn it, her eyes were welling. "Don't say that just to say it, okay? I can't stand bullshit, you know that."

"I'm *not* just saying it. I don't just say stuff. Okay, that's not totally true. I say stuff to Dad I know he wants to hear, and sometimes to set him off because it can be amusing under the right circumstances, but that's different. You know me, Emma, and you know I would totally tell you if you were unlovable. I told you you're a nutter, didn't I?"

Emma couldn't help her smile. "You did." She wiped a lone tear from the corner of her eye. "But that's exactly my problem, Leo. You really don't *know* what I am. You really don't know me at all. No one does."

"Oh, come on, no one knows anyone as well as they think they do. But I know you as well as anyone can know you, right?"

She nodded. If anyone knew her, if only a little, it was Leo.

"Of course it's true. I'm a certified genius, baby. I know this stuff backwards and forwards."

"And you're so modest, too," she said. "That's what makes you truly special."

"Hey . . . you haven't taken anything of mine, have you?"

Emma laughed ruefully and shook her head. "Never. I care about you." She stood up and leaned over him to hug him, and kissed his forehead.

"Okay, all right, stop that."

"I love you, Leo. I love you more than I've loved anyone in a very long time."

A faint blush appeared in his sunken cheeks. "Give me a break," he said, although his eyes were twinkling. "Who doesn't?

I'm, like, super charming. Okay, seriously, get out of the way. I can't see *Days* with you standing right there."

Emma moved back to the laundry.

"Just curious," Leo said when she had started to fold towels once more. "When Jackson went out to LA to tell you about Grant dying, did he maybe happen to leave a tie behind? Purple with green spots? Because I really dug that tie, and he could never seem to find it once he came back."

"Shut up, Leo," Emma said, smiling.

She left later that afternoon when Leo asked to be taken to his room for a nap. He had to sleep with a breathing machine now, and she put that on him, and sat at the window, watching the elm tree sway against a cobalt-blue sky, dislodging thick, wet clumps of snow with each breeze.

When she was certain he was asleep, she stepped out onto the porch and inhaled deeply. The day was crisp but brilliant with light. She jogged down the steps and caught sight of Bob Kendrick salting the wheelchair ramp to keep it from icing over.

He glanced at his watch. "Leaving?" he asked, presumably because it was three thirty in the afternoon, a little earlier than her normal afternoon departure of four or five.

"Leo is napping," she said.

"You got him into bed okay?"

Emma nodded.

"Breathing machine is on?"

"Of course."

Bob looked at the house. "Boy is having trouble breathing and yet I've got to take him to this goddamn football game."

"I'm not crazy about it either," Emma agreed. "But I understand his desire. He can't exist just for the sake of existing, right? There has to be some pleasure in life."

"You think I don't get that?" Bob asked, not unkindly. "I'd do

anything to give that boy what he wants. But I don't want to has-
ten . . ." He clenched his jaw and shook his head, and shifted his
gaze away from Emma.

How difficult this must be for Bob Kendrick. Emma walked
down the steps and put her hand on Bob's arm. He wouldn't look
at her. He was looking away, toward the mountains, the crinkles in
the corners of his eyes indicating a hard squint into the sunlight. "I
wish more of it was in our control," she said. "I wish I could make
it better for you somehow."

He glanced at her sidelong. "Yeah," he said roughly. "Okay,
well, I got work to do." He stepped away and Emma's hand fell to
her side. Bob began to shake salt out of a big container over the
ramp. She wondered why he would be so concerned about salting
the ramp, because it wasn't as if Leo would be going out tonight.
But then it dawned her. If there were an emergency, if Bob had to
carry his son to a hospital . . .

"Okay, I'll see you tomorrow," she said.

"Yep," Bob responded tightly.

Emma didn't think twice about going by the park this afternoon. She knew the kids would be out, and she could see the snow
flying before she turned into the park entrance. She smiled at the
sight of them on the playground hurling snowballs at each other.
Today, two other children had joined her little brood. It appeared
that they had divided into teams.

Emma parked in the lot, maneuvering through the big patches
of snow. She emerged carefully from the car. She donned some
mittens, and began to walk across the park to her bench. The snow
crunched under her boots as she walked, and the bench was covered in snow. She brushed it off and sat, wincing a little at the
wet cold the snow had left behind. Just as she settled in, Quinn
hit one of the boys in the side of the head with a snowball, which
resulted in a shrieking wail. Emma stood up; she heard a door

bang open and a moment later, the kids' mother was hurrying across the street.

"What'd you do?" she shouted as she rushed toward them.

Emma watched in fascination as the children gathered around the mom while she tilted the boy's head back and examined the point of contact.

In the next moment, she was loudly ushering all the children back across the street. Two of them went obediently, but behind the mother's back, Quinn and Brynn tried to snuff snow down each other's shirts. That ended when the mother whirled around and smacked Quinn.

The strike startled Emma. *"Hey,"* she muttered as the mother and her kids went into the house. Quinn held her hand to the cheek her mother had slapped. That most definitely did not mesh with Emma's fantasy family.

"Because it's only a fantasy," she muttered to herself. She glanced at her watch. It was four o'clock. It was cold out, and she thought of going home. But now, in the silence of the park setting, she kept hearing her conversation with Leo.

You're not unlovable.

Maybe he was right. Maybe in some universe, Emma was not as despicable and disgusting as she felt. Was that possible? Was she kidding herself? And really, what was the point of even wondering? She had screwed it all up with Cooper. She'd been playing with a bit of fantasy there, too, she realized, and folded her arms tightly across herself. But the reality was that she'd taken the medal, she'd been caught, and she'd made a fool of herself in front of Cooper. There was no hiding it, no pretending it hadn't happened. There was no way Leo could help her whitewash it—the damage had been done. She'd just have to renew her determination to stop acting out.

If only it were that easy. If only she could just tell herself not to do it anymore and then not *do* it.

She heard the sound of snow under someone's foot and stood up. Probably the teen girls, she thought, and hitched her purse over her shoulder. But when she turned around, it was not teen girls striding toward her, it was Cooper Jessup.

Emma was surprised to see him and, truthfully, a little happy. But as Cooper marched toward her, she realized that he did not look happy to see her—he looked very unhappy. And then she realized where he was—in her park, her private park, at her secret bench. How did he know she was here? Emma glanced around, half expecting an entire audience to leap out and accuse her of stalking children. She took an unconscious step backward. "Cooper? What are you doing?" she asked uncertainly as he strode around the bench to where she was standing.

"Looking for you," he said coldly. "I just have one question, Emma. What the hell is the matter with you?"

"Huh?" His presence, his question, confused her. Did he mean watching the kids? Did he think she was doing something weird here?

"You're the worst," he said hotly. "The absolute *worst.*"

He *did* think she was being weird about the kids, and her hackles rose. "And? So? What the hell is it to *you* what I am?"

"What the hell is it to *me?*"

"What, do you know them?" she exclaimed, gesturing vaguely in the direction of the little house across the street. "Did you meet them while you were running around town with Luke?" That had to be it—he'd met someone who had complained about her watching the kids. The teenage girls! Emma would bet her diamond necklace that Tashi, whoever she was, had said something about her.

"Meet *who?*" Cooper demanded. "What the hell are you talking about?"

"I just come to watch them play, and the last time I checked, that's not a crime!"

Cooper blinked. "I'm not talking about watching kids play," he said, his voice full of anger. "I'm talking about *this*." He pulled something from his coat pocket and held it out to her. She recognized the box that contained Carl's medal.

Emma stared at the box, then pressed her fingers to her temples and tried to understand what was happening. She'd just confessed to watching kids she didn't know, and he was talking about that damn medal *again*? "Okay! You *have* it! You can take it! Go! Fly back to Carl and deliver it on a silver tray for all I care!"

Cooper's expression darkened. "Did you buy it in town? Did you steal it from someone? Because I sure as hell can't figure out where you might have come across it."

"What are you talking about?" she cried. "That is Carl's fucking medal you wanted so badly!"

"Nope, no, it's not, Emma," he said, clearly exasperated with her. "Carl's medal is *blue*. This one is *red*."

Emma felt a surge of physical panic that almost choked her. How could she have made such a careless mistake? She reached for the box, certain he was mistaken, but Cooper jerked it out of her reach. "Uh-uh. Not until you tell me what's going on here. Starting with who does *this* medal belong to?"

She wasn't about to tell him that she'd taken it from a colonel she'd met in Santa Barbara one night. CEM had staged a wedding for the daughter of a very wealthy Chinese businessman, and the colonel had been at the bar of her hotel when Emma had wandered in, very late, exhausted from the day's events. The colonel had taken one look at Emma and had sidled over, a smug smile on his face, so sure of himself and his powers of attraction. Turned out, he was what one would call "highly decorated," with so many medals and insignia and ribbons that he'd laughed at how he could no longer keep track of them all.

Cooper was waiting for her answer. "It's mine," she said, staring at the box.

"Yours?" Cooper repeated hotly. "Just where did you get it? Did you do a stint in the armed forces? Did you have a soldier boyfriend? *How*, Emma? How did you get it?"

"That . . . that is none of your business," she said, her voice shaking. She hoped her heart didn't give out, pounding as hard as it was in her chest. "Look, I gave you the wrong medal."

He snorted disdainfully. "Yeah, I kind of figured that out. I want Carl's medal, and if you don't want to be charged with theft, you'd better give it to me."

Nausea rolled through Emma. She held out her palm to him. "He's not going to charge me with stealing."

"Like hell he won't," Cooper said angrily. "Did you know his mother-in-law's wedding ring was under the medal in that box, or did you just luck into it?"

Emma's wildly beating heart stopped beating so suddenly she couldn't get a breath. *What* diamond ring? She never took anything of value!

"You actually look surprised. Yes, Emma, a four-carat diamond ring. If he doesn't get it back, he's pressing charges."

She was going to be sick. A *diamond*?

She deserved anything Carl did to her. She deserved to be arrested and thrown in jail. She'd just never believed it would *happen*. "I have his medal," she said angrily. "I'll get it. But give that one back."

"No way," Cooper said, and Emma watched the box disappear into his pocket. "Give me Carl's medal first."

"I'll get it—"

"*We'll* get it."

"It's up at the ranch!"

Cooper gestured grandly for her to come around the bench and walk to the car.

There was no way out of this. Cooper was clearly determined and wasn't letting her out of his sight. *"Fine,"* she said, and started for her car.

She walked at a clip, reaching the car before him, and put her hand on the driver's side handle to open it. But before she could, Cooper slammed his hand against the door and held it shut. He was standing very close to her, practically holding her against the car, and glared down at her with eyes so hot with anger they reminded her of smoke. *"I'll* drive."

"You can't just commandeer my car!"

"I'm not commandeering your car, I am commandeering *you.* Give me the keys."

He wasn't kidding. *"No,"* she said, alarmed and angry at once.

"I'm serious, Emma. You've played me enough. I'm done with the games. Give me the goddamn keys."

He looked so serious, so angry! He looked as if he could strangle her right there and was working to restrain himself from doing just that. Emma reluctantly pulled her keys from her purse. She shoved them against his chest, forcing him to drop his hand from the car to catch them. But he was quick; he grabbed the keys and her elbow at the same time, and marched her around to the passenger side before she knew what was happening. He practically stuffed her inside the car, and a moment later, he was in the driver's seat, hitting the gas as he backed out, causing her tires to squeal.

"Hey!" she cried out with alarm. "Slow down! There's snow on the road."

"If you're going to own a car like this, maybe you should learn to drive it," he said gruffly, and sped onto the road.

Emma braced herself against the dash. "You know this is totally illegal, right? What you're doing is called *abduction.*"

"Call Sam," he said with a shrug. "I'm more than happy to let him sort it out."

"Bastard," she said angrily. "Why are you in such a big hurry, anyway?" she demanded nervously as he maneuvered her car around the main drag and onto a seldom-used road that ran along the rail tracks and bypassed town.

"Because I'd like to get on with my life, Emma. I'd like to finish this job and leave the crazy behind—meaning you. And on top of that, I don't trust you."

"I never said you should," she snapped, and folded up into a tight ball, her legs crossed, her arms crossed, and sank into her seat. "I never asked for you at all."

He said nothing to that, but she could see the bulge in his jaw from the clench of his teeth.

They hardly spoke on the way up to the ranch, Cooper driving so recklessly that Emma's breath was snatched from her at every turn. They bounced down the road to the house, and he slowed considerably as he pulled into the drive. He hadn't even stopped when Emma thrust the door open and bounded out, slipping and sliding on a patch of icy snow in her haste, and righting herself by grabbing onto the open car door. She ran through the dogs that had eagerly emerged to greet her, pushing their snouts out of her way and hoping they would close in on Cooper and slow him down.

She opened the front door and slammed through the screen door. It banged loudly behind her.

"Hey!" Madeline said, appearing with a basket of laundry. "What's wrong?"

Emma didn't respond as she took the stairs up, two at a time. She was panicked, her breath coming in painful gulps. She had to get the other medal out of her bag before Cooper saw it. She had no doubt he'd follow her up this time, no doubt that he was right behind her.

In her room, she fell to her knees and reached under her bed. *Damn it*—she'd pushed it far underneath and had to wiggle partially under the bed to get her hand on it. She grabbed the handle and pulled it out, popping up—

"*Shit,*" she muttered.

She was too late. Cooper was at the door of her room, his hand gripping the frame. "What's the matter?" he asked, only slightly out of breath. "Is there a fire?"

"This is my room! You can't come in here!"

"I'm already in," he said, and stepped inside. His hands were on his waist again, and he nodded at the bag. "What's that?" He lifted his gaze to hers. "What's in there?"

He asked it so suspiciously that she wondered if he knew just how crazy she was. "What do you think?" she asked bitterly.

"Nothing would surprise me. Let's have it, Emma. Give me the medal."

"Just wait out—"

"*No,*" he said.

Emma groaned. Or did she whimper? She was dazed with anxiety as she unzipped her bag and plunged her hand inside, her fingers rummaging, trying to find the box. But she had so many things in that bag, she couldn't find it.

"What are you doing?" he asked as she swept her hand blindly along the bottom of the bag.

"I'm *looking.*"

"You're wasting time," he said, and moved forward, as if he meant to take her leather tote.

With a gasp, she grabbed her tote and held it closer. "I have a lot of things in here. Will you stop pressuring me?"

"Look, I just want to get out of here—"

Emma suddenly surged up onto her knees and dumped the bag upside down onto the bed. The evidence of her depravity tumbled out of it, falling and bouncing on the lumpy bed. *All* of it. Ties and tie clips. Medals and pens. The panties she'd stuffed into this bag.

She risked a look at Cooper. He was looking at the pile curiously, not understanding what the strange hodgepodge was. But as Emma sorted through it, looking for the box, his expression changed, sliding from confused to shocked.

She found the right box and clamored to her feet and thrust it at him. "Here," she said, her voice shaking.

Cooper hesitantly took it from her and opened it. The medal was a star with blue ribbons. Cooper pulled the tab of the cardboard bed and lifted it up. With forefinger and thumb, he lifted out a diamond ring.

Emma gasped. How could she have missed it? The answer was simple, really—she'd missed it because the box meant nothing to her. She'd thrown it into this tote with the rest of the things and never looked back.

Cooper was frowning as he returned the ring to the bottom of the little box, the cardboard bed with the medal fastened to it on top. He didn't look at Emma as he tucked it all back in and shut the lid. He didn't look at her as he put it in his pocket. He withdrew the other box from his pocket and held it out to her, his gaze on her bed.

The heat of her shame flooded Emma's cheeks. She took the box from him and began the humiliating process of returning it, along with everything else, to her bag. Cooper watched, studying each item as she stoically put them inside. He didn't lift his gaze until she'd zipped the bag.

She could scarcely look at him as she dropped her bag to the floor and, with her boot, nudged it back under her bed. *What he must think of her!* Emma pushed her hair out of her face and folded her arms tightly around herself. Why didn't he go? He had the medal; he'd seen her brought as low as she could possibly go. Why wouldn't he just *leave*?

She couldn't bear his silence and looked up. Cooper was studying her as if he were trying to figure out how the pieces of her fit together. *They don't fit, obviously! There are pieces of me all over Los Angeles, don't you get that?* She couldn't bear the silence, the scrutiny. "Jesus, Cooper, can we go now?"

"Yeah," he said, his voice low and soft. Ambivalent.

She moved, brushing past him as she fled her room and the evidence of how deplorable she was. She strode down the hallway, down the stairs, gaining speed as she moved.

"Hey!" Madeline said happily as Emma barreled down the stairs, Cooper right behind her. "It's just about happy hour—"

"No," Emma said curtly. "Cooper has a plane to catch."

"Oh." Madeline's voice was full of disappointment. "Well, Cooper, I hope we see you again."

"Not likely!" Emma shouted, and pushed through the screen door, bounding down the steps to the car, ignoring the dogs that were jumping around her, demanding attention she would not give them. They may as well learn it now, too, Emma thought. She had an amazing capacity to turn off, to disengage.

She had already turned the engine when Cooper slid into the passenger seat. He said nothing, just stared straight ahead. Disgusted with her, obviously, but the joke was on Cooper. He couldn't possibly be more disgusted with Emma than she was with herself.

In fact, Cooper didn't speak at all until they were pulling into the parking lot of the park. And then he asked a very simple question, for which there were no simple answers.

He looked at her, covered her hand with his. Gently. Tenderly. "Why?"

"Don't try and understand," she said roughly, her gaze on the trees in front of her. She owed him no explanation, no matter how much she wanted to give him one. No matter how much she wished she had one. She couldn't make sense of it, much less try and explain it. The humiliations ran together, overlapping, until there was no beginning and no end to them.

Cooper opened the passenger door and put one leg out. But then he turned his head and fixed those gray eyes on her.

Kryptonite, she warned herself. *Don't speak, don't speak.*

"Emma—"

"Get out," she said. "Get *out.*"

He didn't argue.

He'd scarcely closed the door before she sped off. She drove blindly, tears filling her eyes. She'd never felt so debased, not even the day she'd found Laura in her father's bed. At least that indignity had faded with time, the edges of it fraying. *This* was heartbreaking and, she was fairly certain, the pain of it would never fade.

Emma had never felt so low.

When she reached the ranch, she ran up the stairs, past Libby and Madeline's chatter in the kitchen. She took a hot shower, scalding hot, and tried to get that thing, that humiliation, off of her. It wouldn't come off, of course, because there was no way she could possibly scrub her own essence from her skin. Leo could say it was okay all he wanted, but Emma had seen the truth on Cooper's face and in his eyes.

It was not okay. It was *not okay.*

SIXTEEN

Sleep was impossible for Cooper in the bizarre Beaver Room. He tossed and turned, wanting desperately to hit something besides a feather pillow.

He closed his eyes, but he kept seeing all the items Emma had—had what, *stolen*?—fall from that worn leather bag. He kept seeing the way she sorted through the things, looking for the box, tossing aside this tie clip, that pen, a tie. His first reaction had been disgust—it wasn't a great leap of logic to figure out how Emma had come by those objects.

But what sort of person *did* that?

He was trying not to be judgmental about it. A lot of people in Los Angeles slept around and, in fact, Cooper had a couple of partners who had fallen into that category before they'd married. God knew Cooper would be a hypocrite to think he was somehow better than that—he'd been through his share of women in his life.

But there was something very disturbing in taking things from one's conquests like little trophies.

Cooper woke up cranky and tired. He didn't want to go skiing, but he was too much a guy's guy to let Luke down. He'd do it, he'd go, he told himself, and then he'd get the hell out of Pine River. He'd take that goddamn medal back to Carl and tell Michael or Jack they had to handle the event up here. Not him. He was going to put the distance of space and time between him and the girl who had, against all odds, crawled under his skin to bite him.

>−+◆>−○−◆+−◁

Luke was in a good mood when he picked up Cooper and chatted on the way to the ski valley about everything and nothing. Fortunately, his enthusiasm for the day didn't require a lot of interactive conversation from Cooper beyond the occasional grunt of agreement or a yes or no.

He couldn't push Emma from his mind.

She was a beautiful, gorgeous, puzzle of a woman. Cooper had never been the type to think too long about personalities or idiosyncrasies. People were what they were, and he never bothered to examine it. But Emma? How weird, how unhappy, how extraordinary could one woman be? He wanted a woman as beautiful as Emma to be reasonable, to have all those things going for her that would make her a perfect mate.

And why did he want that? Why did he need ordinary? Wouldn't that bore him after a time? Didn't it always? Jill was pretty and accomplished and a great hostess (which she'd pointed out to him more than once) and would be a great mother. And yet, there had been something missing for Cooper in that relationship. Jill's perfection held no intrigue for him.

Emma Tyler was the other extreme, however, and not in a good way.

There had always been something about her that had set her apart from all the other gorgeous blondes in LA, but who would have guessed it was something so bizarre? She'd seemed secure to him before this week, but now, he'd describe her as floating without a rudder.

He was granted a reprieve from the endless loop of thoughts in his head when they reached the ski area and strapped on the sticks. It was great snow, great runs, and it was a good and solid diversion from the strange week he'd spent in Pine River. At the end of the day, he and Luke dined on steaks and beer and relived every turn on every run.

At the end of the meal, Luke brought up Emma. "Maddie said you were out at the ranch yesterday," he'd said as they waited for the check. "That you and Emma came together and left together."

"Yep," Cooper said.

"So did you get what you came for?" Luke asked, looking down.

Cooper got more than he had come for, so much more he didn't even know what he had now. "Yeah," he said. "She had it."

Luke looked up. "What now?" he asked. "Are you leaving our little slice of heaven in Pine River?"

Cooper thought of the moment he'd opened his eyes and seen Emma standing at the living room window in that shirt, and the way she'd climbed on top of him, the soft look in her eye that was so different than anything he'd seen from her yet. "I'm going back to LA in the morning," Cooper said. "A couple of days there, and then I'm off to Texas to help my mom with the holidays."

"Bummer," Luke said. "There should be some good snow between now and Christmas. Hey, if you're back this way at the end of the year, I'd love to have you at our wedding." Luke smiled. "I should qualify that by saying that I'm not actually authorized to extend that invitation . . . but I think I can pull a few strings."

Cooper laughed. "Thanks. But I doubt I will make it."

"Nevertheless," Luke said, waving a hand. "It's going to be a small wedding. I'll put you on the list just in case." He reached for his wallet as the waitress deposited the check.

＞━┼◆＞━◯━＜◆┼━＜

The next morning, Cooper was up at dawn, eager to get out of the Beaver Room and Pine River. He figured that if he reached Denver by three o'clock, he could catch a flight to LA and still make cocktail hour at Marnie and Eli's house. It was a four-hour drive to Denver; he had plenty of time.

Cooper packed up the rental car and headed out on Main Street. At the end of the street, he turned right, toward the old Aspen Highway. The route took him past the city park and the bench where Emma sat in the afternoons, watching the kids.

He thought about her knit cap and the long strands of blond hair spilling out from beneath it.

Cooper turned at the next corner and drove around the block, coming up to a stop sign directly across from the park. It was empty; it was cold this morning, the sun made bleak by a thin gray haze that had overtaken the sky. He could imagine Emma sitting on that peeling bench, watching kids play. He recalled with a small shiver how angry, how *livid* he'd been when he'd seen her sitting there a couple of days ago. And yet, at the same time, he'd felt a sense of isolation and loneliness in her as he'd strode to that bench to confront her. Maybe he was reading something into her that wasn't there. She certainly deserved his disdain, but Cooper couldn't shake the feeling that she deserved compassion, too.

He was loathsomely familiar with that incongruent feeling— he'd had it many times for Derek. No matter how charming Derek had been over the years, or the promises he'd make and break, or the assurances that this time, he really had changed, Cooper could always sense that it wasn't so. He truly believed it was beyond Derek's ability to change. It wasn't like Cooper was clairvoyant or anything like that, but he had a strange sixth sense about certain people. He had it about Derek, and he had it about Emma.

Cooper glanced at his watch. He should go, get on a plane, get the hell out of here and away from crazy. But when he put the car in gear, he turned back into town and drove down Main Street to Elm.

Emma's car was not at the Kendrick house. Cooper drove on, to the end of the street, and turned west. Not toward Denver. Toward Homecoming Ranch. He gave a stern talking to himself on the drive up to the ranch. This was a stupid thing to do. Emma wasn't his problem, so what was the point of this? What the hell was he doing?

He liked her, that was what. It was hard to admit to himself because she was so enigmatic and peculiar. Was it because she was beautiful? Was this infatuation because his body snapped to attention every time he looked at her? Was he so shallow? Or was it something deeper than that?

When he turned into the gates at the ranch, he noticed a couple of men were down in the meadow, working on the fence. Cooper drove up and pulled into the circular drive. He stepped out of his car, shoved his hands in his pockets for warmth, and looked around. Wind chimes were tinkling somewhere nearby, and the breeze was chilly. He looked at the house, expecting the sisters to spill out, the dogs to come out from under the porch, to see a tail of smoke rising from the chimney. But the house was silent.

Cooper glanced around. He felt a little foolish being here after all that had gone on between them. A glutton for punishment. A boy with no game, no head for women. But Cooper also knew if he didn't do something, if he didn't reach for her now, he never would, and Emma . . . well, he feared what would happen to Emma if he, or someone, didn't grab her.

SEVENTEEN

Emma filled each dog bowl with a cup and a half of kibble while the four dogs sat anxiously, each of them drooling, awaiting the signal that they were allowed to eat. As she filled Roscoe's bowl, she thought she heard something outside and paused.

Roscoe whimpered.

"Yeah, okay," she said, and finished filling the bowls. "Eat," she said, and the four dogs lunged for their individual bowls.

She sealed the lid to the bucket of dog food—which they now had to keep in the house, as Rufus had chewed a hole through a lid—and pulled on her mittens. She picked up the bucket and walked outside the garage, strolling toward the house, her mind miles away. In sunny California. With a pair of gray eyes. The strain of having Cooper discover her awful secret had taken a toll—Emma felt as if she were moving in a fog, her life as she'd known it fading away, and a new, harsh light spilling down on her.

A movement caught her eye as Emma moved slowly past her car. She glanced up and stopped midstride. Cooper was on the porch, peering through a window. Only then did she see his car, parked just behind hers.

He turned and started down the steps. He'd only managed one stair when he noticed Emma.

Her pulse began to pound. She put her hand to her head and her knit cap, then self-consciously looked down at the big coat she wore, the rain boots she'd donned to walk down to the barn. *Why was he here?* He had what he wanted, he'd been so disgusted—

Emma suddenly panicked and dropped the bucket. The sound of it hitting the hard ground startled her and she said, "What the hell are you doing here?"

"Hey," he said, and put up his hands, palms out, almost like he was surrendering.

"I thought you left. Did you come alone? Who else is here?" she exclaimed, and whirled around, turning a complete circle, expecting someone to leap out at her. *Who, Carl?* That made no sense.

Cooper lowered his hands. "It's just me, Emma. Calm down. I was hoping we could talk a moment."

"No," she said flatly, backing away, her foot knocking into the bucket she'd dropped. *"Why?* About what? We've said all there is to say. I mean *you* certainly have, and I damn sure don't have anything else to say."

"Just humor me," he said, taking a step forward.

Humor him? "Are you kidding? I am completely humiliated, Cooper! What more do you want?"

"I don't want that. I never wanted that," he said firmly. "The medal is behind us," he said with a flick of his wrist. "It is what it is. But I . . . I really want to talk to you." He seemed a little anxious, almost uncertain. As if he wasn't sure why he was here.

His uncertainty only made it worse for Emma. She felt like a leper. She wanted to die, to crawl under the porch or a car until he left. "God, Cooper, do you have to drag this out?" she pleaded, pressing her mittened hands to her temple. "Please, just *say* it, whatever it is you think you have to say and leave me *alone*."

"Could we go inside?" he asked, jerking his thumb at the house. "It's cold as hell out here."

"No! The last time I saw you, you threatened to have me arrested. You *abducted* me."

"I didn't—" Cooper sighed. "I'm not abducting you. I'm *asking* you. I only suggested we go inside because it's freezing."

Emma didn't know what to do. She didn't want to go inside, didn't want to hear whatever he felt the need to say to her now that she'd been exposed. She folded her arms, debating.

"You do that a lot, you know."

Emma looked around her. "Do what?"

"Fold your arms across your body like that. You do it when you're unsure. It's like you're protecting yourself. But you don't need to fear me, Emma. Let's go inside."

How did he see that? Emma dropped her arms. "No. There is nothing left to say, nothing to talk about."

Cooper ran a hand over his head. "Okay. If you're uncomfortable with the idea of the house, what about the garage? Or the barn? We can even sit in my car if you want. Give me fifteen minutes, Emma. What have you got to lose?"

He had a point—she'd already lost herself completely. But why did he care? "I don't understand why you're being so *weird*."

He actually smiled a little. "I find it highly ironic that you, of all people, would say that."

He was right—it was ironic. Emma frowned. She folded her arms again. "Okay, seriously," she said, calmer now. "What do you want? Why did you drive all the way out here? I mean, I lied, I fessed up, you were disgusted, and you left. So *go* already."

"Because I've had time to think. Because I want to smooth things out between us before I go. I don't want to leave it like . . . like it is, Emma. Who knows when we might run across each other again and work an event?"

"I quit, remember? I won't be back in LA, so you don't have to worry about it."

"God, you're stubborn," he said. "Never say never. You know as well as I that you could end up in LA again. Surely you eventually have to work again. I don't want to stumble across you at some event and it be so strange that we're both uncomfortable. Where's the harm? Fifteen minutes."

"We hardly know each other, Cooper. We're not going to see each other."

"We *obviously* know each other," he scoffed.

Emma ignored that. "Is this an intervention?" she demanded. "Did you swoop up here to put a friendly arm around me and tell me everything is okay?"

"I have no idea what all I want to say, but I am pretty sure that 'everything is okay' is not on the list. Let's go inside and talk about this like adults."

"Not until you tell me why!" she demanded.

"Because I care!" he shouted, casting his arms wide. "That's it, Emma! That's all there is—God help me, I don't know why, but I *care* about you!"

Emma's heart slipped from its mooring, then struggled to swim back to safety. She stared at this man, this gorgeous hunk of kryptonite, unable to absorb what he'd just said. "Care . . . about me?" she asked, to be doubly sure she hadn't misunderstood him.

He sighed and held out his hand to her. "Yes, Emma. *You.*"

She looked at his hand.

"I promise not to harass you. I promise not to abduct you. And I promise to leave soon—I have a plane to catch today."

"No lectures?" she asked uncertainly. "No judgments, no condemnations, no surprises?"

"Do I need to draw blood, too? I promise."

He *cared* about her? That seemed so . . . impossible. But at that moment, Emma's heart was racing so badly she was in danger of taking flight. She didn't believe him. She was afraid to believe him. But those words, *I care about you,* banged around in her head with such a clatter that she couldn't ignore them.

She had no idea what to say to that, and she wasn't going to risk speaking and saying something completely wrong. So Emma dipped down and retrieved her bucket, then clomped up the steps, brushing past him without making eye contact. She was afraid to look at him, afraid he'd laugh or disappear if she did. She walked to the door and opened it, then held it open. Only then did she dare to look back at him.

Cooper was quick to grab the door and follow her inside.

Emma dumped the bucket and her boots and stalked into the living room. She was on edge—no one ever said they cared about her, and she was alarmed by how ill-equipped she was to even believe it, much less accept it.

She yanked the mittens from her hands and the knit cap from her head and tossed them down, then unzipped her down coat. She shrugged out of that and threw it onto the couch, too, and turned around to face Cooper. "Okay. You've got five minutes. Start before I change my mind." She punched her hands to her waist and lifted her chin, as if she was preparing for a fight.

Cooper sighed a little. "Does it really make you so uncomfortable for someone to say they care?"

How did he know that? "I just find this all a little suspicious."

Emma unthinkingly folded her arms again—until she realized what she was doing and dropped them. "I mean, what, you just woke up this morning after being furious and thought, 'Yeah, I care about her'? No way."

"No, it wasn't like that." Cooper shook his head. "Look, I'll be honest—I was intrigued by you at the bat mitzvah," he said, looking at her pointedly. "You weren't wrong about my interest in you that night."

Emma's eyes widened. "So you really *did* follow me here like Carl's lap dog!"

"Wrong," he said, frowning. "I didn't *follow* you, I looked for you. I didn't come because of the bat mitzvah. I came because Carl paid me a lot of money to find and retrieve that medal."

"And now you have it. So I'm guessing you're no longer intrigued. Which makes you what? Disgusted? Repulsed? Did you come back out here to get a really good look at this train wreck"—she gestured to herself—"so you can go back and tell your friends?"

He recoiled a little as he took her in. "Are you always so hard on yourself?"

"Yes! Does that bother you?"

"What bothers me," he said, "is that I can't wrap my head around why you would take things from men." He threw up a hand before she could cut him off. "I know it's not my business, I know I'm prying. But I want to know. I want to understand why. Because I'm *still* intrigued with you. Even more so now that I know you're not just another pretty face."

"Oh my God! I don't believe you!"

"Here's the thing—if no one asks, if no one challenges you, then you end up going down a path so far that I don't know if you can come back. I would hate to see that happen, Emma. So I am asking you as a friend."

He looked sincere, but Emma was shaking, mortified to her core. "Don't waste your time," she said low. "There is nothing to figure out."

"That's not true," he said quietly.

She felt her entire body sag with the weight of her dysfunction. How could she ever explain it? "Don't, Cooper," she pleaded. "Don't try and get involved. I am begging you. Because I will probably let you, and you'll end up disappointed. Whatever is going on with me is *really* messed up."

His gaze did not waver from her. "I happen to be pretty good at messed up."

"No, you aren't," she said weakly. "Even your brother can't prepare you for someone like me. You should go back to LA and forget about this."

Cooper shifted closer. "I did want to go back to LA yesterday. I wanted to get as far from you as I could possibly get."

Yes, she had seen that in his face yesterday, and it was painful to remember. She winced and glanced down.

"I thought that I had known women like you all my life, women who will take from and use men without batting an eye."

Who knew truth could sting so bad when it mattered most? No wonder everyone hated Emma's truthfulness. "That's what I've been trying to tell you," she admitted weakly. "I take and I use."

Cooper shook his head and stepped closer. He was just before her now, his presence strong and confident, while she felt like a jumbled mess of nerves. "But then I cooled down and I thought about it, and I don't believe it. I don't know why you do . . . *that*," he said, gesturing to space, apparently unable to find a word for what she did, "but I don't believe that you are really the kind of woman you present to the world."

"Yes, I am. I am *exactly* what you thought I was yesterday," she said, and poked him hard in the chest. "Don't try and romanticize me."

"It's hardly romantic," he said quietly, and impulsively reached out and pulled a tress of her hair from her collar.

She shoved his arm away from her, frantic that he not touch her. "You can't help, Cooper! What kind of trip are you on? You want to figure me out?" She suddenly shoved both hands against his chest. "I *do* it—I use men!" She shoved him again. "But don't get your hopes up, because I don't always *sleep* with them. Believe it or not, it's not a sex thing, it's anything *but* a sex thing. You want to know the whole ugly truth? It's all about my father! It's all about getting older men to pick *me*, to choose *me*," she said angrily, shoving him again. "It's about control! Anyone with a brain and a current copy of *Psychology Today* can see that! So are you satisfied?" she asked, shoving him again, harder still, the fury sparking in her, building, morphing into a monster inside of her. It was fury with herself for ever having allowed this to happen. Fury for ever having believed Grant or Laura, for ever letting their affair screw her up so completely. Emma hated herself for it, despised, loathed, *hated* herself. "Okay, so you've made me say it, you've made me humiliate myself even more." She balled up her fist, hitting him as hard as she could in the chest.

He didn't move.

She hit him again.

Cooper didn't even blink.

Why didn't he move? Why didn't he speak? She shoved him again with all her might and glared at him, looking for the reaction of disgust.

There was none. "It's okay," he said calmly. "I'm strong enough to take it. I'm strong enough for you, Emma Tyler."

No, no, no one was strong enough for her! No one could endure her, and Emma despised Cooper for thinking he could. She cried out and launched herself at him with both fists, pounding them into his chest. Cooper caught her hands, easily held them. "Is that it?" he asked. "Or is there more?"

"Shut up," she said, her voice shaking. "Shut *up*." She launched again, but this time . . . *this time*, her lips met his.

Emma did not know how she went from fury to kissing him. It happened so quickly, in the space of a second. She had definitely intended to inflict pain and suffering—but then her arms were around his neck.

Cooper grabbed her up, his arms sliding around her waist to hold her tightly to him. He kissed her with as much fire as she kissed him, their tongues tangling, their hands sliding up and down each other's bodies. They kissed like long-lost lovers, two people who had been searching for each other all their lives, and Emma would not have been surprised if the house had opened up and rain had poured down on them, just like the movies.

He lifted his head, impulsively kissing the palm of her hand that had somehow found his face. "Where is everyone?" he asked roughly as he nuzzled her neck.

"Town," she murmured, and pushed her knee in between his legs, against his erection. Cooper grabbed her up again, lifting her off her feet and kissing her, then walked with her and fell onto the couch. He pressed his lips against her cheek, her eyes, and her mouth again. "I've been fighting it," he said breathlessly, his eyes roaming her face. "I've been fighting wanting you."

"Me too," she admitted, and pulled his head to hers. She dipped her tongue between his lips, into his mouth, and sparked a prurient wave crashing through her, shoving her out onto a churning sea of pure, unadulterated desire. It was fantastically electric.

Cooper rolled onto his back, pulling Emma on top of him, his hands on either side of her head, his mouth on hers, and on her face, her ears and neck. He devoured her lips and her tongue while his hands explored her body, her breasts, the curve of her hip. His hands moved on her body, but there was something different about this. It took Emma a moment to realize what it was. Cooper kept looking into her eyes. He kept looking at *her*. He wasn't groaning over her body, he wasn't rutting on her. He was actually looking at her.

That realization charged Emma even more, and she was now ravenous for him. Their surroundings—the ranch house, the smell of old smoke, the moan of wind in the rafters—began to fade away. Emma was only aware of Cooper, the scent of his skin, the way he held her, touched her, his movement effortless, the tender look in his eyes. She felt nothing but his taut skin, the hardness of his erection, and the damp heat between her legs.

Their clothing came off, piece after piece tossed away until they were naked. Emma gasped in Cooper's ear as he squeezed her nipple between his fingers, and pressed harder against him, stretching her body the length of his, and it still wasn't enough. Not nearly enough. She had never wanted a man like she wanted him.

Cooper twisted again, putting her on her back on that couch and coming over her, taking her breast in his mouth. Emma was moving without conscious thought, her hands on him, her eyes meeting his, expecting to see the lust dim them. But his gaze remained completely focused on her.

Her body raged for him to be inside her, a new, electric feeling, because Emma never *wanted* sex. But with Cooper, everything had tilted. She was surely imagining things, because she felt as if he was looking past her body, as if he were looking directly into her. He could *see* her.

She wrapped her hand around his cock and began to move. Cooper braced himself and looked down at her. His breathing was uneven, his hair a mess. He surveyed her body, unabashedly looking at every inch of her, one hand trailing behind his gaze. "You're beautiful, Emma," he said with genuine appreciation. "I know that's not news to you," he said, his fingers splaying across her breast. "But you should hear it all the same. You are beautiful inside and out."

That remark made her heart flutter. Emma smiled with pleasure. "You're beautiful, too," she said, and swept her hands up his chest, across his pecs. "You're kryptonite."

"What?" he said, his gaze on her body again, taking in every curve, every exposed patch of her skin.

"Kryptonite," she whispered. Her arms went around his neck, and she pressed her breasts against his chest. She opened her legs to him, one of them hooking around his back. She pressed against him warm and wet, and felt herself unravel completely, caught up in her torrential desire. He slid the tip of his erection into her, and she could feel his heart beating in his chest, the steady rhythm of it on her breast. He skimmed lower, over her breasts, his hand floating down her side and across her belly, then down again, between their bodies, stroking her as he slowly pushed deeper inside her.

Emma sighed with longing and arched her neck, shifting beneath him, opening wider to his body and his hand. Cooper began to move in her, sliding in and out. Emma was falling away, the cracks in her foundation splitting open, letting Cooper seep into her and burn her with an intensity she'd never felt, as if his heat was branding her. She moved against him, her body rising to meet his, urging him to move harder and faster. Her hands gripped at him, clutching him, holding on to him with the strength of a drowning woman.

He was so hard, so hot, moving in her with unstoppable force. And Emma kept pressing back, kept digging her fingers into his hips, drawing him deeper inside her, wanting all of this, everything he had. She was panting, nearing her climax. Just before she came, Cooper took her chin in his hand and said, "Let me see you."

That was it, the thing that tipped her over the edge. Emma cried out, arched her back, and a moment later, waves of pleasure crashed over Cooper, spilling hot and thick inside her.

He collapsed beside her, completely spent, his breathing as ravaged as hers. A few moments passed before she awkwardly, but meaningfully, twined her fingers in his hair, then drew a long line down his spine.

"You better not," he said.

"Better not what?" she murmured, and kissed his shoulder.

Cooper lifted himself up, his eyes the color of a storm. She could fall into those eyes and stay there, bobbing around without a care in the world.

"You better not take anything from me. Because this," he said, stroking her cheek, "is not *that.*"

Emma smiled. She opened her mouth to speak . . .

But the sound of a car on the drive startled them both into action.

EIGHTEEN

They scrambled around the living room, both gathering up boots and jackets and clothes as they dashed upstairs. Emma could hear the slam of car doors, could hear Libby and Madeline's voices on the drive as she and Cooper slipped into her room.

She heard the front door open as she pushed Cooper inside her room, then quietly, *slowly,* shut her door so that the hinges wouldn't squeak. She turned around and put her back to it, then covered her mouth with both hands as laughter erupted. She slid down to her bottom, doubled over with the laughter she wouldn't allow to escape.

Cooper joined her there, his back against the wall, a grin on his face. His chest was still damp with the sweat of their lovemaking, and his hair looked as if a rake had been dragged through it.

"Emma!" one of the women shouted. "Are you here?"

Emma buried her face in Cooper's shoulder to stifle her laugh.

There was the sound of plodding footsteps on the stairs, the movement of feet down the hall toward her room.

"Is she up there?" Libby shouted from the bottom of the stairs.

Emma and Cooper stilled as Madeline stopped just outside the door.

"I don't think so!" Madeline called back, so close that it made Cooper jump. Emma put her hand over his mouth, her finger to her lips, warning him to be quiet.

A moment later, Madeline walked away. "She's not here," she called down to Libby. "Maybe they went down to the bunkhouse." Her steps faded away as she jogged downstairs again.

Cooper slowly pulled Emma's hand away from his mouth. "You're a grown woman," he whispered. "Why are you hiding?"

"Trust me," she said with a smile. "They won't talk about anything else if they know. Plus, you're naked." She reached for his shirt and tossed it to him. Cooper stood, giving her a view of his mouthwatering physique. Had the sex they'd just had been as spectacular as it had felt? Thinking about it made Emma feel a little wonky now, unsteady on her feet. It occurred to her that the things she'd felt only moments ago were things to be feared—how far would the fall be from that pinnacle?

She gained her feet and padded across the room to a bureau. She opened one drawer, found some panties and a T-shirt, and donned them. She reached down and picked up his jeans, holding them out to Cooper. He finished buttoning his shirt and ignored the jeans—he wrapped his arms around her and held her head against his chest. "Come back to LA with me," he said.

What? Was he crazy? Did he think anything could really come from a romp on a couch at Homecoming Ranch? "I can't."

"Why not?"

She put her hand on his waist and pushed away from him. "Because. I don't have a job. And I'm needed here. Madeline is getting married. *Leo* needs me."

"Emma . . ." Cooper cupped her face. "Madeline will get married and get on with her life. And Leo . . ."

Emma's gaze narrowed.

Cooper didn't state the obvious. "I want to see you."

"What are you doing?" she asked, closing her eyes for a moment. "I *can't,* Cooper. You know I can't. My life is too complicated right now."

"I don't care," he said, and kissed the corner of her mouth.

Emma's eyes fluttered shut.

"There is no one like you. And, I think I can help you."

"*Help* me?"

"Help you sort things out."

Her heart leapt painfully, and so did Emma, jerking out of his arms, putting some space between them. He thought he could help her? The moment Cooper *saw* her, the moment he understood how bad she was, he would leave her. How could he not? And this time, Emma wouldn't be able to bear it. "Has it occurred to you that maybe I don't *want* help?"

He stared at her, surprised. "What's the matter? Didn't this," he asked, gesturing between the two of them, "mean anything to you?"

Everything. It meant everything. But Emma, the girl who had been told all her life she was nothing special, who had been rejected by her father more than once, who led men on and then stole their trinkets, couldn't even fathom the possibilities of it. So she said the only safe thing she could say. "Not really."

Cooper looked as if she'd slapped him. Stunned. Hurt. Confused.

"Cooper, listen," she said, and pressed her hands against her heart, one on top of the other. To hold it in, to protect it. "I told you, I can't do ordinary things. I can't be in an ordinary relationship. I can't do ordinary love. What you think I am? What you think you see? It's not real. It's just your idea of real. Think about what I *do.* Think about all the things you've heard me say."

"My God, you are messed up," he said, his voice full of awe.

"Yeah, I know," she said, nodding. "That's what I'm saying. I'm also honest, and I'm being totally honest with you right now. That's why I said you are my kryptonite. It's sick and weird, and you should do yourself a favor and go back to LA before it gets *really* weird."

"Goddammit, Emma!" Cooper exclaimed angrily. She tried to shush him, but he ignored her. "Why are you so down on yourself? Why do you reject something before you've even had a chance to think about it? Do you *like* to hate yourself? Do you *like* being a slut? Do you *like* having no one to rely on?"

Daggers, one by one, he shoved daggers into her. But Emma knew herself too well. "I just know who I am."

"Bullshit. There's no room for personal growth? For a different interpretation of who you are? Of exploring another facet of *you*?"

Was there room for that? Emma thought of the kisses they'd shared, of the lovemaking on the couch, and how explosive it had been. She thought of how she wanted to do that again and again, feel that heat in her blood, feel that connection to another human being. Of how devastated she would be when he left. No, there was no room.

Cooper slipped two fingers under her chin, forcing her to look up. "You don't have to do this with me. Not *me*. I know who you are—I saw you that night in Beverly Hills. I saw you today. I have seen you with Leo. Yes, you've got some really strange shit going on, but there is more to you than that. Whatever it is that makes you do what you do, I don't know, but you don't have to hide from me. I'm trying to tell you I will help you deal."

"I'm not hiding—"

"The hell you aren't," he said. "You hide behind sarcasm; you put distance between you and everyone who tries to get close. I get that you've had some rough things happen in life, that maybe the world isn't as easy for you as it is for someone else. But there is a lot of life stretching in front of you, Emma, and you don't have to keep living this way."

She wished she could believe that, or even just hope for it. But she'd lived too many years in her skin to dismiss it just because they'd had great sex. "Do you know how crazy you sound right now?" she said, exasperated. "A guy like *you*? A guy who could be with anyone he wanted to be with? And you're going to choose someone like *me*? You're crazy! Maybe *you're* the one with issues!"

"I'm not crazy; I'm *into* you. What's wrong with that? Why can't you believe it?"

He was scaring her now. He wasn't thinking, he wasn't understanding how bizarre her life had become. "Cooper, we had a thing! Don't read so much into it, okay? I'm not a nice person. I'm not going to magically turn into someone you'll want to be with. This isn't *Pygmalion*. You can't remake me!"

His face darkened. "Thanks for telling me what I want," he said. "Maybe you should think a little more about what *you* want. You keep telling yourself that you're no good, and baby, it will become the truth."

She stared at him, her mind whirling. "I'm not going back to LA."

Cooper ran his hand over his head. He took the jeans she was holding and pulled them on, then reached for his boots. "I like you," he said angrily. "Goddammit, I don't know why, but I like you a *lot*." He yanked on his second boot and stood up, towering over her. "You don't scare me, Emma. You don't put me off. I'm offering you a chance at something *different*. Something meaningful. So I'll be in LA if you ever wake up." He started for the door.

"Wait! What are you doing? Where are you going?"

"I have a plane to catch," he said curtly, and yanked open the door, striding out of her room and down the hall.

"Cooper!" she cried, but he was already on the stairs.

She didn't go after him; she was frozen. She heard Madeline or Libby cry out with surprise or alarm, their voices rising up almost as one as they pummeled Cooper with questions. Emma heard the rumble of Cooper's voice outside, then Libby and Madeline again. It all sounded so far away from her. Miles and miles from her.

Emma remained standing where Cooper had left her, swaying a little, light-headed with grief and confusion. Her mind was racing as fast as her heart; she was unable to grasp any thought other than *stupid girl. Stupid, stupid girl.*

Emma liked Cooper a lot, too. But she was terrified of disappointing him. How could she not? Eventually, he would see her in all her glory. *Not that cute. Brass tacks coming out of her mouth. An inability to grasp social nuances. Issues with sex.* He would recoil, he would back away. He would leave her! He would choose someone else!

She had done the right thing, rejecting his offer. He didn't know it, but she'd done the right thing. Hadn't she?

She could hear Madeline or Libby coming up the stairs, heard one of them calling her name. Emma sank down onto her bed, her gaze fixed on the floor.

"Emma?" It was Libby beside her, pushing her hair out of her face. "Hey, are you all right?"

"I'm fine."

"I mean is everything okay?" Libby asked, crouching down beside her. Madeline had come in, too, was hovering near the door as if she was uncertain whether to stay or go. "We saw Cooper leave. We didn't know you guys were up here."

"Well, now you know."

Libby put her hand on Emma's knee. "Did something happen? Do you want to talk about it?"

Emma pushed her hair from her face and looked at Libby's pale blue eyes. *Yes,* she wanted to talk about it. She wanted to tell them what had happened, to hear it all again. She wanted someone to know how much she was hurting right now. But Emma couldn't do it. Years of conditioning would not release their hold on her, and she couldn't make herself admit what had happened.

"I can't . . . I can't really talk about it," she said, sounding slightly apologetic.

Libby sighed and exchanged a look with Madeline. That *look*! That *I knew it, I told you so* look.

"Okay, Em." Libby stood up and walked to the door.

"It's not that I don't want to talk about it," Emma tried to explain. "I just can't."

"Come down," Madeline said, and she touched Libby's shoulder, as if Libby were the injured one, as if Libby had just sent her best hope for happiness storming out the door. "I'll make some coffee."

Madeline and Libby disappeared.

Emma looked to the ceiling and blinked back tears. She hated what she'd grown up to be, but damn if she knew how to change it.

She took a breath and looked down. She turned her hand palm up and opened her fingers, stretching them. She'd held her hand in a fist for the last quarter of an hour, since the moment she picked up Cooper's jeans and handed them to him. She stared, heartbroken, at the St. Christopher charm she'd taken from his pocket.

NINETEEN

Cooper called Michael from the Denver airport and asked him to pick him up at LAX when the flight arrived.

"Perfect. Audrey is doing a show at the Wiltern tonight, and she and Jack are throwing a party afterward," Michael said, referring to Jack's pop-star wife, Audrey LaRue. "You can come with us."

"I'm not dressed for that," Cooper said, looking down at his jeans and boots. Not to mention he wasn't in the mood for it.

"Dude, it's the Wiltern. Text me when you land."

A few hours later, Cooper walked out of the LAX terminal. Leah, a vivacious brunette with short, bouncy hair, leapt out of a vehicle and threw her arms around Cooper as if he'd been gone for months instead of days. "I'm so glad you're back! Braden and Brodie keep asking where Uncle Boober has gone."

"What have you done with those hoodlums?" Cooper asked, bending over to peer into the back of the SUV Michael now drove. Gone were the sports convertibles he'd once favored.

"With their nanny," Leah said, and did a little dance move. "'Cuz Mommy's got her party face on!" She grabbed Cooper's hand and did a twirl beneath it, then opened the back door and hopped in.

"Leah, I'll sit there," Cooper said.

"Nope. I'm sure Michael is going to interrogate you about the potential to break your necks, so I'm going to check some e-mail. Go on, Cooper, get in the front and leave me alone," she said playfully, her gaze already on her phone.

Cooper sighed and glanced at Michael.

Michael eyed him curiously, a Cheshire grin on his face. "I wasn't going to interrogate you, but now I am. You looked pissed, bro," he said, and took Cooper's bag, tossing it in the backseat next to his wife.

"Not pissed," Cooper said. *Pissed. So pissed.* "Tired."

"Sure," Michael said, and fist-bumped Cooper's shoulder, smiling a little as he walked around to the driver's side of the SUV.

Michael started in on Cooper the moment they pulled away from LAX. "What happened in Colorado?"

What happened in Colorado? An invisible rug had been jerked out from beneath him, that was what. A rug Cooper hadn't even realized was there until he found himself flat on his ass. That was the thing that had eaten at him on the flight to Los Angeles—not, as one might expect, the way Emma had sent him on his merry way after some of the most incredible sex he'd had in his life—but that he didn't even *know* he'd held this torch for Emma Tyler all these months. Had he really been so smitten that night in Beverly Hills?

And yet, when he'd seen her at the door at Homecoming Ranch, he'd felt a familiar reverberation in his membranes. A recalled ache, a resurrected attraction.

"Yo—Coop?"

"Nothing happened," Cooper said, startled back to the present. "I checked out Trace Canyon. It looks perfect for what we want."

"Oh yeah?" Michael said.

That's how you handled men—give them some sport to talk about, and they were happy to push aside the nasty business of feelings. Michael asked a lot of questions about Pine River and Trace Canyon. How sheer was the rock face, how deep the ravines? What sort of access would they have, and how would they get equipment up to the site? All business.

But as they turned on to Wilshire Boulevard, Michael looked at him curiously and said, "Anything else happen?"

"Like what?"

Leah's head suddenly popped up between the bucket seats. "What my husband wants to know, and so do I, is what about Emma Tyler? What's the deal with her? Did she have the thing?"

"The thing!" Michael scoffed.

"The thing, the thing, whatever it was Carl Freeman thought she took?"

"Yes," Cooper said. He'd called Carl earlier to tell him he'd be personally delivering it to him tomorrow.

"Wow," Leah said, and looked at Michael. "Is she really as loony as they say?"

"She's not loony," Cooper said instantly, and then caught himself. Unfortunately, not before Leah and Michael had noticed.

"No?" Michael asked, a big grin spreading his face. Leah punched Michael on the shoulder. "Ouch," he said with a laugh. "So I guess you had some time to talk to Miss Tyler, huh?"

Cooper didn't smile. He couldn't banter his way out of this. "A little," he said, and looked out the window. "Sorry guys, I'm beat."

He knew Leah and Michael were looking at each other again, the silent questions flowing between them. He felt Leah ease back to her seat, and they didn't ask him more, for which Cooper was thankful.

Audrey's concert was already underway when they arrived, and with their backstage passes, Cooper was able to nurse a beer and enjoy her show in solitude. Without a lot of questions, without having to *think*. Audrey's music could do that to him—carry him out of this world. He wasn't the best judge of musical talent, but to his ears, Audrey had the most melodic and sultry voice of anyone on the airwaves.

The after-show party was a typical Jack-and-Audrey event. The who's who of Hollywood was in attendance, but so were regular folk, too. Audrey always made a point of that. Invitations to these high-wattage parties—which Cooper took for granted—were highly coveted because Audrey was a huge pop star. Yet in spite of fame, Audrey was a down-to-earth gal, and she liked to invite people who typically would never have access to this sort of event. Such as the barista at her local coffeehouse, or the middle-aged couple who owned the dry-cleaning shop she used. Tonight, Cooper recognized two girls from the Whole Foods grocery near their offices chatting with the head of Moonglow Records.

Generally, Cooper was right in the thick of things because he enjoyed these events as much as anyone. Tonight, however, he was not in the mood. He wanted to go home, take a shower, find something to eat. He sighed when Eli sidled over to him and said, "Why the long face?"

"I don't have a long face," Cooper said.

"It's so long it's scraping the floor, Coop. Everything all right?"

Cooper looked at his oldest friend. "Everything is fine," he said. "I'm just tired."

"Sure," Eli said, but his gaze was locked on Cooper's.

Cooper swallowed down the rest of his beer. "Derek's getting out," he said. "I'm flying out at the end of the week to help Mom." That much was true. But it was also a lie—Derek wasn't on his mind. Cooper had never lied to Eli that he could recall, but in all honesty, in the last two days, Derek had hardly crossed his mind.

He hated that Eli's expression suggested he knew that wasn't what was bothering Cooper. But he nodded and said, "Ah. I guess it's going to be a tough transition for him."

"Yep."

Eli's eyes narrowed. "Tell him I said hello."

"I will. Thanks," Cooper said.

Eli looked at his beer bottle, then at Cooper again. "Need anything, Coop? Another beer? A friend?"

Eli and Cooper had been friends for so long—more than thirty years now—that Cooper knew Eli wasn't asking if he needed help with Derek. He couldn't help a small chuckle. Couldn't get anything past Eli McCain. He put his hand on Eli's shoulder and squeezed affectionately. "I'm going to take a rain check."

"Whatever you say, chief." Eli touched his bottle to Cooper's and wandered off.

That was it—Cooper was calling a car. He walked out into the hallway, out of the din, to call up the service. There were people there, too, groups of two and three talking away from the music. Cooper pulled out his phone and was about to make the call when someone tapped him on his shoulder. Cooper turned, and looked into the smiling face of Laura Franklin, Emma's stepsister.

"Cooper, right?"

Unbelievable. What was she doing here? What were the odds? "Cooper, right. Hello, Laura," he said, and stuck out his hand.

"Wow," she said with a laugh of surprise as she took his hand and gave it a shake. "This is weird, running into you like this. How'd you get in?"

"Audrey's husband and I go way back," he said. "How about you?"

"My boyfriend!" she said, and pointed to a man down the hall, talking to a couple. "He's a real estate broker. He sold some property to Audrey LaRue's lawyer."

And with that bit of information, Cooper knew exactly the sort of guests Laura and her boyfriend were. Leeches, Jack called them, people who sought out any angle to get into this sort of Hollywood party.

"So, did you find Emma?" Laura asked. "We haven't heard from her, you know. But that's not unusual—Emma's a flake."

Cooper felt a hitch in his heart; she wasn't a flake. Laura said it casually, with a smile on her face. "I found her," he said.

He didn't mean to show any emotion when he said it, but he obviously did, because Laura blinked. And then she smiled wryly. "I take it that it didn't go quite as you hoped? Trust me, you're not alone, Cooper. Welcome to my world."

"It was okay," Cooper said. "She had what I was looking for, so . . ." He shrugged.

"Well, *that* surprises me. Emma's not very forthcoming. I mean, she's forthcoming with her opinions, obviously. But when it comes to her? She won't tell you anything."

Laura was full of information of what Emma was not, and Cooper didn't like it. "Why do you think that is?" he asked, trying very hard to sound casual.

Laura shrugged. "I don't know. Mom says she's jealous."

"Of . . . ?"

Laura laughed. "Of *me*, silly," she said, as if that should be obvious to him. "It's been a problem all our lives. When we were kids, it was manageable, but when we grew up, and boys came into the picture, she got really possessive and really weird." She wrinkled her nose.

Why was she telling him this? She was Emma's sister—she ought to be defending Emma, not piling on.

"I mean, between you and me? Her own family has always been a lot more comfortable around *me* rather than her." She smiled a little.

Cooper was appalled that Laura would casually toss that observation out there, given what had happened between her and Emma. Not to mention Emma's father and her.

Laura smiled curiously at his study of her. "What?"

"Yeah, I've heard just how comfortable some of her family has been around you."

Laura's smug smile faded. She blinked back her surprise. But she didn't deny it. No, Laura Franklin slowly smiled again, as if sleeping with Emma's father was amusing somehow. Her smile was a come-hither smile, too, one meant to seduce. "No one listens to Emma," she said silkily. "But forget her, because you know what? You're cute, Cooper Jessup."

He gave her a dark look, annoyed that she thought he would fall for that.

"No, *really* cute," she said, turning to face him, her shoulder against the wall. "How come you're not married?" She touched the button of his shirt—the same buttons Emma had touched—and began a slow finger walk up his chest. "You could have anyone in LA if you wanted. You can't be so hard up for company that you'd want my sister."

And Emma thought she was the despicable one.

Laura laughed. "Don't look at me like that. Everyone knows how Emma is. I can't help it if her own flesh and blood found her difficult to be around, can I?"

Cooper reached up and pushed Laura's hand from his chest. "Good night, Laura."

"Hey, don't go away mad," she said, reaching for his arm. "I'm not going to tell Emma. Not yet, anyway."

What the hell was wrong with this woman? "Tell her what?"

Laura shrugged. "That we sort of hooked up," she said, and her smile turned cold.

Laura was a bitch. "We're not hooking up. Nowhere close," he said.

"Whatever you say."

He could tell by the slight sneer on her face that she would do exactly what she threatened. She would tell Emma that she'd met him at this party, that they'd connected. She would imply they'd slept together, and on some level, that was more shocking than anything Emma had done. "Why would you do something like that?"

"Why does Emma keep telling everyone I had an affair with Grant?" she shot back. "It wasn't my fault, you know. I was only eighteen. Besides that, we didn't do anything to *her*. What, he wasn't supposed to live his life because she didn't like it?"

"Wow," Cooper said. "Are you a sociopath? Do you pack your heart in ice every night? I mean, you *do* realize you're talking shit about your sister, right?"

"*Step* sister," Laura snapped, and walked away from him.

Cooper stood a moment, unable to move. No wonder Emma's life had spiraled out of control. Her family was as treacherous as anything she could possibly encounter in the rest of the world.

Eventually, Cooper went outside, away from Laura and her betrayal. Which, in the grand scheme of Hollywood, wouldn't even rank on the list of great family betrayals. It made him a little nauseous.

An hour later, Cooper was home at his little house in the Hollywood Hills. He made himself a sandwich and a drink and sat on his terrace overlooking the glittering lights below. His thoughts were with a beautiful blond woman with enough emotional baggage to fill a dump truck.

He told himself it was best he'd left when he did. That it was mountain air that had him thinking there could be more to the story of Emma and Cooper than a chance encounter at a bat mitzvah, or a few days in Colorado.

When he finished his sandwich and drink, Cooper decided he was truly as tired as he felt. He thought he'd have a shower and get a good night's sleep without any beavers looking at him.

Cooper wearily turned on the shower and as the water warmed, he emptied the pockets of his jeans onto his dresser. A few coins, his wallet, his phone. He looked at the little pile in passing, but halfway to the bathroom, he paused. He walked back and studied the contents of his pocket. Something was missing, he thought, although he couldn't think what at first. His wallet was there. His phone. A few bills and some change.

He shrugged and went into the bathroom and got into the shower. As he lathered up, it suddenly came to him. *"No,"* he said, and banged his fist against the glass shower wall. He pushed open the door and stepped out, striding to his dresser. With soap and water dripping from him, he stared down at his pile of things.

His St. Christopher was gone. Cooper didn't have to think about it. He didn't have to wonder if he'd dropped it or forgotten it at the Grizzly Lodge. He knew Emma had taken it, had slipped it out of his pocket in her room. He knew she had added it to her bizarre collection of things. He was another number, another one in a long line of men who meant nothing to her.

Cooper's pulse began to pound with ferocious fury. Hell no, he would not accept this. Emma Tyler would *not* get away with it.

TWENTY

I know it's taken me a while to get back to you about my most excellent adventure to Denver to see the Broncos play the Patriots. I've been dying to tell you everything, but the trip kind of wore me out, and I had another seizure and had to go to the hospital, which of course Dad said was because I had worn myself out, and then he said, "I'm not going to say I told you so, but I told you so." If Emma were here right now, she'd be all like, *I don't understand why people say that. He clearly means to say I told you so*, and I would have to agree. But here's where Dad is wrong—the game didn't make me have a seizure. I mean, I have seizures when I'm not doing *anything*, so you can't really blame it on the Broncos stinking it up.

Anyway, while we were at the hospital, the doctors said they were going to have to put me on a feeding tube because I really can't swallow much anymore, which of course I know, hello! Who do you think has been trying to choke down Dad's homemade gruel?

But this time when they said it, they looked at Dad instead of me. Like I wasn't there.

Or, like because I can't swallow, that must mean I can't speak English anymore. I wanted to tell that doctor that I'm a genius, and I know exactly what it means, because I'm sitting in this body every day, feeling it give up and the life leak out of me. If it weren't so morbid it would be totally awesome that you can actually feel when life is leaving you. It sort of starts in your fingers and toes. It's hard to describe—kind of like a tide going out.

Okay, well anyway, enough of that. The big news is the game!

So we went to Denver, and even at sub-grandpa speed, which, for those of you who don't know, is about two miles an hour, we made it to the Mile High Stadium in time to actually see the game. My friend Dante was stoked, but he had to walk a really long way to our most excellent seats, whereas I was in a chair. Dante could have had a chair, too, but he didn't want to enter the hallowed halls of football that way, and dude, who could blame him? Anyway, I don't know if it was that walk or all the radiation and chemo he's been taking, or maybe it was just that the Broncos sucked, but Dante got like, *really* sick, and he didn't look to me like he loved the game. Maybe he was just completely depressed that the Broncos lost.

I know, *right*? They lost! All my hard work and then the Broncos went and *blew* it.

Don't you think my story would be so much better if they'd won? It would be like one of those cool sports movies where the cancer kid and the MND guy crawl across mountains and desert to see their favorite team play, and their dying wish is that the Broncos win, and everyone in the audience is worried for those two kids because the Broncos are playing the Goliaths, and you think there is no way they can pull it out, and then, in the *last three seconds* the Broncos kick the winning field goal!

Well, *that* didn't happen. The Broncos fumbled just after the two-minute warning and the Patriots scored. But still, Dad and

Buck, the nurse we hired to accompany us to Denver, said it was a really good game, and it was, I guess, if you think a really good game includes *losing*. Which I totally don't.

And you know what else? The skybox wasn't as great as I thought it would be. I mean, it was nice and all, and Dad said the seats were comfortable, and we could see the field. But we couldn't see it better than I could on my big flat screen at home, you know? Plus, I thought there'd be chicks to serve the drinks and snacks, and maybe even a cheerleader or two to rub my head for good luck. You can imagine my extreme disappointment when it was Dad who served the drinks—Orange Crush, of course, because I *insisted*—and potato chips, which Dante's mom had sent with us because they help with his stomach issues, but of course, *I* can't eat.

The Broncos totally let me down, but still, you gotta hand it to me—*I did it*. I made that trip happen. That may not seem like a lot to you, but try accomplishing something like that from the hell I live in every day. I mean, think about it, the only thing I had was my cunning and genius. I couldn't even hold a pencil to make some notes! Look, I'm not bragging, I'm just pointing out, *that's how good I am.*

I'm *super* proud of myself, but I have to be honest here—it made me wonder what else I could have accomplished in life if I hadn't come down with this stupid disease. I mean, I could have been an astronaut! Not that I would have been an astronaut, because the idea of flying around space freaks me out. I'm just saying, I could have been *anything*.

So I was thinking about all this and feeling pretty sorry for myself while I was in the hospital, because a), once again, they gave me a *guy* nurse, which is a total waste of my time, and b), I guess I'm due.

At first, I thought I was just bummed because the Broncos lost to the freaking Patriots (you really can't say that enough, Bronco fans), but then I realized I was mostly bummed because I've been looking forward to that game for so long. I have spent so much time working and planning to make it happen that I haven't had time to think of other, more unpleasant things, you know? Meaning . . . those thoughts that creep into my head when I'm trying to sleep. You know what I mean. You've probably had those thoughts, too, but maybe not as urgently as I have. Like . . . what's it like to die? Will I know I'm dead? Will it hurt? What's it like on the other side? Is Mom going to be there? Did she find Grandpa? What if she's not there, and it's all black? What if it's *nothing* but *darkness*?

I won't lie, I used to worry about that, but I don't anymore. Maybe because lately, I've been having these dreams of running. I'm just running and running, and I'm impressed by how strong my legs are, and amazed that my lungs are working so efficiently, and my heart is steady as a drum, and it feels *good*. No, seriously, it feels *fantastic*. I would run up and down these mountains if I could. Here's something I've never told anyone but you: sometimes, I want to sleep just so I can run.

If you don't run, you should try it. It's totally awesome that your body can do that, and then make you feel so good about it when you're done.

So I was digging my running dreams, and then this weird thing happened. Don't freak out when I tell you this one, but okay, here goes. When I got out of the hospital, Marisol brought over that little stinker Valentina and her *abuela,* her grandmother. Grandma is visiting from Mexico. She comes up from the interior once or twice a year and cleans Marisol's house and makes tamales for Christmas. At least that's the way Marisol talks about it. Her name is Maria, and she doesn't know a whole lot of English, which is cool, because I don't know a whole lot of Spanish other than *hola* and *besame* and *abuela*.

So Granny Maria was sitting in the corner holding the baby

and watching me like an old barn owl while Marisol combed my hair and made me change my shirt because I was wearing one with holes in it. Granny Maria didn't say much, but every once in a while she'd let loose with a string of Spanish, and Marisol would fire right back at her in Spanish like she was mad, and then she'd say something to me like, "My *abuela* likes you."

Well, of course she *likes* me. What's not to like? And I'd say, "That's a whole lot of Spanish to say she likes me," and Marisol would say, "What, you *habla Español* now?"

And so it would go.

Anyway, Granny Maria liked my blue shirt better than my green shirt. Granny Maria thought I should have some *achicoria* in my food because it's good for the liver. My finely tuned thinking skills translated that to chicory, which I thought was hilarious, because if Granny Maria thinks my *liver* is the problem, she's crazier than her batshit gorgeous granddaughter, Marisol. And I promise you, Dad is not going to buy *chicory* without a fight.

Anyway, when they were leaving, Granny Maria waddled over to my chair—let's just say she's obviously enjoyed a *lot* of Marisol's excellent homemade tortillas—and put her hand on my totally useless left arm. She smiled down at me, and she had these really pretty brown eyes, and they looked really deep to me, like there was an ocean or something under there, and she said, "The light, it is very bright for you in the heaven, Leo."

I was like, "*What?* You speak English?"

She didn't say yes or no. In fact, she didn't say anything else in English. She kept smiling at me with those ocean-deep eyes and patted my arm before she waddled out with the baby, firing off in Spanish at Marisol.

I've been meaning to mention to Marisol that if she doesn't watch it with those tortillas, she might end up with her *abuela*'s hips.

Okay, I didn't know what Granny Maria meant at the time, but let me tell you, I was more surprised than anyone when the doctor called my dad a few days later and said my blood work was showing some liver issues. Freaky, right? I told Dad to get some chicory root, and he looked at me like I was crazy, and he fought it like I knew he would, but he did it, and he's grinding it up and putting it in my gruel.

But wait! *That's* not the freaky thing!

So get this—one day, I'm sitting in my room, staring out the window at the birdhouse Sam made and Dad put up so I could see some blue jays—who of course *refuse* to use our birdhouse, like they are staging some sort of birdhouse protest—and it just came to me. I mean, I suddenly felt all warm and gooey inside, and I had this epiphany, and what Granny Maria had said that day just jumped into my head, and I *got* it. It was like a door opened in me somewhere and light streamed in, and *I got it.*

She was telling me that it's not dark on the other side, that there is light, bright warm light. And there are grass and trees and sunflowers and cows and dogs and places to run. And it's all for *me.* There are no chairs, no feeding tubes, no breathing machines. There's light. Lots and lots of light that goes on for infinity. And there's me, running. My arms and legs are moving, and I can breathe and swallow, and I feel so damn *free.*

No shit, I could see all of this in my mind's eye, I could see me running like Luke and I used to run across that meadow up at the ranch, racing each other. But the totally amazing thing is that I could actually *feel* it. I could feel my dead legs pumping and my dead lungs working, and I could feel my smile and I could hear my own laughter. You know what? I was happy. I was *super* happy!

I was *running.*

TWENTY-ONE

The St. Christopher medal did not go into the leather tote bag with the other things; Emma kept it with her. It wasn't like those other meaningless things—she hadn't traded a piece of herself for this one. In fact, this was actually the opposite of that. Cooper had tried to give her a piece of himself, and Emma had refused it. This time, the trinket meant something.

She couldn't even reason why she'd taken it. To cling to a part of him? Whatever the reason, Emma couldn't bear the examination of her motives. She was too appalled by what she'd done.

For the first few days after Cooper had left, Emma kept expecting his call demanding his medal. Oh, she knew he'd figured it out. He'd probably discovered it on the flight to LA. She had no idea what she'd say when he reached her. *Sorry?* No, she wouldn't say that because she wasn't sorry. She was ashamed, and that was not the same thing. *It's mine now?* No, it was definitely his, and she intended to give it back, just as soon as she could.

But the funny thing was, Cooper didn't call. And when he didn't, Emma's anxiety began to ratchet. She questioned everything that had happened between them. He'd said it was his good luck charm, that he'd carried it for years. Didn't he *want* it back? Or was it more like the idea of having a good luck charm appealed, but that actual charm could be replaced? Maybe he'd had a dozen St. Christophers in his lifetime. Maybe he kept a dozen at home in case he lost one.

Or maybe the charm didn't mean as much to him as he'd said, and he couldn't care less if she had it or not. Maybe he really couldn't care less about her, and he'd said those things—those things that were now firmly lodged in her heart—in order to get sex. Could she have really imagined the connection between them? Had she manufactured the thing that had flowed between their fingers and their eyes, turning back on itself and looping again? Was she really so out of touch with the truth of her emotions?

And she suffered the worst doubt—that he was really just like the others. That was more disappointment than Emma could bear, and she hoped to God it wasn't true.

It seemed liked a lifetime had passed since Cooper had left, and since Leo had returned from Denver and the hospital, weaker than before he'd gone, the toll of another seizure evident in the way he looked and felt. Since he'd been back, Emma had lain in bed with Leo, watching TV. He wasn't his usual chatty self, other than his ongoing post-game analysis of why the Broncos lost. But even that— armchair coaching, his favorite pastime—was a chore for him. Emma didn't like the lines of worry around Bob's eyes, or the way Dani chewed her lip when she came to visit. She didn't like that Marisol was coming by every day, standing at the foot of his bed with her hand on Leo's leg. She didn't like any of it. It wasn't fair. It wasn't *fair*.

Fortunately, things were a little more upbeat up at the ranch. Madeline and Libby were completely caught up in the last-minute preparations for Christmas and the wedding. They'd enlisted Tony D'Angelo, the de facto governor of the Homecoming Ranch Veteran's Rehabilitation Center, and a veteran himself, to build a tent awning over the old paddock in case the barn was too small to include their guests and the buffet. Tony didn't like that idea. If it snowed, he said, the tent would collapse. Which prompted Madeline, Libby, and Tony to relentlessly study the weather forecasts on an iPad.

When they weren't trying to predict the weather, they were making things. Libby made sashes for the chairs just like the ones she'd seen in a magazine, and Madeline and Luke were building an arbor under which they would stand for the ceremony. There were mason jars and ribbons and sashes and candles everywhere.

And Emma?

When Emma wasn't with Leo, she was lying on her bed, staring up at the ever-changing mountaintops, thinking of Cooper and of all the things he'd come to represent to her. Hope, for one. Normalcy. Maybe even love.

Emma had never been in love. Not real, deep love. She wasn't even certain that was what she was feeling—what she felt seemed awfully painful to be love.

She thought of all the things she wanted with every bit of her being, but couldn't have. This painful love she was feeling. A home. Someone to come home to, someone to share her life with. *Children.* All of that had seemed out of reach for her for a long time now, locked up tight as a drum in this body and brain and soul she inhabited.

For a week, Emma was lost. For a week, she hardly remembered to eat at all, unless Libby yelled at her and shoved a piece of chicken under her nose. Emma began to understand that she had no direction, and she hadn't had one in ages. When she was a kid, she'd had these ideas of what she would become—a wife, a mother, a fashion model. A famous painter! Which was more amusing than reality, as the idea had sounded romantic to a teenage Emma, even though she'd never shown the slightest bit of talent. But at least she'd been thinking of a future, of a life. It was as if her life had shuddered to a stop the summer she turned seventeen.

How far from that girl she was now. Look at her—she'd quit her job, she'd left Los Angeles, she'd developed a torch, a flaming bonfire of a torch, for Cooper Jessup. She would be twenty-eight years old in a few months with no destination for her life, and worse, a maddening inability to maintain a single relationship. The only thing Emma had going for her was the money she'd saved and some marketable skills in a certain world. But in the greater scheme of things? She had nothing that mattered. She didn't have anyone to care for or who cared about her.

What would she do once Luke and Madeline were married and settled here? Emma presumed they would—they had no place to go until the fate of the ranch was settled. Libby's life had done a dramatic turnaround since last summer. She was happy now, and she was talking about moving in with Sam and maybe buying in to a partnership with Sherry Stancliff at the Tuff Tots Daycare.

None of them had said a word to Emma about her length of stay at the ranch. None of them had asked her to stay. But then again, she'd made it painfully clear she wouldn't be around long.

Because she was going *where* again? To do what?

Maybe she'd head east, she mused. To New York, to bright lights and high society. Surely there was a management company that could use her experience in Hollywood. But . . . but if she went to New York, did that mean she was starting over? Or did that mean she was still hiding, or whatever the politically correct term was for running away? Would she run to London after that? Then Paris? Islamabad, Hong Kong? *When,* Emma whispered to herself, when would she stop? When would she find the courage to stop and face her issues?

Emma didn't have any answers. She lay there, turning the St. Christopher medal over in her hand, reflecting back on a life that had made her afraid of rejection and disappointment. Of wanting her mother's approval and finding nothing but criticism. *You're not as cute as you think you are. You're pretty enough, but Laura is what I would call cute.* Of wanting a father to want her. *I think we should invite Laura to Vegas, don't you, kiddo?* Of believing someone *could* love her and want her, even once they had discovered the person beneath the face. *I care about you.*

Hope could be a cruel bitch.

>─┼─◆>─•─O─•─<◆─┼─◄

Cooper finally called.

Leo was sleeping, and Emma was lying down on the bed in a room that was considered Luke's on those rare occasions he stayed home with his father and brother. When Emma's phone rang, she glanced at the number on the screen. It was an LA area code, and her heart skipped a beat or two. Before she could talk herself out of it, she hit the talk button. "Hello."

"Hello, Emma."

Cooper's voice dripped into her like warm honey, and she closed her eyes, savoring it. *"Cooper,"* she said softly. "How did you get my number?"

"From Luke." He sighed, sounding tired to her. "I'm guessing I don't have to say why I'm calling, do I?"

"No," she said weakly, and opened her eyes. She heard Cooper release a breath and imagined he'd been hoping she would tell him something like, *hey, you won't believe what Libby found in the kitchen.*

"I'm flying through Denver tomorrow on my way to Texas. I'm asking you to bring the medal to me, Emma. My grandfather gave that to me. I've carried it for years."

"I know. Where do you want me to bring it?"

There was another pause, and she wondered if there was something else she was supposed to have said. Perhaps he'd wanted her to deny it, to offer an explanation. What could she say that wouldn't be empty and meaningless to him now?

"The airport, or some place around there. I have a three-hour layover. So you'll bring it?"

Emma held up the medal and looked at it. "You don't have more of them lying around?"

"What?" He made a sound of impatience. "Of course not. But would it matter if I did? It's mine, it belongs to me, and you took it from me. I'm not another notch on your bedpost."

Oh, she didn't blame him for that, but it hurt. He was anything and everything but that. "No, of course not—"

"I don't care what you have to do, but I better see you in Denver tomorrow. My flight arrives at two. I'll text you when I land."

"Cooper, listen, I—"

She heard the unmistakable click of his phone shutting off.

"I think I love you," she whispered, and clicked off her phone. She gripped the St. Christopher in her hand and turned on her side. A tear slid from the corner of her eye to her pillow. Emma wouldn't allow herself to cry more than that single tear. She didn't deserve tears. She hadn't earned them. She'd brought this debacle on herself and there was no room for crybabies in her thoughts.

She had to get her act together and figure things out. And she had to give Cooper back the piece of him she'd taken without asking.

The next afternoon, Emma waited in the cell phone lot at the Denver airport, having left a message for Cooper to text her when he was coming out so she could drive around to the terminal and pick him up. His text in return was brief: *Here.*

"Okay," she said, and steeled herself.

She spotted him instantly, a head taller than most, heart-stoppingly gorgeous, standing on the curb. He had a backpack slung over his shoulder, one hand in the pocket of his black jeans. He was wearing a leather jacket, and under it, a Seattle Seahawks

T-shirt. He had a cap as dark as his hair that he was wearing with the bill to the back.

Emma tried to tamp down her nerves as she pulled up alongside him. He opened the door, tossed in his backpack, and got in.

He took a look at her in her jeans and boots, the turtleneck sweater beneath a down vest. She had braided her hair, and it hung like a rope over her shoulder. Emma smiled a little at his perusal of her, and when she did, Cooper sighed. It sounded full of resignation. He picked up the end of her braid and toyed with it between his fingers. "You're a mess, Emma Tyler."

"Tell me something I don't know," she said, and put the car in gear.

"Where are we going?" he asked as she entered the stream of cars leaving the airport.

"I don't know. Some place to talk, I guess. There are a few restaurants on Tower Road."

"I'm not hungry."

She looked at him and smiled sadly. "Me either, Cooper." But she kept driving in the direction of Tower Road and pulled into the parking lot of a diner. Where else would she take him? A roadside hotel?

The hostess, a girl with straight brown hair and black pants that rode far too low and too tight on her hips, seated them in a booth. Cooper ordered coffee, black. Emma didn't want anything, but she felt bad for the waitress, an older, plodding woman with gray hair and a stained uniform, so she ordered coffee and a slice of cheesecake. The waitress did not appear to appreciate Emma's gesture.

When the waitress had gone, Cooper arched a questioning brow and spread his arms along the back of the booth. "Well? Give it to me," he said. His gray eyes looked like stone.

Emma unwrapped a straw. "I don't want to give it to you."

"It's mine."

"I know," she said. "I stole it from you, remember?"

Cooper groaned and suddenly surged forward. He took his cap off, ran both hands over his head and then reseated his cap. "I would ask you why you did, but I know you won't give me a straight answer. What the hell, I'll ask it anyway," he said, and looked up, his gaze piercing hers. "*Why*, Emma?"

She swallowed nervously. "I guess that's the million-dollar question, isn't it? If I had a really good reason, a good explanation for taking shit, I probably wouldn't take shit, you know? Catch-22."

"That's a cop-out. Give it back."

Emma opened her purse and reached inside for the charm. She reluctantly slid it across the table to him. Cooper picked it up and looked at it. He laid it back down on the table and lifted his gaze to her again.

His disapproving expression made Emma feel very self-conscious. "It's the only one I have. I know it's the right one."

Cooper said nothing. It was that look, always that look, that suggested he could see right through her, could look right into the strange lands that inhabited her head.

"I'm sorry," she said, her voice cracking a little.

Cooper's jaw clenched. "Unfortunately, sorry won't do. You can't sorry your way out of this one. We had a great time. No, fuck that—we had more than a great time, we had *meaningful* sex. Real sex, Emma. We connected. In other words, we made love. Unless I was on some mind-bending trip and went there by myself. Was that it? Was I the only one feeling it?"

Emma shook her head and swallowed down a nauseating lump of regret.

"And then you did *that*?" he said, wincing, gesturing at the charm. "After that extraordinary moment between us, you could turn around and toss me into a basket with all the other meaningless men you've used? How could you do that? How could you equate what we had with all those . . . *others*?" he asked her, sounding disgusted.

"I don't know," she answered honestly. "I didn't. I know it seems like I did that, but it was different, and I honestly, sincerely, don't know why I did it. It's like a weird compulsion. But Cooper, you have to believe me, that's not why I wanted to be with you. I swear it."

He stared at her, waiting for her to say more, but Emma didn't know what more to say. It *wasn't* what she'd wanted. What she'd wanted, what she *still* wanted was . . .

The waitress appeared with a slab of cheesecake, two coffees, and two forks.

"I thought we were better than that," Cooper said bitterly when the waitress had left. "I thought what you wanted was for there to be something real between us."

"I did," Emma assured him. "I *do.*"

"Tell me," he said, gesturing impatiently for her to speak. "Explain to me what was between us."

"What you said."

Cooper grunted, clearly dissatisfied with her answer. He picked up a fork and took a big bite of cheesecake. And then another before putting the fork down.

"I'm sorry, Cooper—"

"Goddammit, stop telling me you're *sorry.*"

"I don't mean I'm sorry for taking the St. Christopher," she said earnestly. "I mean I *am* sorry for that, but I'm so sorry I've disappointed you."

He glanced up at her, interested.

"You're not alone in your confusion and frustration," she said. "I actually have a family I've been disappointing for a long time. There's just something in me that won't work right," she said, and fidgeted with the end of her braid.

Cooper watched her closely, waiting. He wasn't going to help her explain herself. He wasn't going to tell her it was all right.

"I am not trying to hide anything or be purposefully vague," she said. "It's just something I can't really explain, you know? All my life, from the time I was a little girl, I wanted to be was the girl everyone wanted," she said, flicking her wrist to the vast universe of *everyone*. "I wanted to be the girl my dad wanted to be a father to. I wanted my mother to think that I was . . ." She paused here, uncertain. "I wanted her to think I was as good as my stepsister, Laura."

He looked down when she said Laura's name.

"But instead, I was the kid who never said the right thing. I wasn't cute and friendly like Laura. I wasn't fun to be around. I wanted to be, but I couldn't figure out how to be."

Cooper lifted his gaze again. He was listening. Intently.

"I was—I *am*—really awkward. I always say the wrong thing, even when I'm trying to say the right thing. And God, please, don't ask me if I have Asperger's syndrome. I'm just socially awkward."

"You're not," he said low.

"I *am*. I can say it, Cooper. I know it's true, and I can live with it. But I wish, I *wish*," she said, pressing her hands to her chest, "that I was different. Unfortunately, wishing doesn't make it so."

"I understand," he said.

"No you don't. All that wishing has turned me into someone I don't like very much. I do things I don't even understand," she said bitterly, "things I don't *want* to do. And yet, I can't seem to stop myself."

He reached across the table and put his hand on her arm. "I *do* get it. You think it's easy having a brother who is always in trouble? When he's the kid that the neighbors suspect stole their lawn mower, and by extension, think *you* stole their lawn mower, too, because you're the kid they always see tagging along behind him? I have wished my brother was different. I have wished my dad wasn't as strict as he was with Derek, and I have wished he could have been a little more understanding. I have wished for a lot of things that never happened. But here's the thing I know about my brother. Derek isn't a bad guy. I mean, yes, obviously, he is missing some moral fiber and he does some reprehensible things. But at the same time, he was a great brother to me. He had a big, warm heart, he loved animals, he loved *me*. He was a good guy underneath, but he couldn't make himself fit in like the rest of us. He tried, but he could never seem to do it."

"Boy, do I get that," Emma sighed.

"Maybe that's why I'm so angry with you right now, Emma. Because in some ways, you are like my brother. You've got issues, but underneath it, you're a good person. I always knew with Derek it didn't have to be that way. He could have been anything he wanted to be if he'd only allowed himself to believe it. The same goes for you. I would hate to see you live your life alone and on the fringe."

Emma shook her head. "I don't think it's the same thing."

"Yes, it is," Cooper said adamantly. "Look, I can't begin to understand why you pick up guys and take things. I hate that—it's disgusting, especially because I know you are so much better than that. You *deserve* so much better than that."

She could feel those words squeezing around her heart, holding it tight against the guilt that was roaring up from the bottom of her soul. "Don't kid yourself about me."

"Don't run yourself down," he said. "Who made you think you were less than zero? Who put that idea in your head?" he demanded a little angrily. "Because they couldn't be more wrong."

How was it that he could put into words things she was feeling before she could do it herself? It made her shiver, and she rubbed her arms.

"Remember that night in Beverly Hills?" he asked.

Emma remembered every single thing about it, every moment, every smile. The way his eyes danced in the low light, the way he'd laughed at her recounting of the polygamist anniversary. The way he'd looked at her when she'd left him, the way Reggie kept stroking her earlobe, making her feel like a dog, and most of all, the look in Cooper's eyes when Reggie had rolled down that window.

She nodded.

"You were different with me that night. You were real. There have been moments here in Pine River when you've been that girl. And then you . . ." He made a sound of impatience. He leaned across the table again and grabbed her hand, holding it. "It could be like that night in Beverly Hills with us all the time. Do you get that?"

She wanted to believe it. She wanted that more than anything, but she had no faith in herself. Emma bit her lip and squeezed his hand.

Cooper squeezed her hand, too, and let go, shifting back, sliding away from her. She almost grabbed his hand before he could slip out of her reach, but in a moment, it was too late. "I need to get back to the airport," he said.

He tossed a twenty onto the table and stood up.

"What about your St. Christopher?" she asked.

He picked it up, took her hand, and pressed it into her palm, then folded her fingers over it. "You keep that."

"I couldn't. It's yours—"

"You need it more than me. And when you look at it, I want you to remember what could have been."

Emma's heart stopped. She wanted to say what Cooper wanted to hear. But Cooper wasn't waiting for her to find the right words, to try and put some spin on it. He put his arm around her waist and walked with her out to the car.

Neither of them spoke on the short drive back to the airport. At the curb, Cooper looked at her, his gaze moving over her face, searching for something. Could he see how close she was to tears? Could he feel how certain she was she would disappoint him? Could he understand how hard it was to let him go?

"You're not coming back to LA, are you?"

Emma shook her head. If she spoke, she would cry. She would *not* cry. Because if one tear fell, she would melt, right there in front of the airport, melt away into nothingness.

Cooper closed his eyes a moment, and with a shake of his head, he reached for the door handle.

"I don't want to disappoint you," she whispered. "And I will. I will disappoint you so badly you will hate me, and I can't do that, Cooper. I can't *bear* that."

He suddenly twisted in his seat and cupped her face. "That's where you're wrong. You told me you don't do ordinary love, remember?"

Emma nodded, her vision starting to blur with tears that were building behind her lashes.

"I told you I was strong enough for you, and I meant it. I am strong enough for your extraordinary love, Emma. I'm strong enough for both of us. So this is your loss." He let go of her then and got out of the car. He stepped up onto the curb, then turned around and tapped on her window. Emma rolled it down. "And your sister, Laura? She is no friend of yours," he said. "She's a snake in the grass around you, waiting for a chance to bite. Steer clear of her." He straightened up and walked into the terminal without looking back.

She watched him disappear inside, watching him through the plate-glass doors, certain she could still see him.

A policeman knocked on her hood, gesturing for Emma to move on.

She put her car in gear, her mind twirling around his warning about Laura, but mostly, hearing the same thing reverberate in her head. *I am strong enough for your extraordinary love, Emma.*

She gripped the St. Christopher medal in her fist as she drove.

TWENTY-TWO

Emma drove back to Homecoming Ranch without stopping, even when fat lazy flakes of snow began to fall. As she climbed up over the mountains, the snowfall was heavier, and she had to slow down.

It was ten o'clock when she pulled into the drive at the ranch. She was exhausted, starving, and emotionally spent, having replayed everything Cooper had ever said to her on the long road back.

The snow had spent itself by the time she reached the ranch and was falling very lightly when Emma stepped out of her car. She paused to pet the dogs that had come out from the garage to greet her, then hauled herself up the porch steps and inside. In the entry, she braced herself against the wall and pulled off her boots.

"Emma, is that you?" Libby called from the kitchen, and a moment later, she was standing in the hallway, wiping her hands on a dish towel. "Hey, where'd you get off to today?" she asked cheerfully.

"Is there any food?" Emma asked.

"There's some sandwich stuff," Libby offered. "So where'd you go?"

"Denver," Emma said, and walked into the living room.

Madeline was on the couch under a throw, a notebook in her lap. "Denver!" she said, and yawned, stretching her arms high above her. "How come?"

Emma halted her drive toward the kitchen and looked at her sisters. "Cooper was flying through and I went to meet him."

Libby's face suddenly broke into a grin. *"See?"* she said gleefully to Madeline. "I told you!"

"It's not what you think," Emma said. "I stole a St. Christopher medal from him that his grandfather had given him. He wanted it back."

Libby's very gleeful look faded. "Huh? You stole what? You *stole* something?" she asked, as if those words made no sense to her.

"A St. Christopher medal. A charm," Emma said with a flick of her wrist.

"But didn't you take something from that *other* guy?" Libby asked uncertainly.

"Yes," Emma said. She felt very weak, as if her legs wouldn't hold her. In fact, she felt herself swaying a little.

"I don't get it," Libby said.

"Hey," Madeline said, frowning. She sat up, tossing the throw over the back of the couch. "Are you okay?"

Emma couldn't help the sour laugh. "No," she said. "I am really, seriously fucked up," she said, and her legs gave out. She crashed to the floor in a heap. She heard Libby and Madeline shriek, felt hands and arms around her.

"Damn it, Emma, when was the last time you ate?" Libby demanded.

"I don't know," Emma said, and rubbed her forehead, only now realizing that she had a biting headache as well.

"What is the *matter* with you?" Madeline cried and jumped to her feet, running into the kitchen.

Libby tried to help Emma up, but it required Madeline's help when she came back from the kitchen. Together, they put Emma on the couch, and Madeline shoved a banana into Emma's hand. "*Eat* it," she ordered. "Eat it now."

Emma took one bite of the banana and began to cry. "I'm so hungry," she said tearfully.

Libby disappeared and returned a moment later with a bag of chips. "Eat that! I'm making you a sandwich!"

Emma choked down the banana and a few chips before Libby returned with a slab of ham between two thick slices of homemade bread. "What happened?" Libby asked Emma, stroking her hair.

"I'll tell you," Emma said, tears streaking her cheeks. "But you're not going to like it."

"What else is new? Just tell us," Madeline said. "It is very possible that we could help, you know?"

"I don't even know where to begin," Emma said sadly between bites of food. "Maybe with Grant."

Madeline and Libby exchanged a look.

"You can't really be surprised," Emma said flatly.

"*I'm* not," Madeline said. She settled back onto the couch beside Emma and had a few potato chips as Emma began her story, beginning with the year Grant and Libby had come to Orange County.

She told them how she had been envious of Grant's attention to Libby, and then had felt so overlooked when he had sent Libby back to Colorado. No one had told her, no one had warned her Libby was leaving. Soon after that, he left, too, without a word to Emma. Not even a goodbye.

Madeline uttered something under her breath about that, but motioned for Emma to continue.

So Emma told them about her mother and Wes, and Laura, and how she'd adored Laura, had wished she was like Laura. So had her mother, apparently, always comparing Emma to Laura, wanting Emma to be more like her stepsister.

"That's horrible," Libby muttered.

Emma told them about the summer of her seventeenth year, when Grant had returned to her life, wanting to be the father he'd never been. She had thought him so dashing, and she confessed how excited and hopeful she'd been. "I always wanted him to want me. Always."

"Welcome to the club," Libby sighed.

She told them about Laura and Grant, how she'd discovered them. "It's horrible, right?" Emma said.

"Of *course* it's horrible!" Madeline shouted angrily. "What a pig. What a *damn pig.*"

Emma told them how it was Laura everyone felt sorry for, that Laura was the one who had been devastated by the things Emma's father had done. And how difficult it had been to live with that, and how she'd begun to understand that summer that she'd been playing second fiddle to Laura for years.

Emma admitted that she didn't know when her relationship with men had begun to spiral out of control, but somewhere along the way, she'd begun to lure older men in, men old enough to be her father, and then take something from them. She told them about Grif, a rough man with rough appetites.

Emma could tell by the look of alarm on Libby's face and the shock on Madeline's how disgusted they were by her behavior and it made her feel awful. "Believe me, I hate me, too," Emma said. "I feel so dirty all the time."

"I don't hate you," Libby said instantly. "But . . . you didn't do that to Cooper, did you?" she asked, wincing as she anticipated Emma's answer.

"No. I mean, not at first." She told them about running into Cooper in Beverly Hills, and how amazing she'd thought him. And then here, in Pine River, even though he'd known what she was, he had still cared about her. "He was able to see something in me that no one else had ever seen," she said, her voice sounding as dead to her as she felt.

"Then for God's sake, what happened?" Madeline exclaimed.

"Me! I happened! What we shared that day was . . ." She sighed to the ceiling. "There are no words for how incredible it was," she said. "And he . . . he wanted something more. But I knew, I knew in my gut that even if I wanted it, I would not be able to live up to my end of the deal. I would do something to disappoint him. So I told him to go back to LA. I honestly wanted him to go back to LA. But then, I took his St. Christopher."

"Oh my God, *why*?" Libby exclaimed.

"God, Libs, if she knew that, she wouldn't take them," Madeline said.

Emma looked at her with surprise. "That's what *I* said. But I think I know why now. I think I took it so he would come back."

Madeline and Libby regarded her solemnly. "Well? He did, he came back, right?" Libby said hopefully.

"He did. And we talked. And we . . . well, me—I was honest. I told him the truth about myself."

"Oh, Emma," Madeline sighed.

"I had to, Madeline," Emma said. "Isn't it better that I tell him up front instead of him finding out down the road about the things I've done and all the issues I have? I love him. I really think I *love* him. But I'm my own worst enemy, and a leopard doesn't change its spots, does it?"

"It does if it's important enough. But you'll never know, thinking like that," Libby said, sounding angry.

"Why are *you* mad?" Emma asked.

"Because!" she said, casting her arms wide. "So far, you've told us about Grant, who we all know is a loser, and these other men

JULIA LONDON

who are so disgusting I can't even *think* about them, and this *Grif* guy, who you chose because he was bad news. Don't you see, Emma? You've never been with one decent guy in your life. How do you know you'd disappoint him? How do you know it wouldn't be the best thing that ever happened to you? How do you know that it wouldn't change you somehow and make you a better person? How can you know anything until you've at least tried it?"

"You can't upend years of behavior," Emma argued. "You can't suddenly become socially adept. You know me, Libby," Emma said. "*I* know me too well. I've been wanting to be wanted for so long that I . . .." Without warning, Emma burst into tears. Big, thick tears and gulping sobs, for all that she'd lost today.

The unexpected part of it was that Libby and Madeline wrapped their arms around her and cried, too.

"You're not the only one," Madeline said with a swipe of a tear beneath her eye. "Grant left me with the worst mother on the planet. And then threw you two at me after he'd died. I can see now that even as a kid, so much of my life was out of control that I had to control *something*."

"Me, too," Libby said. "I got moved around so much as a kid that I kept looking for that one place I actually belonged, you know? I needed a family, and when I finally had one, I couldn't let go."

"Did you tell Cooper you love him?" Madeline asked.

Emma shook her head. "I thought it would only make things worse. You know, the old, I-love-you, it's-not-you-it's-me shtick."

"Yeah. Bad idea," Madeline agreed.

"It's so screwed up," Emma said morosely. "The worst is *knowing* that it's so twisted and not knowing how to untwist it." She smiled sadly at Madeline. "I'm sorry that I'm the sister you got."

"Me, too," Madeline said gravely.

Libby gasped.

"Seriously," Madeline said. "All those years of wanting sisters, and then I get one who bashes pickups with a golf club and spends a week in a psych hospital, and somehow manages to turn that around and build an amazing rehabilitation center for war vets. *Plus* manages to raise money for Leo's van. And then another one who is amazingly beautiful and a straight-shooter, which I happen to like, and takes care of Leo every day—for free—and makes big donations to afterschool programs and who finally, *finally* found a way to open up to us. Yeah, I definitely got screwed."

"You!" Libby scoffed. "What about me and Em?"

"Oh, definitely screwed," Madeline said, nodding. "A super-control freak who goes around highlighting little chalk outlines around you two."

Emma couldn't help a sad laugh. "It's not funny, because it's so true. You're very controlling."

Madeline snorted. "God, Emma, never stop being you, do you promise? I think you're the only one in my life I can trust to *never* beat around the bush." She suddenly took Emma's hand and Libby's hand. "Look at us. Three misfits, three sisters. Three women who had one really shitty father. And somehow, I couldn't have created better sisters myself."

"You know what?" Libby said, her voice shaking a little. "I couldn't ask for better, either." She laid her head on Emma's shoulder.

"Christ, I told you guys I wasn't going to let you turn this into some Lifetime movie," Emma complained, but she didn't protest at all when Libby put her arms around her to hug her.

TWENTY-THREE

Emma, Madeline, and Libby stayed up late, sharing a bottle of wine, exchanging tales of their lives until the wee hours of the morning. Before they turned in, Libby asked, "What are you going to do about Cooper?"

"Nothing," Emma said, resigned. "He's given up on me."

There was nothing for her to do but figure out where she went from here, a process that Emma wasn't sure how to even start. But she was determined—she meant to turn her life around, whatever it took.

She was late to work the next day, and she was prepared for Leo to give her a hard time about it as he was wont to do. She dashed up the steps—cleared of the light snow by Bob first thing, she noted—and was reaching for the door when it opened.

Bob was standing there. He had deep circles under his eyes and looked as if he hadn't slept in days. "Dante passed away early this morning," he said low.

Emma gasped. *"No!"* she said. "I thought . . ." She didn't know what she thought, really, other than the fact that Leo was always talking about him. "But he went to the game!"

"Yeah," Bob said, and rubbed his face. "Guess he was sicker than we knew."

"How's Leo?" Emma asked.

Bob shrugged. "Can't tell with him, sometimes. The Methodist ladies are with him now."

Emma nodded and walked in, putting her bag next to the little Christmas tree. She straightened her jacket and took a breath before moving on to Leo's room. She poked her head into the room and lifted her hand. "Hey, Leo. Ladies."

"There she is," Leo said, his voice lacking the usual gaiety. "I told you she'd make it."

The Methodist women—four of them today—looked rather glum as they said hello to her.

"Sorry I'm late," Emma said. "The roads were slow going."

"Gee, what's a little snow," Leo said. "Emma, can you make my lunch? If you could whip up some crème brûlée and that delicious liver Dad was eating the other night, I'd really like it."

She looked at him strangely. He had a protein shake for lunch every day.

"Is it lunchtime?" Deb Trimble asked. She stood up, looking at her watch. "We better go, girls. We want to get to the Rocky Creek Tavern before the noon special sells out."

Leo gave Emma a faintly victorious smile.

Emma made him a protein shake while the Methodists prayed over Leo and said goodbye. They gathered their coats and purses and paused to speak to Bob on the way out.

Emma returned to Leo's room with the shake. She adjusted his bed and fit the container into a contraption Bob had installed on the side of his bed, then moved to insert the straw into his mouth.

"Not yet," Leo said.

"It's not liver," she assured him.

"I'm not hungry. And anyway, isn't it time for *Wheel of Fortune*?"

Emma picked up the remote and turned on the television. She put down the remote and considered him a moment. "Leo?"

"I'm not upset about Dante, if that's where you're headed," he said instantly, and drew a labored breath. "I mean, yeah, it sucks, and I'm really going to miss him. But he's in a better place."

"Yes, of course," Emma muttered.

"No, don't say it like that. I'm not saying he's in a better place just because that's the kind of thing you say when someone dies. I mean I *know* he is. I've seen it. And it's awesome that he's going to be there when I go." He smiled a little. "Kind of selfish, right? But I always hated going to a party alone."

Emma's heart sank like a rock in her chest. She tried to swallow her grief, but with no success. She sat on the edge of his bed and laced her fingers through his curled ones. "I'm sorry about your friend."

"You don't believe me," he accused her.

"I honestly don't know what I believe."

Leo snorted. "Trust me, when you're sitting in my chair, you're desperate to believe anything. Solve the puzzle," he said to the television. "Power broker!"

"What about your lunch?"

"It'll still be there after *Wheel*. Come on, let's watch."

Emma crawled onto the bed and lay on her side next to him, her head on his shoulder. She could hear his breath in his chest, but she could also hear a faint rattle she'd not heard before. Bob was right—Leo hadn't been the same since that trip to Denver. How ironic was it that the thing he'd wanted the most had turned out to be so harmful for him? That was the deal with desire, wasn't it? It didn't hurt if you didn't want it so.

"Are you going to leave me in suspense all day? How was Denver?"

Emma lifted her head to look at him. "How'd you know I went to Denver?"

"Because, doofus, Cooper called Luke to get your number. He said he was flying through and needed you to bring him something. So when Dad said you called and said you wouldn't make it in yesterday, I figured you'd gone up there. Okay, so?"

She lowered her head to his knobby shoulder again. "It was okay."

He drew a breath. "Is that all you're going to say?"

"Yes."

"Fine," he said, trying to sound perturbed. "I guess I'll have to resort to my superior fiction-writing skills when Dani comes." He paused to catch his breath again. "Everyone wants you two to get together, you know."

"God," Emma said with a moan. "Yes, I know, I *know*. It's like a regular Peyton Place around here."

"Well, I hope you do, too. He's a good guy, that Cooper. I'm hoping he comes around for Luke."

"For Luke?"

"Yeah. Luke's going to need someone to hang out with when I'm gone." He drew another breath, as if he couldn't quite catch it.

"Leo—"

"Come on, Emma, it's obvious. I'm having trouble swallowing and breathing. I know I'm weaker. And you know, when I can't swallow, the words will disappear. I've already compromised my standards to drink Aunt Patti's brownies. But no talking? Unable to share my genius with the world? Forget it. I'm not sticking around for that."

Emma bit her lip. She wouldn't cry—nothing made Leo as irritable as tears. She just clenched her jaw, using her own power of swallowing to choke them down while Leo tried to solve another puzzle.

"Damn it. That dude should have bought an *I*," he said. "So why can't you be with him?"

"Do we have to do this now?" Emma asked wearily. She was emotionally drained.

"Yes, now. Marisol is bringing the stinker, and I only have so much time before she gets here."

Emma groaned and sat up. "Do you want the short version or the truth?"

He smiled.

"I mean, you've surely heard enough by now to know how screwed up I am, right?"

"Sure," he readily agreed. "Nutty as a fruitcake. Go on."

"Thanks," she said wryly. "That's it. I'm too weird. I would end up screwing it up, and while I don't mind screwing guys up now and again, I really don't want to do that to Cooper. Because I really like him. I like him *so much*."

Leo smiled and drew a shallow breath. "Did I ever tell you about the time Luke and I went white-water rafting after that big spring storm?"

Emma frowned with confusion. *"Huh?"*

"I think I was thirteen, which made Luke about sixteen. There'd been this huge storm and it dumped like six inches of rain on us. We decided that would be the best time to go rafting."

"I am so confused. What has that got to do with Cooper? And that sounds totally dangerous, by the way."

"It was! That's why we wanted to go. Stay with me, here." He drew a breath. "So, like a couple of idiots, we don't tell anyone and we go and put our raft in the water. We start off, and we think it's the best time we ever had, and we're such *studs*, running the river on storm water. But then the water got really rough, and we lost control of the raft and slammed into an uprooted tree that had fallen over the river."

He paused, took a couple of breaths. But his eyes were bright with the eagerness of telling his story. "Em, I thought I was going to *die*," he said. "Luke kept shouting at me to move my paddle here and there, stroke it backward, and I won't lie, I was bawling like a baby, I was so sure I was going to die. But somehow, we got off that tree before getting sucked under, and the next thing you know, we're floating down the river again."

"Where were your parents?" Emma demanded.

Leo grinned. "Conspicuously absent. Anyway, we're flying down the river again, and the next thing you know, we get shoved right up against a bunch of rocks. Here we go again—I thought I was going to die." He paused to breathe. "The raft was banging up against those rocks, and one good puncture, that would be it for us. Luke was shouting that the rocks were going to sink us, and we were pushing and trying to get away, and this rope line got caught."

"Oh my God," Emma said.

"Right? I thought, that's it, we're done. I think I even pissed myself. But somehow, by some miracle, we got out of *that* and went crashing down the river again."

He paused for a moment to rest. "All we had to do was get past the worst of it, and find some calm water so we could get safely to shore. That was it. Just keep fighting and fighting downstream until we found calm water and could climb up on shore."

He stopped there and looked at the TV.

Emma waited for him to continue. When he didn't, she touched his arm. "Hello? What happened?"

"What, you don't get it? We found calm water and got out."

"Okay . . ."

"Do I seriously have to spell everything out around here?"

"Yes."

"It's the river of life," he said, and drew a breath.

"The river of life is where you almost died more than once?" Emma asked skeptically.

Leo drew another long breath. "Yep, now you're getting it. You know, you're floating along and you get hung up in these trees or on those rocks, and you think you're going to die, and you fight and fight, and you get away, you get another chance, and you keep going downstream. And then you hit up against another snag that's even worse, and you think you're going to die again, but then you somehow manage to get out. And eventually, you move away from those things that seemed so life threatening and so important at the time, right? And the farther away you get from those trees and rocks, the less important they are. The only thing that's important is what's in front of you. That search for calm water so you can climb up to a safe shore. You have to have calm water to get out, Emma. You can't get out when it's churning around you. You have to forget what happened and get to safe shore to avoid more death traps downstream. Get it?"

Emma could hardly speak. Her heart was aching, her thoughts whirling. "I get it," she said solemnly.

Leo smiled and turned his attention back to the TV.

"I love you," she said and kissed his cheek.

"Yeah, I know," Leo said matter-of-factly. "Look in my drawer in my nightstand, will you?"

She leaned over and pulled the drawer open.

"See a compass?"

There was a small brass compass inside, one that might have been earned as part of a Boy Scout exercise, she thought. She picked it up and held it up for Leo. "This?"

"Yep. It's awesome. I won that at science camp in the sixth grade. I want you to have it."

"What? You want me to have your compass?"

"Yes," he said, and paused to catch his breath. "Take it and keep it with you at all times. You need a compass, Emma. You need a way to find your calm water and safe shore."

"Oh Leo," she said, and tears began to quietly slide down her face. She clutched the compass to her chest and closed her eyes.

"Stop that, stop that," Leo chided her. "If Marisol sees you, she'll think I asked you to marry me and kick my butt."

But Emma couldn't stop crying. She lay down beside him, the compass in her hand, silently crying on his shoulder while he solved the *Wheel of Fortune* puzzle and pronounced himself the winner of the trip to the Bahamas.

TWENTY-FOUR

Cooper flew into Dallas, rented a car, and drove west, past Abilene, to his mother's house in Sweetwater. The little red brick house with blue-and-white striped window awnings was all decked out for Christmas, with a tree in the front window, and a mantel full of Christmas cards.

His mother was in a jovial mood. She'd made fried chicken for him, which Cooper didn't have the heart to tell her he hadn't eaten in years, mashed potatoes and, of course, green beans that she'd poured out of a can and into a pan to warm. She bustled around her kitchen humming Christmas carols. "It's the first Christmas I'll have both my boys since your father died."

"You won't exactly have Derek," Cooper reminded her. "He's going to be in a halfway house in Midland."

"I know, but I have plans for that day. We can take him out for three hours. That's plenty of time to take him to church and get him a decent meal," she said. "That's just what we'd do here, so essentially, it's the same thing as having him home."

It wasn't essentially the same, no matter how badly his mother wanted to believe it was.

Cooper spent the night on his childhood twin bed, the light of his mother's computer modem blinking at him all night. The next morning, they left very early for the six-hour drive down to the Texas town of Huntsville to pick up Derek.

It was two days before Christmas.

Derek walked out of the gloomy monolith that was the correctional facility with a sack in one hand. The clothes he'd been provided for the occasion were ill fitting. Derek was hard and lean now, his neck and arms painted with prison tattoos. He was missing a tooth, too, and Cooper wondered how and when that had happened.

"I've got some clothes for you at home," his mother said once they were on the road. As they drove away from the place he'd called home, Derek was antsy, jumpy.

Cooper drove so that his mother could pamper his brother. Derek was quiet at first. He sat behind Cooper's mother and stared out the window. "A lot's changed since I went down," he said. "I can't believe how big Austin is now."

"Just wait till you see Sweetwater," his mother said proudly.

"How about a beer, Mom?" Derek asked, his head suddenly appearing over the console between Cooper and his mother. "It's been a long time."

"No, sir," Mom said firmly. "I'm not buying you a beer. You haven't had any all these years, so why would you want to start up now?"

"You can get booze on the inside, you know," Derek said absently, and turned his head to look at Cooper. "So what's up with you, Coop? Married yet? Got a girl?" he asked, and playfully tapped Cooper on the back of the head.

"Not married. I'm still in LA. We're still training stunt performers and thrill seeking—"

"First thing I'm going to do is get a job," Derek interrupted. Cooper didn't know if it was because he truly hadn't been listening, or he didn't want to hear about Cooper's prison-free life. "One of the guards told me that oil fields are hot again. That true?"

"Oh yes," his mother said. "And they pay good money, too. Nicole Fruehauf's son got a job there, and he just bought himself a new truck."

"That's what I'm going to do, Mom," Derek said. "I'm not afraid of hard work, you know."

Cooper glanced out the window at cactus thick as weeds. If Derek was truly okay with hard work, maybe he wouldn't have held up the convenience store with a gun. Maybe he would have gone to school and found a job like everyone else.

"I'm going to make some money and get a little house and maybe a girl. I miss women."

"Derek," his mother said. But she was smiling.

"Worst thing I ever did was break up with Tammy," Derek continued.

"I always liked her," Cooper's mother said cheerfully. "She married a boy from Anson and they moved to Fort Worth."

"You remember her, Coop?" Derek asked, shoving at the back of Cooper's seat.

"Of course," Cooper said. "I had a huge crush on her." He glanced over his shoulder at Derek and smiled.

"You were a squirt," Derek said, and laughed. "Tammy was *hot*, man. I'm telling you, letting that one go was a mistake. If I'd been the kind of man Tammy wanted me to be, I would never have gone down. Never."

No one argued that.

Derek grew quiet again and sank back into his seat.

They stopped at a steakhouse in Abilene and watched Derek eat two steaks, then drove on, to Midland. When Derek was checked in, Cooper waited for his mother at the car so she could make sure Derek would be okay inside. The plan was to return on Christmas day for what Cooper's mother said was "Christmas with presents."

On Christmas Eve, Cooper rattled around his boyhood home, fixing things for his mom. But they were little jobs, and there was not enough to occupy his thoughts. While his mother kept up a steady stream of Derek talk—where he could get a job, how he could meet some girls, her sincere hope that he wouldn't keep smoking, etc.—Cooper thought about Emma. He thought about the first time he'd met her, and the day she'd stood on the Kendricks' porch looking so beautiful. About their lovemaking and how forlorn she'd looked when she told him she'd disappoint him, so certain of it.

It was frustrating enough to make a man want to put a fist through a wall.

But then Cooper would tune in to what his mother was saying, all the hopes she still held for Derek, and Cooper knew that Emma could never disappoint him as she believed she could. That was impossible; Cooper had scraped the bottom of his trough of disappointment with Derek.

On Christmas Day, Derek appeared at the door of the halfway house dressed in the Dockers and button-down plaid shirt their mother had bought him. She was very happy with his appearance and gushed over him, telling him how handsome he was. Derek smiled thinly at her.

He sat through church with one leg bouncing, glancing around. Cooper couldn't help but notice he was checking out the women at the service. Their mother, seated on the other side of Derek, smiled and sang the hymns louder than anyone.

She was so happy, truly happy, and Cooper's heart bled for her.

He didn't know when exactly they had ceased to be a family, or the precise moment their choices in life—Derek's crimes, Cooper's leaving Texas—had splintered them apart. His mother desperately wanted to put them back together again, but Cooper knew it would never happen, not in the way she dreamed. He knew even before Derek coaxed him outside of the Chinese restaurant after church what he would say.

Derek dragged on a smoke and said, "Listen. You're going to have to watch after Mom. I'm not sticking around."

Cooper bristled. Like he hadn't been looking after their mother all the years Derek had been running from the law or was incarcerated. Like he hadn't been the one who was there when their father had died of lung cancer.

"You don't look surprised," Derek said, eyeing him.

"Nope."

Derek laughed. "You could always read me pretty well. But I can read you, too, Coop, and you know what? I can see you're relieved I'm moving on. I think you're glad you don't have to deal with it."

Cooper was mildly surprised. "I guess you do read me pretty well," he said. "Okay, I'll own it. I just don't want you to drag Mom through the wringer."

"It's bound to happen if I stick around," Derek agreed, and drew on the cigarette.

"I didn't say that," Cooper said. "I don't *believe* that. You could choose to make it the right way, you know. You could choose to get a job in the oil fields and a girl, like you said. You could choose to make up all these years to Mom."

Derek laughed at him. "When did you get so soft? I can't change, Cooper. Anyone who says I can hasn't walked in my shoes. I'm forty-two years old. I've been in and out of the system since I was fourteen. I ain't changing, bro, and if I stick around, I'm just going to disappoint her. I don't want to do that. Mom's been through enough. So, best that I move on." He tossed down the smoke and ground it out with his heel.

Any other time, Cooper might have tried to talk him out of that belief, but Derek's words struck too close to what Emma had said to him, and it made Cooper angry. "Just curious . . . do you still have the St. Christopher medal Grandpa gave us?"

"Huh? *No*, man," Derek said, and laughed. He suddenly threw his arms around Cooper, giving him a big hug. "You be good, bro," he said, and patted Cooper's cheek before strolling back inside, beneath the green tinsel, to the table where their mother was sitting, waiting on their meal to be served.

Cooper would later think about how angry he'd been that day. How frustrated he was with the excuses Derek had been using for years, but mostly, how angry he'd been with Emma. She was using the same excuse as Derek and was going to rely on it—just like Derek. She was going to let her life spiral out into loneliness and isolation because, like Derek, she was too afraid to try something different.

Perhaps most frustrating of all was that Cooper had never been able to convince Derek to try for something greater. Did he honestly think he could convince Emma?

Inside the restaurant, Mrs. Jessup handed out Christmas presents to her boys. Sweaters and socks for both, a new watch for Derek, and a belt for Cooper. Derek had a gift for her, too. Somewhere, he'd picked up a figurine of an angel and had put it in a bag. It looked like something one could get at a convenience store. Cooper had given his mother some perfume and earrings. On that Christmas afternoon, his mother was so happy, she practically oozed it. All those years of worry were gone and she kept saying, over and over, "I have my boys, that's Christmas enough for me."

When they drove back to the halfway house, Derek gave his mother a tight hug and kissed her cheek. "Love you, Mom," he said.

"Oh honey, I love you too," she said, pressing her palm to his face and smiling up at him.

Cooper broke the news about Derek to his mother the next day. She took the news well enough, Cooper supposed, almost as if she'd been expecting it, too.

"Well, he'll get out there and run out of money, and he'll come home," she said, and gripped her coffee cup.

"Mom . . . why don't you come to LA with me?" Cooper said. "I've got plenty of room."

"What?" She laughed. "No, honey. I'm from Sweetwater, Texas. My church is here, my friends are here, my husband is buried here. I'll be all right." She'd stood up from her chair, leaned over Cooper, and kissed the top of his head. "Don't you worry about me, Coop. The best thing you can do for me is to keep doing well for yourself. I never have to worry about you. That was the one thing Kurt and I always agreed on—we sure don't have to worry about our Cooper. But Derek? Well, I need to be here for him. He will always need to come home, won't he? He'll always need me."

Cooper was grateful a day or so later when Eli called him to tell him they had a meeting with a new director after the first of the year to discuss some stunt choreography. Cooper had the excuse he needed to leave his mother and her disappointments behind and headed back for LA. And honestly? She seemed ready for him to leave. "I've got bridge on Wednesday," she kept saying, as if she couldn't play bridge with him underfoot.

He packed up his things, said goodbye to his mother, and started the long drive to Dallas to catch a flight.

Along the way, Jackson Crane called him.

"Hey buddy," Cooper said. "What's up?"

"How are you, Cooper? Hey, glad I caught you. I've been assigned a task by the happy couple, Luke and Madeline."

"Oh yeah?"

"They gave me the invitation list. I'm calling everyone to tell them that the wedding has been moved to four o'clock, New Year's Eve, at the house on Elm Street. Party to follow."

"Ah . . . I'm not going to make it, Jackson," Cooper said apologetically. "What happened, too much snow up at the ranch?"

"No," Jackson said. "You don't—oh man, you don't know about Leo. Yeah, he's not doing very well. He's not well enough for the trip up to the ranch, so they've decided to do it at Elm Street."

Cooper didn't say anything for a moment. He stared at the road stripes clicking by on that empty stretch of highway.

"You there?"

"Yeah," Cooper said. "Sorry. I didn't know it was so . . . I didn't think things were going that fast."

"No one did," Jackson said. "And honestly, I don't know how bad it is. I just know they don't want to take him up there, and they've asked me to call everyone and let them know. So consider yourself informed. Everything all right?" he asked. "You got in some skiing before you left, I hear."

Cooper managed to talk about skiing, but his mind was racing. He was stunned by the news, his heart going out to Luke and his family. And to Emma, too—he knew how important Leo was to her.

"I'll let you go," Jackson said after chatting. "I've got about ten more people to call. So let me know when you're back up here, will you? I've got a couple of guys who would love to talk to you and see if there's any work for them as part of your event."

"Sure," Cooper said.

He drove on to Dallas and the airport, turned in his rental car. As he waited for his flight to LA, he reached in his pocket for his St. Christopher charm to fidget with it, and remembered where it was.

He took out a nickel instead, turning it over and over between his fingers.

TWENTY-FIVE

Marisol returned to work the day after Christmas, bringing her baby and an automatic swing with her. She had worked it out with Bob, apparently, who explained to Emma that Leo needed a nurse full time now. "Nothing personal," he said.

"No offense taken," Emma replied. "But I'm not leaving. There's enough work around here for four people, much less two."

"But there's not enough room for four people. Or two," Bob said wearily. "This is a tiny house, Emma. Come by and visit, but I've got to have Marisol day to day."

It was devastating to Emma. She had come to rely on Leo and, she liked to think, he had come to depend on her. Who would watch *Jeopardy* with him and discuss how Alex Trebek and his crew had landed on the day's categories? Who would listen to him talk about what the Broncos needed in the playoffs?

What would she do to keep her mind off Cooper? The incessant reel playing in her head of all the things she'd said, then all the things she should have said?

The weather had turned cold; Emma's kids weren't in the park these days to distract her. She wandered around Pine River looking in storefronts and drinking fancy coffees, seeking a purpose and found none. There were too many unanswered questions about herself. How could she find purpose without finding herself first?

She was at the Grizzly Café one afternoon, nursing a cold cup of coffee. She noticed an older man seated by himself near the window. He kept shifting his gaze to her, a hint of a smile on his lips. On his lapel he wore an American flag pin.

Emma stood up, put a few bills on her table. She sauntered toward the older man; he sat back, his smile widening. But the remarkable thing was that Emma averted her gaze and kept walking. She walked right past him and his little American flag. She had no desire to tempt him. She had no desire to add that pin to her collection. She had no desire for anything or anyone but Cooper.

It was Leo who rescued her from aimlessness. He must have known she wouldn't handle Bob's rejection well, because Bob called her a day or so later and asked her to come back. "Leo's got something he needs."

What Leo needed was a party. "A big one," he'd said. "You know, with balloons and marching bands."

A party. That was so like Leo. Emma pushed down her grief and agreed. "You want a party, Leo Kendrick? You're going to get the best party this event planner knows how to throw."

As part of her planning, Emma explained to Bob that she had things to do around the house. "The house has to be decorated, Bob," she'd said firmly. "First and foremost, you're going to have a holiday wedding here, and Luke and Madeline deserve this place to be what they envision."

Bob had puffed out his craggy cheeks. "Fine," he'd said. The man knew when he was defeated.

Marisol was not as easy to persuade.

"There are too many things," she said when Emma showed up with an armful of crystal beads and chiffon sashes. She suspiciously eyed the box Emma was holding. "No room for these things."

"There's no room for a baby, either," Emma pointed out. "Who's to say this is less important? I will put up all the decorations, you don't need to worry about a thing."

"My baby comes with me!" Marisol snapped. "I will take down this tree," she threatened, gesturing to the tiny tabletop Christmas tree in the living room.

Emma sighed. She put down her box and turned around to face Marisol. "You don't like me, Marisol—I get it. Trust me, you're not the first woman to dislike me, and you won't be the last. But you know what? You and I could be friends. We're very much alike."

"No!" Marisol protested hotly. "I'm not like you!"

"I guess it's a good thing I don't get my feelings hurt easily," Emma said to Marisol's visceral reaction. "Look, we both love Leo," she said, holding up one finger.

Marisol glanced down the hall, to Leo's room.

"We both tell it like it is," Emma said, lifting a second finger. "And neither of us will tolerate nonsense. Do you know how compatible that makes us? We should get a drink after work and talk about how many jerks there are in the world."

Marisol eyed her up and down. She looked at Emma's box and waved at it. "Nothing in the way of his chair. And not fussy. Mr. Kendrick, he does not like fussy."

"Fair enough," Emma said. "But you don't touch what I put up until New Year's Day."

"I will agree," Marisol said. "The night nurse comes at five," she said. "The Rocky Creek Tavern is on the road I take to my home."

Emma's brows lifted with surprise. Marisol was apparently ready to have that drink. "Okay," she said. "What about Valentina?"

"She goes!" Marisol said, as if that was a ridiculous question.

"That's completely weird, but far be it from me to question your mothering skills. Okay. It's a date."

Marisol said something in Spanish, picked up her baby, and disappeared into the kitchen.

Emma got down to work.

As the best man, Leo wanted some of the decorations in his room, too. "Maddie's garter belt would be *awesome*," he said.

"The garter belt isn't available until after the wedding. And besides, I'm not sure she'll have one. She's doing this sort of bare bones."

"Then her bra," Leo said from his bed. "That would be just as awesome."

Emma smiled at him. "Pig."

"You know I love it when you call me that," he said wearily. "Could you put it on ESPN?" he asked, his gaze finding the television again.

It was so difficult to lose two men Emma had come to care for. It was the cruelest reality—after all the years of being unable to connect, of sabotaging any chance for true happiness, Emma had found two chances here in Pine River. And both of them were gone. One, gone from her heart, and one who would eventually be gone from her life.

Emma kept stumbling toward the wedding, almost blindly putting one step in front of the other, her heart breaking with each step. What else could she do? To stop was to surrender to her grief and let it consume her.

The tent that the veterans had hauled up to Homecoming Ranch for the wedding came down the mountain to the house on

Elm Street at the end of the week, along with the chairs Libby had worked so hard to dress in silk and the arbor Madeline and Luke had built together. "What do you think?" Madeline had proudly asked Emma as she'd admired the arbor.

"I think it's ugly as hell," Emma had said.

Madeline had laughed.

The day before the wedding, the tent was erected in the middle of a driving rain that was forecast to turn to sleet overnight.

"This is a disaster," Madeline groaned ruefully. She was standing at the kitchen sink at Homecoming Ranch, peering out the window. Just yesterday, she'd arrived home from Denver where she'd gone to collect her best friend and maid of honor, Trudi Feinstein.

"It will be fine," Libby said. "This will pass and tomorrow will be beautiful. It always happens that way."

But it didn't happen that way. New Year's Eve was just as cold and as wet and dreary as the day before.

Sam came up to the ranch that morning to collect the women. "I don't like the way the roads are looking," he said. "I don't want any of you driving down. We need to go on before the roads are impassable."

"But where will we dress?" Madeline exclaimed. "I have to get ready, Sam! I've got a wedding dress and flowers, not to mention my *shoes*. Oh my God, my *shoes!*"

Sam looked uncertainly at Libby for help.

"Well?" Libby snapped irritably. "What about her shoes?"

"I . . . I don't know about her shoes," Sam said carefully. "I just know if you want to get married today, Maddie, you've got to come down this morning."

"Listen, I'll just call Bob," Emma said. "I'm sure he won't mind if we use a couple of rooms at the house."

But Bob did mind. "I got every relative here right now and then some," he said. "I got three rooms, two tiny baths, and a living room that will hardly fit Leo's chair. Where do you suggest I put all these people, Emma? Where do you suggest I put all this gosh-dern food?"

Emma's years of event management problem solving kicked in. "Bob," she said calmly, "it will be okay. A little hectic, I agree, but I'll figure something out."

"I guess you better," he said, and clicked off.

Emma called Jackson Crane. "I need an RV," she said.

"Okay," he said without missing a beat.

"I mean today, Jackson. Right now. I need one on Elm Street, plugged in, ready to house at least four women who need to dress for a wedding."

"Oh. As in, this is an emergency," he said. "Got it."

"Can you deliver?" Emma asked him as she stuffed herself into Sam's truck next to Trudi. "Because if you can't, I need to know right this minute."

"Give me a little credit, Emma," Jackson said jovially. "Go worry about something else, like the weather."

An RV—one of the big ones, with pop-out dining—arrived an hour later. Jackson himself maneuvered it into the drive directly behind Leo's van. Behind him was the truck with the propane space heaters Luke had thought to arrange when they'd decided to move the wedding to the house for Leo.

Emma donned a heavy down coat she'd borrowed from Bob, and together with Sam, they rolled out tarps for the ground and set up the chairs under the tent and arranged the propane heaters. The sleet was coming in sideways, so Sam and Jackson rigged some plastic sheeting along one side of the tent. The arbor that Luke and Madeline had built was also covered with tarps to keep the bride and groom and pastor dry. "That's a good thing," Emma said to Luke. "That way, it won't spoil your pictures."

Luke had looked a little startled by her thoughts on his arbor, but Sam had laughed.

The best man—Leo—would stay dry by remaining just inside the kitchen door. As maid of honor, however, Trudi would be forced to hold an umbrella.

When at last the backyard was made as ready as it could be, Emma paused to look around. She'd worked so many weddings that she never thought about the significance of them anymore. But today's wedding, in the middle of a driving sleet, in a tiny house up in the mountains of Colorado, made her tear up. Not because it was her sister—Emma was happy for Madeline—but because she had never realized until she met Cooper just how badly she wanted this for herself. And she felt galaxies away from it.

Emma at last made her way to the RV to dress. Madeline was wearing a robe, but she'd had her hair arranged in a gorgeous chignon and her makeup applied. "Are the chairs up?" she asked anxiously when Emma came in.

"This is what I do for a living," Emma said. "The chairs are up. Everything is under control. You look beautiful."

Madeline smiled. "Wow. Thank you. So . . . so everything is going to be okay?"

Emma snorted. "No. It's going to be horrible and wet and cold. You should have eloped."

Madeline's brows sank into a vee. Behind her, Trudi's mouth gaped open with shock. "You really, seriously, have *got* to get a filter for that mouth of yours, Emma," Madeline said.

Emma shrugged. "You asked."

"You don't have to say everything you think!" Libby cried, obviously just as startled as Trudi.

Emma smiled a little. They might not see it, but Emma thought she was making some progress. For example, she hadn't mentioned out loud that Trudi's dress was way too small for her.

"Well . . . she's kind of right," Trudi said, surprising Emma.

"Don't agree with her, Trudi!" Madeline begged. She shook her head. "Okay, I should have eloped, but I didn't. So what are you wearing, Emma?"

Emma hadn't brought anything formal to Pine River, and she hadn't had time to go to Colorado Springs for anything, either. At the last minute, Libby's mother had lent her a dress. It was pale green silk with dark pink embroidery on the hem and on the plunging neckline. It wasn't the sort of dress Emma would choose for herself, but she had to admit—she really liked it.

"Who cares what I'm wearing? You're the bride, and you are all anyone will see."

"Right." Madeline puffed out her cheeks and let out a long breath. "I can't believe it. I *am* the bride." She glanced at her watch. "Three hours. Libby, where's my task chart?"

Only Madeline would make a chart of tasks for her wedding.

"According to your list, it's snack time!" Libby said. "I'm going to pop into the house and get our snacks. Trudi, can you help me?"

The two women went out, leaving Madeline, her task chart, and Emma.

Emma sat on a little built-in bench directly across from Madeline. "You're beautiful, Madeline. Truly beautiful."

"I really must be if *you* say so, because we all know you only say what's true." She laughed. "You know what sucks, Em?" Madeline asked. She had taken to calling Emma that of late. "Even on my wedding day, I am not as beautiful as you. It's not fair. How's Luke holding up?"

"Great!" Emma said. "Last I heard, he was talking about plans to expand the house."

"*That's* what he's thinking about? Well, I'm glad to know he's not nervous or anything!" She shook her head. "And Leo? Is he okay?"

Emma averted her gaze. "He's okay," she answered truthfully. "He's in his chair and he's talking. But he looks exhausted. Maybe because Marisol put a tux on him. He is pleased with the outcome and apologized to Luke for upstaging him, but I think it took a lot out of him."

Madeline frowned and looked down. It was like that now. When anyone mentioned Leo, everyone looked away, too afraid to see what was coming. Leo had explained that to Emma one evening when they were planning his party.

"And how are you, Em?" Madeline asked.

"Me?" Emma said. "Okay."

Madeline smiled sadly at her. "I wish Cooper was here."

Emma stilled. Her first instinct was to brush that off, but her shoulders sagged. "Me, too," she said. More than she could ever convey.

The door of the RV opened and Libby hopped in with a tray of finger foods.

"Where's Trudi?" Madeline asked.

"She decided she needed something a little more substantial, so she's making a sandwich."

Madeline laughed. "That's my Trudi."

"Hey," Libby said. "I need to tell you guys something."

"God, no bad news, Libby! No drama, please! It's my wedding day!" Madeline pleaded as she reached for a pita square from the tray.

"Nothing like that," Libby scoffed. She was beaming, Emma noticed. An ear-to-ear grin. "I know it's your day and all, but I can't wait another minute."

"For *what*?" Madeline cried, fearing the worst.

Emma knew. Actually, she'd guessed it quite a long time ago. "Libby . . . that's fantastic."

"What?" Madeline demanded.

"I'm *pregnant!*" Libby squealed.

Madeline gasped. And then she leapt up and threw her arms around Libby. Libby managed to keep the tray from spilling, and Emma grabbed it from her hand. Libby wrenched partially free of Madeline's grip and grabbed Emma's wrist, forcing her to stand and join them.

"Oh my God, I *hate* group hugs," Emma complained. But she laughed when Libby threw her arm around her neck and pulled her in close.

It was a joyous day, Emma thought when they finally untangled from each other. When she could forget her own troubles, she felt truly joyous. She had never really experienced a day quite like this, because for once, she felt part of something bigger than her narrow world as Libby talked excitedly about her and Sam's plans.

She looked at her sisters chattering about Libby's news. So much had happened to them, and yet look at them—they were family now. One marrying, one expecting, one drifting, but okay, Emma was here, she was *present*. In a strange way, that asshole father of theirs had made this happen. Not that Emma believed for one moment that Grant had intended to bring them together when he'd left the ranch to them. What he'd meant to do was unload a bothersome property and say he gave his kids something. But in spite of his intentions, he'd given them each other.

Not only was she part of this family, Emma *wanted* to be part of it. It was such an odd feeling, to want to be part of something instead of apart from it. It was a rusty emotion in desperate need of oil and buffing, but that's exactly what she was feeling. She still hadn't learned to trust her instincts entirely, but so much had happened to her here. For the better. It was remarkable, really. Emma had some gaping holes in her—one in her heart she could drive a truck through—but maybe there was enough here to fill it. *Maybe.*

And it felt good. It felt as good and real as anything had felt since . . . well, since Cooper.

The sisters dressed for the wedding together, chatting about everything. The weather was so bad that when the guests began to arrive, the Kendricks had no choice but to let them gather in the house. Trudi reported that there were too many of them—so many that the house was quickly too hot.

Emma had braided a green ribbon into her hair, then had the stylist wrap it into an artful chignon. "Wow," Libby said, nodding approvingly at Emma's dress. "Trust me, that never looked so good on Mom."

"You're adorable," Emma said, admiring the short blue dress Libby had worn with her very high heels.

"It's not exactly right for the weather," Libby said, staring down at her stockings. "But what are you going to do? Adorable? Or warm?"

"Adorable, every time," Emma said.

Madeline was more than adorable—she was gorgeous in a pale cream silk that skimmed her body, and pearls woven into her black hair. "My God," Emma said approvingly. "I can't believe that's you. You're stunning."

Madeline laughed. "I can't believe it's me, either," she said nervously.

"Well *I* can," said Trudi. "Come on. You can't keep a guy like Luke waiting."

In preparation for the exchange of vows, everyone was ushered out to the tent. Naturally, the guests wore big parkas and huddled together like a herd of penguins. Emma and Libby stayed behind with Madeline to hug her once more and wish her the best, and then they dashed out, too. Libby found Sam, and Emma ducked into a corner, out of view of most, but with a line of sight to the back porch. It was the place she normally took—on the fringe, as Cooper had said.

The pastor appeared wearing a down coat. Luke followed, choosing not to wear a coat and looking very handsome in his tux. Behind him, also dressed in a tux, Bob wheeled Leo to the door. Someone had tucked a blanket in around Leo, so only part of his tux was visible.

The musicians Madeline had hired had set up in the shed. It was not exactly convenient, but at least the music could be heard. A little, anyway.

When they began to play the processional, Trudi and Madeline came around the corner of the house, holding their hems, smashed together under the umbrella. It was such a comical entrance that the guests couldn't help but laugh.

When Madeline stepped in under that arbor, she looked as radiantly happy as Emma had ever seen any bride. Everything about her glowed with love for Luke. And Luke? The expression on his face, the pure joy, the pure adoration, made Emma's heart stop. She had to look away before tears of happiness for the couple and bigger, messier tears of regret began to slide from her eyes. Her gaze landed on Libby, who was standing next to Sam, her head on his shoulder, her hand on her belly, her grin irrepressible.

Good Lord, just put a dagger through her heart! It was wretchedly, selfishly painful to see such happiness brimming from her sisters. As Luke and Madeline expressed their vows to each other, Emma felt a growing emptiness inside her. She imagined herself as the clichéd chick-flick friend, the one who attends wedding after wedding and never has one of her own. But unlike a character in the movie, no Prince Charming was going to come around the corner and sweep her off her feet. Emma had made a point of removing herself from everyone and everything, so that now, in a moment like this, when she should be clinging to someone's hand, she was utterly alone. As far removed from what Madeline and Libby had found here in Pine River as anyone could possibly be. It was a bit astonishing to understand on that bitterly cold afternoon that what Emma wanted was to be loved. That she ached to love someone.

Emma was crying. Dani smiled at her sweetly, and Emma knew Dani thought Emma was the type who bawled at weddings. Emma was *so* not that type. These were not tears of happiness. These were tears of deep regret.

After Madeline and Luke were pronounced husband and wife, the guests spilled back into the house, packing into it. Emma lingered behind, sneaking into the shed, trying to put her face back together again before the whole world saw the splotchy skin and knew she'd lost it. By the time she came in through the back door, there wasn't air to breathe. People were in the living room, the tiny kitchen, the hallway, and in the back, Emma could see some of them had even taken up space in Bob's room.

Dani Boxer had enlisted the aid of the Methodist Women's Group to help serve the champagne and finger foods. There would be no sit-down dinner here—money was as tight as the space. Emma made her way to Madeline and Luke and congratulated them, and wiped a bit of perspiration from Madeline's temple. Someone had opened the windows, so if one was unlucky enough to be standing next to one, it was freezing. Any deeper in, it was boiling.

Leo was in his chair in the living room, strapped in like a baby in a car seat. He was smiling, but he didn't seem to be talking much. Emma debated escaping with him to his room, but this was Leo's element. He would never consent to leaving the party.

Emma stood in a tiny space where the living room turned to hall, nursing her champagne, feeling the prickly heat on her nape, watching everyone celebrate Luke and Madeline. But as she stood there, that prickly feeling grew stronger, and she began to realize it wasn't the heat. She felt as if she was being watched and glanced over her shoulder, into the kitchen.

Her heart stopped beating. And then began to race so desperately she could hardly hold on to her flute of champagne.

In his dark trim suit and black silk tie, Cooper smiled at her. Emma all but tossed the champagne onto a small table in the hall. She pushed past a beefy man and dipped under the arm Bob had braced against the kitchen doorframe as he chatted with Leo's aunt. She emerged on the other side of Bob to stand just before Cooper, crammed into the small dining space between several other guests. "You *came*."

He nodded and touched his knuckles to her face. "Are you okay?"

"*No*. No, I'm not okay. It's so hot in here I might throw up."

He smiled warily. "Please don't throw up. Madeline would not be happy."

Emma doubted anything could douse Madeline's happiness tonight. "That's not even it. I'm not . . . I'm *lost*."

He didn't say anything to that, just held her gaze.

"I didn't think you'd been invited," Emma said.

Cooper chuckled. "Luke invited me without authorization. I hadn't planned to come, but then I heard about Leo and I worried."

"I know," she said, nodding adamantly. "Everyone wants to see him."

"Yeah, I can imagine," he said. "But I was worried about you, Emma. I know how much he means to you."

What was that, wrapping around her heart? "You did?" she asked weakly. "After everything, you still worried about me?"

"After everything. Before everything. During everything."

Emma closed her eyes and sighed with longing. That was possibly the kindest thing anyone had ever said to her. She opened her eyes to Cooper's soft gaze. It was liquid silver. Molten kryptonite. Her mouth went dry. "Was your brother released?" she asked, searching for something to say.

He nodded. "He's already gone. Took off a couple of days ago."

She hardly noticed that she'd twined her fingers in his. "I'm sorry."

"It's okay. I've known for a long time that Derek is never going to do the things that most people do. He is never going to change his ways. It's too late for him."

"That must be hard for you."

He shrugged a little. "It was too late for him, but not for me. *I've* changed, Emma. Seeing Derek, hearing him—it made me realize that you do the same thing he does. And I realized I can't make you change, either."

Her racing heart began to slow with dread. "I know," she admitted. "I'm hard and flinty, I get that."

"Hard and what?" he asked when she dipped backward as two men edged into their space. They were moving, shifting out of that tiny dining area and back into the living room.

"Flinty," she said.

Cooper shook his head. "I don't know about that, but what I am trying to say is that I realized Derek uses disappointment as a crutch. He was disappointed in Dad, so he acted out. He doesn't want to disappoint Mom, so he takes off. I didn't fully get it until he actually said that. But you know what was so ironic? Those were almost the same words *you* used. He was so scared of disappointing Mom he couldn't stay, he had to leave. He didn't even try. And neither did you, Emma."

All the warmth and happiness at seeing Cooper had now bled out of Emma. He hadn't come here to forgive her, he'd come here to get things off his chest. Today, of all days. She glanced down, away from those eyes, and took a step backward to allow one of the Methodist ladies to pass into the kitchen with an empty tray. "I understand," she said low.

"Derek doesn't know what he is capable of if he doesn't try."

That brought her head up. "You're right," she said. "Same goes for me. But I *want* to try."

Cooper looked as if he wanted to believe her. But he also looked skeptical.

This, Emma thought, was one of those famous make-or-break moments Leo liked to talk about in his analysis of the Broncos season. How many times had she heard him say it on Sunday afternoons? *This is a make-or-break moment, Emma. Gotta make it here or hang it up—the game is over.* Emma reached for Cooper's hand and took it between both of hers. "Cooper Jessup, I think I love you."

Cooper blinked with surprise.

"I know, I know, it surprised me, too. I have thought all this time that it wasn't in me, that I was missing some gene that allowed me to feel that way. That I can't do ordinary relationship things, like fall in love and yearn to touch someone."

"Emma—"

"What, am I saying too much after all that's happened? I'm sorry if I am, but if I don't say it now, I never will. You . . . you don't have to love me back." If he didn't, she would be completely crushed. "Actually, I'll be surprised if you do, because I really *am* hard and flinty, Cooper. I know that I am. I've never been able to be one of the gang. I say the wrong things, and most of the time I'm okay with that. But you're right—there is more to me than that. I really *do* care, even if I don't look it. It took you to make me see it. And for that, I love you. For a lot of other stuff, too, but for that. And I have to say it. Before you go, I have to tell you what you are to me."

"I don't know what to say," Cooper said. "I'm a little skeptical, to be honest."

"Believe me, Cooper. I'm telling you the truth. Look," she said, and suddenly dug out a necklace that she'd tucked into her bra. She held it out to him. On a long chain was the compass Leo had given her, and Cooper's St. Christopher medal. She'd had Tag weld them both onto the chain so she could wear them always, keep the two men she loved, closest to her heart.

Cooper looked at it, confused. "A compass?"

"I got this from Leo," she said. "He gave it to me. He told me—" How mortifying that the tears would come at this crucial moment. She'd turned into a regular waterworks display in the last week. Emma swiped at one that fell down her cheek now. "After you left, Leo said I needed to stop thinking about the past and find calm water so I can get to a safe shore. He gave this to me so I could find it. But Cooper, I was already *there*. My calm water was right here, with you," she said, touching the St. Christopher. "It was here in Pine River and that stupid, useless ranch, and with sisters I never knew. And you? You are my safe shore! You know what I am, and you *still* care about me. *You!* A man who is handsome and smart and accomplished and stubborn and demanding—"

"Demanding?"

"In other words, you're perfect," she said earnestly. "You can look past the physical and see the person inside. You did it with Leo the first day you met him. You didn't look at him like there was something wrong with him, you looked at him like you saw the person he was. You are without prejudice, Cooper Jessup, and you are everything I never believed I deserved in a man. You are everything *any* woman would want, and look, you're standing here with *me*. And I . . . I love you for it." She pressed her fist to her heart. "I *love* you," she said again, her voice breaking. "So much."

Cooper stared down at her, almost as if he was waiting for the *but*. Waiting, Emma supposed, for her to say he should leave now like she had so many times. She was overcome with emotion. It was as if some internal dam had burst, and all the hopes and desires she'd secreted away came spilling out, washing over this man who wouldn't give in to the barrier she'd erected. Who waited patiently until he could see over it. "And if you never love me, that's okay," she blurted. "You deserve real happiness. If that's not me, I understand."

Emma stopped there, before she managed to ruin her speech by saying something painfully truthful.

After a long moment, Cooper let out a breath of relief. He put his arms around her waist and drew her in. "Okay," he said. "Okay. *That's* what I'm talking about, Emma. You just made a giant leap forward in the quest to change the direction of your life. And if you're serious, if you really want to put your life back on track, I'm here for you. And while you're trying, you should know that I love you, too, Emma. I love the unordinary. I love hard and, what, flinty?" He laughed a little at that. "I love you."

"Cooper, really?" She thought she could actually feel her heart swelling. "I promise, I *swear* to you I will try and be what you need."

"I just need you to be you, Emma. Just you." He picked her up to kiss her as he turned them in a slow circle.

Emma kissed him, and quite passionately, too. She heard the cheers, heard Luke shout *Yes!* But she didn't realize that the shout was for her and Cooper until Bob put his hand on her back and said, "Knock it off. This ain't the time for that."

Emma lifted her head and laughed. She laughed as brightly and as fully as she'd ever laughed in her life. This was *exactly* the time for that. This was the time for shouting and singing and dancing and whatever it was people did when they were delirious and drunk on love.

With Cooper's arm securely around her, Emma joined in the raucous toasts to the newly married couple, lifting her flute of champagne, smiling at Cooper when the wishes for a long and happy life were tossed out. She kept her hand in his as they inched around that crowded little house, mingling with other guests. He was there beside her when conversation became stilted and she didn't know what to say, stepping into the conversation to save her. He was there beside her when Leo declared dancing was in order, and everyone tried to move in that tiny room, their laughter pealing over the strains of holiday music.

Emma couldn't take her eyes off Cooper. She couldn't believe this man, this gorgeous, wonderful man, had come back for her. And every time she looked up, there was Cooper, looking at her. *Seeing* her. The one man who could look past her exterior and see what she really was, the sweet and the sour. And he loved her.

Emma had never felt so easy in her skin as she did that night. For that, she loved Cooper all the more. She would never let him go. She would never let this magical night go, either. She would carry this moment forward and not look back, because Emma believed with all her heart she'd finally found her calm waters and safe shore.

EPILOGUE

The memorial service for Leo was held on a mild early-February day at the Methodist church in Pine River, and it seemed to Emma as if the entire town packed into those pews. There was hardly any room for the marching band.

The service was short and sweet, with "nothing too political," as Leo had advised her when they'd planned this, his final party. "You know how some of them can get," he'd warned her.

Emma was never sure who "them" was in that sense, but she'd gone with his wishes.

Only family and close friends were invited to the burial service, which was held at the Kendrick family cemetery halfway between Pine River and Homecoming Ranch. This was where the Kendricks had been laid to rest since the turn of the century. "It's just like the Kendricks to make it, like, *super* inconvenient for anyone who wants to stop by and chat," Leo had complained of its location.

Per his wishes, his send-off was not a maudlin affair. "I swear to God, Luke, I will haunt you like Rosemary's Baby if you let them all get weepy-eyed on me," Leo had threatened in the last few weeks. With Luke's help, Emma had convinced the local high school marching band to come and march around the cemetery playing the theme from *Rocky,* just as Leo had wanted. "I'll be in fighting shape then," he'd explained.

Leo's death had been terribly painful for all of them to watch and excruciating for Leo to endure. He'd lost his ability to swallow, as the doctors had predicted, and suffered horrible bouts of choking. Shortly after that, he lost the ability to talk, his breathing labored and shallow, and as Leo himself had warned, that signaled the end.

Bob was desperate to take him to a hospital, but unbeknownst to him, some time ago, Leo had asked Jackson to prepare an advance directive, in which he'd said he did not want to be kept alive by artificial means. *Because you know you won't be able to let me go, Dad. But I will be ready. I am ready,* he'd said in the note that accompanied the legal document.

"I want to die at home, Dad," Leo had said through an endless bout of wheezing a few days ago.

That plea had nearly put Bob Kendrick on the floor. But he had given his boy what he wished.

It was a merciful death when it came one Tuesday afternoon, right after *Days of Our Lives* and before *Dr. Phil.* As heartbreaking as it was, Leo's family and close friends gathered around and felt nothing but relief for him. His suffering was over. Most of all, Emma thought, Leo must be relieved. He'd once told her the first thing he was going to do on the other side of life was run. "I mean, *run,* like Usain Bolt. You saw him in the 2008 Olympics, right? *No?* Seriously, now, how big is that rock you live under? Like, is it a *meteorite?*"

God, how they would miss him.

When the service was over, and the marching band dispatched, and the party balloons released to the sky, and the streamers thrown, they all trooped back to Homecoming Ranch for the real party. A local band had come out to play, and the Grizzly Café had set up a buffet in the old barn.

It was Bob who started talking about his memories of Leo, from the time he was a boy and got himself hung in barbed wire trying to escape a bull, to the day he called home from college and mentioned in passing that he couldn't grip a football. Before long, everyone was laughing at the memories of Leo, repeating the things he'd said, the messages he would get across in the form of sports parables. It was a fabulous send-off, just what Leo wanted.

But Emma wasn't ready to laugh yet. Her memories were still swollen and bruised and tender. She owed so much to Leo. Along with Cooper, Leo was the person who had slowly convinced her to open herself up to the possibilities life offered. To let go of the prison she'd put herself in, especially because Leo couldn't. He'd convinced her one cold afternoon to stop looking back and to start looking forward.

The dance was gearing up when Emma walked out onto the porch and sat on the steps. The dogs came out from under the porch one by one to be petted. She heard the screen door open and close behind her. In the next moment, Cooper sat beside her. "You okay?" he asked, putting his arm around her.

"I am," she said, and she meant it. "You know, the last thing he said to me was to laugh at his funeral. But I can't laugh, Cooper."

He smiled. "The last thing he said to me was to take care of you."

Emma's eyes widened with surprise. "Really?"

"Yeah," he said, and looked out over the meadow. "He said you are horrible about asking for help and probably need it more than anyone. And that you're super hot and guys will always be hitting on you." He chuckled. "It's no wonder the two of you were lovebirds over there. Probably had a great time together, calling it as you see it."

Emma laughed. "Yes, we did."

"There, you see?" Cooper said with a wink. "He made you laugh."

"He also wanted me to promise to never leave Pine River," she said. "But he finally gave in and said it would be okay to go back and forth between here and LA."

Cooper kissed her temple. That was their plan for the time being—they'd go back and forth between LA and Colorado until the solution of where to settle presented itself. Neither of them felt an urgency to make that sort of decision. They were okay in flux for the time being, because the big decision had been made—they loved each other, and they were going to give this a go. That was challenging enough, given Emma's past and the need to build trust with Cooper. But Emma had never felt so wanted as she did with Cooper, and she basked in the feel of that. She wanted Cooper to feel as secure as she did, and was devoted to making sure he knew every day how much she loved him. Truly, deeply, *loved* him.

Leo would be so proud of her. And he would be the first to congratulate her that in spite of the somber note of the day, she could see just how bright and shiny the future was looking.

Emma hadn't told anyone but Leo that she'd taken her tote bag with its contents and thrown it in a Dumpster by the Wal-Mart. The past was a fallen tree on the river of life, and so far behind her now that it wasn't important.

"You know what he told me?"

Cooper and Emma started—they hadn't heard Libby come outside. "I was holding Marisol's baby, and he said I should have some stinkers of my own. Lots of them, because Marisol was not the sharing kind." Libby laughed. "I'm so glad I got to tell him I was pregnant."

"Tell who what?" Madeline had followed Libby outside and sat down beside her.

"I got to tell Leo about the baby."

"Oh," Madeline said, and scooted over to make way for Sam, who'd come out, too. He sat behind Libby, and she leaned back against his knees.

"He asked me to promise not to put a birdhouse on his grave," Sam said. "Apparently, he had something against blue jays and doesn't want them hanging around."

"What's the last thing he said to you?" Libby asked Madeline.

"Oh, what did that man *not* say?" Madeline sighed and looked heavenward. "He said, 'Blue Eyes, Luke has had to take care of us his entire life. Promise me you'll take care of him and Dad.' I said, 'Of course I will, I love Luke and Bob.' And he proceeded to tell me that Bob was used to being in charge and might try and boss us around, and to let him." She smiled.

"What's going on out here?" Luke asked from the door. He walked out and stared down at them all. Madeline reached her hand up to him, and he sat on the step behind her, wrapping his legs around her.

"We were talking about the last thing Leo said to us," she said softly, and leaned back into him. "What did he say to you?"

"A lot," Luke said with a snort. "You know Leo, full of unsolicited advice." He laughed a little, but tears were glistening in his eyes. "He told me that in some ways he was glad it was over. But that he wished he could stick around a little longer because he'd built such a great team. He was taking full credit for all of us, you know, and more. Most of Pine River was on his list."

Emma laughed.

"He also told me to hang on to Homecoming Ranch," Luke said, and paused a moment, looking out over the lawn. "I was set to argue with him about that, but Leo pointed out that we'd all come home to it. I hadn't looked at it that way, but he's right. We all found home here."

No one spoke for a very long moment. Emma stared out over the meadow and the mountains across the valley. She imagined Leo running, his legs and arms pumping, that crooked smile of glee on his face.

"I guess he really was a genius."

With surprise, they all looked back to see Bob Kendrick on the porch. He was sitting in a chair off to one side, alone and unnoticed.

"He was, Dad," Luke agreed. "What's the last thing he said to you?"

Bob Kendrick squinted skyward. "He said, 'Thank you.'"

No one spoke, all of them lost in their private thoughts, remembering.

Cooper was the one to break the silence by lifting his beer bottle. "Here's to Leo, the world's greatest armchair quarterback."

"To Leo!" the rest of them echoed.

"And Homecoming Ranch," Libby offered. "His home. *Our* home."

"To Homecoming Ranch!" the seven responded.

"While we're at it, we better include the Denver Broncos," Luke said. When everyone hesitated, Luke laughed. "I forgot to mention that's another thing he made me promise. To make sure Dad never missed a game and to explain the nuances of a nickel defense because Dad didn't get it."

"Good God, that kid had a mouth on him," Bob said.

They laughed, and raised their glasses once more. "To the Denver Broncos!"

ABOUT THE AUTHOR

Julia London is the *New York Times*–, *USA Today*–, and *Publishers Weekly*–bestselling author of more than thirty romantic fiction novels. Her historical romance titles include the popular Desperate Debutantes series, the Scandalous series, and the Secrets of Hadley Green series. She has also penned several contemporary women's fiction novels with strong romantic elements, including the Homecoming Ranch trilogy, *Summer of Two Wishes*, *One Season of Sunshine*, and *A Light at Winter's End*. She has won the RT Bookclub Award for Best Historical Romance, and has been a six-time finalist for the prestigious RITA Award for excellence in romantic fiction. She lives in Austin, Texas.

IF YOU ENJOYED THIS BOOK,
CONNECT WITH JULIA LONDON ONLINE!

Read all about Julia and her books at: http://julialondon.com/

Like Julia on Facebook: https://www.facebook.com/JuliaLondon

Sign up for the newsletter: http://www.julialondon.com/newsletter

Follow Julia on Twitter: https://twitter.com/JuliaFLondon

Read about Julia on Goodreads: http://www.goodreads.com/
JuliaLondon